Figures of Enchantment

Zulfikar Ghose

Figures
of Enchantment

1817

HARPER & ROW, PUBLISHERS, New York
Cambridge, Philadelphia, San Francisco, Washington
London, Mexico City, São Paulo, Singapore, Sydney

FIRST U.S. EDITION

Library of Congress Cataloging-in-Publication Data

Ghose, Zulfikar, 1935–
   Figures of enchantment.

   I. Title.
PS3557.H63F5 1986   813'.54   85-45637
ISBN 0-06-015575-2

86 87 88 89 90 10 9 8 7 6 5 4 3 2 1

I

A Brightness Elsewhere

The only sheet of paper that remained on his desk at the end of the working day was the one on which he had made several calculations during the coffee break in the morning, filling the page with numbers. There were a dozen narrow columns of them on the page with its black heading—*Bureau of Statistics Memorandum*. The figures at the top, just below the heading, were inscribed neatly; but away from the center, and especially toward the bottom right-hand corner of the page, the sums seemed to have been worked out by a hasty, or a desperate, hand, as if it were eager to arrive at the elusive answer before the final seconds of the break ran out and one had to return to the obligatory work of the office.

He picked up the sheet of paper and began to fold it up in order to put it in his pocket, but unfolded it and stared at the numbers; he felt pained by the injustice to which he believed himself condemned. He looked up from the page and glanced around him at the plywood partition of the small cubicle in which he worked. There was space only for his desk and chair; to his right there was a gap in the partition—his entrance and exit—which opened to a passage across which was the Supervisor's office. He had pinned on the plywood wall in front of him color pictures from magazines showing islands in the Pacific whose blue and green perspectives offered a little relief from the oppressive feeling of being confined in a narrow cell, one photograph, that of an albatross floating high above a cliff with the ocean below it, now catching his attention as if it represented the opposite of his present situation. That there was a brightness elsewhere, a landscape which was daily comforting, renewing its warm charm with each sunrise, in a million little proffers of light and color, he knew but was not tormented by its remaining always inaccessible, for it was not his soul that dreamed, only his eyes.

He could hear chairs being pushed back and the mutterings of his colleagues as they went out of their cubicles; some of them were wishing one another good night, and others expressing relief that the working week was behind them and discussing their weekend plans.

He looked again at the little sums on the paper in his hand as if they were calculations attempting to prove some immutable law of probability or the working out of a complicated theorem with a clear, and a satisfying, proof at the end; but several of the numbers were multiplied by twelve, and indicated a common, and futile, form of daydreaming. His own life seemed encoded by the numbers, his existence caught in a not too puzzling arithmetic of wanting more than he possessed.

If only there were another zero at the end of his salary! In one magical stroke all his problems would disappear. He would move his family from the noisy little apartment, which was so close to the disreputable Rua Miraflores, to a sumptuous duplex in one of the tree-lined streets of Quinteros, buy a car—possibly one of those beautiful new Fiats with a sunroof—to take his family on weekend trips to the seaside or to the mountains, and have money to spare for a college education for Mariana. It invariably thrilled him to read the classified ads in the paper where just looking at the impossible rents demanded for apartments in Quinteros dazzled him: to pay out more money in rent each month than he earned—what must it be like to be so rich! He knew by heart the prices of the different models of cars, including the extra options available on each one, and he never failed to work out exactly what the Fiat of his choice would cost after the latest price increase, each time first stunning his mind into a fine ecstasy over the price of a luxuriously appointed Mercedes Benz by comparison with which his modest little Fiat seemed the cheapest thing in the world. But even so it always remained far beyond his means.

In his obsessive calculations there was always the sum

representing what he would be willing to sacrifice—resigning himself to a used car one day and on another determining what could be saved by being content with a less sumptuous apartment—in order to have the money for Mariana's education. At the end of each such calculation he resolved that he would give up everything for his daughter's future, and the thought filled him with a high esteem for himself, convincing him that he was the most selfless man in the world. But he always added a postscript to each of his calculations: figures hastily and surreptitiously scribbled, as if he feared to be caught at an illicit activity, a quick placing of noughts at the end of the earlier figures that added up to a grand sum which made him so rich he could afford the world.

His fingers moved to fold the sheet of paper again but instead he tore it up in a sudden surging of resentment and anger. What use was it to dream of the impossible? His eyes fell across the passage to the door of the Supervisor's office. He had been summoned to it twice during his twelve years in the department and received perfunctory praise for work over which he had labored in his own time, hoping that such a demonstration of his mental abilities would reveal him to be distinctly superior to his fellow workers and reward him with advancement. But all he had received had been a limp handshake from the Supervisor and two words of thanks uttered in the absent manner in which one acknowledges a servant for bringing a glass of water. During the few minutes in the Supervisor's office he had been impressed by the relatively grander environment—a carpet on the floor, a potted philodendron, a window that looked out on the building across the street—before returning to his own enclosed cell.

And then, only a month ago, the Assistant Supervisor's position had fallen vacant. For a week he had been made thrillingly dizzy by the daydream of filling it and surrendered himself to elaborate fantasies by working out sums based on the Assistant Supervisor's salary, deriving from the numbers a deep secret pleasure. One day his friends Ribera and Salazar, with whom he habitually sat over a beer after work on Fridays, had said to him that they and everyone they knew had no doubt that he was the best candidate for the job, so that his idle wish, echoed by his friends as a possibility, became converted in his mind into a conviction that he alone was suitable for the job. If others had been thinking of him as the best candidate, then surely he had not been harboring a delusion about his merit but only acknowledging a truth about himself?

He had written a carefully worded letter of application to the Supervisor, consulting his friends over the language to make sure it was sufficiently lofty and showed a cultivated mind. Ribera was full of praise for the final draft, which included his own suggestion that the words "my experience in the department" be replaced by "the execution of my duties in the professional service of our most prestigious department," and Salazar declared it a masterpiece, giving it his highest accolade—"Not even the King of Spain could have written better."

Two days after he submitted his application the Supervisor came and stood by the entrance to his cubicle. A charming smile fixed on his face, he said, "The department is not unaware of the exceptional quality of some of its staff. Keep up the good work, Gamboa!"

The men in the adjoining cubicles had picked up the words and by the end of the day every worker on the floor had heard them repeated. Although it was not a Friday Gamboa insisted on taking Ribera and Salazar to the bar, saying, "Come on, be my guests, we have important matters to discuss."

What had the Supervisor's words meant? They repeated them again and again to see how they were to be interpreted. Ribera thought that the key lay in the words "not unaware" —and he slapped the table, marveling at the Supervisor's subtlety. But Salazar said, "No, no," and, emphasizing the words he quoted, declared, "'*exceptional quality*'—there you have the heart of the statement."

Gamboa asked them to think of the worst interpretation that could be put on the Supervisor's words, saying, "I don't want to be blinded by my own enthusiasm." Could there be a catch in the statement? Could "keep up the good work" mean keep working in the same position? Gamboa invited the most pessimistic speculation. But his two friends were dumbfounded. However hard they tried to see the idea of rejection in the Supervisor's statement, they could only find in it a most emphatic approval. And then Salazar said, "Who can praise you and not be on your side?"

"That's right," Ribera said enthusiastically. "You are not chosen for praise unless you are the chosen one."

The remark struck Gamboa as containing an irrefutable truth. It was as perfect in its construction as a proverb and, hearing it, he felt himself rise above other mortals. Advancement was within his grasp. And if hard work made him deserving of this prize, then what other, more glorious heights could he not conquer in the future until he rose to the very top of the Ministry? Another twenty years, and he would have three decorations to wear on his breast.

After a couple of beers Gamboa asked if the gentlemen would not prefer rum. Ribera called for a toast. Salazar responded with, "To the new Assistant Supervisor!" Gamboa stood up, the glass raised in his hand. "To the Assistant Supervisor *designate!*" Ribera said solemnly, making the toast sound like a formal announcement. They clinked glasses and drank. The rum intoxicated Gamboa less than the title. When he went home that evening, wherever he caught a reflection of himself he observed a man of civic importance and solid substance who walked with a strikingly dignified air about him. The Assistant Supervisor *designate.*

A fortnight of tense anticipation passed. There was a paragraph in the political gossip column of the evening newspaper: The Supervisor had met the Minister to make his recommendation. Gamboa's friends seized upon a phrase from the column, "a man of proven experience," and uttered it repeatedly, emphasizing *proven* and smiling at him in felicitation: the words could mean only one thing. The Assistant Supervisor *designate.* "Let's not jump to conclusions," Gamboa said, trying to look unaffected by his friends' congratulatory tone.

For several days, while the Minister deferred his decision, Gamboa remained outwardly serene, presenting to his colleagues the appearance of a humble man who expected no extraordinary rewards in his life, who was devoted to his present job and only desired to continue at it with no thought of advancement, thus superstitiously guarding himself against the bad luck that must follow a presumption of deserving more or any manifestation of pride. He said nothing to his wife either but rehearsed in his mind how he would break the news to her—"Sonia, here is an ad for a four-room apartment in Quinteros that we should go and look at. It's only on the seventh floor with a slightly restricted view of the mountains, but maybe we should take a look, what do you say?" He knew how she would answer. "Have you gone mad, Felipe?" He would look at her with a sly smile and say, "I thought that with my new salary we could afford to move to Quinteros. It's not going to be too grand, mind you, but still, Quinteros is Quinteros." She would stare at him a little scornfully. "What new salary? You're always dreaming of a great fortune." He would finally take out the letter of appointment from his pocket and place it in her hands. "This just arrived at the office, Sonia. I must say it took me quite by surprise." And she, unable to read, would call Mariana to read the letter to her, so that he would have the double pleasure of seeing his wife's disbelief turn to amazement and his daughter run to him in her joy to hug him for the happiness he was bringing to her life.

Gamboa did not see the announcement when it was published in the morning paper. When he arrived at the office he did not at first notice that the people he passed by in the corridor looked a little embarrassed as they took their eyes away quickly from his cheerful greeting which they interpreted as the forced bravado of a humiliated man. A little later, working in his cubicle but finding it difficult not to think of the dazzling raise in pay when the promotion came through, he saw the Supervisor's door open and a group of well-dressed men emerge. There was laughter and handshaking, and when the group left, in the moment that it took the Supervisor to close his door, he saw that a younger man stood with him and the two exchanged congratulatory glances. He understood at once. The group had been a ministerial delegation which had arrived before he did. There must have been a little ceremony behind the closed door.

Afterward Ribera would console him with, "It's not a reflection on you, Felipe. Everyone knows your worth. The Minister had a political debt to pay." And Salazar would say,

"The Supervisor's hand was forced by the Minister. That's politics for you!"

And now Felipe Gamboa stood up, his hand clutching the torn pieces of paper on which he had, in a mood of bitterness during the morning break, worked out sums based on what his salary might have been had justice been done and he obtained the appointment. And, becoming even more bitter when he saw what he had been denied, he had added more noughts to the sums, punishing himself with the imaginary sight of a wealth so tremendous it produced a momentary ache in his brain and blurred his vision. Then it occurred to him as a negative sort of consolation that more than double though the other salary was from what he received, all his dreams would not have been fulfilled had he got the job. He could have moved his family to Quinteros, but the expense of living in such a high-class suburb would have left no money to send Mariana to college and it was unlikely that he would have been able to afford a car as well; and if he had sacrificed his own and his wife Sonia's comfort for the education of their sixteen-year-old daughter by remaining in their present apartment, it would have been humiliating for a girl of Mariana's sensibility to have to confess to her fellow students that she came from one of the city's poorer districts, next to the infamous Nuevo Soho with its Rua Miraflores full of Bohemians, prostitutes and gambling dens. The extra money simply would not have been enough for a real happiness.

For a few moments, as he thought of his daughter, his bitterness diminished and he wished he had a rich uncle or some great aunt who suddenly left him a fortune so that he could do credit to Mariana's quick mind and her beauty. Why else was a child with such perfect attributes born—surely not so that the parents may helplessly witness poverty mock her growth, letting her mind stultify and her flesh early lose its bloom? But no rich relatives existed in his family of which he, working as a petty clerk in the Ministry of Labor's Bureau of Statistics, was the first member in several generations to rise above the condition of a peasant. Sonia's bachelor brother, who worked as an electrician, gave her presents of a little money twice a year, on her birthday and at Christmas, which she invariably put aside for items of need. Gamboa could see no real money coming his way, and his dear Mariana deserved so much more than he was ever going to be able to provide! The best he could hope for now was that she was lucky in marriage, that she found someone from a better background. He had dreamed in the past of some rich young man falling in love with her, but he scornfully dismissed that thought now, for his own daydream of a higher salary had been futile, proving the foolishness of all such dreams. He was not in a mood for the consolations of magic, having spent so much of his life expecting the incredible to happen.

He thrust the torn pieces of paper into the left pocket of his trousers, not wanting to leave in the wastebasket the mutilated evidence of his daydream. Most of his fellow workers had left the building and he realized that he had deliberately, though unconsciously, been delaying making his own exit in order not to have to countenance glances of pity, especially when that pity was only the mask of triumphant glee, as he knew it must be in the case of two or three of his colleagues who in their own hearts despised anyone who committed the error of working hard and proving himself superior to them. He understood, as he walked down the corridor, that crueller than the failure itself was the humiliation of being extended sympathy: it was as if the person embracing one out of compassion had claws instead of fingers and that by pressing them into one's back he wounded some vital organ.

Deciding not to take the elevator, which at this time was bound to stop at each of the eleven floors below the one on which he worked, imprisoning him with someone who might know his story, he began to walk heavily down the stone steps, which were illuminated by a window at each half-landing. He stopped at the first one and looked out through the begrimed glass. The distant view was of the still water of the bay which continued to the left where the docks were and widened out toward the ocean on the right; directly across from him at a distance of some seven kilometers was Isla Blanca and he could see a ferry, overcrowded with workers, laboring in that direction. Down below, the sidewalks were massed with people, thousands at the waterfront, thronging toward the next ferry, with those who had reached the vessel clamoring for a foothold in crevices between the packed bodies; rows of buses crept up the wide avenue, each one already full, destined for the city's outer suburbs. Still more people poured out of the side streets and the buildings to join the thousands on the sidewalks to endure there an hour's struggle to secure a passage home. He saw himself in that crowd and was filled again with a resentment against the injustice of his existence, for he had no choice but to repeat this terrible journey day after day for the rest of his life. His only immediate consolation was that it was Friday when he habitually had a couple of beers with his friends in the bar on the square, thus avoiding the worst of the rush hour. It was the one indulgence his wife did not begrudge him, for she knew him to be a good man who restrained his own pleasures for the comfort of his family.

As he descended the stairs a shudder ran through his body when he thought of the crowds scrambling to catch the ferry to Isla Blanca, the habitation of the poorest workers, a rocky lump of land on which there was not a single edifice with foundations but only shacks and huts vulnerable, should the ocean turn malevolent, as had happened fifteen years ago, to being wiped out by a tidal wave. And there people were obliged to live, raise families among whom the boys could not wait till they grew into men and then had the further good fortune of obtaining a job on the mainland that committed them to the twice daily crossing on the overcrowded ferry. The few who escaped could find life only in the mainland's underworld, a vast, invisible and pitiless bureaucracy which in its admission of criminals and prostitutes was stricter and more exacting than the army in its recruitment of soldiers and in the administration of its affairs more viciously vigilant than a secret police. The thought should have comforted him, for at least he was not so low in the hierarchy of human beings; but instead, Gamboa, turning round the landing to descend the steps from the second floor, was filled with a loathing for the abstraction in his mind that he identified with the ruling class—managers, industrialists, politicians, the military, and those despicable idlers who were born to wealth and used their money to manipulate power—for why, he wondered, should millions have no expectation other than the raw struggle to exist?

He came out into the street among the crowds hurrying toward the waterfront or the bus stops. Cars creeping out of a multistorey car park were joining the buses in the street, the congested traffic creating a haze of smoke, the fumes attacking one's nostrils with their odor and permeating one's lungs. The only noise in the street was that of the throbbing diesel engines of the buses and the loud roar as they labored forward in low gear together with the muffled noise of automobiles in several of which suited gentlemen sat alone absorbed in the contents of a newspaper. The great crowd of humanity on the sidewalks made scarcely any noise while it walked hastily toward the bus stops; it was almost as if the people had spontaneously agreed to suspend their existence for the next hour, cease to be while their bodies were precariously transported to their homes. Gamboa had the sensation that he was watching people in a dream, a body of mankind that was flowing impetuously, and without thought, toward another world where an intenser misery awaited it than it had known, but that in its thoughtless drive it was sustained by the belief that it proceeded toward a land of enchanting pleasures, an expectation supported by examples of the few who had won a sweepstake of which the grand prize was a fortnight in Disney World.

He joined his friends Ribera and Salazar at a sidewalk table in the bar on the square some distance from the waterfront. The roar of the traffic was somewhat subdued by the high buildings beyond which it ran. At one end of the square the larger-than-life statue of the country's liberator sat on a huge horse, his cocked hat silhouetted against the sky in a gap between two buildings and his hand raised in acknowledgement of the cheers of an invisible crowd. A fountain in the middle of the square with the bronze figure of a naked woman at its center, a virginal maiden poised upon a Venus shell, jets of water falling in loops about her shoulders, splashed incongruously, its suggestion of Baroque splendor and Arcadian bliss inconsistent with the scraggly and dust-laden nut trees and the stone benches on which beggars lay asleep.

"The dice were loaded, that's for sure," Ribera said when the waiter had brought Gamboa his beer.

"Yeah, the cards were stacked against you," Salazar remarked. "The Minister was just paying back a favor. What do you expect?"

"It was just politics," Ribera said with a look of disgust on his face. "The Supervisor's words didn't count. It had nothing to do with being the best candidate."

"Believe me," Salazar said, suddenly pounding the table, "the King of Spain wouldn't have got this job on merit with the Minister having to pay back a favor."

"I hear the man they appointed is only thirty and owns a car dealership," Ribera said. "And you know something? He presented the Minister's daughter a new Fiat when she turned eighteen three months ago. It's incredible how open the corruption is. Anyone with money can get away with murder."

"What's more," Salazar recounted, "I hear this so-called Assistant Supervisor isn't even married. It's not that he needs the job. And his mother has income from a ranch. Can you beat that? The ones who don't need it get it, and the ones who do get screwed. That's the way life is, the bitch!"

The sarcasm and bitterness of his friends consoled Gamboa, and after he had drunk his beer he offered to buy a round of rum. The liquor warmed the men to greater eloquence and Gamboa discovered a delicious pleasure in his friends' denunciation of the world, as if their abuse were a form of generosity to himself, or that the extent of their attack were a measure of his own martyrdom, the extremity of it giving him the appearance of having been singled out from all the people on earth for a special and singularly unjust punishment. In the pleasure of believing that his suffering was unique and monumental he bought several more rounds of rum, forgetting that he no longer had even the dream of advancement to afford such an indulgence.

A commotion at another table distracted them. A lottery vendor had passed by their own table, displaying the brightly colored tickets and inviting them to buy one. It was a common occurrence and as usual the lottery vendor was saying something about the numbers he offered to make them sound interesting; and they had, out of habit, waved him aside without paying him any attention. At the other table, however, the vendor had captured the notice of the four men sitting there, morosely sipping from their glasses of beer without

having anything to say to one another. And now the four
seemed to be vying with one another to purchase a particular
lottery ticket. Gamboa and his friends watched with sudden
curiosity as the four men finished their loud argument by
agreeing to draw lots with some matchsticks. Men at other
tables looked too, and the waiters stopped with their trays in
their hands and stared at the four men drawing lots, while
the lottery vendor stood next to them, holding a ticket in one
hand and rubbing the back of his other hand, in which he
held the remaining tickets, across his chin. The drawing
completed, the winner took out his wallet, pulled out a note
from it and handed it to the vendor who exchanged it for the
lottery ticket.

Several people went and crowded round the man who had
purchased the ticket and who now had a self-satisfied smile
on his face. Ribera hastened to join them and presently
returned to tell his friends what the noise had been all about.
By a remarkable coincidence, the number of the lottery ticket
had been DD12101492. Salazar screwed up his eyes, not
seeing a connection, and Gamboa's face asked for an explanation. "Twelve ten, don't you see, that's twelve October,
Columbus Day in America, and what was 1492 if not the
very year in which chance brought Columbus to the New
World!" That wasn't all. The serial letters DD stood for
Discovery Day. Wasn't that an amazing piece of luck?

It was well known that such coincidences sometimes proved
exceptionally lucky; the example was on everyone's mind of a
man who had bought, on the day on which there was a total
eclipse of the sun, a ticket the number of which was readable as
that very day's date with SOL as its serial letters, and that man
now drove around in a Mercedes Benz convertible.

Gamboa stared ruefully at the man who had purchased the
ticket and it seemed to him that the man was already in
possession of a fortune.

Salazar slapped his forehead and said, "To think the vendor
came by here first, and we told him to move on!"

Gamboa felt as though the chances of life had cheated him
once again and ordered another round of rum.

Ribera shook his head in disbelief and remarked, "Fortune
came right by me and I told it to shove off!"

The three men were silent until the waiter served them the next round of rum, and in the silence each man stared at enormous figures and saw images of himself in an immaculate suit catching a plane to a foreign country or driving with a young mistress to a hotel frequented by illicit lovers or walking across the marble hall of a bank and cashing a check which, though it was a large sum, represented only petty cash to be thrown away on idle luxuries and made not the slightest dent on the mountainous reserve accruing interest in the account.

They looked about them when they heard the waiter talk sternly to a beggar who had wandered among the tables, and Ribera sighed, "Ah, life, the bitch!"

"You know what I think," Salazar said. "When something bad happens, something good has got to follow. Something really good."

Gamboa was in no mood to be cheered by homely wisdom and muttered irritatedly, "There's no justice." And then, looking at Salazar with anger concentrated on his face, he said with great bitterness as though addressing a judge who had just sentenced him to hard labor for life, "Where's the justice in anything? What did I do to be punished? Did I lie to my parents? Did I spend nights in adultery? Did I rob a bank? Did I join the communists?"

Salazar put a hand across Gamboa's shoulder. "No, Felipe," he said, gently patting him below the neck, "you didn't deserve this."

Ribera grasped Gamboa's hand and pressed it, saying, "You'll come through, my friend. You'll see for yourself how strong you are."

When they left the bar and were walking toward the buses, Gamboa put his hand in the pocket in which he usually carried his coins. There was only a thin five-centavo piece there. He knew there was nothing in his wallet since he had just paid out his last note for the drinks. He was obliged to borrow small change from his friends for his bus fare.

Buses going to the district where Salazar and Ribera lived came before the one Gamboa needed to take, and he stood alone on the sidewalk, leaning against the lamppost. All that money spent on liquor and he did not even feel drunk! What was he going to give Mariana for her pocketmoney? What was he going to tell Sonia? His throat hurt with a fresh thirst. His head throbbed with anger.

Other people had loitered up to the bus stop, a crowd of thin, poorly dressed people. Across the road the day's last ferry to Isla Blanca was about to leave and two middle-aged men were running to catch it. Cars and taxis went past with solitary drivers looking ghostly in the failing light. Darkness was falling. By the time his bus came enough people had collected to catch it for all the seats to be taken, and although he managed to get one the crowd packing the aisle seemed to press down upon him with its combined weight, inducing within him a sense of being suffocated. The man sitting next to him by the window kept clearing his throat loudly and, each time the bus came to a halt, retching and spitting out of the window.

Going out of the business district, which was comparatively free of traffic, the bus entered a shopping area where, the night now fallen, brightly lit stores and boutiques were still open, attracting crowds of people to their dazzle. The bus jolted forward in short, anxious jerks in the congested traffic, its engine loud and whining. The liquor finally began to have its effect on Gamboa; it was not, however, a belated intoxication that might have relieved him from his present oppression, but a dizziness and an ache in his head and a distinct swelling within him of nausea. Some of the passengers had alighted and he moved to a seat by a window and stuck his face out for a moment for fresh air. The odor of diesel fumes attacked him like a physical blow and he quickly withdrew his head. A bright red convertible was creeping along with the bus in the thick traffic and Gamboa noticed, when he withdrew his head from the window, the young woman who occupied it alone. She wore an evening dress with a plunging neckline that exposed nearly all her bosom to the sooty air; precious stones sparkled from the five tiers of her necklace and a wide gold bracelet clasped the wrist above the hand that held the steering wheel; Gamboa watched her move her other hand from the shift to the radio where she played with the tuning knob, and he gazed at the white fingers with their polished nails, feeling within him a longing to be caressed by her hands. Although she appeared to be looking anxiously for an opening through which to speed away, she was obliged to remain next to the bus for three more blocks. Her beauty distracted Gamboa from his dizziness and he continued to stare down at her until she turned into an empty side street with a sudden burst of speed and accelerated out of sight, leaving him in the mist of diesel fumes which had now thickened with the presence of regret and envy. If he had ten lives to live, at his present salary he would still not be able to save enough money for his Mariana to wear those jewels and possess that car and afford for two days to live in the style of the woman in the convertible.

The bus began to move more freely, and he leaned back from the seat in front of him against which he had been resting his aching forehead and turned to face the window where there was now a rush of air. They had left the commercial area and were driving along the ocean on an avenue of expensive apartment buildings. None of the passengers in the bus needed to alight there and the driver had to stop only once to pick up a stout middle-aged woman in a maid's uniform. On the opposite sidewalk, above the sea wall, joggers went past and young lovers strolled, and in the distance, on the dark sea, a well-lit ocean liner was moving out of the bay with its party of rich foreign tourists on the monthly excursion to the islands nine hundred kilometers out in the Pacific where the tourists would take pictures of the giant turtles, the blue-footed boobies and the albatross.

The nausea was now stuck in his throat like a lump of lard, and Gamboa tried to distract himself by thinking of the lives led by the rich, forcing himself to remember images from movies seen when he was a bachelor and could afford such a pleasure—people in formal dress in casinos raking in a fortune that was won so casually and with so much apparent certainty, a beautiful woman in a gorgeous dress and a spectacular hat patting a horse who had just won the Derby for her—but the renewed jolting of the bus as it now entered the ill-lit narrow streets of a poorer district wiped out the pictures in his imagination.

He got off the bus nearly an hour after he had boarded it. The journey took half as long again on days when he did not go to the bar after work. And now there was half a kilometer's walk up the hill on the narrow sidewalk of the cobbled street. Cars were parked with two of their wheels on the curb, leaving just enough space for pedestrians to proceed in single file. There was a low wall between the sidewalk and the apartment buildings, the enclosed space, five meters wide, filled with oleanders, philodendrons and palms. In the little nook by the entrance to two or three of the buildings lovers stood embracing and whispering to each other.

Gamboa trudged on wearily, cursing his fate that he had to live so far from the city center in a neighborhood where rents were cheaper; and cursing, too, the fact that though he had taken an apartment at the top of the hill in order to benefit from the sea breeze, he had only been able to afford a second-floor apartment which was too low to be affected by the breeze. He passed by another embracing couple; in the dim light he saw little more than the shadowy form of the lovers, but just when he was walking past them a car drove by and the diffusion of light from its headlamps suddenly illuminated the couple. Gamboa stopped. His heart seemed to bound up and hit against the knotted lump of nausea in his throat and to drop back, filling his chest with a deep pain with its sudden violence. Could it be his Mariana, his girl of sixteen whom he dreamed of giving away in church to a rich aristocratic husband, messing around with some local lout?

The lovers, unaware of the passerby, were kissing passionately, and for a moment Gamboa stood frozen in rage. Another car passed by, confirming that it was indeed his daughter at whom he stared. The rage and the frustration of his dreams became transformed into a terrible power, and he flung out his hand and clutched the young man by his shoulder and tore him away from Mariana. She gave a scream seeing her boyfriend being pulled back violently, being turned around with rude force and then being slapped hard several times before being pushed to the ground and kicked, all very rapidly. She gave another scream when she recognized that the perpetrator of the violence was not some wanton criminal but her own father. He now turned to her, catching her as she made to move away. He stared at her, his mouth open, panting. She squirmed as his hands tightened on her arms. He wanted to crush her in that moment, to destroy her for having betrayed his dream of her great worth. He raised a hand to slap her. But a limpness entered his hand which only waved past her face, his fingertips barely brushing her chin.

His hand would not punish her and in his helplessness he shouted, "For you I slave away my life in an office, for you I sit three hours in a bus every day with a crowd of the lowest of the low in order to save money to give you, and this is what you have to give me in return? You go right back home this instant!"

She went away, crying, and Gamboa turned back to the young man who had stood up and was in a state of confusion, not knowing whether he should strike back at the man who was the father of the girl he loved or run away humiliated.

"It's you!" Gamboa recognized him. "Chagra's son, Federico? I should have known nothing good would come out of that family of idlers and gamblers! Get out of my sight!"

The insult to his family on the top of the blows he had received momentarily gave Federico the resolution to strike back, but he sensed the power of an enraged bull in his adversary and withdrew behind the parked cars.

Gamboa arrived panting at his apartment. The front door opened directly into the small sitting room. His wife Sonia sat staring at the door and, as soon as he entered it, she said accusingly, "What have you done?"

A loud wailing came from another room. Gamboa slammed the door behind him and said angrily, "What have *I* done? Why, I have only brought up a girl who's set on becoming a whore. I have only paid a fortune to doctors and dentists so that she has a pretty body to give to any fool who comes her way. What have *I* done? Oh, I have not done enough! I should make more money and set her up in a fancy apartment where she can receive her lovers."

"What are you talking about, Felipe? Oh God, you've been drinking!"

"Yes, I've been drinking!" he shouted, suddenly conscious that he was absolutely sober. "And if this room were filled with money, I'd spend every penny of it on drink. What have I got for being sober and good? Who has rewarded my virtue, my hard work, my sacrifice? What has been my prize in this life? A wife who couldn't have a second child, and the child she did have is turning into a cheap whore. What has been my prize, ha? My little reward? Oh, stop whimpering and snivelling! Go to your slut of a daughter and beat her vice out of her. Go and do your duty, dammit, instead of gaping at me like a fool!"

She looked at him in between sobs, not knowing what had come over him to say such terrible things, speaking them with so much anger, and not understanding the demand he was making of her. "What do you want me to do?" she asked softly.

"Get up and do your duty, you heard me!" he shouted, advancing toward her and pulling her up forcibly and pushing her toward Mariana's room. "Thrash the cheap little bitch before she brings more dishonor to this house!"

Sonia stopped outside the door and appeared to be completely bewildered. He flung it open and, snatching her wrist, pulled her into the room. He looked wildly at Mariana who sat on the bed huddled against the corner, her eyes filled with terror. "Little whore!" he shouted at her. Sonia had not been able to decide whether he was in a drunken rage or had reason behind his obscene accusations when he dragged her into Mariana's room, and she found herself caught in the current of her husband's violence.

Gamboa began to hit and yell incomprehensible oaths at his wife who dashed to the corner and, grabbing hold of Mariana's arm, pulled the girl toward her and started to slap her. Mariana squirmed backward, trying to escape the blows; her mother pulled her fiercely so that she fell off the bed. And now there was a wild confusion of blows and noise and screams, with Gamboa beating his wife, she beating the daughter, and the girl throwing her fists across her face to protect herself.

At last Gamboa held back and stood by the door. Mariana lay crying on the floor, her face scratched and bruised, her exhausted mother next to her looking like a round bundle of clothing. He glanced at Mariana's face, recalling in that moment how often, when she was younger, he had held his daughter in his lap and touched the flawless skin of her cheeks with his lips and taken great pleasure in recognizing that she had inherited his large black eyes and that her nose and mouth closely resembled his. He would never be able to see that face again without feeling some of the repulsion that he now experienced; and he realized, too, in the same brief moment of his glance, that when she again became a dutiful daughter and her cheeks healed from their present beating, he would never see her face again, even when she had transformed it with make-up, without seeing the scratches and bruises that now covered it. If only things had been different and one's reasonable expectations not frustrated, he would not now be in the middle of this misery. The thought was futile but persisted nevertheless, and he wished that somehow another existence had been granted him—not that of immense wealth, but one of simple happiness, one in which the same Mariana was his daughter but was a Mariana whose chaste beauty would be his jealous possession to bestow upon a chosen suitor.

His wife moaned, rising from the floor, heaving up her fat little body with difficulty. Mariana sobbed where she lay. Gamboa turned to leave the room and, his anger flaring again before he did so, found himself saying harshly, "Worthless little slut!"

Monday morning at the office was more than doubly trying for Gamboa. In his mind he had come so near to being promoted that to return to his usual little cubicle was a sharply painful experience, especially as it was accompanied by the knowledge that that was to be his lot for many years to come. And secondly, the weekend had been a form of imprisonment in his small apartment with his wife, Mariana and himself as one another's jailors: he could not go to the local bar for a beer on Saturday afternoon, not having any money; his wife produced frugal meals to dramatize the fact that there was a limit to how far she could stretch her meagre budget; also, she had not understood the cause of the Friday night's violence, Gamboa remaining silent, and she sensed that some form of abstinence was necessary, as during a time of grief; and Mariana, who remained in her room all Saturday, turned on her crackly transistor radio on Sunday afternoon, driving her mother to the kitchen where she began to scrub the pans, banging them against the sink, and the combined noise of the abominable rock music and the furious activity in the kitchen made Gamboa go out for a long walk.

He walked past the corner where the bar was and realized that there was no comfort for him outside his apartment either; for the outside world showed him a succession of images of what he could not do, having no money. He could not enjoy the simple pleasure of stopping at the bar for a beer. Everywhere he looked people were buying things or were engaged in superfluous and indulgent consumption. His aimless wandering took him past the cemetery where people were purchasing flowers from the vendors outside the gate; he turned back when he had walked as far as the city zoo where swarms of children were crowding around the ice-cream vans while their parents shouted at them from the soft-drinks booth. The streets were now full of cars packed with families who had spent the day on the beach or the weekend camping in the mountains, and he took a bitter sort of interest in imagining the lives of these people who could afford to enjoy their weekend.

His worst moment, however, came on the Monday morning when, rising at six o'clock to catch the bus half an hour later, he had to ask his wife to give him some change from her housekeeping money so that he could afford the fare to his office and back. She gave it to him without speaking a word, for she had become convinced in her own mind that the weekend's trouble came from his spending more money on drink than he should have; and he felt her silence to be a worse rebuke than any abuse, even blows.

Taking the little brown bag in which she had put his lunch, he walked out of the apartment feeling like one who is merely being transferred from one prison to another, and his journey to his office was a cruel form of punishment, transporting him through other people's freedom where they lived in propertied splendor. At the office he found it difficult to concentrate on his work, but during the morning break when he had not gone out to fetch himself a coffee, a worker in an adjoining cubicle had brought him one, placed the cup on his desk and, laying a gentle hand on his arm, had said, "I know how you feel, Felipe. Believe me, you're a kind of leader to us. You'll make it."

The man had gone away and Gamboa, grateful for the coffee, felt himself overcome by an emotion that had the effect of imbuing him with a new resolution; the gesture and the words of his colleague made him feel that he was one of a larger community of men, that his suffering was not wasted when it evoked a genuine sympathy in his fellows, and that perhaps, after all, he was indeed singled out for some special fate for which his present setbacks were a form of preparation; so that he found the resolution to work with a determined energy: if he could not achieve the pleasures he desired for himself and his family, then he would display a silent form of leadership through his devotion to work without ever again expressing an interest in a reward.

But, when the lunch hour arrived, he found it difficult to go and sit where most of his companions did; he had been touched by one man's sympathy, but was not yet ready to receive too large a measure of it from several. And so he walked out of the building to go and sit on a stone bench in the square. He needed to be alone for the present to let the internal wounds heal so that he could be among the men again without the pain showing on his face. The phrase the man who had brought him the cup of coffee had used, *a kind of leader*, came to his mind and he wondered how different things would be if workers' unions were not illegal in the country. They had no rights at all. Salary raises came not because merit was rewarded or there was fair negotiation between the management and the workers but merely because the government had devised some statistical formula that tied wages to the rate of inflation; but since the government itself decided what the rate of inflation was and, in order to make a favorable impression on foreign banks from whom it borrowed heavily, inevitably made the rate seem lower than it really was, the buying power of the wages consequently diminished each year. If only they could have a union! As he walked through the streets Gamboa was excited by images in his mind of an underground movement springing up with himself as *a kind of leader*. The phrase kept returning. But what could a union do? Strikes, too, were illegal. Whenever newspapers reported on strikes in Europe, it was always to show the harm they did to the country, the chaos they created in daily life, and how inconsiderate the workers were to be making such excessive demands. The implication always was that the outlawing of unions was an economically sound policy and the best thing for the nation; and by a clever trick of argument the newspapers invariably managed to conclude convincingly that the people who most suffered from the existence of unions were the workers themselves. How wrong, how wrong! Gamboa almost cried aloud. All that happened was that, with luck, the government put you into a job and kept you there for the rest of your life. You could move if you got a job at a factory, but there you labored with your body for no more money; and if you lost a limb or your sanity, then neither the state nor the company had the conscience to pay you a pension. He had read about job training in other countries, where the employers actually trained workers on the job to give them the chance to move to a higher-paid position. Gamboa was filled with pleasure at the thought of such a just system that gave each man an opportunity to improve himself. This is what he must do now, he who was *a kind of leader*, slowly and quietly bring the men together, and see if a new, fairer life could not be won for themselves. Thus, lost in his thoughts which were renewing his confidence in himself, he arrived at the square, his little brown bag in his hand.

There was an unexpected crowd of people in the square. Someone standing on the pedestal on which was mounted the statue of the country's liberator was making a speech, but the sense of his words could hardly be followed for each time he uttered a phrase a great roar went up from the crowd. More people arriving behind where Gamboa stood just inside the square in his idle curiosity had the effect of gradually pushing him deeper into the crowd, and soon he found himself in a thick press of humanity, voices shouting all around him, arms gesticulating, fists beating the air. The man beside the statue shouted a slogan; the crowd roared. Gamboa vaguely imagined they formed some political party and felt uncomfortable. He had himself, only a few moments ago, been thinking of a kind of political organization, and now, accidentally finding himself fallen in the midst of one, he felt uneasy and realized how unsuited he was for such action. He really wanted to be left alone to eat his lunch. The crowd had thickened behind him and his attempt to extricate himself from the mass of men proved impossible. And now a strange transformation occurred in him.

The crowd's shouting made him unexpectedly want to shout too; he was astonished to see his own arm fling itself up involuntarily as others about him did. He heard the words *justice* and *human rights* and was amazed to discover that he himself was shouting them with the crowd. And then an extraordinary intoxication possessed his brain, giving him a sense of belief in what his mouth was shouting. It all happened very suddenly, and the thought that he was Gamboa, a man with his own problems which had nothing to do with the troubles of others, who had only come here to eat his lunch in peace, the thought of his individuality had vanished and what seemed important was that he shout and gesticulate as forcefully as the rest. The man on the pedestal cried aloud, "When will we be free?" and Gamboa shouted back in one voice with the crowd, "*When, when, when?*"

"What more sacrifices do they want?" the man cried.

"*What more, what more?*" Gamboa shouted with the crowd.

A part of him felt that he should not be there. A political rally was illegal and if the generals had allowed it they probably planned to trick the opposition leaders to come out into the open the easier to discredit them. In any case, he did not belong to these men whose particular grievances he well might share if he knew what they were; but it was contrary to his nature to be an activist in a public spectacle. The ideas he had just been having were speculative; they were a new daydream, or that energy-giving illusory preoccupation necessary to keep a man working, replacing the one that had preoccupied him until recently, the one of a larger salary that for the present had to be excluded from his mind. The reality of a mass movement was one that he would never have associated himself with voluntarily. But now there was the other part of him over which he had no control, for it was possessed by the emotions of the crowd and kept on shouting passionately words that had no precise relevance to his own individual life.

And then a new commotion rose in the air. Those on the outer fringes of the crowd heard it first, and their cries, different from the general shouts continuing among the people closer to the statue of the nation's liberator, came in waves to the center of the square, so that a moment later there was a brief silence, as if some leader had signalled a cessation of noise, and in that moment the insistent sirens of police cars from the four sides of the square filled the air. And now an altogether different sort of shouting was heard, the general voice of panic, and there were people running in all directions. Gamboa found himself in a group from which he could not detach himself, trying to make a wild dash from the square and finding it impossible in the great crush of men.

They were suddenly hit by water and knocked back. Now there were screams in the square. Gamboa had fallen near a stone bench and he put his hand out to hold the foot of the bench and dragged himself to get his head and as much of his body as he could under it. Dried orange peel lay in the dust near his face. He heard shots being fired. Everywhere people were being hit by the water cannon and the screams were of people who were being trampled by the wildly rushing crowd. The dust under the bench smelled of urine. He was filled with the horror of his situation. He had only come to the square in order to be alone! What was in his fate that such a simple desire should be the prelude to a catastrophe? He was an ordinary person, with no ambition other than the wish to do well for his family. "Why, then, this punishment?" he cried into the vilely smelling dust.

A silence fell on the square and he put his head out from under the bench. Scores of people lay on the paths and the grass, some knocked unconscious, some probably feigning that state, and some very probably dead. He saw that the entire square was surrounded by armed military police and behind them stood Jeeps, police cars, vans and armored vehicles. An officer shouted into a megaphone for everyone to rise immediately, giving them precisely two minutes to surrender.

Gamboa began to walk with a line of others, and although it was obvious that he had no choice but to follow the others and be packed with them in one of the vans, he had the thought, incongruous and trivial in the circumstances, that he had lost the brown bag containing his lunch; he no longer had any appetite and his immediate longing was only for water with which to wipe the urinous dust from his face, but the loss of his cheese sandwich and apple filled him with an enormous grief.

He stopped by the rear door of the van and said to the soldier who stood there with a rifle in his hand, "I was only here to eat my lunch."

The soldier stared at him with expressionless eyes, and Gamboa added, "I had nothing to do with the rally. I am innocent, see?"

The soldier turned his rifle around in his hands and barked, "Inside, scum!" As Gamboa climbed into the van the soldier struck a painful blow to his back with the butt of his rifle.

An armed policeman stood just inside the van ordering those who had already entered it to stand closer together to make room for others. Soon the door was closed and the van moved off. It was dark and oppressive where Gamboa stood in the crush of bodies. Four louvered windows let in some air and very little light and were so formed that nothing of the outside world could be seen from within. In the near darkness one or two lamented their fate, but the rest, realizing the futility of protest when there was no one to listen to them, stood silently, and if one cursed his situation it was only the immediate aspect of it, the uncomfortable pressure of other bodies and the lack of air.

Gamboa tried to think that it was not he who stood there but some real enemy of the government, someone who had indeed cried out against the repression of his natural desires and was being punished for his arrogance; but the memory came to him of wanting to punish his daughter and finding his own hand unable to strike her, so that he was obliged to transmit the punishment via his wife; and that memory released in his mind the chain of events that had begun with his desire for promotion and ended with his coming to the square in order to escape the pity of his colleagues; and it seemed to him that somehow each succeeding event that apparently had no link with what preceded it was in fact a logical effect, manifesting itself obscurely and unpredictably, caused by the earlier event with which it had no predictable connection. Perhaps the real cause went back to a time much more distant

than the recent weeks during which the only sin he could really
accuse himself of was one of pride in his sense of his own value;
he tried to think if he could remember, from the forty years of
his life, some fact, some grave error from which his sorrows
sprang, but if there were one he had no memory of it.

The coincidence of the thoughts he had been having about
becoming a leader struck him now as bitterly ironical. Had
he really been an activist and had organized the men into a
union, and were now being taken to jail for breaking the law,
then there would be some merit in his present situation. At
least men would know what he had done and what was to
happen to him: he would be a martyr, and some international
brotherhood, meeting in England or in Switzerland, would
pass resolutions supporting him. But now? He was a nobody,
and no one in the world knew where he was—or, knowing,
would come forward to help him.

His thoughts came confusedly in the jolting and suffocating
van, interrupted by the oaths of his fellow men or by an
awareness of their silence. Most of them seemed to have a
premonition of their destiny, and Gamboa thought that they
were either resigned to it or were saving their energy for a
future revolt. It was pointless, in the present circumstances,
to inquire what their cause had been that the government had
moved with such rapid brutality against them. He had read
in the newspapers of dissidents, liberals, and communists—
all rather abstract and existing in his mind in the imagery
of popular cartoons in which they were depicted as boa
constrictors, alligators or fire-breathing dragons, whereas
these men appeared to be no different from himself.

After a while he heard two men near him talking. One
mentioned the name of an opposition leader who had been
rumored to have returned from exile, and said that the
generals themselves had encouraged the rally to let him know,
by crushing it so easily, what power they had and how
openly they could exercise it. The other man said he thought
differently: the opposition leader had called for the rally
knowing workers would be killed—it was the only way to
get the foreign press to take him seriously.

The van proceeded to go faster over an unevenly surfaced
road, throwing the men against one another with greater

force, making it difficult for anyone to talk. Gamboa began
to be afraid for himself. Men unknown to him were engaged
in a brutal strategy and would make of *his* body a convenient
statistic to suit their separate ends. How was he going to get
anyone to listen to him and to believe his story? I am only a
poor man. The one who stands in the crowd when the
procession goes past. And whether it's a king or a general or
a civilian president, I am always the same, waving and cheer-
ing. The complete patriot, flag in hand. Just a blur to you.
Who would listen to him? Who would believe anything he
said? And then he started to berate himself for his savage
treatment of Federico Chagra; he should not have beaten him
so ferociously. He had never raised a hand to anyone in his
life. What had come over him? It would have been more
proper to have gone and spoken to the boy's father. Chagra
was an idler and a gambler but as a father he would have
respected another father's concern for his child. That would
have been the correct thing. If only he had had money and
they lived among families of a superior class! Mariana would
have found her young man in some elegant drawing room.
Not in the street. It was not her fault to want to escape from
their tiny apartment. But he had seen other girls in the
neighborhood thrown into an early marriage. More children,
more misery, and that was all. He had not wanted that to be
Mariana's fate. Sonia never understood him. Always accused
him of having grand ideas. But she was kind-hearted, though
ignorant. He cringed now to think how hard he had struck
her and in what awful language he had cursed his daughter.
What would become of them if no one believed his story? His
throat felt as if choked with dust. He would apologize to
Federico, he would ask his daughter to forgive him, he would
never again dream of a promotion or of being a leader—if he
could only have his ordinary life again.

When the van finally came to a stop and its rear door
opened, and a soldier ordered the men to alight and line
themselves behind the three rows of prisoners who had already
arrived, Gamboa saw that they were inside the compound of
a military base on the edge of the ocean. While they stood in
line within an asphalted, fenced-in area, the prospect around
them was a pleasing one, momentarily making them forget

the terror that attended their situation. Beyond the fence were well-kept lawns, the paths bordered with flowering hibiscus bushes; flamboyant trees covered with vermilion blossoms and palm trees with their lower trunks painted white almost concealed a large stone building and the several barracks behind it. And then there were the glimpses of the blue ocean. Gamboa was reminded of some pictures of a holiday resort he had seen in a magazine at the barber's. But just then he saw rising in the sky a large military cargo plane that had just taken off from the runway which must presumably be on one end of the base but invisible from where he stood, the four turbo-prop engines of the plane making a loud whining sound. The eyes of the other prisoners were turned to the plane too, many of them taking the opportunity of the overhead noise to talk to each other, and Gamboa heard a man behind him say to a companion, "That plane has a door on its bottom that flaps open. They're not wasting time giving anyone a trial."

"What do you mean?" his companion asked.

"I heard," said the man, his voice barely audible over the roar of the engines as the plane flew directly above them, "they pack the plane with prisoners, fly over the ocean and open the door."

Gamboa found that hard to believe and would have laughed it off in another situation, but now a cold fear ran through his body. He heard the other man say, "No, the plane would crash if they did that. They must make you jump out without a parachute."

"Don't be stupid," the first man said. "It would take too long that way, and it would be too much trouble to force everyone to jump. They fly the plane low, see? And just let everyone fall out."

The noise of the plane decreased and Gamboa observed that as it gained distance over the ocean it scarcely attempted to gain height. Other prisoners had also been looking up at the plane and exchanging their thoughts on the matter: everyone seemed to know the economical forms of execution the government had invented for its unwanted citizens.

A Jeep drove up, an officer sitting in the front passenger seat, and halted beside a group of soldiers. They conferred for some fifteen minutes. The officer finished giving his orders and drove away. The soldiers formed themselves into a line, rifles held against their shoulders, and marched toward the rows of men. There were ten soldiers, led by a sergeant who had the distinction of carrying a machine gun. Gamboa looked to his left and to his right and at the rows of men in front of him. There were perhaps a hundred prisoners, certainly between twenty and thirty in each row. In the two distant corners of the compound, where more vans had been arriving, there were more lines of prisoners, two large crowds of them with a lot of soldiers herding them about and the officer in the Jeep driving toward them. Another three hundred, Gamboa thought, perhaps as many as five hundred. He tried to find a way of calculating the number precisely, finding his mind relax when it distracted itself with numbers. But he was brought back to his immediate reality, hearing the sergeant give a command. There was a brisk movement among the soldiers, who came to attention in front of the first row.

"Every tenth man when pointed to," the sergeant shouted, "will fall out to form a new line."

He himself began to walk between the rows, taking slow, ponderous steps, and raised his machine gun to point at each tenth man. A line of twelve men was now formed and two soldiers were ordered to march them away to one of the vans that had brought the prisoners. The sergeant waited to see the twelve loaded and the van drive away in the direction from where the plane had earlier taken off, giving the remaining prisoners plenty of time in which to conjecture both the fate they had been saved from and the nature of the alternative fate that awaited them.

The sergeant walked grimly between the rows and, coming out to the front again, paused for a minute and then shouted, "Next, the third and seventh man in every ten."

He resumed his solemn march through the rows and pointed to the men thus counted. Now a group of twenty-one emerged, and these prisoners, too, were driven away in the direction of the airfield.

First every tenth man and now third and seventh, Gamboa pondered, and it struck him that, since three and seven made ten, the sergeant was doing nothing more original than carrying out an old-fashioned decimation. Somehow Gamboa felt pleased to observe that a rule governed the apparently sense-less action.

The sergeant followed two more procedures, but now making the selection so random and arbitrary that the logic Gamboa had perceived a moment earlier collapsed, replaced by barbarian thoughtlessness that generated only the cruelty of unpredictable chance.

The sergeant paused for a good five minutes between each of these random drawings, so that the men who remained looked to their right and counted their position in the line and waited in tense apprehension although none knew the next method of selection. They could only presume that there was some secret code which the sergeant followed—thus making them the victims of a larger design—and not that he simply shouted out a number that happened to come to his mind, making them the victims merely of the whims of a lowly officer.

As the sergeant stood pondering his next formula, the remaining men worked out the possibilities that could be their lot: the ones chosen first were either the luckiest or the most unfortunate, and in their anxiety the men still standing wanted to believe that to have been missed out by the random pro-cedure so far was a good sign. It was always a privilege to be saved, for it was to be among the chosen who were favored to receive some poignant honor; but even the most optimistic could not suppress the doubt that the ones to be kept to the end could well be marked out for some hideous experiment in the infliction of pain.

The third and fourth groups to be chosen were driven away in the direction of the barracks. Just then a cargo plane, similar to the one they had seen taking off earlier, quite possibly the same one, came into the men's view as it made a wide arc over the ocean in its descending approach to the airfield.

Now only twenty-eight men remained, among them Felipe Gamboa. The sergeant walked up and down in front of them, the two remaining soldiers behind him. Gamboa's fear of what was to happen to him alternated with boredom. Although a breeze blew from the ocean, it was hot under the sun, and he had also begun to feel hungry. He found it odd that no one had really said anything. The officer in the Jeep had scarcely looked at them as he drove past to give his orders. The sergeant appeared to be conducting a drill. It suddenly occurred to Gamboa that he and his fellow prisoners did not exist in the eyes of their military captors, and hence they were being disposed of without question or ceremony so that the government could believe that the opposition had no substance at all, that the fire-breathing dragon was indeed the farcical creature of a cartoonist's imagination. As the sergeant pondered his next move, Gamboa wished he would put an end to the suspense; while the sergeant's playing with numbers had a certain fascination for Gamboa, by now, however, he was becoming quite bored with the game and, did his life not possibly depend upon the outcome, would have ceased paying attention. But he realized that cruelty took many forms, of which being made to stand hungry under a hot sun was a banal version, for which relative kindness he ought perhaps to be thankful. The pain that was beginning to circulate within him, attacking his brain with sudden rushes, contained in its bitter chemistry the sharp acid of anger that fate should have trapped him in the evil of others and the dark lead of sorrow that his life should lose all its promise at one unfortunate stroke; but he remarked on the extraordinary phenomenon that, given such pain on the top of his physical discomfort, his keenest sensation at the moment was that of boredom.

The twenty-eight men stood in one long line. Now the sergeant pointed at random to anyone who took his fancy and asked him to step forward. Gamboa was selected. He then ordered these men to return to the line but each to a place other than the one he had earlier occupied. The sergeant followed this crazy move two more times. It was like shuffling a pack of cards. Satisfied, he let the men stand for another five minutes.

His boredom and hunger worsening, Gamboa paid no more close attention to the sergeant's game which would have been childish and silly did not some mysterious dread attend its outcome. His head hung low under the heat as he waited for the sergeant to come up with his next trick. Only a month ago he had been a happy man, given to idle dreams of wealth, certainly, often wishing for a magical power that would transform his condition, but no more, really, than any other ordinary human being whose simplest desires possessed the aura of extravagant fantasy because so little was accessible to him. Sometimes the sense of misery was oppressive, sometimes the lack of money filled him with despair and the reality of his life was difficult to bear; but he had been content. Well, more than content—happy. *Happy*, he repeated to himself without irony, suddenly filled with a nostalgia for his past life.

The sergeant marched to the beginning of the line and then began to walk slowly past each man, counting as he proceeded. He called out each number in a clear but low voice. When he came to Gamboa, he stopped, took a long look at the man, and shouted as if in triumph, "Thirteen!"

The muscles on Gamboa's face twitched; a burning coal seemed to have lodged itself in his throat.

"Number thirteen, step forward," the sergeant cried, staring at Gamboa. "You are the lucky one," he added with a grin that appeared to Gamboa to be ironical and malicious.

The process of random selection had made it his fate to be the one chosen to be put aboard one of the Navy's ships on which an accident had resulted in some dangerous chemical being spilled, making it necessary for the Navy to find a man whose health it did not value to do the job of cleaning up. More importantly, the Navy did not wish anyone to discover the kind of weapons its ships carried and therefore, when Gamboa had finished the job at the end of the fourth day and the ship had sailed some eight hundred kilometers out into the Pacific, making for an island base, he was put on a small boat and abandoned in the ocean.

During the next three days, as hunger, thirst, and the ferocious sun above the equator seemed to be extracting his life from him one cell at a time, he wondered why he had not simply been shot and thrown overboard instead of having inflicted upon him the captain's cruel idea of a sporting chance.

He found unbearable the fierce light that shone upon him from the great empty sky. He was at the center of an enormous circle of water whose surface was a chaos of reflected sunlight. He had been cast out of the world known to humans, thrown into that immense ocean in which the sun, too, was obliged to end its voyage sinking on the western limit of the globe.

He should have drunk the chemical they had made him clean up; instead of wearing the plastic suit, gloves and a mask, he should have gone naked to the poison; he should have leaped into the pool of poison on the ship's iron floor and lapped it all up greedily. It would have been sweeter than the sorrow he must continue to drink.

A number of times he thought he should lean over from the drifting boat and let his body fall into the water. But either he did not have the strength for even that little action or there was something in his mind holding him back, perhaps nothing more than an unwillingness to die or, in the extremity of suffering, some perverse inclination to endure it, as if a time had to come that offered a justification of what he had had to experience.

Late on the third afternoon the sky grew cloudy, and with the blinding glare gone he began to perceive shapes in the gloomy light. There appeared to be a dark form on the horizon, a thin jagged line. He had no doubt that he was hallucinating, that, after so long a time when the light had been so intense he could see nothing, he was now dreaming a new world into existence. Surely he must be close to death for his mind to spring upon him a desperate fantasy of life? But a little later he saw something else. There seemed to be a large dot in the sky that was looping around in wide circles. It was a bird, he realized, floating free on the air currents. So, that jagged line must be land!

The bird floated lower, and he saw it clearly now. He recognized it from the picture he had pinned in his office. It was an albatross, exactly like the one floating high above a cliff with the ocean below it in the picture that he had stared at so often while working on little sums with their round numbers that held within them the promise of a free life.

II

The Amulet

"Where in the world have you been?" his mother cried at him when Federico Chagra returned home after Mariana's father had pulled him away from her embrace and beaten him. "Look at those pants I only ironed this afternoon, and that white shirt! What have you been doing, playing football in clothes my hands are red from washing?"

"I had an accident," he said in a low, sullen voice.

"An accident?" It was then that she saw his face. "Oh my God, Federico, what happened? There's blood on your chin and a cut on your forehead."

"It was nothing, just a stupid accident."

"Nothing, he says! He looks like he walked through a shop window, and says it's nothing! Tell me, Federico, what happened?"

"I fell on the sidewalk. It just happened, all right? There was oil from parked cars, and I hit against the bumper of one when I fell."

"Don't you look where you're going?" his mother demanded. "I know, that Gamboa girl has turned your head. You're always in a dream nowadays."

"Oh Mother!"

"Well, didn't you say you were going out with her?"

"Yes, and if you'd only given me the money I asked to take her to the movies, then maybe this wouldn't have happened."

"Oh, so it's my fault, is it? You walk around in a daydream, and it's I who am to blame if you fall on your face! And where do you think I'm supposed to find the money for your young girl's amusement?"

"It isn't too much to ask," he said, "and it's not that I pester you for money that often."

"No, you don't," she said sarcastically. "Only last week it was to go to a football match, and then you sulked for two days as if your world had come to an end because I couldn't spare the money for a new pair of sneakers. Oh no, you never pester me for money!"

"Oh, what's the use!" he muttered.

"You'd better go and change," she said. "And wash yourself well. You don't want your father to see you in this state."

"Where is he?"

The innocent question made her heart jump, but she said after a moment, "Working late."

"On a Friday?" Now he could be sarcastic in turn. "Oh, yes, poor Father is working overtime in order to take his family on vacation. Come on, Mother, you know very well he's out drinking with his friends, throwing money away on booze and cards that he should be bringing to his family."

"Federico!"

"Maybe not all of it on booze, but on women, too. Isn't that what you shout at each other about in your bedroom at night?"

"Federico," his mother said, forcing her voice to remain calm, "I think that cut on your forehead needs to be dressed. You should go wash yourself and put some iodine on it. And leave your dirty clothes in the basket."

Later that evening he remained in his room when his father returned, and long after he had switched off the light he heard' his parents talking feverishly in their room. It was always the same thing—bicker, bicker, bitch and wail, or they would go on and on in a low monotone that was more irritating than being kept awake by a dog barking. Other kids had fathers who worked hard and saved to buy the family a car or a color TV, but his father gave the impression that he even resented having to buy food for his.

He could not go to sleep after the parents had fallen silent, for his mind was filled with a confusion of ideas—schemes of revenge against Mariana's father that would neither harm her nor make him appear bad in her eyes. He realized that they should not have stopped in the entranceway to a building on the same street on which she lived, but they had just passed two buildings where lovers stood embracing and, coming to a third whose dark and deserted entrance appeared to have been reserved for them, they had stopped spontaneously. Mariana had quickly tugged at his hand and, without thinking that it was about the time when her father usually returned from work, they had seized the opportunity. It could not have been two minutes before the old bastard came up and snatched him away from Mariana. Federico suffered the brutal punishment again in his mind and, filled anew with anger and hatred, wondered how he could pay back ten times for every blow that he had endured. In his mind he played out the imagery of several barbaric fantasies: tying Gamboa to a bed and setting rats on him; coating his body with honey and throwing him on an ant heap in a field buzzing with wasps and bees, etc. Then he had a more practical idea. He should get Mariana pregnant and then abandon her, and let the old bastard solve that one! But he was immediately repelled by this idea; he could not do such a vile thing to Mariana. The notion of pregnancy, however, discarded as a contemptible trick, was followed by an association of idyllic images in which he and Mariana made love in some vaguely charming setting which contained pink flowers and a blue sky, a conjoining of bodies that represented pure love in his mind and was quite unrelated to copulation and its consequences—as if the two bodies, locked in an eternal embrace in which each gave all of itself to the other, nevertheless preserved their original innocence.

So far he had not gone beyond kissing her, and it had only been on this evening, during the few minutes in the dark entranceway, that the sudden spontaneity of their embrace had made her open her mouth when she felt his tongue against her lips. The memory of that thrill made him perspire now. What was more, she had then pressed her tongue into his mouth and pulled up his hand and placed it firmly against her breast. How sweet it had been to have been wanted by her, to have been drawn so freely to her secret body! Another moment and he might have brought out his secret, guided her hand to give her a full possession of it. The very thought of it was too much and, imagining his own hand to be hers, he turned to his side, whispering her name, Mariana, Mariana, imagining too her little breasts pressed against him, sweet sighs escaping her lips as he ran his tongue over them, Mariana, Mariana, and her thighs raised to receive . . . *Mariana!*

He tiptoed quickly to the bathroom, going past his parents' room, his cupped hand wet and sticky. What a perfect life he could have with her, he thought, returning to bed. But for that old bastard. And his own parents. He hated them all. Stingy, mean old bastards. His father could give him more money if he did not spend so much on drink and gambling. Probably spent it on whores, too. Federico was disgusted when he thought of his father. Never gave him any pocketmoney unless he begged for it or told a clever lie, like inventing some special project he had to do for school. Never took him on a vacation or even to a football match. He might as well not have a father. It was horrible to have to obey a person who did everything to make you want to hate him. The way he ate! *Chup-chup-chup*, fat lips smacking at each bite. The way he slurped his coffee or leaned back in his chair and scratched his balls right in front of everyone! It was revolting. And what a way to talk, like everyone was a servant who had to be scolded loudly all the time, always making out he was some big shot. Disgusting it was. And you were supposed to love your father and look up to him. God, what a punishment! He wished he could lay his hands on a bundle of money and put ten thousand miles between himself and his father. He wondered how much money he would need to go away. Five thousand contos, and he could be free. At least make a start on his own. Ten thousand contos, he could really be free—wouldn't that be something? A million contos . . . He fell asleep mentally working out complicated sums with an ever-growing running total in his mind alternating with images of stacks of bank notes and heaps of gold coins that were magically at his disposal.

The next morning he was surprised to see an unexpected conviviality between his parents. They behaved as though they were a young couple who had made up after a quarrel and, in the glow of a new understanding, threw frequent loving glances at each other. Federico watched with amazement. What a pair, really revolting! Top marks for total *yuk!* From their conversation, in which his father was again describing his winning streak at cards the previous evening, talking for a change like a civilized man, Federico understood that the cause of their reconciliation was that he had won a lot of money. So, that's how it was. You gamble and whore, but all that gets wiped out as soon as you win big. The nasty old wife-beating bully is a good guy again, the old lecher is a homely hippo with a totally stupid grin because he's brought home a bundle of money—and no questions asked. Totally and absolutely and positively revolting.

Finding his parents even more unbearable now that there seemed such a renewal of affection between them than when they had nothing but sarcasm and abuse to express to each other, Federico went out of the apartment and found himself walking up and down the street where Mariana lived. She usually came out of her apartment around ten o'clock on Saturday mornings, but on this occasion she did not appear, although Federico waited a good forty-five minutes past that hour. The old bastard must have locked her up in her room, he thought, and rehearsed new situations in which he could inflict unendurable tortures on the man who had come between him and his girl. Finally he walked away, frustrated that he was not likely to see Mariana until Monday morning when her parents could not prevent her from going to school. He had no desire to return home, nor did he feel like going to the park where his friends would just be beginning a game of soccer. He walked about the streets without thinking and found himself in a place that his father had often told him to avoid, in Rua Miraflores, the main street of a small district famous for the number of artists who lived there, the first of whom had been attracted to the area by its cheapness some twenty years earlier. The chance of one of them becoming a much-honored national artist led to many more artists making their studios in the same street, as if it possessed a magical quality of imbuing each one of them with the talent of a genius; shops that appealed to the taste of pseudo artists, especially the young sons and daughters from wealthy families who enjoyed believing they were poor, neglected artists, had sprung up together with houses of prostitution, and thus a district had developed to which a trendy journalist had given the name Nuevo Soho. There was also a number of gambling houses in the area, all but one of them offering the usual games of chance with playing cards and dice; the other house, the one where Federico now saw many men entering, ran cock fights twice a day.

He followed a group of men to the entrance and, seeing that no one noticed him, let alone questioned his presence, he continued with them into a courtyard. Here a small dusty square had been roped off and a crowd of men stood around talking loudly among themselves. There was a booth where many people went and handed over money in return for a ticket. Federico had heard the older boys at school talk of this place and had a general sense of what the game was. And, soon enough, the first cock fight was on, with the men shouting for the one they had backed. All he could think of while watching the fight was that the weaker cock was Mariana's father and the one who was tearing his flesh out was himself. Apart from this fantasy, what caught his attention most was the sight of two men who cashed in their tickets at the booth for what looked to Federico to be considerable sums of money. He knew basically how odds worked at gambling, but had no knowledge of the particular complications introduced at this arena to make it more difficult for the gamble to pay off. He got the erroneous impression that all one had to do was to guess which cock was going to win, and just like that, in a matter of minutes, there was a pile of money to collect. When the second cock fight ended, he saw one of the men who had won on the first fight and had then bet again on the second collect what seemed to Federico—to whom an American dollar bill that a school friend had once shown him represented real wealth—a small fortune. He had not seen that the man already held a quantity of notes in his hand to which he had added his winnings, and, noticing only the outer bill that was of a large denomination, and that too for just a moment's glimpse of it, Federico concluded the man had made a killing. All that money, made so quickly, with no effort at all! Total paradise! He could hardly believe that, had he had some money to play with half an hour ago, he could now be walking away from the booth with a fortune in his hands. Totally rich and away from that revolting slum and free from that slimy hippo. He idly imagined coming in for the afternoon's fights, winning like he had seen the man do twice, doubling and quadrupling his money, and going away with Mariana before the sun set to some perfect island in the Pacific.

He left the arena, dreaming of the paradise that could be his; his vision might have been different had he stayed and observed the man he had seen win twice lose all his money on subsequent fights.

He hastily walked back along the street, going past a gaming house where groups of men were coming out, some with the contented look of those who have had a modest run of luck and others, the majority, whose faces betrayed wretchedness and despair. A restaurant at a corner, with tables on the sidewalk, had filled up, and a smell of roasting meat and broiling chickens was in the air. Young men and women, many of them presumably artists, sat engaged in serious discussions, with bottles of beer before them. The ground floor of a number of houses had been converted to art galleries or to shops which sold artists' materials, and through some of the upper windows could be seen glimpses of paintings hung on the studio walls. Voices or music from a stereo came from the windows. Federico hurried on, his blood agitated, fascinated by what he imagined to be the life led in these houses—independent of parents, exciting, and sexually loose—and also scared by the vague idea that here there were no distinctions between good and evil.

A block away from the end of Rua Miraflores he was back in his familiar environment of shabby old houses, many replaced by apartment buildings that lost their newness within a year, with here and there an empty space where a house had been knocked down, a hole dug for the foundations of an apartment building but left abandoned.

Back home he found his parents in the kitchen. His father sat with a beer at one end of the table on which were heaped little mounds of chopped onion, sliced squash and a cut-up cauliflower. His mother had opened the oven and, holding the rack, which she had just pulled out, with a cloth in one hand, was brushing some dark brown liquid on the roasted meat. Federico went to his room and sat down with an exercise book and the algebra problems which he had to solve for his homework.

He stared at the page without understanding what he read and realized that he would have to reread the chapter before attempting the problems. He had the whole afternoon and all of Sunday ahead of him. The homework could wait. He went to close the book, but his eyes fell on a page in a later chapter, one which they had not yet come to in class. It was covered with letters and signs, some of the symbols new to Federico. Total chaos! He was astonished to see what complicated problems, the very terms of which were unknown to him now, he was expected to master before the year was out. He kept the book open, staring at the signs and symbols, converting one formula into a secret account number in a Swiss bank, imagining another to be the licence plate on his Mercedes Benz, and seeing a whole series of calculations as the numbers on the certificates of the shares that he held in a dozen international corporations.

He was opening a dozen envelopes, each containing a six-figure check for the quarterly dividends, when his mother called him from the kitchen and asked him to carry the trash out. She seemed to be making a special effort, for it was unusual for her to clean the utensils she had used before serving the meal. Her normal procedure was to throw everything in the sink and leave it there until she had to cook the next meal. No one paid any attention to the squalor while they rapidly gobbled up the food. An overflowing trashcan in the corner, giving out a vile stink, was routine decoration in the kitchen even as they ate. But now she had apparently made a resolution to introduce a new style and, when he returned with the empty trashcan, he saw that she had cleared the table, wiped it clean and was spreading a tablecloth over it. She asked him to carry two pans she had scrubbed and to hang them from their hooks while she brought out the set of china that they hardly ever used, usually eating off plastic plates.

"Ah," his father exclaimed, "what we need today is a bottle of wine!"

Federico saw his mother look at her husband with a mixture of amazement and admiration. "Well, why not?" the father said, answering her look. "We can afford to celebrate. A bottle of Concha y Toro. Yes, a nice bottle of red Concha y Toro."

His eyes seemed to go into a dream and he smacked his lips after swallowing some beer. "Federico, go get my wallet, will you? It's in the pocket of my coat, hanging from a chair."

Federico went to the parents' bedroom. He felt embarrassed

by the way they seemed to be going on. Like a honeymoon couple. It seemed so unnatural, it made him tense. He missed the usual atmosphere of quarrels and noise. As he entered the room he saw the coat hanging from the back of the chair; he walked to it, pulled out the wallet without needing to stop, turned round from the chair, and was making to return to the kitchen, all in the automatic, surly manner of the adolescent who resents slave labor for his parents who appear to him to be too lazy to lift themselves from their fat behinds, when he suddenly halted. He looked at the wallet. Retreating from the door, he looked inside the wallet. He had never seen so much money! Total wealth! There must be some fifty bills there, he thought amazed, each one of the highest denomination of five hundred contos. He touched the edge of the notes with a finger and found himself pulling one out. It was a crisp new note with a lovely sharp edge to it, the number "500" inscribed on each of its corners. Five hundred contos! Ten times what Alberto Reubios, the richest kid in school whom everyone hated for talking so glibly about the stock market where his father worked, got for a month's pocketmoney. More than enough for the best seats for two every night at the movies for an entire fortnight. So much money in one note!

He held the back of the wallet open in order to replace the note, but stopped. The thick wad of notes looked no different from before he had reduced the number by one. He quickly took out another note, closed the wallet and opened it again to see if he could tell the difference. Hardly any; none, in fact. He folded the notes and put them into his pocket. Unless his father took all his money out and counted it, he would not be able to tell; besides, he had been drinking beer. But he would know sooner or later, Federico thought, walking to the kitchen and trying hard to breathe calmly. It occurred to him that the first explanation that would come to his father would be that the man who had paid him had cheated him or that he himself had made a mistake in calculating his winnings and that he had won no more than what was contained in his wallet.

The father opened the wallet, enjoyed the momentary

pleasure of staring at the money, plucked out a note and, closing the wallet said, "Here's five hundred contos."

"Don't you have anything smaller?" his wife cried at him as if alarmed.

"Small notes are for poor people, my pet," the father said, and chuckled. Federico cringed on hearing the endearment: it sounded silly coming from his father's lips.

"Make sure you get the correct change," his mother advised Federico when he took the note from his father.

"Yes, you better count it carefully," the latter said, irritating Federico by assuming his normal loud voice and scolding manner. "Double check it, yeah, remember that, double check it. Everyone's out to shortchange you nowadays, the world is full of crooks. A bottle of red Concha y Toro. *Red*, you got that? Hurry along. There'll be a tip for you if you return in ten minutes but not if you take a minute longer."

"You want me to put your wallet back in the coat?" Federico asked, seeing his father was again holding the wallet open and fingering the notes.

He folded the wallet closed and raised his hand to give it to Federico, but withdrew his hand, saying, "No, I'll keep it."

As Federico was walking away from the kitchen he heard his father say, "I'd better count it and put it away in the strong box."

And just as he was about to leave the apartment, his mother's voice reached him: "You can't be too careful."

Closing the door behind him, Federico made a dash for the stairs, rushed out of the building, and ran down the street. He did not stop until he had come to the main street where there were shops and bars. He stood panting outside a super-market where the wine was to be purchased. Surely his father would have counted the money by now. Was he sitting there in a rage and cursing him? Was he going to wait for him in the apartment and beat him into a pulp when he got back or was he already coming after him? On the other hand, he might be thinking that he himself had made some mistake and not have the slightest suspicion that his son had been a thief. But Federico decided that he could not take the chance. If only his father had given him the wallet to put back in the coat, he would have replaced the two notes—though in his present mood of fearing the consequences of the discovery it did not occur to him that, had his father indeed given him the wallet to take back to the coat, he was more likely to steal another note from it, seeing that the father had not noticed any missing from the thick, original total.

His only hope now was to buy the bottle of wine, return home promptly and confess by saying that he had only taken the money as a joke, intending all the time to return it. There would be a slap or two, but the worst of it would soon be over. But no: no one played jokes with money; and if they did, the person at whose expense the joke was played was never amused. He could not expect to get away with a mild rebuke and a gentle slap. He would be beaten like never before. His father was a great one for teaching him lessons meant to last a lifetime. He repented now having taken the money. It was a stupid thing to have done —what had come over him? It was going to be his father's thick belt on his bare back, lash after lash until his kidneys exploded. That's what you got for fooling with money.

Then he remembered the morning's cock fights. The image came to him of the man he had twice seen collect his winnings, and he recalled some talk about twelve-to-one and seven-to-one which he naively figured must have been the odds. His mind began to flash a dazzling array of numbers like a pinball machine. Supposing he had first bet fifteen hundred contos; that would have given him eighteen thousand; and putting eighteen thousand on the second fight would have produced 126 thousand contos! Maybe the kind of luck that the man had had, winning twice in a row, was exceptional, but the fact was—he told himself, thinking of the fortune that could have been his—that he had seen it happen with his own eyes.

Federico was mistaken, however, in what he believed to have been the evidence of his eyes, for as an inexperienced observer he had jumped to simplistic conclusions, understanding what he saw only in terms of what he already knew, which was practically nothing; and moreover, his knowledge embraced nothing of the complicated betting rules and restrictions applicable at that arena. He had heard some numbers repeated without knowing the context in which they had been mentioned and had erroneously convinced himself that they were the odds; and then, in his ignorance—one digression from the true facts leading him into a labyrinth of false impressions—he had believed that one man's winnings were related to those odds. In short, his perception had absorbed nothing but a series of distortions of the reality before him.

Having thus mistakenly concluded that, had he had fifteen hundred contos in the morning, he could have made 126 thousand, he was led to begin to believe that he had made a voluntary sacrifice; and in this curious progression of illogical ideas he ended up by convincing himself that, as a consequence of his sacrifice, as a kind of reward for not being greedy, he had a claim, indeed a right, to make a modest winning: fate owed him a small prize for his virtue. This thought, which seemed to him to be perfectly reasonable, prepared the ground for his next conviction, that the only condition on which he could return home was one in which he had a lot more money in his pocket than when he had left.

Rua Miraflores was much more crowded than earlier in the day. People from other parts of the city came there for their Saturday afternoon amusement, loitered on the sidewalks, finding diversion in the art galleries, the curio shops, and the dark little bars in the streets which led off Miraflores. Some artists had set themselves up on the sidewalk and offered to draw a charcoal portrait of anyone who paid them. When Federico arrived at the building where he had observed the cock fights, he found a crowd of people waiting to enter it. Apparently the doors had not yet opened for the afternoon's session.

He felt impatient and tense, and walked about nervously, going a little distance down a side street. He stopped at a café and had a roll and a cup of coffee. The proprietor was dumbfounded when Federico brought out one of his three notes to pay him and, calling to his wife to mind the cash register for a moment, he went across the street to get some change, cursing as he went. Federico saw him enter a shop that had above it the single word POPAYAN and painted in gilt letters with black edges across the top of the glass front were the words *Gold, Silver, Antiques, Theater Costumes*, and below them, in the center of the window, an enormous eye surrounded by lines representing the rays of the sun.

Federico was surprised not to have seen the image before, it was so powerful, staring at him all this time.

Collecting his change, he walked across the street to look in at the shop window. There was no carefully arranged display but a confusion of objects apparently simply thrown in a heap. Federico could make out a tarnished silver coffee pot, some ornaments made of ivory, others of brass, several packs of tarot cards, wigs, garlands of paper flowers gone ghostly with dust, a cracked china clock, a stuffed owl lying on its back with its large eyes staring up, a black cape with red lining, half a dozen volumes of old books with their leather bindings peeling off, a human skull, and several rumpled costumes. Behind all this the shop itself was dark and only blurred forms could be seen. Federico looked again at the objects in the window. That silver coffee pot. It would look beautiful when polished. His mother had always wanted one. Wouldn't it be nice to buy it when he went home? But what was he thinking of? The doors must be open by now. He had to go and make money before he could dream of buying presents. He rushed off to the cock fight.

Most of the crowd had already gone into the building and he joined the line at the door. He saw a sign on the wall that he had missed earlier. There was an admission charge for the afternoon session. This fact should have served as a warning that, while entrance was free in the morning, when only the local regulars had the compulsion to gamble, the place, like every other establishment on Rua Miraflores, was out to rob the hordes of tourists who came in the afternoon, to take from them even their small change, using whatever pretext seemed not too outrageous. Federico, however, saw in the charge only the slight inconvenience of being held up in a line while each person bought a ticket to go in.

Two men sat at a table in the entrance, selling the tickets. When Federico held out his money, the man was about to tear a ticket from the roll in front of him, going about his business mechanically, but he stopped, let his hands fall to the table, stared at Federico, and said, "How old are you?"

"Why?" Federico asked, wondering what age he should say he was.

"Come on, don't hold up the line!" the man said sharply.

"Eighteen."

The man leaned his head back and said, "That means sixteen, right?"

"No, I'm eighteen, I tell you!" Federico exclaimed.

"Oh, all right," the man said, taking his money and giving him a ticket. "But just don't try betting, that's all."

It was only when he reached the courtyard and saw the crowd of people at the betting booth that Federico realized that if he could not bet then he had wasted his money coming here. The courtyard was filled with noise, with groups of men talking loudly. There were a few well-dressed women in the crowd who looked about them with mildly ironical smiles as if to disassociate themselves from the absurd passion of their men for a ridiculous blood sport.

A hand fell on Federico's shoulder. He turned cold. A middle-aged man with a close-cropped gray head and a thick black mustache was grinning at him, his eyes narrow slits.

"So they won't let you bet, eh?"

"I just came to watch," Federico answered.

"You said you were eighteen," the man said, and gave a short laugh. He had been standing by the entrance and had followed Federico after having heard his exchange with the ticket seller. "You got to be twenty-one to be here," he added. "I bet you aren't even sixteen."

"I'm not harming anyone, am I? I said, I just came to watch."

The man smiled and said, "You should have gone to Popayan's and got yourself a costume. Old Popayan would have made you up, too, to look any age you want. He's like a magician when he's in the mood to trick the world. You've got to learn the little gimmicks, boy, if you want to make it big in the world."

"Who are you?" Federico demanded. "You're not a cop."

"Call me a friend," the man said, smiling again. "You want to bet? Put some money on a sure bet? I could help you. I could do it for you, see, so you won't be breaking the law."

"I told you, I just came to watch."

"And you've never heard of people winning money here," the man said. "Big money. And you never thought you could make money, too, eh?"

Federico felt uncomfortable under the bemused stare of the man and, affecting a show of bravado, said, "I know all about winning. There was a twelve-to-one this morning that paid off."

Federico's remark, calculated to show off his familiarity with betting, proved to the man that the boy knew nothing about it. There had never been a twelve-to-one. The boy was an ignorant fool. It was going to be easy working on him. He gave Federico a friendly pat on the shoulder, saying, "Hey, you're no kid, you've been around!"

"You're damn right I have," Federico said, pleased with the self-confidence he had suddenly acquired.

"So, you just came to watch?"

"Well . . . yes." Remembering his parents brought back the hesitation to his voice.

The man detected the shift in his tone and said, "Or maybe you'd like to play some? I know this place, see. I can tell you wouldn't mind making a little money to take home." He paused for a moment, thinking he must keep it simple for the kid, make him a proposition that he could understand. "There's a five-to-one that's certain for the first fight," he said, and watched the effect on the boy, seeing his mind begin to do the easy calculation. "I know the men who raise the cocks, see," he added. "I make it my business to know. I don't fool around with frauds. Say what. You want to put twenty contos on the five-to-one?"

He watched the boy through his narrowed eyes. He could not have made it simpler. An easy sum to compute. A nice hundred for an answer. A tempting hundred before his eyes. He could see from the look on the youth's face that figures were running through his mind. The kid was going to be easy prey.

Conflicting thoughts were running through Federico's mind. His instinct told him that he should not trust the man talking so smoothly to him. But the image of his father hunting for him made him want to carry out his earlier plan. The man could be a devil tempting him. But then providence could be on his side: he realized in this moment that he himself would not have known on which cock to place his bet and, probably going for long odds, would have lost his money. He was really lucky the man had come along, a convenient agent of fate that had placed before him a series of extraordinary chances since morning; he really was very lucky.

The man was again grinning at him, and said, "You want to put twenty on or not? There's not much time left."

"Five-to-one?"

"Yeah, five-to-one, and a sure bet," the man said, looking around to make certain no one heard this preposterous statement.

Federico put his hand into his pocket, and the man said, "Make that twenty-five. Five for my services."

Federico kept his hand in his pocket and said, "What if I want to bet more?"

The man was glad he asked, for in order to work out how he should operate on the boy he needed to know how much money he had. Guessing from Federico's question that he might have quite a bit, he said, "I'll do a deal with you. Ten per cent commission on the winnings and no service fee. How's that for complete trust in my judgement? I don't get a cent unless you win."

"Okay, here's a thousand," Federico said, suddenly pulling out the notes that he had been holding in his pocket.

The man kept his astonishment to himself, thought very quickly what approach he was going to make to pocket that thousand, swallowed hard, and said, "Come on, let's go, we've got business to do!" He walked quickly to the booth and Federico kept at his heels. As they walked through the crowd the man turned his head toward Federico and said with a grin, "Where'd you get the thousand from, your father's wallet?" He laughed aloud, seeing Federico's face darken. "No one fools me, see," he added, "I know everything."

Federico watched him in the crowd at the booth and saw him over the shoulders of other men when he was placing the bet at the window but without being able to see exactly what he did there.

"You just stay close to me and you'll do fine," the man said to Federico when they went to the arena.

Federico felt surprisingly calm as he watched the fight. It was as if he had no doubt of the outcome. Everything would be all right. It had to be. Things were going to work out just great. He would give three thousand to his father and take him two bottles of Concha y Toro as well as maybe that silver coffee pot to his mother. Make them both happy. Make his own life with them a bit more tolerable. Maybe give the old man only two thousand, not three, that was enough profit for him in one day. Save the rest. Buy a present for Mariana, for himself too, why not? Some really sexy clothes. Making his mental calculations, Federico remained indifferent to the bloody spectacle before him and the shouting of the men around him that made it seem there was a brawl going on. He could not have told afterwards what he had witnessed, for what appeared in his eyes as a sharper reality than the wounded cocks was money.

"What did I tell you?" the man was saying as they walked to collect the winnings. "I don't fool around with frauds, no sir!"

He disappeared into the crush of people at the betting booth. Federico waited, tense and alert, the thought having come to his mind that the man might collect the winnings and disappear. But the man emerged from the crowd surprisingly quickly, holding up the notes in his hand and grinning at Federico. "Here's your forty-five hundred and here's my five," he said charmingly. "It's a pleasure doing business with you, young man!" And he held out his hand, showing Federico his widest grin yet. At that moment, Federico thought him the friendliest and most honest man on earth. "What are you going to do now," he asked, warmly shaking Federico's hand and slapping him on the shoulder, "run home with a little present for your mother? Or do you want to play some more? Make some real money?"

"Do you have any more tips?"

"Tips?" the man threw up his hands in a gesture showing he was repelled by the word. "My business is with sure bets, I don't go in for *tips*."

He advised Federico not to bet on the next fight. He had doubts about his information on it, and when he wasn't certain he preferred not to risk any money. They sat out the fight which Federico found very dull—not because he had become a discriminating spectator but because his perception was influenced by what the man said. Federico derived a greater excitement from the images in his own mind which showed him his present profit multiply to an astronomical sum as he won on subsequent fights. In the middle of the dull fight the man went away for five minutes and, returning, said, "This fight's a pisser. You know why? It's so boring everyone goes and takes a piss during it. There was a long line back there." The fact that hardly anyone else had left the arena during the fight went unremarked by Federico.

In the interval before the next fight he said to Federico, "Well, now you're going to see the big one on which you can make seven-to-one. Can you believe that," he repeated to give Federico time to make his calculation, "*seven-to-one*! You want to put something on it? Five hundred, a thousand?"

The prudent part of him that had whispered that, now that he had more than three times the money that he had stolen from his father's wallet he ought to go home and be thankful that he had been saved had long been silenced within Federico's head. Instead he had been calculating what he could win with four thousand contos at various odds and, hearing the man mention seven-to-one, he unhesitatingly said, "Here's four thousand."

"Boy, you really like thinking big, don't you?" the man said, looking impressed when Federico handed him the money.

Just then someone in the crowd whistled and the man turned his head and stared at a person standing to the right of the booth. Federico saw a serious look come over his face as he said, "Just wait here a minute, will you?"

"Where are you going?" Federico called after him, seeing him march off. "You've got my money!"

Federico was suddenly stricken with panic, the idea rushing to his brain that the man was playing some trick on him in order to disappear with his money. Maybe he had accomplices scattered in the crowd, all of them carrying on a carefully planned operation. Had he really gone to the toilet just now, or had it been to arrange some signal with an accomplice? Was there some kind of sleight of hand that he didn't see? He went to follow the man, but stopped, seeing that the man was standing by the booth and talking to someone, maybe receiving important information from him; while turning his ear to his companion, the man gestured to Federico to wait.

The two talked, their faces appearing very grave. Then the man walked back to Federico and said, "Here's your money, keep it."

"Why, what happened?"

"The fight's been fixed. A lot of people are going to lose a lot of money."

"How do you know?" Federico asked.

"I told you a couple of times already, I don't fool around with frauds. Certainly not with a client's money."

Federico was vexed at losing the chance to make twenty-eight thousand contos and felt as if he had been robbed of that sum. But soon he was grateful to the man when he saw the fight turn out exactly as he had predicted—though what Federico saw was what the man told him—and he chided himself for having doubted the man's integrity. There was one more fight which offered a three-to-one according to the man.

"You're sure about this one?" Federico asked.

"Listen, have I done *any*thing wrong? Have I lost you a single cent? If you don't want to bet, that's okay with me, go on, go home to your mamma."

The thought of Mariana had come to Federico. He could make thirteen thousand contos, a bit more. They could go away somewhere and start a life together. And so, smiling, he handed to the man the four thousand five hundred contos he had won earlier, saying, "You're damn right I want to bet!"

The crowd at the betting booth was larger than before and, after waiting at the back for a minute, the man said, "This is ridiculous. I'll go and see my contact. It won't take two minutes."

"Where will you find him?" Federico asked, following him as the man hurried away to behind the booth. Some people got in Federico's way but he kept the man in sight. He saw him undertake a quick transaction with someone just behind the booth. The other nodded his head. Federico had disengaged himself from the people blocking him and had nearly reached the two men when he saw his friend turn round and come toward him.

"That's settled," he said to Federico, grinning. "That's the way to do business, quick and easy. Here's your ticket, you want me to keep it?"

"I'll have it," Federico said.

"As you like."

Just after the fight had begun he said, "Listen, I'm going to see a contact for a minute. This fight looks okay, your bird's winning already. I'll meet you by the booth when this is finished, okay?"

"How will I find you, it gets so crowded there?" Federico asked.

"Listen, *you* have the ticket and *I* will need to collect ten per cent from *you.*" His index finger pointed back and forth with each emphasis. "Therefore, if you will pardon my saying so, you can bet your mother's coffin that *I* will find *you.*"

He went away and Federico felt a little ashamed to have given the impression of having distrusted him. But his thoughts were soon distracted. His bird was indeed winning. That two live creatures were being yelled at by men who urged them to tear each other apart, that one had already been blinded and blood poured from the sockets of his eyes, that the crowd screamed for more blood—the spectacle of the murderous sport evoked no emotion in Federico, neither of sympathy nor of horror. He was thinking of the thirteen thousand five hundred contos, less ten per cent. Not bad at all. He'd keep ten thousand for himself and Mariana, and send the rest to his father in a registered envelope. That would be just over two thousand, a good deal more than he'd taken from him; and besides, his father himself had won it gambling.

He ran to the booth when the fight was over. Other people were hurrying to it, too. He looked around for his friend but could not find him. Soon, a crowd had gathered in that area and it seemed pointless for Federico to look for the man: for all he knew, the two could be going in circles round the booth. Federico decided that he would join the line at the booth and, if the man did not turn up by the time he got to the window, he would have a go at presenting his ticket. The man in the booth had a wire mesh in front of him and might not notice Federico's age if he looked at his face; as far as Federico could tell, his preoccupation was mainly with tickets handed to him and the counting out of money.

His friend had not turned up by the time Federico presented his ticket at the counter. The man held the ticket in his hand and, instead of proceeding, as Federico had anticipated, with counting a pile of money, he turned the ticket around in his fingers and then slapped it down on the counter and shouted, "What the fuck is this?"

"My ticket," Federico said. "I bet four thousand five hundred."

"You bet what?"

"Four thousand five hundred contos. Three-to-one on the winning cock."

"Three-to-one! Where the fuck you come from, asshole? Forty-five hundred contos at three-to-one! Where do you think you are, at the Jockey Club? Shit, can't you see what it says there? Limit one hundred contos on all bets. And no one's heard of three-to-one."

"But that's my ticket for the bet," Federico insisted.

"Shit, fucker, this looks like some cloakroom ticket from a theater. And *you,*" he shouted, suddenly peering closer through the mesh, "you look like you still get your breakfast, lunch, and dinner at your mamma's titties. Who let you in here?"

Federico snatched the ticket from the counter and quickly stepped aside. Surely there must be some mistake. His friend must have given him the wrong ticket. But then why hadn't he come for his ten per cent? That is when he saw the notice at the front of the booth which had earlier remained hidden by the crowd gathered there and which, among other official information, confirmed what the man in the booth had said about the one hundred contos limit on all bets. He realized, too, that the betting procedure was different and much more complicated than he had thought it. This discovery put an entirely different complexion on the afternoon's events, and at last the truth about his situation dawned upon him. He could never, with the best of luck, have won more than a hundred contos; he had lost a thousand.

He left the building when nearly everyone had gone. It was almost five o'clock and the crowd of strollers on Rua Miraflores had increased. Groups of teenagers in blue jeans and T-shirts with symbolic images—the Eiffel Tower, the

Sugarloaf—and names of foreign cities printed across them gawked incredulously inside doorways or through the windows of galleries where paintings of nude men and women were hung or where a group of artists seemed quite openly to be smoking pot, and, exchanging glances of amazement, the teenagers shrieked and ran up the street in their sneakers with red and blue stripes until some other scandalous image arrested their attention. Some artists, who had come to live in Nuevo Soho too long after it was discovered to find a studio on Miraflores itself, or were too poor to afford one, and consequently lived in the adjoining streets which the tourists tended to ignore, displayed their paintings on the sidewalk, sitting near them on folding chairs and staring at the passersby with looks of cultivated arrogant disdain.

But Federico hardly observed the scene around him as he stood outside the building, its front door locked, from which everyone had now departed. If only he could have his original thousand contos returned to him, he would go back home and accept the inevitable punishment as his just due. He could not believe that he had been such a fool. To think that he had actually had four thousand five hundred contos in his pocket, together with the change from the other five hundred, and he had been dumb enough to fall for a simple confidence trick! The man must be laughing to himself at how easily he had tricked him. The whole thing had been based on gaining Federico's confidence by handing over to him four thousand five hundred contos; now that Federico thought about it, he had not actually seen the man collect the money from the betting booth—he had only seen him go into a crush of people and emerge from it holding the notes in his hand. The real game had been not that he had been placing bets for Federico but that he had been betting his own money to empty Federico's pockets. He had coolly placed three thousand five hundred of his own in Federico's hands in order to make him part with his thousand—a much more certain profit than if he could have put all his money on the cock fights where the betting restrictions made it impossible for anyone to win a thousand contos. He had cleverly not disappeared soon after Federico handed him the thousand the first time, for that would have provoked alarm in the boy, but instead had engaged him in a protracted distraction; and it had been a subtle stroke, leaving Federico with the money, as if he himself had no claim to it, and going to the toilet for five minutes, or pretending to do so; Federico now realized—understanding comes fast in misfortune—that he was probably watched all the time and, had he decided to leave with the money at that point, he would quickly have been stopped.

He had not even found out the man's name, and when he tried to describe him to the person who had been selling tickets at the entrance his verbal sketch evoked no recognition; the only reply he received was, "Aren't you the kid I stopped and asked your age? So, what happened with this guy, took your money, did he? Serve you right for breaking the law!"

Federico had left him, pained by his cynical laughter. The money that remained in his pocket would buy him meals for a week or so, but that was about all. When it came to having to exist on what one had, the money, which had seemed a generous supply in another's possession, suddenly could buy so little when one's life depended solely on it. There was no answer to the basic questions—where was he to sleep, where find a bathroom, where a change of clothing? And if he sneaked into his neighborhood on Monday morning to see Mariana when she went to school, what could he tell her? Everything had gone wrong ever since that old bastard of her father had pulled him away from her! It was all his fault! However, the discovery of a scapegoat for his troubles did not make them go away. He realized that he had only two alternatives before him: go to the river which ran at the back of the park and jump into it or return home and accept all the horrible consequences. He began to be resigned to the latter idea.

What were humiliation and pain after all? They would pass after a few days. The bruises of his father's blows would heal. It was a small price to pay to be with Mariana again. She would love him all the more intensely when he told her how he had thought only of her when he bet the money on the cock fights; he would share with her what he now began to convince himself was the true motive for his actions: to release her and himself from the tyranny of their parents. To her at least he would be a hero and, imagining her admiration for his attempt, the fact that he had stolen money from his father became transformed in his mind into a heroic action that had demanded extraordinary courage.

He was about to go home. But at that moment he remembered that the man who had disappeared with his money had mentioned Popayan, saying something about getting a costume there to look older. It was the only reference he had made to another person and suggested that he was familiar with him. Federico decided that, before he went home, he would follow this one lead.

A bell jingled behind the door when he opened it. It was dark in the shop. The only illumination came from the waning light of day that fell through the murky front window. Federico stood just inside the entrance after closing the door behind him. In a moment or two he began to distinguish objects. Cloaks and gowns hung from the walls and from a cord stretched just below the ceiling, giving him the impression that he had entered a cave. Here and there a point of light reflected back from a sequin or some ornament embroidered on a gown. He took a few steps forward. There were several tables in the room with narrow passages between them. They were heaped with objects that he found hard to make out in the poor light, but he was able to discern some items of pottery and a few articles of silver and gold.

Suddenly a light was switched on in the far end of the room. Federico saw a table lamp with a green shade cast a glow on a large wrinkled face whose tightly closed mouth and angle of the jaw suggested the absence of teeth. Above the deeply scored forehead the curve of the bald head seemed a dull yellow, while the eyes, round and opened wide, were black. Federico took a step forward but halted. Now he could see a little more clearly. He assumed that the large man who had stood up behind the table was Popayan, and unaccountably felt a little afraid in his presence and could not think how to broach the subject of the man who had taken his money.

Popayan had seen the boy earlier, standing outside and looking at the articles in the shop window a few minutes after the café proprietor from across the street had come to change a note. The boy had a haunted look, the kind he had seen on people who had the compulsion to flee, an anxiety to be leaving some place, without knowing what they were running away from and, in the majority of the cases, not even knowing that they were engaged in flight. He himself had known the demon that could suddenly possess the soul and draw it to some alien landscape as if it were a bird migrating from a dusty scrubland, where it had twittered and warbled, that can discover the full range of its singing voice only when it finds itself, after a journey forced by blind instinct, in a cool, dark forest that is as unlike its native habitat as is the terrain of the moon from that of the earth.

He switched on a floor lamp that cast a more general light in the room. Federico thought he observed a flickering on the old man's pale white-yellowish skin: the shadows cast by the wrinkles twitched about the face and the eyes blazed as though the man stood in front of a roaring fire. Federico formulated the question in his mind. Did Popayan know where he could find a man who . . . ? But inexplicably he could not utter it aloud.

"Is there enough light? Can you see?"

Popayan's deep voice was somehow reassuring and Federico quickly answered, "Oh, yes, it's really very bright in here."

Popayan sighed and sat down, saying, "Well, look around and see if there's anything you want. Take your time. See what you can buy."

Popayan took advantage of the light on his table to ponder again the two sheets of paper that he had been looking at earlier in the day. One was a folio from an old German manuscript book that he had found many years ago in a shop in Heidelberg when he had been a student of antiquity; there was no mystery about the image—a common enough representation of the Voyage of the Sun; thirty years earlier he would have been interested in identifying the temple in ancient Egypt from where the image had been copied, but his present interest was far from scholarship: he was wondering how best he could treat the paper to make it look older in order to pass it off as a rare print to sell to a collector. The other sheet on the table perhaps suggested a reason for such an unscrupulous preoccupation. It was an account of the week's takings at the shop. Popayan's early interest in scholar-ship, his studies in Germany during his middle twenties and a short tour of the ancient countries, followed by a professor-ship after he returned to South America were passions of a soul now extinguished; he had concluded one day that learning had failed him, and had come to the belief that the quest for knowledge was a monstrous chimera created by the imagina-tion of man. There could be no wisdom because there could be no relief from the body's pain; and the mind's bemusement with abstract thought was only a strategy to distract itself from an infinite despair.

Become hard, cynical and calculating, the passion that now drove him was avarice. But though now money, and hoarding it in interest-paying accounts, wholly preoccupied him, from time to time the spirit of the student who had touched the stone monuments in the ancient world would rise within his breast and he would, in a flashing moment, be puzzled again by the startling recognition that some fragment of a destiny unfolding before him belonged to a scheme whose pattern he had known, and that, unpredictable though the next event was, the final outcome already existed and had been recorded as past history, that indeed he himself had deciphered the hieroglyphic text.

"I was thinking . . ." Fedrico began tentatively.

"Yes?" Popayan stared back at him in the manner of one whose time is precious and can indulge the visitor only for a few minutes. "Is there money in your pocket? How much do you want to spend—twenty contos, a hundred?"

"I was wondering," Federico tried again, but Popayan, finding the boy's presence summoning thoughts he did not wish to confront and wanting him to leave quickly, interrup-ted him with, "A present for your mother, is that what you're looking for? Something for a girlfriend? How much do you want to spend? Do you have any money?"

"I really only came to ask if you knew a man who . . ." Federico rushed the words through his mouth to tell his desperate story, and concluded with, "I thought you might know him. You see, he mentioned you."

"He stole *all* your money?" Popayan asked, irritated to be wasting his time on the top of having his mind troubled by thoughts of destiny. "You have *nothing* to spend? You have *no* money?"

"Yes," Federico answered, but, finding it difficult not to tell the complete truth to the man staring at him, quickly added, "except for the four hundred or so that I had in another pocket."

"You still have the four hundred? You have *four* hundred contos in your pocket?"

"Well, yes."

Attempting to suppress the abstract thoughts from his mind by concentrating on the material objects around him, Popayan rose from his chair and cast his eyes about the shop, the scattered items quickly suggesting to his mind an inventory of things priced around four hundred, and, thinking that young boys were fascinated with weapons, he wondered whether he could not pass off as a colonial antique a pistol too rusted for use in a theater where for two decades it had fired blanks in melodramas. But just then Federico, who had interpreted his pensive and calculating glance about the room as concern for his predicament, said, "I don't know what to do."

Popayan had begun to walk toward a table where the pistol lay. He stopped and turned round to stare at Federico, realizing that it was impossible to escape the inflexible form of the ancient catastrophe. Normally another human being's plight did not touch him, and he who in his youth had been moved to tears by a text narrating the death of Osiris and, coming out of the library in Alexandria, had seen the beggars in the street as creatures in a myth, a people chanting a lamentation at the death of a god, was now a man without emotions. But in this moment, seeing Federico's face in three-quarter profile, the light catching only one side of his face and giving the eye there the appearance of painted stone, as if the boy had become an image on a frieze, Popayan suddenly gasped. He had not thought that his mind would play such a trick on him. He saw himself standing in the museum in Cairo looking at the relief of the boy Horus. He took a step toward Federico. Behind him, suspended from a cord, hung some theater costumes, and two gowns, their material falling in haphazard folds so that the shadows fell upon the cloth as triangles, making it appear like the skin of a crocodile, framed the boy. Popayan shook his head violently as if trying to rid himself of an illusion. Federico remained still, not knowing what else to say to him.

"Four hundred contos!" Popayan mumbled to himself as though uttering a magic formula to dispel the troubling thought from his mind.

Now Federico said, "I will be punished."

Popayan had taken another step toward him. "Punished?" he cried, startled by the word—as if the boy had expressed a premonition; but could self-knowledge be so transparently ambiguous that one did not see the true consequences attending a seemingly casual perception, and therefore could never comprehend a revelation of the self? "There's money, *money* in your pocket," he said aloud, but the words would not exorcise the thought that filled his mind.

Federico did not move. Popayan went and sat at his desk and held his large head between his hands. It had been an error, all that learning; he was trapped by it now, unable to escape the affliction of time; but he understood that even if he knew nothing, and were as ignorant as the Indians who brought produce to sell at the market, he would still be under the same obligation to history.

"The man had closely cropped gray hair, a black mustache," Federico prompted him.

Popayan nodded his head, his eyes closed. Federico imagined he was trying hard to remember the man's name. But Popayan was remembering something else and the thought that had seized him with the memory of the boy Horus would not leave him. Why should he concern himself with destiny, he was only interested in the boy's money. Four hundred contos. Not much, but something to add to the week's income. It had not been a very good week. Four hundred would make it a little better, just a tiny bit better. The boy had stood there outside the window earlier in the day; even then he had struck him as someone compelled to flee, someone caught in a circumstantial web of which the events were only a progression of seemingly logical or surprising occurrences but which, however, were only the surface camouflage of a cunning fate. The insights given his intellect had been so outrageous! How they mocked him still, suddenly depriving him of a deliberately self-imposed solace of attending only to material things! As if in a voluntary exile, after making his own the language of another tribe, his own forgotten words were suddenly remembered, evoking broken images of an abandoned homeland. He saw him again, the present twin of the past, the Other only beginning to manifest itself in him, with a terrible future to endure. The reality had already happened in the ancient world and we the late arrivals could only suffer it by believing in the uniqueness of experience injecting into memory a drug that put knowledge to sleep. He had come again, and entered this time, the game of the afternoon creating the circumstances to give him a plausible reason, an illusion merely of cause and effect, that was an illusion also of the self, when the truth was buried behind laws inadmissible to logic. But he was not the boy Horus, whose destiny had been a cosmic burden; just this mortal who had lost not a father but only money, a trifling amount—and yet who stood now before him hoping for the revelation of a name, not knowing the mystery his existence incarnated, a future locked into his body which several thousand years ago was already recorded history. No, not the boy Horus, whose carved image outlined in this boy had only served to touch off a buried memory, enliven again processes of thought he had long suppressed, but that other commonplace life of enormous sadness that came disguised as the fulfillment of fantastic desires of the goatherd who, touching a talisman with his lips, had uttered an evil wish: and he saw on the wide bank of the ancient river, on a narrow beach at twilight, the conclusion of that tale, deciphered with such anxious passion in the glare of the naked bulb, that old parchment with its dreadful lacunae where the worms had been, hardly being able to hold it still, the boy become nearly a liquid form, all his will gone, falling against the Other and the Other against him in a final transformation of substance in the violet glow of sunset.

Suddenly, Popayan said to Federico, "Your father, what did you do to your father?"

Federico stared at him, his lips parted but unable to produce a word.

"The money you had," Popayan said, "who gave you the money?"

"I stole it," Federico said in a low voice.

"What do you want? The love of beautiful women? Power over men?"

Federico did not understand these questions and found himself repeating his earlier words: "I will be punished."

Popayan gave a roar of demonic laughter and rose from his chair. Like blood, time was trapped in the human body where its implosions caused a sickness in the brain which the self, in its arrogant obsession with identity, dismissed as merely a dream; he could express no warning to the boy nor wish for him that his blood could endure the pain: only send him away. Curious and afraid, Federico watched him as he walked to a chest of drawers and, bending to the ground, pulled out the lowest one. He stood up, turned round, and walked toward Federico, holding out an object in both his hands.

"Take out all your money," Popayan said, standing in front of Federico, his arms stretched out, the glinting object before the boy's eyes. "You want to kill your father? The love of women? Empty your pockets, take out all your money."

Federico stared at the object in Popayan's hands. A tiny brass rectangle in the shape of a book on a chain. "What is that?" he cried aloud, inexplicably alarmed. "What are you doing to me?"

"Empty your pockets of money. You have desires, no? Wishes that you utter in secret? You want your own life. You left your parents' house looking for your own life. You took money to make your own life, you took *money*, no?"

With his hands stretched out, holding the two ends of the chain, Popayan moved closer to Federico.

"What is that?" Federico asked again as Popayan brought his hands over his shoulders and clasped the chain behind his neck.

Federico held the brass rectangle between his forefinger and thumb where it now rested at the base of his throat. Its size and thickness reminded him of cough lozenges. Popayan moved back from him and Federico, without thinking of what he was doing, took the money from his pocket and placed it on a counter behind him.

"An amulet," Popayan said, "or a talisman. It's been so long, I've forgotten these things. I've wiped out the words. So many words. But these images!"

"What will it do?" Federico asked.

"My memory fails me," Popayan said, though he retained it all too sharply, but he was not going to reveal to the boy that it was with fear and enormous loathing that he was committing the inescapable act, giving him a long-dead future of riches, bitterness, and sorrow. "I put my knowledge to sleep many years ago. But I must still know—obscurely, dimly, in snatches—what I have known. I am afflicted by partial visions in a world become suddenly old."

He stopped himself and gazed at Federico. These were meaningless words for the boy, who looked pitiable and who could not know that the sense of unease that made him speak those words was a terror that his life had already been lived. Popayan turned round and walked a few paces between two long tables heaped with theater costumes. A world become suddenly old—why should he, in his own old age, concern himself with it? He had long concluded that the more the human race accumulated of the past the less it remembered; memory, without which there could be no knowledge, became imperfect and began to be concerned with trivial matter. Lapses; long forgetfulness: and vitiated passions turned to elusive dreams, as monuments to dust, and truth was overwhelmed by fiction.

He picked up a garment from a table and walked back toward Federico who was still fingering the tiny brass book at the base of his throat.

"Here, take this, throw it round your shoulders," Popayan said, giving him the garment.

It was a cloak made of two pieces of thick cotton, black and red, and when Federico put it on the black section fell from his left shoulder and the red half from his right. Yellow satin crescents covered the black half and stars the red.

"It will protect you," Popayan added on seeing Federico wear the cloak. "It might be turning cool outside. There is no more I can do for you."

He went and sat in his chair.

"That man . . ." Federico began, but he saw that Popayan

was examining a piece of paper and did not hear him. He realized in the same moment that he could not remember the man's face. Had his hair really been very closely cropped or had he been bald? He could not be certain which. The color of his eyes, the shape of his mouth—he could recall no detail. He approached the desk and, standing in front of Popayan, said, "What can I do?"

Popayan continued to contemplate the figure of the Voyage of the Sun for a minute. When he looked up, his face appeared more deeply wrinkled than before.

"Nothing can protect you from your desires." His voice seemed to come from a great distance. "You will wish and you will receive more than you can bear to possess."

"I don't understand."

Popayan pressed his lips tightly together and took a deep breath. "Consider that your good fortune."

"I've lost all my money," Federico said. "How could I ...?" He stopped himself, and then shouted, "Why do you pity me so much and do nothing?"

Popayan was surprised the expression on his face was so obvious even the boy could read it, and, not having an answer to his question, resorted to evasion: "Perhaps everything has already been done for you."

Federico snatched at the amulet, but it was securely clasped.

"Go now," Popayan said in a soft voice, and looked away from the boy. He did not glance up when he heard him walk to the door, nor when the sound of the little bell tinkling filled the room as the door opened and closed again.

To be punished for errors we have not committed! Popayan found it hard to return to the comforting thoughts of avarice that had preoccupied him before the boy had come. What became of the *self* when the afflictions one suffered were only a coincidental occurrence of another life within one's own, depriving one's vanity of its most poignant gratification, that the pain it endured was a unique experience? He looked up and cast his eyes dreamily about the shop. Theater costumes, jewelry, old china, silver and gold, so many disguises for the intrepid or the weary. He saw the money lying where the boy had left it and went to pick it up. A fit of laughter suddenly seized him before he could reach the money, and he stood, a hand on a table to support himself, letting the laughter fill the room with its demonic sound.

The light was momentarily blinding when Federico came out of Popayan's. The lowering sun, reflecting from many windows, seemed to have set the buildings ablaze, and he had the impression of things having become transparent, fragments only of light, without substance. In that brief moment he had the illusion that the world he had known had vanished and been replaced by another. But soon enough his eyes grew accustomed to the brightness and he remembered which way he had to go in the familiar street.

He began to walk in the direction of Rua Miraflores but stopped when he saw his reflection in a shop window. He cut a ridiculous figure in the black and red cloak with its yellow crescents and stars and was reminded of a conjuror at a fair who had dressed himself like a clown. He put his hands up to the large button below his throat which held the cloak in place over his shoulders and, in the moment before he could free the black loop of twisted canvas that was held by the button and remove the absurd garment, a complex of images and thoughts rushed through his mind, and he stood at that moment, a finger and thumb holding the bit of twisted canvas behind the button, staring vacantly at the people wandering in the street. What had he done? The question compressed all the perplexity of his situation. How he wished he could be with Mariana in some other world where they possessed a complete happiness! But he had lost all his money and there was going to be hell to pay. His father stood above him, become a huge man with red, flaming eyes. His life was going to be unbearable. If it were not for Mariana he would not return home. But he didn't have a cent on him! He had emptied his pockets completely. He could not believe the stupid things he had done. Should he go back to Popayan and ask for his money? He wished he lived in a wonderful house by the sea where a beautiful woman loved him. What had Popayan meant, clasping the chain round his neck? Probably just a trick to get what was left of his money. Weird old man. He raised his hand from the button to the tiny brass book and held it between his thumb and forefinger. Ah, to live where the ocean broke against the shore all night and a beautiful woman pressed her naked body to his! He shook his head, freeing his mind of its confusion of fears and fantasies, and let go of the amulet.

He saw just then a young man come out of a house dressed as a Viking, go to a motorcycle parked on the sidewalk, mount it, start the engine, and drive away. A pickup truck came roaring up the street, a noisy crowd of young men and women in the back, all of them in fancy costumes with heavily painted faces and one or two wearing masks. He heard some music coming from Miraflores and was curious to see what was happening there. Forgetting that he still wore the ridiculous cloak, he hurried toward the main street.

He came to Miraflores and saw, as he stood on the sidewalk near where an artist displayed small paintings of churches, a convertible go past in which people sat in fancy costumes, two of them playing on trumpets and one, who stood in the middle behind the front seats, beating on a drum. Federico watched the car disappear up the street. A stream of cars was driving past and he stood on the curb, waiting for a gap in the traffic in order to cross the road, trying not to think that the reason why he needed to cross the street was that he had decided to go home: he was working himself up to enter some sort of a trance in which a Federico experienced what was coming to him while he himself, the real Federico, knew nothing of it; while his substitute suffered the pain of succeeding hours he wished for himself a timelessness until the moment arrived when all suffering would have vanished and he lived with Mariana in perfect happiness.

There was a slight gap in the traffic and he stepped down from the curb. But the car at the head of the next group was coming too fast and he hopped back onto the sidewalk. Suddenly, some twenty meters from where he stood, the car swung toward the curb and came to a squealing halt next to him. The back door was flung open and at the same time a head appeared through the front window and a voice shouted at Federico, "Want a ride to the party?"

Someone in the back seat cried, "Come right in!"

Federico stepped toward the back door with the intention of closing it and informing the people inside that they had

mistaken him for someone else, but a hand with a gold
bracelet at the wrist came out and held his which he was just
then raising in order to close the door. It was a gesture of
gently assisting him to get in, and also one impelling him to
make haste, and before he knew it Federico found himself
squeezed in a tight space next to a young woman, and the
car, its stereo drumming loudly with rock music, shot off to
overtake the traffic. Two blocks up the road one of the men
in the front pointed to an approaching corner where a man
stood in a fancy costume with his hand raised and said,
"There's another guy waiting for a ride." But the driver,
shouting over the stereo, said, "There isn't room for a flea in
here." He drove on, harassing the vehicle in front of him to
let him overtake.

There were seven others in the car apart from Federico.
One girl sat in between the two front seats, almost on the
gear box, with her arm across the driver's shoulder; another
girl sat next to her, resting herself on the thighs of the
man who sat by the window. The four in the back were
uncomfortably packed until the young woman next to Federico raised herself, let him make more room for himself, and
turned herself to sit sideways across his lap, putting an arm
round his neck and letting her head lean against the top of
the window through which some of her hair floated out on
the wind.

No one talked; the stereo was too loud. They were all
dressed in costume, though crowded so closely together it was
impossible to see the disguises each one wore. Only something
of the driver's dress was recognizable for what it represented;
there was a sort of wide collar around his neck which resembled a breastplate at the front, molded from yellow plastic
which was unmistakably meant to look as if ears of corn were
embedded in his flesh.

The man to Federico's left had been absorbed in rolling a
cigarette which he now lit and, after taking a long puff from
it, passed it to Federico. He held it gingerly, never having
smoked before, and hoped that no one noticed his inexperience when he seemed to end by kissing the tip of the cigarette
rather than drawing smoke from it. He passed it to the girl
in his lap who inhaled deeply from the cigarette and hung

her head back, out of the window, and blew the smoke
out into the universe. Her action had the effect of raising her
chest, so that her left breast was pressed against Federico's
chin.

They were driving on a highway outside the city, going in
a wide loop around a military base next to the ocean. The
girl in Federico's lap suddenly looked at him and said, "You
didn't put any make-up on!"

The faces of all of them were gaudily painted—lips glisten-
ing red, eyes thickly lined in black, cheeks glossy pink. "You
can't go to Daniela's with a colorless face," she said, speaking
close to his ear so that he could hear her over the music. "Let
me help you out."

She pressed her slightly parted lips to his cheeks at several
spots, leaned back to look at the effect, and laughed. "You
look as though you have a dozen blind eyes! But the mouth
is too pale."

She brought her lips to his mouth and pressed them against
his lips, holding his head tightly, and pulled her face back and
said, "There, that's better, now you look like you're going to
a party."

The car was at that moment swinging round a curve and
climbing fast up a hill, and Federico's eyes were dazzled by
the flashing of the low sun over the ocean, a golden radiance
that momentarily flooded his perception, extinguishing everything else from his sight.

The car swung from side to side up the winding road for
two kilometers when they came to a straight stretch, high
above the ocean. A little later they entered a gravel drive
bordered by acacias and arrived at a white stucco house with
red tiles. They drove slowly to the side of the house, looking
for a place to park, for all the space at the front was already
taken and, coming round the corner, Federico saw that the
house stood on a cliff and enjoyed a glorious view of the
ocean. The driver stopped between two trees and they all got
out.

Enchanted by the girl in his lap, whose feminine odor
reached him in spite of the smell of the perfume and make-up
that everyone wore, Federico had passed the forty minutes of
the journey in a dream of sensuality as though he had entered

a world of forbidden pleasures and his mind had suppressed images of the earlier events of the day.

The others walked away toward the house and Federico followed them. It was a beautiful house and, looking at the ocean above which it stood, he saw the sun, like a great red eye, poised precisely on the line of the horizon. He had, he felt with a thrill, arrived in the world of his dreams, but he walked cautiously and looked like someone whose feet scarcely touched the ground.

The party overflowed from the drawing room to the wide terraced garden which had been laid out in three tiers, the third one ending with a low stone wall on the edge of the cliff. A number of musicians had arranged themselves on the tiled patio, and a crush of couples danced in the drawing room and as great a crowd improvised a riotous carnival out in the garden. Not everyone wore a costume, and among the casually dressed were young men who wore a pair of shorts and nothing else, and a number of girls in bikinis, one of whom seemed quite unconcerned that the top half of her attire had fallen away during the dance. Some of the older guests were in formal evening dress, and they stood together talking disapprovingly about the young crowd, finding it loathsome to be among them and yet not leaving the party, determined that the hostess take notice of their unspoken protest.

The group Federico had come with was soon absorbed in the crowd, but since the dancing was more a tribal affair than one that required a particular partner, its chief characteristic being that many people threw themselves into a communal frenzy inspired by the music, and only occasionally, by chance, one held another person in a momentary embrace, Federico was restrained neither by convention nor by his own timidity and soon became one of the throbbing mass. In the intervals when the musicians rested, finding himself spontaneously become one of a group, standing near the large table in the dining room selecting delicacies to eat, or wandering about the house with some others, a glass of wine in hand, opening doors in the upstairs rooms to see in one a child's nursery and in another a large bed on which two couples were making love in an astonishing quaternate formation, Federico put together from the talk of his acquaintances the story of the hostess, Daniela.

She had given the party to celebrate her divorce from a banker to whom she had been married for sixteen years. All those years she had held what to many was an enviable position in the country's high society, and had been a perfect hostess to military generals and ministers of government. The present house, which had come to her in the divorce settlement, was a monument to that splendor; the blue and pink nursery, lovingly decorated by Daniela herself, created in expectation of starting a family, had remained empty. And then Daniela had had a crisis. Everyone called it her breakdown. No one knew exactly what had gone wrong. She went on wild binges with young people, almost willfully attracting damaging publicity, or shut herself up for months on end. Society people sympathized with the husband when he filed for divorce, but she did not appear to care and gave the impression that that was precisely what she wanted. Her oldest friends, proud of their Spanish blood, deplored her scandalous desecration of family honor; some others, who found rebelliousness charming in another, provided it did not threaten their own traditional ways, were a little more tolerant of her wild excesses; but no one paused to consider if her sensational behaviour might not be caused by some internal disorder.

Federico had not yet seen her and, as he was coming down the staircase when the music was beginning again, someone pointed her out to him in the center of the crowd that was commencing to dance. She wore what he thought was a bizarre costume: a black tunic with a wide yellow band at the collar which had embroidered on it a snake motif; stitched across the front of the tunic, just below the line of the bosom, were four little naked dolls made of pink cloth, each with yellow yarn for hair, black stitches for eyes and mouths and tiny black buttons for navels; the lower end of the tunic had three overlapping yellow bands with a pattern of fish scales on them. On her head was a papier-mâché mask: the face black, the eyes a vivid green; huge white front teeth painted to protrude from thick wide lips gave the face a viciously predatory appearance; a long tongue of thin leather came out of a slit in the mask just below the teeth and was covered with images of flames; and on the top of the head was a crown made of pointed green cones.

"Why has she made herself look like the devil?" Federico asked.

"No, it's not the devil," his companion said. "I asked her earlier. There's an island in the Pacific where she once saw a remote tribe. In one of its ceremonies, probably a purification ritual, a witch, wearing that costume, comes to the tribe and plays out a nightmare fantasy. She is called the Thief of Children."

The late morning sun cast spots of light through the trumpet vine climbing the sides of the gazebo and drenched the interior with a greenish glow. Below the cliffs, the ocean, which in the early hours around dawn had been knocking noisily, slithered in a slow sinking movement, its surface undulating rather than rising in swells, and filled the air with a less menacing sound. Federico awoke when a beam of light fell on his eyes. It took him a few minutes to realize where he was and how he had got there. He had the sensation of having enjoyed a long dreamless sleep, as if he had somehow discarded the body in the night and been only a spirit that had lain unmolested and unburdened by physical weight. And now the diffusion of green within the gazebo together with the sound of the sea created a sense of enchantment, suggesting to the awakening consciousness that the self it was beginning to identify was encased not within a body, whose hand now moved to grasp the edge of the hammock, but lay within an interplay of light and shadow, finding its true being in a dream of substances.

Federico pulled himself up and climbed out of the hammock. Late in the night, when groups of people had begun to leave the party, he had come out to the garden; unaccustomed to drinking, the wine had begun to overpower him and, staggering about the garden, he had found himself in the deserted gazebo and thrown himself into the hammock that hung there. Had he, at some opportune moment, run into the group he had come with, he would no doubt have accepted their offer to give him a ride back to the city and proceeded at some stage, he assumed, to return home; it was the chance only of his drunkenness and of his encountering no one while he staggered nearly blindly through the garden until he arrived in the gazebo and fell gratefully into the hammock that had kept him overnight at Daniela's house.

Patting his rumpled clothes, he saw the cloak that he still wore, and all the events of the previous day flooded into his mind. He looked amazedly about him as he left the gazebo and climbed to the middle tier of the garden. Here there was a herb garden with a winding gravel path through it; currents of fragrances rose into the air and swirled about him as he walked. He stopped beside a bank of rosemary that grew next to the low stone wall, above which was the lawn in front of the patio with flowerbeds and scattered groups of pots with nasturtiums and geraniums. That is when he saw her.

She sat in the patio beside a white table, eating breakfast. Ferns in hanging baskets suspended from the beams turned gently in the air, the shifting light on the foliage casting across her round face a sparkle that alternated with a faint greenish shadow. Thick black wavy hair, falling loose to her shoulders, framed the white curving outline of the face. Sunk comfortably in her chair, her neck hardly showed above the collar of the light blue dressing gown, the lower part of which, raised and heaped about the thighs, added to the difficulty of making out her figure. Her large black eyes, darting about the garden when she raised the cup of coffee to her lips, suddenly saw the youth stepping up to the path that ran across the lawn, and for a moment it seemed as though he was rising out of the ocean. She laughed, seeing the ridiculous cloak he wore.

There was still a bemused smile on her face when he came up to her feeling much as he felt with his mother when he had done something wrong or foolish.

"I don't know what happened last night," he said, standing just outside the patio and staring at the dimples on her fleshy cheeks. "I just woke up and found myself in the gazebo."

"Better come and have some breakfast," she said, remarking to herself that he was only a boy. "You're probably too young for that kind of a party. I wonder who thought of bringing you." Before he could attempt an answer she turned her head back and called, "Sylvia!"

Federico entered the patio and, taking a chair opposite her, said, "You must be Daniela." In the same moment he remembered someone at the party telling him that she had been married for sixteen years until her divorce, and he wondered how old she was. Hearing her own name made her throw a bright glance at him. He thought her extraordinarily beautiful.

"Wherever did you get that funny cloak from?" she asked, but just then the maid came from the house, and she said to her, "Sylvia, we have a guest. Bring more coffee and some rolls, will you?"

Federico stood up, removed his cloak, and, folding it, placed it carefully in his lap as he sat down again. "I'm sorry," he said, "I'd forgotten I still had it on."

"It hardly passes for a costume," Daniela said. "Had I spotted you last night, I'd have denounced you for a fraud."

"Without it, I could never have come here," he said.

"Oh, everyone tells me the wildest stories!"

He began to tell her how he happened to be standing on the sidewalk, waiting to cross the road, when . . . but he stopped himself with the reflection that such an absurd story could hardly interest her, and spoke instead of his admiration for her beautiful house. The maid brought a tray with rolls and butter and a steaming pot of coffee. They talked of the party and the inventive imaginations of people when they dressed in a fancy costume.

"Yours was terrific," he remarked to her. "I was scared every time I looked at you. That long tongue with flames on it! It was just sensational."

He struck her as naive, but she was amused by his company. His thin cheeks and rather full lips gave him an air which in her own youth had been considered poetical or soulful in a young man. Certainly his dark brown eyes had the potential for that sort of sentimental melancholy, she thought. He only needed to shampoo his straight black hair and comb it in place to acquire that look so many young men of her generation had cultivated of being a sensitive soul in a world in which the mildest breeze was a searing torment to the flesh. Federico, whose serious gaze was really only the entranced look of someone who cannot believe that his present experience is indeed happening to him, was wondering if the wish he had idly made in his despair after coming out of Popayan's—that he live in a house by the ocean where a beautiful woman loved him—had not begun to come true. He had not actually made a deliberate wish, but he remembered holding the tiny brass book at his throat between forefinger and thumb and, desperately wanting to forget the misfortune he found himself in, wishing for the impossible—a house by the ocean, a beautiful woman—but wishing in a way one so often did, by expressing a vague and a general desire while knowing it was only a foolish and futile attempt to escape the immediate anguish. What had Popayan called the little brass book? An amulet or a talisman. He had used both words. He had resorted to abstraction and ambiguity; Federico had been puzzled by what he said. But could such a thing conceivably have the power to grant wishes? It was nonsense, of course; ridiculous. And yet here he was, sitting beside a beautiful woman in a house by the sea!

The fact that he thought her extraordinarily beautiful was a consequence of his expectation that, since he had wished to be loved by a beautiful woman, therefore the one who, by a wonderful coincidence, happened to live alone in the house and was possibly the woman destined to love him, had necessarily to be beautiful. When she stood up to stroll about the lawn, he, walking with her, did not observe that she was rather short and stout, indeed fat, her unsupported breasts too far down on her chest, her hips too wide, but saw instead a voluptuous attraction in her figure, converting the impressions of her body in his mind into a form altogether different from the reality.

What magic was it that had placed him in this enchantment? Of course, it was not magic. Impossible! Had the lights at the far end of Rua Miraflores not been green and the traffic not rushing down, he would have crossed the street and not be here now. The funny thing was he had not even needed to cross Miraflores and could have gone home if he had proceeded along the sidewalk on which he stood; only he had had the thought of using the opposite sidewalk as a change from the morning

and, once having had the idea, he had stood stubbornly determined to cross the street. That was what led to the accident of
his being picked up. But here he was with the ocean in his ears.
He was beginning to believe that he had received a gift, and had
no doubt that he absolutely deserved it.

"I don't intend to go to town before Monday," Daniela
was saying. "I hate leaving my house unless I really have to."

"Please don't worry about me, I can hitch a ride." He spoke
nervously, fearing her immediate assent to the idea, and yet
longing for a sign that he had indeed acquired the gift of
having his wishes granted.

"Oh, I know! You can be my weekend guest!"

He was thrilled by the suggestion and thought hers the
sweetest voice he had ever heard, and when, her eyes scanning
his face, she added, "I don't know what it is about you, but
you seem to awaken a curious memory in me," her words
struck him as being incredibly romantic.

Inviting him to make himself at home, she went to her
room. What she had remembered was not a particular person
but a general memory of the time of her breakdown when
some obscure urge within her drove her to be with younger
men. She had been shocked at first by her own behavior and,
expressing self-reproach during the sober reflections when the
earliest attack had passed, had wondered at the madness that
had overcome her: for there she was, a woman of position in
society, perfectly happy in her husband and hoping each
month for incipient motherhood, and it was sheer folly to
plunge herself recklessly into a world of vice. But the impulse
had returned, recharged while it remained suppressed, and on
each succeeding occasion became more intense the greater the
determination with which she had attempted to check it. At
the same time she developed a horror of her husband's body:
he seemed to have aged and looked to her as though he
belonged to the bed of a woman of her mother's generation,
not her own. She could not tell him what repelled her, for
that would have been both cruel and manifestly false since he
was almost exactly her own age. She was obliged to invent
excuses or fabricate a sequence of deceptions or find some
subterfuge, often contradicting herself or pretending she had
not said what she had or entering into a long silence. The

husband was in turn enraged and solicitous, confused and sympathetic, and finally wild with anger.

But all that was behind her now. Her father, living in England in a self-imposed exile while the clear light of his beloved Andes was made murky by a military dictatorship, could have counselled her; but he refused to talk to her because of her friendship with the generals to whom she owed her position in society; and she in turn, imbued by the same stubbornness and pride that affected the father, remained determined not to seek his help although the image often stormed into her brain of herself as a child running into her father's arms. Had she been able to be with him—oh, not to beg of him to reveal to her the secret of her blood, not to plead for a knowledge that would expel the dark spot that had entered her soul—she might not have suffered the breakdown that had turned her reality into a fantastic chaos. She had seemed to her friends to be rebelling against convention; no one could know, and she herself could only have a vague intuition of it, what possessed her. The divorce had freed her from the necessity of lying to her husband, but if there were a truth to reveal to herself she had no idea what it was.

Even to herself she could be quite scandalously irresponsible. If she was crazy, well—she pouted her lips, standing in front of the mirror, and shrugged her shoulders—so be it. There was a certain pleasure in letting the body go, to let it rise, if that was its inner compulsion, to some great height of moral righteousness, or to let it sink into debauchery, if that was its natural inclination. In her discovery that there was an element within her over which she had no control, and realizing too that any deliberate attempt to check her whimsical passions could well be one of the disguises taken by the emergence of the irrational, deluding her into thinking that she knew perfectly what she was doing when in fact it led her into greater indulgence of what her rational self would consider abnormal behavior, she had ended by professing the belief that all manifestations of the self, whether they conformed to the bourgeois conventions and were therefore applauded as normal, or transgressed them and were consequently condemned as bohemian wildness, were a true expression of its real will. She no longer wanted to think; only to be. If there were complexities buried in her psyche, obscure images that sometimes made poignant and tormenting a dream, in which the sun, become a great round boulder, fell into a dark and fathomless ocean, or a swan flapped its huge wings over her body in a loud, terrifying shudder accompanied by a shriek that made the flesh want to slither away like a fish and be carried to a great depth on some current, then she did not want to know about them. Why desire madness, or even be distracted by its overtures? She was rid of her husband whose body had made her inexplicably afraid; and for some time at least she had been free of the compulsion to find a youthful man to satisfy an enraged craving to lose a sense of her present self. It was not, she was convinced, the crisis of entering her forties, fashionable though it was among women in her society to go into a depression on their fortieth birthday or, in an attempt to counter it, to profess the belief that they were exceptionally gifted to enjoy a prolonged younger age, for she considered tediously banal, and beneath her contempt, the notion that a youthful sexual partner somehow gave substance to the illusion that one had not really grown that old. There was a deeper anxiety within her, but she was determined to avoid the desperate remedy, and also a fashionable one, of consulting a psychiatrist. If the mind was riddled with guilts, so be it; and if madness was the price of independence, so be it.

Federico was sitting in the drawing room, reading a magazine, when she came down after having changed into a dark blue cotton dress that hung loosely from her shoulders and indicated no definition of her body, a comfortable kind of dress in which a fat woman could believe herself to possess a striking figure. She had parted her black hair at the center and plaited it in one thick rope that fell below her neck; her round, fleshy cheeks emphasized the essential circularity of her face, with the curving hairline making a perfect quarter moon of her forehead. None of these details were visible to Federico in their particularity, for he saw only the abstract shape of an exquisitely beautiful woman. He had washed himself in the downstairs bathroom, grooming himself as best he could by wetting his hair. He was embarrassed by the few black hairs that stuck out from his chin and about his jaws because they looked untidy and yet were not too numerous for him to have begun shaving, giving his face the marked appearance of adolescent immaturity which he feared a beautiful woman must consider repugnant.

In order to find something to do Daniela took him on a walk round her property. They went past the gazebo and proceeded along the cliff, watching the frigate birds circling high in the air. Sometimes there were pelicans here, she informed him, and once she had even seen an albatross. They circled back through the wooded area, going past the cottage where Sylvia, the maid, lived with her husband Diego who worked as a gardener and general handyman on the property.

"It's a charming little world, isn't it?" she said when they had returned to the house and sat in the patio. "Sometimes I see myself leaving it in a boat that has come and docked there by the cliff. I just sail away on it and feel sure that I could reach the farthest point in the west before the sun got there. What stupid things we think of!"

Federico enjoyed hearing her voice and whatever she said sounded to him beautifully poetic. When she remarked later in the afternoon, "The poor flowers, how thirsty they get in the sun!" or declared in the evening, "It's heaven here under a full moon. What a pity it's only a crescent!" he felt his pulse accelerate as though her expressions were not merely poetical but were in fact complete poems with so subtle and lovely a music in their language as to make him breathless with astonishment.

During dinner she said to him, "You mustn't hold your knife as if it's a pen, and please, Federico, chew slowly and keep your mouth closed while doing so."

He was only a boy but she realized, seeing him color slightly, that she must not talk to him like a mother, for he was her guest after all, and in order not to give him the impression that she was scolding him she quickly changed the subject. "You know, I'm really glad to have you as a weekend guest. It's such a treat to have someone to talk to."

Federico could hardly utter more than a brief phrase at a time: his head was entirely possessed by fantasies. His imagination would not let him sleep when he went to bed in the spare room. He expected Daniela to come to him at any moment, and during each instant that the door did not open and her wonderful form, which he saw in his mind as outlined in a transparent nightgown, did not appear and advance toward him, he rehearsed the manner in which she would come to him: she would float across the room and sink beside him, drawing his body to hers; or she would hold her arms open as she walked slowly, swaying her hips, a low moaning sound escaping her lips; or ... He whispered her name repeatedly, touching the consonants with his tongue and feeling himself being caressed by the vowels. He thought of his schoolfriends Roderigo and Jorge and imagined himself with them in a few days, telling them of his extraordinary romantic adventure, giving them the details of the pleasures he had enjoyed. Mariana came to his mind. But she was only a girl, he argued with himself, temporarily rejecting her; Daniela was a real woman, a fully developed lady. Besides, if the unbelievable manner in which he had found himself in his present situation suggested that he had acquired a mysterious power or been singularly blessed by nature or perhaps specially selected by God to have what he wanted, an arrangement to which all the forces of the universe seemed to have consented, then his future could be of his own choosing; he could wish to be with Mariana any time he liked. He wanted to taste the world first.

The roar of the ocean outside his window woke him up early in the morning. For a few minutes he had the impression that he was in the middle of a storm. His fantasies had become so elaborate before he fell asleep that his first waking moments seemed like a sudden return to reality in which one knew there were demons waiting to exert their sinister influence. But remembering where he was and seeing from the window that it was only the ocean crashing against the cliff, he breathed in the moist air with the exhilaration of one just released from captivity, one who has hiterto only had vile and obnoxious vapors on which to draw breath.

The door to Daniela's bedroom was closed when he went past it as he walked across the hall on the second floor, stepping noiselessly on the blue carpet. He was thrilled by the ambience of luxury. There were paintings of Indians in colorful ponchos on the wall, potted ferns near the top of the

stairs; to Federico, who had known life only in an overcrowded apartment building, even the plastic imitation of a
crystal chandelier was a dazzling object. A window at the end
of the hall looked down on part of the garden and to the
ocean on the left; how glorious it was, he thought, to have
such a prospect to oneself, and he remembered the view from
the windows of his parents' apartment—another building
with its open windows through which one saw the confusion
in which large families lived. But here there was light and
beauty, space that sparkled.

The door to the room opposite Daniela's was open and
Federico wandered in; it was the nursery, with two pink walls
and two that were light blue. Large pictures of animals hung
on one wall; on another were ten framed photographs, from
each one the same girl of four or five with curly dark hair
stared out in a variety of expressions, mischievous in one or
entirely indifferent in another, with a nonchalant pout of her
fleshy lips. Her black eyes reminded him of Daniela's. Perhaps
she had a daughter who was no longer with her; Federico
remembered people talking of her recent divorce but he did
not know that she was childless. There was no crib in the
room, but a normal single bed with a pink and blue canopy
making an arch over it and several little round or heart-shaped
cushions covered in satin of matching colors piled above the
pillow. Next to the bed was a small table covered with toys
—dolls which made a squeaky sound when turned over,
mechanical birds which bobbed their heads, matchbox cars.
The view from the window was of a wooded area at the back
of the house with a glimpse through the high trees of one of
the mountains far to the east of the city. Near the window
was a dresser whose drawers were crammed with clothes,
ranging from a baby's things—tiny frocks made of so fine
and soft a material they seemed to be woven of air—to a
sailor's costume for a boy of five. There was more in the room
that Federico did not see: a cupboard full of toys and games,
another with stuffed cartoon figures, a shelf of picture books.
He was amazed by what he had already seen; his own childhood had been spent crawling about the floor of the apartment, mostly in the kitchen where his mother kept up a
harsh monologue about the abuses she was obliged to suffer,

escaping from that environment when he was five or six years old and could spend his days out in the street with the other children.

Daniela saw him on the patio when she came down for breakfast and quickly covered up her surprise at seeing him. She had forgotten during the night that she still had a guest, there was so much else on her mind. The change in her life had not as yet made a full impact upon her. She tended to forget that she was no longer the wife of a banker whose position had guaranteed hers, and she had assumed that her relationship with the society she knew would remain unaltered, believing that she had been valued for her own self. But most of the more prominent people had declined to come to her party; instead, a great crowd of bohemians, many of them uninvited, though not discouraged by her, had descended on her. And then, last night, when she had phoned a particular friend to tell her that she expected to be in town on Monday, instead of the usual invitation to drop in for a drink, she had received what was clearly an excuse, expressed moreover in a coldly formal manner that left no doubt that it would be pointless for Daniela to call again. Her former life seemed finished, but there had been no rebirth; a dreadful heaviness weighed her down, draining her of her will.

Now here was this boring boy to whom, her education insisted, she must remain polite and convivial. She regretted not having let him hitch a ride to town the previous day. But even in the morning's weariness of spirit she knew she could never escape her upbringing which had taught her an extreme politeness to guests. For the present she found an escape from him by saying that she had letters to write.

Federico did not mind hardly seeing her all that morning. Her disappearance only increased for him the mystery of her being, and when she appeared, to take a breath of air in the garden or to go and gaze with a melancholy look at the roses just outside the patio, she seemed to him a figure out of some legendary romance, a woman of great virtue and pure passion, worthy both of profound admiration as well as everlasting love. As he saw her large black eyes move from one rose to another, he speculated whether the enormous sadness that he saw in her face was not an indication that she had already fallen in love with him.

Seeing him when she re-emerged from her bedroom a little after noon, she remembered that she had promised to drive him into town, and while she was vexed that she had to perform a chore, for her own desire to go to the city had been replaced by a wish never to have to go there when she had heard her friend make a transparently feeble excuse for not wanting to see her, she was, at the same time, glad that the boy she had made the mistake of asking to stay for the weekend was at last to be removed from her sight.

It was soon after lunch when, wearing a loose white cotton dress and a straw hat with a pink ribbon, she drove out in her Peugeot, having thrown open the car's sunroof. Federico, clutching his folded cloak in his hands, sat beside her in despair, wondering, now that his dream was obviously at an end, whether he had not merely been mocked by the illusion that he had acquired the power of having his wishes granted. He had only been the victim of coincidence, he now thought; of the many thousands of events that could have taken place, that had happened which temporarily gave the impression of a precise answer to a wish. That surely was the way human beings deceived themselves into acquiring beliefs for which there was no real rational foundation; and did not a super-stition tease the mind until it was allowed the status of conviction? He had been a fool once again—as he had been with the man at the cock fights who had stolen his money. He felt a bitter resentment against men who promised him wealth only to reduce him to penury. He was worse now than before he had stolen the money from his father's wallet. He had been shown the dream of luxury but must return to his sordid reality and live there in a perpetual state of regret, knowing the world that could never be his. The thought of his father deepened his despair, for he felt that all alternatives had been taken away from him but that he must return home and face an awful punishment. All that he had gained was two days of a glorious intoxication, like one who had gone on an alcoholic binge but must return now to his family and bow his head to the insults and blows that would be aimed at it. Even the thought of Mariana offered him no consolation;

rather, remembering her, and then her father's brutality toward him, he could not help reflecting that she was somehow ultimately to blame for his present misfortune.

Daniela paid him no attention, driving fast, plunging into the dangers of speed on a winding road in order to relieve her mind of boredom and the thoughts that afforded her nothing but discontent. But then, coming down to the coastal plain and the straight stretch and accelerating to 160 kilometers an hour, she saw the road blocked in the distance, and threw the car into a snaking movement on the road in order to lengthen the short distance in which to come to a stop, working the gears down rapidly before she risked applying power to the brakes. She brought the car to a halt within half a meter of the armored vehicle that was parked sideways across the road with four soldiers standing beside it. One of them came up to her window, shaking his head reprovingly, and, lowering himself so that his face was in front of hers, said, "The speed limit is eighty."

"Well," she answered, "what do you think I was doing, a hundred?"

The soldier grinned at her and, turning his face to his companions, shouted, "José, the lady wonders what speed she was doing. What do you guess?"

The three others came and stood behind the soldier by the window. They made whistling sounds and one said, "Nice car. Imported, too."

"Great stereo system," a second soldier said. "I think we'd better see the lady's papers."

"Yeah," the third one added, "a *lot* of papers."

The three laughed nervously and the one by the window, his head still lowered and his face now almost inside the car, flashed another grin at Daniela as if to suggest that she surely knew what they were talking about. She opened her purse and took out from it a cutting from a newspaper that she carried for just such an occasion. It was a society column with a photograph that showed her sitting at a dinner next to the general who was the country's Minister of Defence. In the picture the general was smiling at her with his glass raised in his hand.

"There," she said, unfolding the paper and presenting it to

the soldier at the window, "you can read all about me, and you can tell me if you want to keep your jobs or if you would rather take up shoe shining in Plaza Independencia."

Within half a minute the soldiers were standing at attention, the three at the back raising their hands in a spontaneous salute.

"Now perhaps you can tell me," Daniela said, putting the cutting back into her purse, "what on earth is going on."

"It's orders from the general," the first soldier said. "All traffic to the city has been prohibited till further notice."

"Why?"

The soldier hesitated but, thinking that he could do no wrong by revealing security orders to one who was intimate with the general, said, "We're rounding up communists in the city."

"But why should this road be blocked?" Daniela demanded.

Again he hesitated for a moment, but gave away the information he had: "No one's supposed to know where they are taken. The highway is kept free of witnesses. Besides, it's quicker when there's no traffic."

"Where *do* you take them?" she asked.

"Perhaps the señora can put that question to her friend in the picture?" the soldier remarked with a smile on his face.

Daniela turned the car around and drove back at a slower pace to her house, saying on the way, "We're trapped in our own country, victims of no one but our own selves."

But Federico had not heard her. He was clutching his cloak close to his chest and passing a forefinger over the surface of the tiny brass book at his throat and wondering whether the country's affairs had not been ordered to give him more time with Daniela so that his wish might be fulfilled. He whispered to himself, "I wish to God it were true."

Arriving at the house, Daniela said with a forced and ironical cheerfulness, "Well, here we are back in the godforsaken paradise!"

She went to her room and phoned her friend Susana, who was married to one of the general's aides. "What's going on? Why are the roads to the city blocked?" she asked. "The cops told me some story about rounding up communists, but what *is* going on? Is someone attempting a *coup*?"

Susana regretted having answered the phone: she ought to have let the maid pick it up even if her hands were wet just then. "Daniela, I don't know how to say this," she said, deciding to speak what was on her mind. "I did not call to thank you for the party."

"Oh, but I understand!" Daniela interrupted. "You don't have to be so formal with me."

"No, you do not understand," Susana continued in a firm voice. "I had not realized our usual friends were not to be there. I was most disappointed to be included among hippies. I don't know how I'll recover my reputation."

Daniela was stung, and before disconnecting the line said vindictively, "I'm sorry if you'll have to sleep again with General Osorio to recover your reputation."

She phoned two more society friends. The maids answered and obliged her to wait for an answer which in each case was identical: the mistress was indisposed and would call back when she was better. One of them had declined to come to the party, and Daniela realized that the few friends of her own superior social position who had come had wasted no time informing the others of that group of their outrage. She suspected, too, that her former husband had encouraged such social climbers as Susana to put the most malicious innuendoes to the gossip they spread. It was a sure way of having her ostracized.

While she remained in her room, Federico wandered about the garden or walked along the cliff, looking at the ocean, his thoughts fluttering about his brain like birds in a forest which busily dart among the bushes for berries and worms, fly up over the trees and come swooping back to alight on a branch where, caught by the sun for a moment, they sing. He saw Daniela come out to the patio at last. She had said nothing to him since returning and he had remained out of the house, not knowing what he was expected to do, and now loitered about the garden, hoping that she would notice him.

"What are you doing?" she called, seeing him walking out to the garden.

"I'm sorry to be so much trouble to you," he said.

"Oh, nonsense!" she quickly exclaimed, and then thought to herself that the phrase was an automatic response and conveyed the opposite of her true feeling. But she noticed for the first time the look of helplessness in Federico's eyes, reminding her of a dog that had come to her parents' house when she was a child. They had ended by adopting the dog after attempts to drive it away had failed, naming it Flick. "I ought to find a change of clothes for you," she added, and was herself surprised by what she had said. Federico interpreted that as an invitation to stay on in the house. She was struck by the smile that came to his face, and she went into the house pleased with the effect of her kindness. She would take him back to the city when she had nothing better to do and felt like a drive. Tomorrow or the next day. Her friends had closed their doors to her; why should she close hers to the boy? He looked like he came from a poor family; why should she not be kind to him? She felt exceedingly pleased with herself, discovering what a good-hearted person she was.

That night Federico kept waking up and looking at the closed door of his bedroom, imagining that he had heard a sound and that the door was just about to be opened. After the fourth or fifth time, he could not sleep. He exhausted himself with fantasies and longed to sleep. Hours passed; the first gray light began to appear outside the window. He tossed and turned. The ocean seemed to him to be especially turbulent and he decided that it was its noise that kept him awake. He sandwiched his head between two pillows, but the ocean still roared in his ears. It was like being on the floor of a factory where massive machinery was at work. He could not endure it. A bird began to sing somewhere. Federico realized that if he was to find some sleep that night then he had to go to some other room, away from the ocean. There was the nursery across the hall. He quietly went there and closed the door behind him; the ocean could still be heard in the distance but its relatively muffled sound seemed to him like a silence and he soon fell asleep.

Daniela did not find him in the house in the morning. She assumed that he had risen early and gone for a walk. When there appeared to be no sign of him by eleven o'clock, she wondered whether he had not decided to make his own way to the city. But Sylvia had not seen him and Diego, who was watering the potted plants when she had breakfast on the patio and had been working about the garden since soon after dawn, had not seen him either. Perhaps he had left early, before Sylvia and Diego came to work, Daniela thought, dismissing the matter from her mind.

She was more preoccupied by her own new and vexing situation, of being rejected by her friends, and had spent a disturbed night bothered by the thought that her freedom might prove to be a terrible form of imprisonment. But, happening to go upstairs to fetch something from her room, she was struck by the closed door of the nursery. It was not unusual for it to be closed, but a curious compulsion led her to look into the room. She saw Federico's clothes lying on the floor and walked to the bed. The sheet that he had drawn over his naked body had slipped below his chest. His black hair was ruffled; his profile against the pillow, with his lips open, gave him the appearance of a young boy, a child. But he moved just then to turn to his other side, and in the process the sheet slipped off his hip and she saw his swollen penis and observed the transformation of the child into a man.

She pulled the sheet up and gently placed it across his waist. Still fast asleep, he moved from his side to lie flat on his back. She watched the profile disappear, and his whole face, with the head thrown back so that the chin was tilted up, presented itself to her view. His cheeks were slightly sunken but the lips, just sufficiently parted to show the tips of his upper teeth, compensated with their rosy fullness for the somewhat emaciated impression of his thin, longish face. She still could not believe it was not the face of a child, but suddenly she longed to see his eyes, as though they held the secret of his age. She put one knee on the edge of the bed and leaned over him to pass a fingertip over his eyelids. Her hand was raised over his face when he opened his eyes. She kept her hand suspended for a moment and then put it just above his shoulder against the pillow. He flung up his arms round her neck and drew her to him, believing her to have come in answer to his wish. "I was in such a dream!" he exclaimed.

Her cheek was against his but she raised her face to look into his eyes. Why, he was truly only a child! For she saw the brightness of his eyes, the wide, unbelieving look, as the innocence of childhood. But just then, still in his embrace, she moved the rest of herself from the position that had become uncomfortable, and consequently her right thigh fell against his legs where she could have no doubt that she lay against a man. He continued to hold her in a close embrace—like a child must, she imagined, when, hurt, it came to be comforted by its mother; but then there was an emotion within her that she could not identify: her mouth was at his cheek, she had shifted to let her thighs lie against his: the throbbing generated in her heart was hardly caused by maternal tenderness.

She quickly lifted herself from him and stood up, noticing in the corner of her eye that the sheet had again slipped off and that his penis stood erect. She turned her face to the door and began to walk away, saying, "You've missed breakfast, and if you don't come down soon, you'll miss lunch, too." She turned to face him from the door, and added, "It will be a pity to miss it. Sylvia is baking a lovely fish." Saying so, she left the room, closing the door after her, but in the slow turning around of her large body she had again cast her astonished eyes on the naked man-child who had come to her house from nowhere.

Federico got out of bed and danced about the room. He possessed magical power!

The months that followed confirmed his belief. Daniela was affectionate, stroking his cheek or ruffling his hair when they sat together during meals. She held his arm when they strolled in the garden, spoke to him tenderly, and often turned to stare into his eyes. When they walked above the cliff and stood watching a sunset, she let her head fall on his shoulder and pressed her breast against his arm. Once, when they had sat in the hammock in the gazebo, swinging gently, she had stopped the hammock's motion by digging her heels into the ground and, holding his head, had kissed his eyes. Federico had no doubt that she had fallen in love with him, and the more he believed her to be ardent, the more he found her beautiful, although during the time that he was with her she added three kilos to the considerable surplus her body already carried.

He continued to sleep in the nursery which had become his room, lying in blissful contentment and enjoying beautiful dreams. One night he was awakened by her lips touching his. For some days after she had first discovered him in the nursery and observed in him the man-child who drew from her ambiguous emotions, she had derived an amusingly wicked enjoyment from flirting with him; but on this night, alone in her bed, she was suddenly filled with a passion that was neither lust nor desire for tenderness but a hunger brought on by the unconscious awakening of a memory too deeply lodged in her past ever to be acknowledged by her rational self. Lighting a candle, she glided out of her room to the nursery, leaving the bed in which she had rejected her husband, having an association just then of her father and his exile. She placed the candle beside Federico's bed and awoke him with a kiss. He saw her leaning over him in a thin nightgown.

It was his first experience of pleasure with a woman. There was so much flesh on her body when, after removing her gown, she lay beneath him! But her enduring compulsion when she went to him on subsequent nights was to have him below her. She sat up on his chest with her eyes closed and head lifted up, and it was only when she had shifted herself so that her knees were against the pillow on either side of his ears and the bushy triangle of hair against his mouth that she looked down, seeing his head as far as the nose as if he were just emerging from her womb. Slowly she moved herself down along his body, letting his face, his shoulders, and chest emerge out of her as it were, her heavy, pendulous breasts sliding over his sweating flesh as she leaned over him, until she was at the end of the bed, below his feet, and could see all of him, newly born. Then she suckled him, lying on her side, holding her heavy breast with both her hands and squeezing it with increasing agitation. And then, her breathing labored and punctuated by moans, she let him tear his mouth away and mount her, his throbbing penis bursting its tension inside her womb from where he must be delivered again the next night. The serenity that came over her mind then was profound; no drug offered such a deeply satisfying relief. Night after night she devoured the flesh she had given birth to, putting out the fire of the unacknowledged memory with its secret terror, consuming her man-child.

Federico enjoyed this ritual for two months. Sometimes during the day Daniela went to the city and returned with presents for him, always some expensive items of clothing. She liked to see him dressed in a suit at dinner with patent-leather shoes, but for his afternoon wear she gave him T-shirts, shorts, and sneakers. Federico found her whims charming.

But then one night, when she again began her ceremony of climbing upon him, he felt slightly repelled by the odor from her vagina and had to force himself to behave as he normally did, finding unpleasant the taste in his mouth. When she began to slide down his chest, her weight seemed to be crushing him. Her breast thrust into his mouth made him feel he was suffocating. But he participated in the motions without giving an indication of his diminished interest. For her the performance had never been an act of sexual intercourse; it was no longer going to be that for him either.

Seeing her the next day and finding no change in her behavior toward him, thus proving to himself that she had not noticed his dissembling of passion during the night, he was eager to give her his affectionate attentions. After all, it was likely that his loss of interest had only been a freak condition of his own body, some obscure chemical change within him which would soon accustom itself to the more regular experience of his life. But then he noticed her face. The full, rounded cheeks which he had found so beautiful, their flesh seemed to sag on either side of her mouth, and the places where dimples appeared when she smiled had lines on them. There were lines, too, at the corners of her eyes and even on her chin. Her black hair had lost the sheen he had observed it to possess and was wiry. A little later, when she walked across the room, he saw her enormous breadth for the first time, and when she turned round, her lips, which he had considered so perfectly contoured, were in fact thick and, remaining partly open, showed a row of predatory teeth. He had been making love to a monster!

Seeing her enter with her candle that night, he tried to imagine what she had been or, rather, what she was not and had never been—some perfectly voluptuous woman, the embodiment of a dream, and not, oh God, this unbearable weight! He kept his eyes closed and tried his hardest to play out the performance to its end without giving away the disgust he had begun to feel. He lay gasping for breath when she had at last gone, and stared wildly into the dark. His nights had become a torment, bringing to his body, in the guise of love, an unendurable affliction. Was this suffering the price he had to pay for the luxury of having a wish granted, that the beautiful should be nothing other than masked ugliness and reality a discovery of what was false at the core? Why could there not be a precise correlation between the expression of a wish and its fulfillment?

Suddenly he was startled by the realization that that was exactly what had happened. He remembered that, coming out of Popayan's, one of the thoughts in his mind had been expressed as a wish that he should live in a house by the ocean where he was loved by a beautiful woman. His wish had never stated that the woman remain beautiful for ever, nor that he love her. What had happened was *exactly what he had asked for!* This conclusion had the effect of strengthening his belief that his amulet gave him a magical power. The thought cheered him, for he could always leave a world become intolerable and find happiness in another. But he did not want to rush into making another wish, for he had the superstitious notion that the power he had was not inexhaustible and had to be used sparingly. He must not be so foolish as to trap himself by indulging the excessive desires of his vanity: he must not be like the man who plays the lottery and, deluding himself that he is bound to win a fortune, spends his meagre savings and ends up becoming a pauper. He feared the power he believed he had acquired; something told him that he would have a terrible price to pay for it: he could not hope to remain lucky for ever.

Three months had passed, and not one of her former friends had called Daniela. Instead, the voices that spoke to her seemed to come from within herself. She felt as if a tribe of demons had entered her blood and that she had lost control over her body. All she could do was to sit and eat all day long and wait for the night when she could possess her man-child, producing him out of her flesh in a terrible agony of creation, the walls of her womb shuddering with pulsations, and thrusting the created flesh back into herself until there appeared to be only her own body heaving and convulsing on the narrow bed, the man-child entirely devoured.

But now she looked at herself in the full-length mirror in her bathroom and said, "You look a mess." She stared and, revising her opinion which had been too kind, exclaimed aloud, "You look like a damned witch!" The old life was killed at last; the Daniela who had appeared glamorous and been talked about in the society columns had been laid to rest. She had no desire to be her again; but nor did she wish to remain the witch reflected in the mirror. She had to do something. She left the bathroom, emerging from it like a diver from the deeps who has seen a mysterious world full of fantastic phenomena and has been fascinated by the shapes beneath the ocean's surface, but who is relieved nevertheless to be breathing air again on a land whose geological structures and meteorological patterns have long been charted and understood.

That same day she received a letter from a lawyer in London. Her father had died and had been cremated, according to his wishes, without ceremony. She felt neither shock nor pain. Grief did not touch her. But these feelings would overwhelm her later when she finally realized what had driven her to her madness, making her mind find relief only when her body was penetrated by a man whom she had first given birth to and suckled as her child, and the understanding came to her of a confused projection of roles, the woman-daughter so horrified by the long-suppressed desire for the man-father that she could only see a disguised reality, when the woman-daughter's passion transformed itself to the false one of the woman-mother.

A few days later she packed her bags, giving only the briefest information to Federico: "I'm going away for a couple of months."

"Where to?" he asked automatically.

"Don't you worry about it," she said, and added, patting his face, "Be a good boy."

He was relieved to see her go. At least his nightmare was temporarily over. Her parting remark indicated that she did not expect him to leave her house; he had two months in which to work out a future for himself. In a way that was both exciting and depressing he had lived a magical existence, indeed, an entirely improbable life that he would not have believed in had he been told it as a story about someone else. He fingered the chain at his neck and wondered whether the time had not come to wish for a new life. Perhaps he should make a small wish, as an experiment to prove that the events of recent months had not been merely a wild coincidence.

His first thought was to wish for Mariana to be with him. A month's visit, say. They would have a perfect idyl. They would love each other, their two youthful bodies intertwined the whole month without either feeling a moment's exhaustion or the boredom of satiation, and at the end she would go away with her virginity magically restored, so that when the future time came when he would desire her to be his wife she would have been touched only by him but as if in a dream or in a former life. The idea dazzled him. Other wishes that came to his mind seemed too uninteresting by comparison. But he hesitated, afraid that some hidden peril lay behind each innocent wish and fearful of mocking the magical power by asking it to perform a little experiment. He decided to do nothing for the moment, that inactivity would best serve his present time; besides, he needed—he told himself triumphantly—a rest from women!

A few days later he had no choice but to sit around doing nothing. The rainy season came in a series of tempests from the Pacific. He had enjoyed an undisturbed sleep for some nights, being amused by the reflection that it was such a relief not to have to make love; then, one night, almost precisely at the hour when Daniela had been in the habit of gliding into his room, candle in hand and her black hair spread over her shoulders, he was woken by a great crack of thunder. Heavy rain fell all night, a strong wind blew; waves of the storm's intensity were accompanied by lightning and thunder. He sat by the window, finding it exhilarating to watch the bent trees when they were lit up by the lightning and to hear the roar of the wind through them, and returned to bed exhausted. In the morning the storm had abated but the rain continued to fall. The sky cleared around noon, the dry air had a clean

edge to it; although it was too wet to go for a walk there was
pleasure in just looking out at the sparkling colors of the trees
and the ocean. Later in the afternoon the sky clouded over
again, the air turned humid, and thick drops of rain began to
fall intermittently. All went silent with the coming of night,
but the heat and the humidity intensified. It was difficult to
sleep in a bed damp with one's own sweat. And then, when
sleep had at last overtaken him, Federico was again awakened
by the rolling, crashing thunder. The storm seemed more
powerful than on the previous night.

When he got out of bed in the morning, tired after a night
of disturbed sleep, he saw from his window that several
limbs had been torn from the trees, some of them dangling
precariously. From the patio he could see that the rose bushes
had been nearly stripped bare. The lawn was littered with
twigs, little branches, and bits of torn bark. There were
puddles of water everywhere. But again there was an hour or
two of clarity, of brilliant sunshine in the afternoon, and if
one did not look at the ground the world appeared perfectly
tranquil, with not even a hint of potential menace in its
elements, and one could not imagine a superior environment.
The impression was a temporary one, however, for again the
night brought back the savage fury of wind and rain.

The exhilaration Federico had experienced on the first night
of the storm turned to loathing by the fifth night; he could
not go to sleep for fear that lightning and thunder would
strike, and he lay staring at the dark window being rattled by
the wind, expecting it to be lit up by lightning at any moment
and for the thunder to begin to hammer its blows upon his
head. The violent weather continued for a fortnight. Federico's days were filled with anxiety, his nights with terror.
There was nothing for him to do but haunt the various rooms
of the house during the day, looking out of the windows at
the pools of water with trees fallen in them, and go to bed at
night, approaching his bed with the neurotic apprehension of
one who is certain that sleep will only bring a resumption of
nightmares.

On the day the sky cleared early he thought he ought to
come to some resolution, for he could no longer endure the
meaningless life in which he found himself. He must come

out of his apathy and do something. Take a step in a new direction. The present situation brought him nothing but mental pain. He passed a finger over the chain at his neck until it reached the tiny brass book; touching it produced a thrill within him, and also a fear. He walked about the room wondering what he really wanted for himself. It occurred to him that the best thing he could wish for was to return to his former life; all he needed to ask for was a little money to repay his father, and nothing else. No, no, he must use the power he had! Why settle for a dull existence, for a life of endless struggle to earn money for basic necessities when he could acquire wealth and live in luxury? Images invaded his mind of driving sports cars, flying to foreign cities, being surrounded by beautiful women. But they were soon replaced by a dread of something that must come after the immersion in luxury. It could not be that a price had not to be paid, that he could escape an ultimate retribution. No, his former life with its simple practicalities was preferable. He would catch up with school, amaze his friends with stories of his fantastic experiences, and renew his courtship of Mariana. The thought of such an existence made him enormously happy. He imagined himself working hard, obeying his parents, and making himself so worthy a person that even Mariana's father would approve of him and himself propose that he accept his daughter in marriage. He would produce brilliant results at school and perhaps win a scholarship to a college, even to a foreign university, and give Mariana and the many children they would have together a great future. He would take the amulet and the cloak back to Popayan, or bury them somewhere; he did not want gifts for which he had done no work.

Having made the resolution to return home, he was in no immediate hurry to do so. The thought itself was so pleasant, the images it evoked so wonderful, making him feel virtuous and cleansed, that he wanted to enjoy the reverie a little longer. That night only a light rain fell. Federico slept soundly, and continued all the following day to dream of the beautiful life to which he was going to return.

The sun shone brightly, drying up the pools. Diego went about the grounds, clearing the debris and restoring the garden to its earlier order. Sylvia made a delicious chicken in garlic for dinner. The sky remained clear even after the sun had set. Bright stars and a quarter moon appeared, and, looking out of the window before going to sleep, Federico thought that this was one aspect that he would miss back home—hardly any sky could be seen out of his apartment room. But before falling asleep he enjoyed again the reverie of the happiness that surely awaited him there, and he resolved that the next day he would make the wish to be restored to it.

The weather now turned perfect. Diego had cleared away the fallen leaves and, carrying a ladder from tree to tree, had begun to cut away the broken limbs. Sylvia made a chocolate cake decorated with almonds for dessert. Federico had tasted nothing like it. And though he went to bed feeling like an aristocrat, images of the simpler pleasures at home played in his mind before he fell asleep.

Each day was a marvel of contentment. The acacia trees were in bloom. The lawn, just mowed by Diego, was a deep green. Little yellow-throated birds flew among some trees that had recently begun to bear green berries. The ocean was calm, undulating very slightly with gentle swells. Sylvia cleaned the windows of the house and waxed the tiled floors. Federico savored the enchantment in which he dwelled, telling himself that it was only proper that he should experience as much of it as he could before he returned to the simpler world of his own people. There was no real urgency in carrying out the resolution. Sylvia and Diego treated him like the master of the house, and why should he not enjoy this privilege, which life might never again grant him in so refined a style, at least until Daniela returned? And thus passed the two months of her absence.

Realizing that she was expected to return any day, Federico became apprehensive. There was not a little terror in making what had to be an irrevocable move. He had thought so frequently of returning home, played out little affectionate dramas with Mariana in his mind, seen himself receive the top prize when graduating from school, rehearsed many possible or probable events so repeatedly, that he sometimes had the impression that all that had already happened. At other times, when beginning a particular scene with Mariana in his imagination, he found himself bored with the repetition of a

scene of which the conclusion was known in advance, and
chided himself for having nothing else in his mind.

He was walking along the cliff one morning and stopped
when he saw a large bird, floating above the ocean, tip its
enormous wings and swing in a wide arc above him and then
be carried away high into the sky on a current of warm,
spiraling air. When he returned to the house, he saw Sylvia
polishing the silver. She held a large scallop-shaped serving
spoon in one hand and was rubbing it with a white drying
cloth. The sight of the spoon evoked images in Federico's
mind of the countless helpings of many delicacies that he had
served himself with it, and as he went up to his room he
thought how he had taken this life of elegance for granted.
There would be none of it when he returned home. The
thought made him feel disconsolate. He summoned to his
mind a succession of those images of life at home that had
recently given him pleasure. Mariana—her brutish father
seemed to be standing above him and kicking him. His own
parents—he could hear their bickering, their constant complaints about not having enough money. School—algebra!

What happiness had he been thinking of? It was a life of
misery! Why, he was a fool even to think of it when he had
access to a superior existence. He must at least give that power
one small try before running like a coward to his miserable
former life. Thinking of what he should wish for, he went to
touch the amulet; but he remembered that when he had left
Popayan he was also wearing that red and black cloak with
the crescents and stars on it. Perhaps wearing the cloak was
vital to success? And, in a sudden compulsion to be decisive,
he brought out the cloak and flung it over his shoulders. He
did not see the two or three moths that flew up above his
head. He held the cloak's ends together against his heart and
walked about the room, the tiny brass book held between a
thumb and forefinger. An ecstasy possessed him. He did not
know what he was doing. "I wish for excitement!" he cried
aloud. "For beautiful women, for wealth!" The words themselves seemed magical and he was driven to shout aloud
repeatedly, *"Excitement, women, wealth!"*

He stopped and stared at his two hands trembling against
his chest. He wanted to say more, express a careful qualifi-

cation of the words that had uttered themselves spontaneously, but found himself unable to speak a syllable. He came out in a sweat and, dropping the cloak to the ground, went and fell into bed. What had he done! Spoken without thinking. Shouted out words like a madman who did not know what he was saying. Perhaps the amulet had no power and it was only his delusion that believed in its magic. Very likely. But supposing it did have the power? Once again each speculation came with its opposite twin, and if he believed one he was terrified that the real truth might be the other. Perhaps not all was lost; he had spoken aloud nothing since the wish rushed out of his mouth and he could still qualify it.

He got out of bed and went to pick up the cloak to start his little ceremony again. He lifted it from the ground and slowly swirled it around to put it over his shoulders. In the moment that his right hand was over his head, placing the cloak on his left shoulder, his eye caught a yellowish glint from the floor. Several of the crescents and stars sewn on the back of the cloak had fallen off. Instead of putting it on, he spread it out on the bed to examine it. There were half a dozen gaps, like a toothless grin, where the yellow satin crescents and stars had been, one next to the other in a straight line a quarter of the way up the garment from its ragged bottom. He gently stretched out the material to look at it more carefully. Just then a moth, which had remained caught in a fold, flew out. In the same moment Federico heard a car door slam outside the house.

He quickly picked up the cloak and went to replace it in the dresser and, in that second's inattention to the details of the objects around him, the cloak, floating over the side table next to the bed, got caught in a corner of the table: the pointed little triangular area of the table was neatly trapped in one of the newly created holes and, before Federico could check himself, the tension tore the small area between the hole where the corner was caught and the one next to it; even as he realized what was happening, the entire length where the crescents and stars had been was torn off. Federico began to laugh. The thing was worthless, nothing more than a rag. What a fool he was to think it was partly responsible for giving him a magical power! Would he never learn to face ordinary reality? It had all been nonsense, how could he believe in a rag possessing magic when it was not fit even for wiping dust; and the chain round his neck with its little tablet which he had thought of as a magical amulet was another piece of junk. What was the matter with him that he was taken in by foolish ideas? He reminded himself that he lived in an age of computers, not witchcraft. There had been no magic at all, only a convenient explanation of an otherwise inexplicable series of improbable and fantastic coincidences. There was nothing for him to do now but to go home. Forget all this junk.

Going down, he saw that a slim woman with reddish hair, wearing a pink taffeta dress with two rows of red, diamond-shaped buttons across the bosom, had just entered the patio with a tall, balding man in a beige double-breasted suit. Red patent-leather shoes stepping across the tiled floor caught his attention, and he saw her narrow ankles and firm calves; a handbag that matched the shoes drew his eyes to slender tanned arms. She was altogether beautiful, and Federico felt an instinctive jealousy of the man who escorted her. He was obviously a man of position and taste; even the manner in which he stooped slightly to indicate his polite deference to the lady he accompanied showed superior breeding.

"Federico!" the woman called at him from a distance when she saw him. "Now, *how* did I know you would still be here? I hope you have been a good boy."

The voice, and the laughter in it when she asked the question, was Daniela's. Federico could not believe it. The woman who had left just over two months ago had been fat and, as he had discovered after his first blind infatuation, ugly. But coming closer, he saw that the eyes were the same. The tiny wrinkles at the corners were gone, but there was no doubt about the large black pupils. The dimples had vanished and the round face with the fleshy cheeks was now squarer and narrower with the diminished flesh giving a new prominence to the cheekbones.

"This is Federico," she said to her companion, "the young man I told you about." And as he stepped forward, holding his hand out to Federico, she said to the latter,

"This is Ernesto Vivado. We met on the plane from Los Angeles."

Federico glanced cursorily at Vivado, offering him a limp hand, and turned to stare amazedly at Daniela.

"What's the matter," she said, smiling, showing a row of perfect teeth, "you haven't lost your tongue?"

"You *are* Daniela?"

She laughed aloud, raising her chin. Her laughter filled him with its erotic charm, but when, after pausing for breath, she continued to laugh, its power seemed to him to be essentially malevolent.

"Ernesto has no doubt," she said.

"That's right," Vivado confirmed. "I hadn't seen Daniela in eighteen years, and there she was, the only other first-class passenger on the plane, looking *exactly* like she did at graduation. It's incredible!"

"You used to be such a shy boy at school," Daniela teased him, "I would never have recognized you."

"Time hasn't stopped for *me!* What do you expect?"

"Let's not start on our secrets," Daniela declared. "Life's too boring without mysteries. You should know, you're a dealer in sensations."

She went away to her room to change. Quite confused by her little dialogue with Vivado, Federico wondered whether her last remark did not imply that Vivado dealt in drugs. But the latter was saying after Daniela, "Only a middleman of other people's dreams."

Now he looked at Federico and added, "That's the truth. I find locations and extras for movie producers, exotic settings for fashion photographers. I arrange expeditions into Amazonia for Scandinavians, package tours to Disney World for Brazilians. There is not a man alive on earth who is not eager to buy a fantasy, who doesn't want a portion of the earth to be his whore."

Federico was startled by his words, for he was reminded of the wish he had himself made. Vivado was struck by his nervous, shy aspect, his appearance of a sensitive youth whose eyes expressed a desperate longing for the unattainable, the forbidden, and asked, "And you, what do you dream for?"

"I . . . I don't know," Federico mumbled, avoiding the

words of his recent wish that had again come to his tongue.

Vivado walked about the room, looking at the interior from different angles, and then stood by the door to the patio and glanced out at the view. Daniela returned, wearing jeans and a T-shirt, reminding Federico of the girls at his school. They went out for a walk around the property, and from each perspective, whether looking across the herb garden to the woods or from the woods at the house with the ocean beyond it, Vivado declared it to be a perfect location. Federico heard him talk of money and was dazzled by the tens of thousands of dollars that he mentioned, wondering to himself whether his future held a new life with Daniela and a share of her wealth.

When they returned to the house and sat down to lunch, Daniela agreed to the figure she had been discussing with Vivado. "It will have to be approved by the management, of course," the latter said, "but that's only a formality. Your house will be famous after the movie comes out. You could make a fortune charging people to peep into the room where the hero and heroine made love."

He raised his glass of beer, and Daniela, who was only drinking water, nodded her head, smiling at him. Federico noticed that she did not touch the rice and beans, nor the chicken which he and Vivado were devouring in large quantities; she only ate a little salad with a thin slice of bread. Instead of the creamy dessert, of which Vivado had two helpings, she slowly chewed on a quarter of a green apple, and when Sylvia brought in the coffee, Daniela asked her to make her a cup of weak tea.

When they were rising from the table, Federico was surprised when Daniela unexpectedly said to him, "I put a suitcase in your room. Why don't you go and pack whatever you need to take with you?"

He was about to say that he was not going anywhere when it occurred to him that he had no claim to stay in her house. Seeing it from her point of view, he realized that it must be a terrible bore to have a guest who never leaves; only he had long ceased to think of himself as a stranger to her house, and the realization that she was now politely asking him to leave came as a shock. It was apparent to him that she was going to ask Vivado to give him a lift into town. Feeling resentful that he was being dismissed just when she herself had been transformed into a desirable shape (by what magic? by what science?), he slowly climbed up the steps and entered his room.

There, seeing the bed reminded him of the scenes enacted upon it, and the memory of how an enchanting passion had turned to a nightmare came to him; and the thought that if he had once been deceived by her form then he ought not to lust after her present beautiful appearance, which might only be a new disguise taken on by temptation to inflict a more painful suffering than he had experienced before, gave him the resolution to go. He became philosophical as he packed, telling himself that he could not be the inhabitant of a dream for ever.

He wanted to say a few words to Daniela before leaving. After all, she had fed and clothed him for so many months, been a mother and a lover who had shown him the essential ambiguity that constituted the mystery of life, revealing itself in maddening contradictions that came as alternating experiences of beauty and terror. But his lips remained open, he could say nothing, and only stared sadly at her. Then it was she who made the necessary gesture—suddenly hugging him and saying, "You *will* be happy!"

He drove away with Vivado who had put a tape of an Italian opera into the cassette player and was loudly singing the arias in it. When they had driven past the military base, Federico observed that Vivado had not taken the turning for the city but continued to drive along the coast.

"Where are we going?" Federico cried aloud.

Vivado was just then singing with the tenor on the stereo, his chin jutting out, his head moving from side to side with the rhythm. He glanced at Federico, his eyes rolling, and continued to sing until the aria was finished. There was a moment's silence and Federico repeated his question. The orchestra burst into sound, and Vivado, raising a hand from the steering wheel, conducted the music with his forefinger, and then, using a bass register in his voice, as if he recited the words that were about to be sung, and attempting a deep sonority, chanted: "Excitement, women, wealth!"

III

Exiles from Appearances

The timber cottages built in close proximity to one another above the small beach had weathered to an ashen color. A gray mass of volcanic rock rose behind them, strewn here and there with the debris of ancient eruptions. Ash covered the ground, and ashen dust hung in the air. The late-morning sun blazed down from a deep blue sky; diamonds of light jostled on the deeper blue of the ocean. Rocks formed a cove at one end of the beach; sea lions rolled on the sand among the rocks where the water lapped over them and receded in the continuous motion of the tide. Dozens of marine iguanas lay motionless on the rocks, their dark gray backs, mottled with red, turned to the sun. At the other end of the beach a huge jagged rock jutted out of the ocean, its irregular higher protrusions crowded with long-billed, white-crested birds and its dark gray sides streaked white with bird droppings. Occasionally, a sea lion barked, or a flock of birds, raising a shrill cry, flew up from the rock, glided above the ocean in a wide curve and then dived into the water, rising out of it with a flapping of wings, the tail of a fish wriggling from a beak. Two children, naked and sunburnt, played on the beach; another swam in the bay.

One sat hunched over some shells in the sand, and the second, with blonde hair and green eyes, standing nearby, was saying, "Come on, Neva, we've got to go home now."

"Diana, you're always in a hurry," Neva said, looking up. Her eyes were green too, and she appeared to be Diana's younger sister. "Herminia's still swimming," she added.

Diana cupped her hands around her mouth and shouted at the ocean, "Herminia, we're going!"

A head with straight black hair raised itself from the water and the face and shoulders that appeared were tanned a deep brown. "Don't wait for me," she called, and plunged back into the water.

Diana repeated her command to Neva, who said, "Oh, all right!"

Springing out of the water and throwing herself to float on her back, Herminia saw the two girls walking away from the beach. She looked up at the sun. It must be nearly noon. Time to take her father his lunch. Almost time. A few more minutes in the water, and she'd go.

Hearing a sea lion cry loudly, she looked in the direction of the cove: he had climbed up a rock and with his nose up in the air was waving his head from side to side as he made a high-pitched sound. Two of the females and several of their pups were clambering up the rocks. Stroking the water to turn her body around, Herminia looked at the distance where four bare islets which were nothing but rounded bald rocks, each shaped like the back of a whale, stretched out in a line and formed a protection for the small bay in which she swam, and saw nothing at first but the shimmering light in the swelling water, but then, observing a murky area no more than a couple of meters wide but from that distance hardly more than a spot, she did a quick somersault and swam rapidly to the beach. Standing on the wet sand, she looked back at the ocean and saw the tide slowly pushing the spreading stain toward the beach. The sea lion was still howling from his rock. Some sharks must have got a sea lion, she thought, observing the widening red, which in the immensity of the blue which surrounded it appeared nearly violet, coming in her direction. She stood there, watching it and searching the ocean to see if there were any indications of the sharks still being present.

Her black hair, which had naturally parted itself at the center when she came out of the water, stuck to the sides of her face, covering the ears, and followed the indented contours between her cheekbones and jaw. Drops of water trembled about her forehead and small, straight nose, and ran down the curves of her cheeks. Her black eyes, scanning the ocean's surface, seemed large for the small-featured face of an eight-year-old.

She ran off in the direction of the cottages. Doña Adriana, her gray-haired grandmother who lived next door and who had looked after Herminia ever since her mother had died when she was two, had prepared the lunch for her to take to her father. After rinsing herself at the communal well behind the cottages, Herminia put on a smock and took the basket from her grandmother, and, stepping past the hens scratching the dirt in front of the door, she proceeded toward the narrow road covered with ash-colored dust. From the top of the hill she looked back on the view of the ocean. Far on the northern horizon, visible only in the clearest light, was another land mass, the large island of San Bernardino, from where, three or four times a year, a ship came to take away what her father and the other men dug in the pits and delivered in return meagre supplies of household goods. She turned her gaze from the ocean, which from that height seemed only a great expanse of blue broken here and there by rocky protrusions, and, going over the top of the hill, came to the ash pits on the western slopes of the extinct volcano that dominated the center of the island. The men had stopped working and sat about in groups under the scattered trees. As usual, she found her father sitting alone.

Darkened by the sun and the ashen dust, he wore a brooding expression, keeping his eyes generally lowered, occasionally raising them to show a look of mistrust or a refusal to be convinced that what he saw was not a subtle form of deception. Herminia had only recently begun to understand that a world of incredible marvels and enormous spaces existed beyond the island of Santa Barbara where she had been born; Diana had been telling her this morning on the beach that out there were people who did not need to wait to go to sleep at night in order to have dreams, they could see them any time of the day on a box simply by pressing a button. Herminia stared at her father. What did he know about *that*? He looked at her gloomily and ate some more of the hard-boiled egg. She chatted on gaily. Could there be so many people in the world? What did they all *do*? And another thing Diana had said. Everyone out there had to make money. It was very important. Without it, you couldn't live. What was that, *money*?

She was growing fast, he thought, and he had not known a child who asked so many questions. It was as if she had been born with a knowledge of another world and, surprised that the one around her was only an imperfect copy, faintly representing an intenser impression, desired to see the imagery of the true reality. Her questions persuaded him that he could no longer content her with the symbolic truth of fairy tales, and he began to tell her the story of the world he had come from, keeping his head lowered, raising it when he paused, and not knowing, when he saw her, whether it was great happiness or great sorrow that he felt within his breast that his daughter Herminia, in this world, looked exactly like his daughter Mariana, in the other.

The resemblance had struck him when Herminia had turned one, seven years ago, and during each succeeding year it became more precise in its definition, sometimes, when he momentarily forgot the circumstances of his immediate life, creating in him the illusion that the intervening years had not passed and that his idea of the past was merely a foreknowledge of the future, that in fact he was still in the city and Mariana still a child; and for a few concentrated seconds his past would become a blessed present, all its anxieties and passions replaced by a contented calm, for time, becoming stationary during this brief withdrawal of memory, suspended its eternal pressure, and the question of how the future was to be survived was made redundant.

But now, telling Herminia of the life that must lead to the fathering of Mariana, he did not, when looking up, glance at her face, not wanting to be confused by the double mirror image of the future, and knowing what he must reveal to the motherless child, or acknowledge to himself, for he was talking more to himself than to the amazed and precocious girl, it was necessary to repress the image of the one left fatherless, and so he looked past her at the line of cacti on the undulating land beyond the ash pits toward the desert that comprised the low-lying land on the western part of the island. *My darling child*—the phrase came to his tongue as he spoke slowly while the large-eyed child listened, but he did not use the words; rather, he could not, for the little bubbles of blood that carried the words of endearment to the brain had long been burst, and passion had left his flesh. But the necessity to explain was really a necessity to love, if only, in the end, a form of self-love that cried pitiably *Do not forget me, do not bury me under the unbearable weight of silence.* The story of the self must be told, eternally. He would speak to her for years, his voice would carry her into her adolescence.

Herminia watched with amazement her father create his own life, was dazzled by vistas of luxuriant landscapes through which broad rivers flowed carrying sweet water, and she found herself plucking one of the millions of wild flowers and holding it to her lips to discover that the dew on it tasted of honey. And so, afternoon and evening, for a long succession of months, of years, Herminia listened to the father's story, each image that he described of his world becoming in her mind a fantastic fiction, but the wonder at what she imagined sometimes gave way to terror.

It was ten years since Felipe Gamboa, nearly dead of heat and thirst, had drifted through the whale-backed rocks at the mouth of the small bay and come to the island of Santa Barbara in a battered boat that could not have carried his weight another day. In the hallucinations that passed for consciousness he had the sense that he had died already, or that the death he had suffered had somehow been insufficient and the fantasy of a world that was not all water was to be the final crushing blow. Some children playing on the beach saw the tiny boat bobbing up and down, and went running to the cottages, raising a cry. Doña Adriana, who nursed him, told him later that he had remained unconscious for a fortnight, waking in fits of delirium in which he called Mariana's name and wept, or sitting up coughing when she had tried to feed him some goat's milk and then falling back to his profound sleep. Doña Adriana's husband, a white-haired man named Domingo Maturana, who like the other adults on Santa Barbara had known life on the continent, had also sat beside him and talked to him when he had begun to recover. You must not bewail the loss of the past, its happiness will never return, its sorrow will never depart, you can only be, only demand of the air another breath, the sky here is infinite in its generosity, and what humiliation cast you out of your world, what treachery sent you into exile, what vicious chance threw you into oblivion, they are nothing to this air that still offers you breath, to this light which comes to you with its glorious dazzle, and even the birds cry aloud, Come, *be*, let us sing because we must, we have to endure. He had a soft, soothing voice, Domingo Maturana, and a persuasive tone, and Gamboa felt that his words had a power that carried more than an ordinary meaning. Oh, who can deny your uniqueness, your singular suffering, but know, my friend, how the sharpest of our pains calls to us that we do not exist —how absurdly beautiful is this paradox! Memories sleep within you, no doubt; no doubt a history, documented, verifiable, lives in your flesh and bones; but only to remind you of what you have not been, the wrong that you wish to be undone, a longing that the errors had not been committed, an expression in the end of a desire not to have existed. Oh, I will not dwell upon the soul! But the white light is trapped between the blue sky and the blue ocean and your heart still throbs, claiming its little measure of air, what existence else? The voice, reaching him in his semiconsciousness as from some great distance, seemed to be summoning him to return to the land of the living though the flow of his murmurous speech was more and more checked by warnings. It was with Maturana that he took his first steps on the island, walking a little distance out of the cottage. The older man, stooping as he walked with the help of a cane, held his arm and, turning his face to look up at Gamboa, said, "I know your feet still do not trust the land, but believe me, it is solid." He prodded the earth with his cane and added, "And as you can see, it is indifferent to the additional weight it must bear."

It was an island of no more than some sixty people, twenty of them children born there. Santa Barbara was both too remote and also of little interest in its species of wild life for the naturalists to want to visit it and was therefore excluded from the protection given the other islands. Some men and women, exiled there several years before Gamboa's accidental arrival, formed a crude society on the narrow plain along the northern shore where they could cultivate corn, grow vegetables and keep goats and hens. Much of the rest of the island was uninhabitable: the central volcanic mass was barren, the land to the west a desert and the coastline rocky. The southern coast, which could be reached only by going through the desert—unless one climbed the precipitous slopes of the volcano—was exposed to the open ocean where the tide swept high over the small beaches, flinging against the rocks and the sand dunes quantities of crabs and stingrays which, when the tide had receded, lay decomposing on the sand. The community remained on the sheltered northern shore just above the island's only safe beach, its common memory of a former life on the mainland becoming a folklore to transmit to the new generation and its general desire to return to it the object of its prayers.

A chemicals company on the mainland had seized the opportunity to exploit nature as well as cheap human labor and employed the men originally put on Santa Barbara by the government: what the men, working in the area locally known as "the ash pits", took from the land was nitrate, their primitive tools allowing them to extract so little at a time that there was never a sufficient sum to pay for the goods the company sold them, so that their perpetual indebtedness gave them no prospect of freedom from their labor.

The first time Gamboa saw the company's ship send out its boats with outboard motors from where it lay at anchor just beyond the whale-backed rocks, he pleaded with the foreman, who made a detailed account of the supplies he had brought, which on this occasion were primarily the materials needed to sink a second water well, and the quantity of nitrate that was being shipped, to allow him to return to the mainland. When Gamboa hurriedly explained his situation, the foreman looked at him suspiciously and did not believe a word of what he heard. Others before Gamboa had begged to be taken away from the island. "I'll have to talk to the captain," he said, finding an excuse to get away from the man whose story was so implausible he wondered if the man had not gone mad in the isolation of the island. Twice more, on the ship's subsequent calls, Gamboa had tried to seek his escape, being motivated by the desire to right the wrong committed upon him and to return to his family; and when the ship visited the fourth time, when he had already spent a year on the island, he did not attempt to tell his story but simply requested to send a message to his wife. The foreman gave him a sheet of paper from his notebook; Gamboa wrote down his wife's name and address on the top and, pausing a moment to think how he could convey his situation in a few brief phrases, looked up and saw a smirk on the foreman's face. He dropped the paper from his hand and walked away.

But now, narrating his past to Herminia—who stopped him frequently to ask, "What's an apartment?" "An office, what's that?" "Stores? Bar? Buses?"—while he put the images together of a life in the city, there existed simultaneously in his mind a history of the ten years already spent on Santa Barbara, its pictorial details making him stop even when he was attempting a picture of the other past, so that in mid-sentence he had to make the effort of suppressing one memory in order not to lose the facts of the other. And when a glance from Herminia was too perfect a mimicry of Mariana, he had to close his eyes to separate the two and, doing so, saw the two mothers, who were not at all alike, merge into one, a person whose features could not be distinguished, as if she were seen walking out of the ocean with the sun behind her low on the water, throwing up its golden brightness before it sank, and that very brightness took away from things their identity. Some time after he had dropped the paper with Mariana's mother's name on it, he had taken Paulina for his woman. She was Maturana's daughter, twenty-one years younger than Gamboa. Maturana said, not then, but three years later when Paulina had died, "Take this cane and beat me on the head till I howl, I am too numb with pain to cry." But Gamboa sat silent, staring at the old man and hearing Doña Adriana's moaning from the cottage. Who was there to beat *him*? Such exuberance of passion she had renewed in him, a carnival of sexuality, his second woman, who was all flesh, even her voice and laughter could embrace him from a distance, his Paulina, whose body was agog with desires and pulsed like the music of carnival.

He heard the first spray fall into the tin can and her voice, still girlish, still so warmly melodious, make jingling and clicking sounds, the tongue tapping the teeth or rattling off nonsense words, *Dimmy-dimmy, dimmy-dimmy, hola, tupi-tupi, there now my girl!*; the goat must have stopped kicking, he thought, lying in his room, wakened in the early morning by the woman walking at the back of the cottage to milk the goat, walking too in his dream, the sound of her long skirt,

just a swish as the coarse cloth brushed past the bush on
which green berries had been turning red, just a touching of
a fold of the material against a small branch, and from where
he could not see her he saw the woman's strong legs, still
girlish, the browned skin smooth and taut as a sail in a stiff
breeze, walking, already calling to the goat, *Dimmy-dimmy,
dimmy-dimmy*; and now she must be drawing the milk in
streams, watching her hands from where he lay in the room,
his arm thrown over his closed eyes, she must be stroking the
udder firmly, her long brown fingers among the teats, and he
began to whisper her name, Paulina, Paulina, until she had
to come to him, though that was later, until he had to take
her and close her large black eyes with his lips, still girlish in
their curiosity, still so maddeningly bright, take her for his
woman. Little russet-colored wrens flew under the eaves of
the cottage, little yellow-breasted finches flew into the light
of the morning, of the evening, and the brown-feathered
owl called in the middle of the night, and the girl Paulina
shuddered, her skin trembling with hesitations, and he spoke
to her lips, he whispered to her breasts, and the woman
Paulina pulsed beneath him, throbbed, convulsed until the
saturated womb calmed the passion, the desire, the longing,
sensations newly discovered but suddenly so familiar, like life
itself, a long history of being surprised by time. Her black
tresses hanging loose, her plain cotton dress bulging out in a
wide curve below her bosom, the skirt much higher at the
front than at the back, she walked on the beach, now toward
the cove where the sea lions rolled in the water, now toward
the rock where the white-crested birds sat in rows in their
eternal observation of the surface of the ocean, and he with
her, in the cool of the evening, greeted by the islanders. In the
drowning light, in the dissolving sunset, veils of clouds, falling
over the past, floating across the future, turned the present
into a ghostly mist, his feet sinking into the sand, the soft
lapping of the receding water like an unheard sound from far
away, and he thought himself the unborn child his woman
beside him carried, alive but not yet born, already hearing the
cries of the bull sea lion, already losing knowledge of a
previous existence, suspended merely in liquid, nourished by
blood thick with memories that were not his own. He heard

her with her hoe in the patch of corn at the back of the
cottage, the hens clucking about her, and the first time he saw
her, she was standing, leaning upon the hoe, the light full on
her face, greenish in the tall rows of the stalks of corn, and
then she turned, hearing her mother Doña Adriana call, and
dropping the hoe walked away, going, from where he saw
her, into the light, her passage through the corn rows agitating
the stalks so that he looked at swaying green speckled with
sunbeams, little circles of light enlarging until he was dazzled.
Longing to finish his own workday at the ash pits so that he
could be with her, he was bemused to think of himself, in his
forty-second year, again become the ardent lover he was at
half that age, which was Paulina's age, but at least a second
life had the advantage of allowing him the knowledge that
there was a pleasure in restraining eagerness, that the greatest
ecstasy was in the desire itself, and if the body wearied it was
not because it had achieved what it had desired but because
it had lost a desire for desire, and so he could be both the
lover in his original experience and also the lover seeing
experience as original. Sometimes Paulina was the bride
Sonia had been, receiving him as the woman desiring motherhood, all her ambitions concentrated in the longing to be a
fruitful wife, her naked and lascivious body resplendent with
virtue, but sometimes also one whose instinct informed her
she must act the whore to provoke his lust to procreate and
must therefore invent the sweetness of variety in calculated
profferings of perversion, to use the tips of her teeth where
he must cry in his pain at the pleasure, and the rich, throaty
laugh that entered as a tide into his blood. She could demand,
be the imperious mistress, or she could whimper beneath him
like a child. And he whose lust in recent years had been for
money, who had gazed with greater longing at automobiles
and mansions than at women, wondered whether he had ever
known love before, and wondered, too, whether the thought
were not another subtle consequence of his condition, his
second life in which he must live as never before, without ever
being able to repress completely the consciousness of the prior
existence, but certainly this impatience with the working day,
this jealousy of the presence of others, was a measure of love,
not just an anxiety that the woman, now in the kitchen with

her mother while he sat outside the cottage with her father, be the continuing bride, making of her body an entranceway into hope that there could still be remission for the committed errors that made the past such an enduring outrage. He built a cottage next to Maturana's to make room for the children who must come, became involved again in new beginnings and expectations, and there, before the roof could be built, she drew him to a corner where the sun did not fall and, standing, raised her skirt, laughing softly, whispering to him her innocent wickedness, and then, when he had finished and moved away from her, she held her hand between her thighs and, collecting the wetness that oozed there, went and smeared the entrance of the cottage with it. There was no door there yet, and he decided he would not put one in.

He felt no bitterness at having lost the other world and had long exhausted the despair he experienced at what Sonia's and Mariana's condition must be, but, with his new child growing within Paulina, he dimly thought sometimes whether the chances of his departure from the other world had not been a deliberate design, each seeming error carefully worked out in advance, but then, if that were so, there were larger, more abstract questions that remained unanswered. If one suffered, why, and if one were saved, then also, why? And why the terrible knowledge that came in dreams, of a past become ludicrously improbable, of a future too certainly incredible?

A voice, a memory, a living friend, a dead man, Domingo Maturana, the father of his nightly renewed bride, dead now, alive still, the father and the daughter too dead, though each morning revived their breath, the voice persisted, the mind's phantoms strolled solidly on the beach, the warm breath of the voice came and went like the tide. Another's past is your past, the other that you now are is not of the self you formerly had but of some other. Oh, do not call it destiny! Just because the stars remain true and you can navigate your course by them does not give you the liberty to believe in certainty. Who then are you? A story told by a Frenchman in Paris a hundred years ago, by an Indian in Delhi a thousand years ago, or by a man sitting in a cave ten thousand years ago, can coincide in all its details and hold you within its triple mirror. The past springs its surprises as the dull events of our present. There's no mystery to it at all, only a boredom that we must somehow endure. Only these paradoxes, this casuistry, with which we are pleased to puzzle ourselves, for the exquisite amusement they offer. You will learn to envy the lives of those iguanas, silently sunning themselves on the rocks, letting time pass in a resigned acceptance of nothing. Domingo Maturana, all his several pasts buried in the ashen earth, journalist once, chronicler of squalor, poet of the shanty towns, and finally an exile from appearances, from the terrible insult of scholarship, letting the burdened body bend under labor, calling for blows on his head to the end, a voice, a memory, extinct as the volcano under which he lay interred, speaking still. Nor can you call it fate, luck! Nor can you proceed, as if building a wall, brick upon brick. The heirs of confusion are tormented by a desire for order, for circles and squares, for the dimensions that confine the infinite. Domingo Maturana, man of the ashen earth, tapping his cane in the dust, also thought that eternity was time in its many reversals, bouncing back from the horizon with each sunset, and this life you have with its continuations, its progressions, is also, like the nightly voyage of the sun in the underworld, obliged to discover in the darkness that constantly overwhelms it those reversals that appear as dreams, that take you back to timeless origins, that drowning you in nothingness startle you awake in a new and subtly teasing awareness of time.

On another part of the island, five kilometers beyond the ash pits, the land rose and then fell precipitously into the ocean. The mass of rock was fissured in places, or broken into large boulders against which the water smashed itself, crashing in fountains or rushing up in a straight column from a fissure. Stepping among the boulders, Gamboa found a cave-like hollow where, the breeze blowing into it over the wet rocks, it was wonderfully cool. He would take Herminia there on some days and they would have a picnic of goat's cheese and bread, gazing out at the ocean that stretched out uninterruptedly to the horizon. He had come there many times with Paulina—*Our little cave*, they had called it. And it was there when he was once with Herminia that he had noticed little Baltazar, who had been born with a dome-shaped head, a tiny flat nose and a jaw that jutted out, loping among the rocks, lying across crevices through which jets of water spurted, imitating bird calls, and, when he saw Herminia, staring at her as if her form contained the incredible mirror image that transformed his own ugliness to beauty. Baltazar hung around outside Gamboa's cottage, undertaking any labor he was commanded to perform, his grotesque, short and stooping body, his head hung low and looking sideways if Herminia happened to be present, clumsily dragging the firewood, the thick-lipped mouth panting.

Past the little cave and into the interior of the island was a desert where only thorny bushes and cacti grew, the latter as large trees with massive thorn-studded trunks, and making an excursion there once with Herminia, drawn into that forbidding land by a fascination of the terror it provoked, the silence around them was suddenly broken by Baltazar springing out from behind a bush, giving Herminia a terrible scare; but he had leaped out to defend her, having seen from a distance the snake Gamboa had not, plucking it up by its tail and swinging it round his shoulder and smashing its head against the trunk of a cactus tree. He had disappeared soon after, but Gamboa knew he remained in the vicinity: he always did, having developed a faculty for remaining discreetly, sometimes even invisibly, present from where he could see Herminia. An orphan of the island, the older couple who had begotten him long forgotten, Baltazar was known among the children as the monkey boy and sometimes simply as the animal. He was the object of the other children's derision and consequently kept to himself. The older people treated him kindly, even indulgently, as if he were a domestic pet, giving him food and clothing. He invariably discarded what clothes he was obliged to wear and had to be forced to keep on a breechclout. Since he performed what was demanded of him, he apparently understood what was said; but when he used his own tongue the sounds that came from it were the calling cries of birds, the barking of sea lions, or noises of his own invention.

On one occasion they crossed the length of the desert and came to the southern coast where the rocky edge of the island was broken by sand dunes and tiny beaches. Thousands of iguanas lay motionless on the rocks, on the lower, wetter parts of which red and yellow crabs moved about slowly.

Coming out of the unbearable heat of the desert, Herminia ran over the sand dunes and dashed to the beach, wanting to fall into the water. A loud yell stopped her and Gamboa saw where Baltazar had suddenly appeared from behind a sand dune, and recognized, as had Herminia, his cry to be a warning. Baltazar came loping up to where Herminia had stopped on the edge of the ocean and pointed to dark shadowy objects floating in the shallow water. Gamboa, coming up, looked too, and saw that the sea was infested with stingrays. But Baltazar had understood Herminia's desire to be in the water and he beckoned her to follow him. At one end of the beach a natural distribution of rocks had formed a hollow that was filled with water at high tide, leaving there, when the tide receded, a pool of transparent water free of any malignant sea creatures.

Listen, and Gamboa was listening, still listening though the voice that spoke had long been silenced, Domingo Maturana said when his own memories were most vivid. Some light verses, a satire, to fill some empty space in a newspaper, describing a general as a crane, an amusing piece that told the corrupt truth and was therefore harmless, and he was done for, hung naked from a steel bar, electricity shot through his balls. It is terrible to have to scream, Maturana said many times. A crowd of them, men and women, packed off in a boat. You should have seen our drained faces. Terror had worn off, pain squeezed out, eyes gone blank after being kept open with intense light, tongues hard as dry, untreated leather, you should have seen this new citizenry of the world afloat on the indifferent ocean. If the whooping crane who then ran the country had any idea of founding a penal colony, he soon forgot it, but trust a commercial enterprise to smell out any quick easy profit to be made. Do you know of Andaman Islands, have you heard of Sakhalin? There are places surrounded by black water where human shapes sit staring into their laps. You don't have to tell me of the wrongs done by others, how your body was dragged from wrong to wrong. The spirit is overwhelmed by dejection, I know. And each little push of a malignant fate engages you in that capricious nudge which becomes a cause for the next wrong and that in itself for the one that must follow, and there you are, in the darkness of the dream, in the flashing glare of your lit-up being, as if the body hurtling through black space were outlined in pink neon. But if you bemoan the black water in which your soul has fallen, observe the simple miracle. Here we have the blue ocean, really quite an enchanting blue, and we ought to be relieved we do not need to concern ourselves with the world that failed us. Only this, though; this other thing that I have understood. The Other stalks you, continuously making tiny encroachments on the self, not he who already possesses you, but another, and behind him there is yet one more, a line of them that will not be exhausted until there are no more worlds for you to inhabit, no more fictions in which to make your appearance.

The baby Mariana crying in the crib, Sonia's movements before bedtime twitched with hesitations, something she had to tell him, walking heavily to draw the curtains, her hair, luxuriant then, hanging loose, her eyelids lowered, and he noticed her bare feet, how uncertain she seemed whether she should stand or walk, the toes tapping the ground. What is it, is it the baby crying, come, Sonia, it's getting late, what's wrong? Female fret, earthly sorrow, taking his mind back to his own origins in the village of coconut palms and corn, half a day's walk from a market town, speak, Sonia! The three-month-old Mariana crying in the room, Sonia raised her woman's sad eyes then, spoke in phrases that sobbed, for she had seen the doctor that afternoon, she must never conceive again if she wanted to live, she would never give him the son he desired, but she would give him her body if that is what he wished, pray for a son to the moment of her death. Was that why, even before she spoke, the image of the village had come to him, a premonition of what he must hear making him retreat from the present to his own origins where another mother had died in childbirth? Was it then that his exile had begun?

Sonia grew fat and old in her voluntary barrenness, but Paulina, who shed so much blood at Herminia's birth, conceived again and miscarried, and conceived once more and died. In his village a woman went crazy during her pregnancy, believing that she carried a monkey in her womb, and another woman became constipated the day she discovered she was with child and had nightmares in which her stools fell as lizards, so that she remained constipated for a full nine months. He had known the suffering of women to be fantastic from the day, in a grove of coconut palms with his friends, an older boy had exhibited his phenomenal erection and described to the amazed younger boys how he had split a girl in half with it. How much energy Paulina had given to procreation! She was beautifully shameless in her lust for impregnation, provoking a fresh erection when he thought he was exhausted, her lips and fingertips had such a magical restorative power. She could not breed enough of life and her suffering was that it should run out of her in a stream of blood, her shame that her body not be solid.

Domingo Maturana gave him his cane and lowered his head. Gamboa sat clutching the cane in both hands as if about to break it, hearing Doña Adriana in the cottage talking to the child Herminia. Baltazar, then an ungainly boy of five or six, whose speech flowed out of his mouth in a wordless whine, passed by, staring at the two men. Shoulders stooping, his back bent, he dragged himself across the ashen dust, moving sideways in a stealthy gait. Maturana looked up, hearing the sound of his feet. Baltazar sprang up and turned round and began to run in the manner of one who is lame, throwing more weight on his right foot. The maimed, the incomplete. Words came to Maturana's lips. And some, whole of body, gifted with beauty, a physique that measured grace, but was there one who could not count himself among the maimed? He remained silent, however. The journalist who had been a critic of society, the philosopher with a Sunday column, the poet of the shanty towns suppressed the pity that language had to offer, the irony in an observation that could console, and lowered his head to gaze at the dust between his feet.

The buried bride called to Gamboa in his sleep as during life after the first timidity when the shivering hesitations of the skin had tautened with desire and she would not let her sated lover sleep, flickering her tongue into his ear with hot words that awoke his blood. He must kiss her chin, her neck, her shoulders, he must keep kissing in widening circles around her navel. When some of the semen discharged in her womb dribbled out of her, she collected it in the palm of her hand and then rubbed her hands together as with some lotion, softening the hands made hard by milking the goat and working the hoe in the corn patch, and stroked her breasts with her moist palms and invited his lips to them and in a moment his body was charged with a new tension. She was alive with a boisterous lust, driven by a mad rage for pro-creation, provoking him into frequent arousal with her fingers, with her lips, with her teeth. He had not known so much innocence. Long buried now, her memory was more distant than his memory of Sonia, for Paulina seemed to have come to him in some previous existence, and yet, though her voice reached him from so far away, she seemed more present in her absence than was Sonia, for Paulina was the greater fantasy that engaged his mind.

But now Herminia was hearing him speak of her half-sister Mariana, whose form, as he had last seen it, she incarnated in such matching detail that he imagined their fingerprints must be identical, and when he saw in her face the eyes of the sixteen-year-old Mariana, the girl who stood in a dark entranceway embracing a young man, the girl whom he had not been able to beat and whose mother had to be dragged to her room to punish her for having damaged his fantasy of her ideal future, he wondered then what catastrophe awaited him in his love for the second Mariana, not yet sixteen.

He worked with some dates and arrived at the precise number of days in which Herminia would reach exactly the age that Mariana had been on the day he left home for his office and never returned. After that, life with Herminia would be a resumption of life with Mariana, as though the intervening years had never been, or, if the improbable twists which had led to the present circumstance were not just a meaningless series of unconnected accidents but were logically linked, and some mystery must finally reveal its meaning, then this reappearance of one life in that of another, giving him a second chance, must contain in the complex fabrication of its design, folded within some crease, a sign that could at last comfort, at last make the breath come more easily and soothe the pain growing in his chest.

Baltazar lurked about wherever he took Herminia on the

island. He lost his monkey features as he grew older. His nose remained flat but more flesh on his cheeks made his jaw appear less prominent. What primarily distinguished him from other men was the great quantity of hair that grew on his body. His head supported a rather untidy mane and fine black hair covered all his body. His long front teeth protruded and rested on his thick lower lip, giving him a menacing appearance. But for all his resemblance to a beast, he was the most harmless soul on the island. It had not escaped Gamboa that from an early age Baltazar was fascinated by Herminia, and by now he stared at her as at some divine image. Once, when he was on the beach with Herminia, and Baltazar came and sat nearby, Gamboa pulled him up from the sand and, holding his arm, dragged him to where Herminia sat. "Twelve paces, see?" Gamboa shouted at Baltazar, walking away from Herminia, still clutching Baltazar's arm, and measuring twelve long steps and stamping the ground a few times where the twelfth step fell, added, "Understand? You must never get closer than twelve paces." The boy nodded his head and grinned. But just to make sure, Gamboa knocked his knuckles on Baltazar's head and repeated, "Understand?" The boy nodded his head vigorously and grinned some more. He was in awe of Gamboa, and in the future, whenever Gamboa saw him trying to come closer, he had only to raise a finger and say, "Twelve!" and Baltazar would hang his head down and retreat.

Some time after Domingo Maturana's death the ship stopped coming to collect the nitrate. By now the island had established a basic form of agriculture and had a sufficient flock of goats to feed its inhabitants, but the absence of the link with the other world, even though they had never been allowed to communicate with it, disturbed some minds. It was as if a vital element of their reality had been removed. The men gradually abandoned work in the ash pits; some took to fishing, but the majority hung around outside their huts, sitting listlessly in their boredom after they had exhausted all conjectures why the ship did not return: perhaps great quantities of the same material could be mined more cheaply elsewhere, or the company had gone into liquidation or had been taken over by a foreign corporation which had simply eliminated areas of business that were not highly profitable;

or perhaps there had been a change of government in the country, a new freedom or a new tyranny, revising its laws. The men, sitting outside the huts, said the same things again and again until there was no point to repetitive speculation. A few occasionally got together and discussed schemes for leaving the island, and for weeks they went about chopping down trees and devising ways of constructing a vessel which would transport them at least as far as San Bernardino, the larger island on the horizon that had commerce with the mainland; but each scheme ended in failure: the trees on Santa Barbara were all of a dwarfed variety with thin, twisted trunks, the bigger trees all having been cut many years earlier for the building of the cottages. And each failure added to the sense of oppression among the islanders, of fate having doomed them to a life that offered nothing. A number of them died during this time, among them Doña Adriana—she of old age, but among the others were men who had appeared to have nothing wrong with them and who seemed simply to give up living because life offered them only an endless waiting for that which each succeeding day proved was not going to happen.

Gamboa escaped the general gloom by going on excursions with Herminia to different parts of the island, sometimes going away for two or three days at a time. Invariably Baltazar lurked in the vicinity and, whenever it was time to eat, Gamboa shouted his name and the loping figure appeared and, sitting a dozen paces away, shared in the meal. It became such a routine that Gamboa began to employ Baltazar to carry the food and things they would need for the excursion, thinking that if the youth was going to follow them in any case, he might as well be useful. They were like a group of naturalists studying the habits of birds, collecting fossils, examining the variety of cactus and the shrubs that sprouted pink flowers at certain seasons, but without the tools of the modern naturalist and without the previously developed theory with which the scientist enters the field of investigation, and without, too, the aim of arriving at some conclusion which revealed why things had reached their present state. It was only something to do, this absorption in the land, this making up of diverting games that led to useless discoveries, the subtle anxiety with reality always the compelling force.

Once, when they returned to their hut after being away for three days, they discovered the other islanders to be in a state of great excitement. A launch had come to Santa Barbara from San Bernardino! Four men had sailed right into the bay. No, they were not from the company wanting to resume the export of nitrate; they had actually come to offer them a passage to the mainland. It was incredible. They were all going to be free! The women had gathered in groups and were animatedly discussing the future that was within their grasp, the children, not really understanding what was happening, were running around screaming, "Free, free!" and the men were exchanging bright glances and saying, "Ah, now we will be able to live!" A ship was to be sent within the month to transport them all.

Gamboa talked to Herminia. It was natural for her to be excited by the idea of going to a new world, but she must not expect too much of it. "Oh, but I shall be able to marry!" she cried. Some extraordinary young man that her imagination saw. In the big church he had talked about, its altar adazzle with gold. Yes, you will, my child! Her excitement inspired his enthusiasm, reviving the dreams he had once had for Mariana, seeing now that Herminia was not a copy of Mariana but Mariana herself, coming unblemished to her sixteenth year, and very soon now—in some months—Herminia would be exactly the age Mariana had been when he last saw her. He marvelled at the coincidence that when he returned to the mainland it would be to see Mariana a moment after he had left her, it would be as if he had returned home from his office on that Monday, and in Herminia it would be a Mariana as he had wanted her, chaste to her fingertips, and again those fantasies revived themselves of giving his daughter to an eminent suitor, of performing his fatherly duty to perfection. How much better it would be for her than on this barren island! She had never seen him look so cheerful. She had a thousand questions for him. Where will we live? Shall I have beautiful new dresses? What will we do there? Her questions brought back the bitterness and resentment that he had experienced in his former life, for he would be returing to the world in which there could be no life without money. How could he make Herminia happy with what he had earned at his old job? But he suppressed this new anxiety, resigning himself to what had to happen, not wanting to spoil the dream that possessed her. And then he, too, began to dream. Perhaps he was finally to be rewarded by a perfect happiness. Why, of course, the government would have to compensate him for the years of exile! A lawyer would present his case before a judge. It had been a mistake of the soldiers. He had only gone to the square to eat his lunch. Compensation. A conto for each day he had lost. He began to calculate, to see rows of numbers in his mind. No, *ten* contos for each day. It was only fair the government pay for causing him suffering. Damages, that's what it was called, a lump sum over and above the payment for each lost day, ten thousand contos perhaps, no, it had to be more, *punitive* damages, yes, that was the proper term, the government had to be punished for the wrong it had committed against one of its most upright citizens, a hundred thousand, *five* hundred thousand contos, that was more like it, half a million contos! The more he thought about it, the more his conviction grew that he was bound to be paid damages, so that within the month his mind acquired the certainty that he was going to return to an enormous wealth, the earlier computation of half a million contos having become two million by the end of the month. The ten contos payment for each lost day changed to twenty-five, and the sum for the punitive damages altered each day. He intoxicated himself with calculations, the sum growing larger at each successive reckoning; he spent hours making speeches in his mind, seeing himself stand in the nation's supreme court and talk with such eloquent passion about his suffering that even the judges wept.

And for a month after the visit of the four men in the launch the islanders had daily feasts, slaughtering the goats and chickens. But four weeks later no ship had come. Much of the corn had been eaten. Five goats were left. Six or seven chickens. Had anything gone wrong? Had they made a terrible mistake having a month-long festival, almost like pagans, in the expectation of certain departure? Men climbed up the highest point on the island and kept a lookout for the ship. They set fires whose smoke would be visible from San Bernardino. But the horizon remained dead for another month. It could not be, they said repeatedly to one another, that the four men in the launch had come to play a joke on them. And it had not been a dream. All of them had sat there in a circle listening to the man who made the announcement. There must be some obvious reason for the delay; perhaps no ship was available just then; or perhaps the ship had broken down and awaited spare parts from the mainland. It should be here any day now, we must remain ready: that was the important thing, to remain ready, to live in the expectation that the ship would come tomorrow.

When still another month had passed and the ship had not come, the community began to become nervous and frightened. Some began to plant new rows of corn, some to tend to small vegetable patches, for the unspoken fear of starvation pulsed within them. Gamboa stopped his nightly calculations of the compensation that was his just due; and once again he felt that he had been robbed of wealth that was already his. He was pained to see Herminia, who had spent so much time talking with her friend Diana about their exciting future, look so dejected. Wanting to escape the intense gloom that had fallen on the community now that the promise of liberation it had received daily went unfulfilled, and anxious to provide Herminia with a distraction, he decided to take her on another excursion, even if it was only to their little cave where they could spend a few days in the surroundings of a past already remote and already possessing the charm of a former happiness.

Herminia raised the obvious question: "What if the ship comes while we're gone?"

"We're bound to see it," he answered.

"Not from the little cave, it faces west."

"Well, if you don't want to go." He shrugged his shoulders.

She saw that he looked disappointed. She was herself frustrated and bored with the waiting. The same old talk every day with her friends, the same old expectations that never came to anything. Now she wanted to go because she could see that he was sorry that she had not wanted to go. She came up with an idea. "I know, I'll ask Diana to come and tell us as soon as they spot the ship."

She went away to speak to Diana. Gamboa remarked how precisely she looked like Mariana. His mind, accustomed to calculations, quickly played with some numbers and he was astonished to find that in another forty-two days she would be exactly the age Mariana had been when he last saw her. It was as if a countdown had begun for some fearful event and, finding his forebodings exaggerated by the gloom that prevailed among the islanders, he was glad to have the opportunity to escape to the cave. When they went, Baltazar followed a dozen paces behind, his eyes, as always, on the miraculous form of Herminia, now walking up the sloping path and appearing to him as if she were entering the immense blue of the sky.

Some of the islanders saw the three of them go and not too long after they had climbed over the hill and disappeared out of sight, a man who had been sitting on the rock at the end of the beach came running, shouting with his hand pointing to the ocean, "The ship, the ship!"

The coincidence of Gamboa, Herminia and Baltazar going and the ship's coming struck those who had seen the three depart as significantly connected, as if it had been a necessary form of sacrifice, and they remained silent about them. Diana said to her mother, "I promised Herminia I'd go and call her when the ship came. I'll run up the hill, they can't be far. I'll be back long before they send out the boats." Her father heard her and, quickly stepping to her just when she was about to go, held her arm and said, "You'll do nothing, you hear me!" He had always hated Gamboa because Domingo Maturana had made him out to be someone special, giving him his daughter. "But I promised her I would!" Diana cried. "All I have to do is run up the hill and shout for her to hear me. It won't take a minute!"

"You stay right with your family until we reach the mainland," her father ordered, and seeing that he was ready to slap her if she did not obey him, she did not go. Some other men who had heard the exchange remained silent; they, too, disliked Gamboa: he was aloof, uncommunicative, never shared in the natural camaraderie of men. The women in the group said nothing either, for he had been the object of contempt among them for many years, after Paulina's death, because he remained unattached when there were young women in the community who were without a man, two of whom in fact had taken the trouble to give him more than obvious hints only to be humiliated by his cold stare; they weren't good enough for him and so why should they care about him now?

And thus, when later in the day the ship lay at anchor beyond the four whale-backed rocks and the islanders were taken to it on boats, and the ship finally set sail for the mainland, no one mentioned the three who had been left behind.

Gamboa, Herminia and Baltazar returned four days later to the empty settlement. Coming down the slope they sensed the silence even though, just then, the cries of sea lions filled the air. Baltazar grasped the situation first and went running down in his clumsy gait, more a succession of leaps than a run. Herminia quickened her pace, shock and alarm on her face, crying, "No! They could not have left without us!" Gamboa stopped and stared at her rapid steps and at Baltazar, who had now reached the cottages and was looking into them one after another. "Oh God, no!" Gamboa whispered, realizing that something far worse than his own dream of rehabilitation had been destroyed: how could he ever look again into Herminia's eyes and not see there her despair at having lost her chance at life? Wanting to be kind, taking her away to divert her from the oppressive gloom of the community, he had ended by inflicting upon her a lasting hurt. If he had beaten Mariana that day so long ago, broken her teeth and disfigured her face, he would not have been more cruel than his simple act, inspired by love for Herminia, now made him appear. He saw her stop by the first of the huts and turn round to stare at him and from the distance he could see hatred blazing in her eyes as she screamed at him, *"What have you done?"*

It was useless for him to try and comfort her, as he did, with the notion that someone was bound to notice the mistake and send a boat for them. "We were away for . . . *four* days," she cried. He understood what she meant: if the ship had come on the first day of their absence, it must be nearing the mainland already. "They must all be in their new homes by now," she added bitterly, and he was pained on hearing the anguish in her voice when she spoke the words "new homes",

giving him a sharp sense of the loss of her dream. Baltazar
sat on the ground in the distance, his arms around his knees,
looking sideways at them. "What do you want me to do
now," she cruelly asked her father, "have children with
Baltazar? Breed a new race of monkeys?"

Though they could not escape the misery of each other's
presence and the silence that was worse than a loud flow
of abuse, they gradually adopted routines that kept them
preoccupied and their lives going. There were the goats and
the chickens and the corn to attend to if they were to have
anything to eat in the future, and, without prescribing a
division of labor, each found an appropriate task.

Baltazar, who wore loose coveralls that Gamboa had found
left behind in a hut and made him put on instead of the
piece of cloth he carelessly tied round his waist, went about
gathering firewood. When he came back with his load,
Gamboa always kept an eye on him to make sure he kept his
twelve paces from Herminia. She, however, treated him as a
child, insisting, when he came for his meal, for example, that
he finish his glass of milk. He drank, his head raised, his eyes
on Herminia. Gamboa watched.

His poor girl. She had learned so much so soon. The hatred
bred of the father's love. The treachery of her closest friend
Diana who had not kept her promise. An existence become
entirely meaningless. But the gentler instincts had surfaced,
too. She knew what had to be done to go on. She acquired
skills that no one had taught her, milking the goats, grinding
the corn and preparing the meals, though she must have
absorbed everything as a child when she played in the kitchen
while her grandmother worked, for her hands now mimicked
Doña Adriana's gestures. While it was some happiness for
Gamboa that she should have matured so quickly and become
resigned to her empty existence that had no promise of a
future, he was greatly grieved that that should remain her
condition indefinitely. And then the thought came to him:
what if he should die? As he must long before her and Baltazar.
What had he to leave as her inheritance but an eternity of
solitude with a beast for a companion?

He himself did not work as hard as she did, for he soon
wearied of the task he undertook, crushed by thoughts of the

pointlessness of the future, and he sat in front of the cottage like a tired old watchkeeper talking to himself.

He was sitting there one day feeling utterly defeated with not even the ghost of Domingo Maturana's voice to comfort him or images of Paulina to reassure him that in unexpected places, as in this wilderness, life had the potential to surprise one with beauty and wonder. His misery was so great he was scarcely alive to the world around him. He awoke from his stupor on suddenly hearing Herminia running out of the cottage, crying, "The boat, the boat!" She stood a few paces in front of him, saying, "I heard the sound of a motor, where is it?" He rose and walked to where she was. Had he heard the faint distant drumming of a diesel engine? He could not be sure. They looked at the bay and the four whale-backed rocks and the ocean beyond them. There was nothing there. But then why was Baltazar coming down the hill in his awkward leaping run, gesticulating wildly and shouting incomprehensibly? All at once the sound of a diesel engine burst into the air as a white boat came from behind the largest of the four whale-backed rocks and entered the bay. Gamboa held his breath: it seemed too large a boat to be risking the submerged rocks that made entrance into the bay hazardous and the person navigating it must be ignorant of the danger he ran. But the boat sailed in unimpeded.

"They've come for us, they've come for us!" Herminia exclaimed, jumping excitedly. Baltazar was almost down the hill. "We are saved!" Herminia cried, and hugged her father in her joy. He held her tightly, tears in his eyes through which he saw over her shoulder the blurred image of the boat, and in that moment numbers filled his mind, did instantaneous leaps in the circuitry of his brain, and in a second gave him the solution to the question he had not consciously asked, and just when, wiping his eyes with Herminia still in his embrace, he saw two men on the boat, the numbers informed him that Herminia was on that day exactly the same age Mariana had been sixteen years ago, the last time he had seen her.

IV

Poor People, Rich Lives

She unlocked the door with the master key and dragged in the cart on which were piled white sheets and towels, with a section on its side that contained sponges, cloths and a bathroom cleanser. The TV in the room had been left on. She walked to it and switched it off, seeing, as she took the few steps to the box, that it was showing a gray-haired, obese man, his lips open in lascivious anticipation, hold a beautiful young woman's face in his hands, her look indicating the expression of one who has lost all hope and must unwillingly submit herself to the ultimate sacrifice. Turning away from the set, the woman walked back to the corridor and fetched the large vacuum cleaner. She was short and heavy, her stomach bulging out below the belt of her white uniform, and she moved laboriously as she went about her work. Her eyes were dull, as if she no longer needed to see what she did, her black hair, streaked with white, was pulled back and held untidily in a rubber band, and her face, with no make-up on the loose, coarse-grained flesh and the dry, swollen lips, appeared exhausted: her general manner seemed that of a person whose body has been subjected to indiscriminate and callous suffering, who has unreasonably had to endure extreme hardship and who has no expectation of being released from misery.

The ashtrays were all full. An empty bottle of Scotch lay upside down in a trashcan which was otherwise full of balled-up paper tissues. The bathroom floor was wet with soaking towels abandoned on it. She had seen the couple leave in the morning—a young woman, a middle-aged man—but now, as she went about cleaning after the storm of their passion, no image came to her of what the room had witnessed during the night. She pulled off the rumpled sheets without imagining what physical agitation had disturbed the bed. She had no interest in the affairs of others; it meant nothing to her that men were driven by brute passions and women by whorish cupidity, though sometimes perhaps both were ruled by love. She herself had only known different forms of violence, including the animalism of her own desires: to her, existence had proved itself to have been a fraud, giving her such beautiful expectations when she was sixteen and then compressing within her next eighteen years experiences each one of which was the opposite of what she had wished for herself in her projections for the future, making her now, at the relatively young age of thirty-four, a fat little woman who mechanically went about performing the repetitious motions each day of cleaning and making up the rooms of a hotel, rooms that were briefly occupied by people who must live extraordinary lives but which were always empty when she entered them.

Sometimes, when looking out of a window from a room on the eleventh floor, she imagined her body falling through the air, but though the thought produced the chilling sensation of a peculiar thrill, she was invariably left staring at the image of her three girls and her aged mother for whom she must continue to provide. There was Pascual, too, the father of her youngest daughter, who periodically abandoned his own wife and threw his huge body on her bed where he snored night and day for weeks on end, rising to eat half the family's food and threatening to beat her if she did not spend on liquor the money she had been saving to buy new clothes for the children. He was the most despicable of the men she had known, a bully and a parasite; and yet, when he was not with her she would wish he would lose his job again and quarrel with his wife, and she could not explain why she missed the loudly snoring body that left so little space for herself on the bed. The gross, sweaty mass of his flesh, his bloodshot eyes and unshaven face, and the harsh voice with which he spoke to her, all filled her with disgust, but when he went away she missed even the smell from his armpits that, when he lay next to her, forced her to keep a handkerchief crushed against her nose. Perhaps her attachment to him was only a habit that had grown, for Pascual was, after his fashion, the most faithful of the men who had loved her. His manner was rude, his language foul, and whatever he did was the whim of the instant, performed without premeditation. No words or gestures of endearment preceded his sexual assaults on her—he simply thrust her into the position he fancied and threw his enormous weight upon her. The coupling was invariably brief, merely a rapid succession of blows, and gave her no pleasure, but still, when he was not there, she sometimes longed for his rough hands to twist her around and renew the shock of penetration. When he was not drunk or asleep, he would sit with her mother, giving her his opinions on topics that ranged from the performance of the local football team to world politics, none of which meant anything to the old woman whose mind had long exchanged the facts of reality for a small packet of obsessive images of its own invention. When Pascual paused after some long statement about the economy or the corruption in government, the old woman would remark, "It was all that money he came into." Or Pascual might have described how the football team lost a match by its own mistakes, and the mother would declare, "It was all that money that fell into his lap." Though sometimes she added a phrase or varied a few words, her contribution to the conversation was always the same irrelevant sentence. And even when no one sat talking with her she would be heard muttering from her corner, "With so much money, he must live in a palace. He got his money and ran, Mister Millionaire. It was all that money he came into. Just like that."

Only she had a clue to her mother's derangement, tracing the shock back to eighteen years ago on a Monday night when the father did not return from work. After the tense weekend that had begun with the father forcing the mother to beat her, his absence on that first night was attributed to the plausible hypothesis that he had gone and got drunk. The mother knew that he did not have any money on him, for he had been obliged to ask her for his bus fare. She had concluded at first that he must have borrowed from his friends or got an advance from his office; but later she came to believe that his telling her he did not have the money for his bus fare had been a clever lie in order to prevent her from having any suspicion of the wealth that had suddenly come to him. When he had not returned the next night, Sonia had begun to be anxious, but did not know what she should do. The idea of going to the police filled her with shame. What could she tell the police —that her husband was a drunkard who had got himself into trouble somewhere? When a few more days had passed and her anxiety had turned to alarm, she decided that she should go to the city and inquire at his place of work. She knew he worked for the Ministry of Labor and had little trouble finding the building, but once there realized in her bewildered way, for her mind comprehended such matters with the frightened awe of the illiterate for whom the commonplace was a complex of baffling mysteries, that the Ministry was an enormous structure made up of divisions, sections and subsections together with satellites of departments. Had some officer at any one of the innumerable desks to which she applied taken a few minutes to check with the personnel section on the fifth floor of the building, the first problem of discovering in which department Felipe Gamboa worked would have been solved; but all the people she approached, talking timidly, hesitantly and almost inaudibly, took one look at her undistinguished presence, glancing tiredly at her cheap clothes and hearing her clumsy speech confirm the impression of an illiterate poor person, jerked their heads and told her she was in the wrong place. Most of them did not even hear what she was saying, for they assumed from her appearance that she was soliciting money for some charity and told her to move on. With two or three she started to speak again, but the men did not even look back at her. She was obliged to return home in utter frustration.

Her state of mind had progressed now from alarm to despair. Two weeks had passed and Felipe had not returned. Dust had accumulated in the apartment, dirty clothes were piled in the bathroom; pained by her inability to do anything, she had been lost completely in her worry. For two weeks Mariana had been saying something about Federico. That he had disappeared too. And she had obviously been crying. But Sonia could not concern herself with the problems of the young, for each minute that passed without any news of her husband intensified the horrifying thought in her mind—that very soon, certainly after the next month's rent was paid, she would have no money left of her little savings. She must go and see her brother. She must start looking for a job. She must do *something*. But she sat in a stupor, staring at images of herself sleeping in doorways with only her old poncho to protect her against the cold nights. Suddenly she sat up and slapped her forehead, telling herself how stupid she had been. There was the small box in the bedroom in which Felipe kept some papers. The slips of papers that his office gave him with his wages. He was always careful about keeping those. Every year he brought them all out and spent a Sunday morning adding sums, calling to her across the room, "Sonia, can you guess how much tax I've paid this year?" She never could and always expressed astonishment at the sum they had lost. "And what does the government give us for our money?" Felipe always asked, and proceeded to recite a catalogue of deficient services. She hurried to the box. The slips must contain some identification number, some information that could help to trace him in that huge building. When she looked at them, at first she saw only rows of figures without understanding what each sum represented. She would have to ask Mariana to read the words above them. But then she noticed that there was one number that was repeated in all the slips. That must be it, his work number. She decided to go to the Ministry again on the next day and see if she could not discover the office in which he had worked. There must be other workers there who must know him. Someone surely would be able to tell her what had happened to Felipe.

But before she could set out the next morning a letter addressed to her husband arrived in the mail. An official seal, printed in blue in a corner of the envelope, alarmed her and she went to Mariana's room where the young girl was getting ready to go to school. Annoyed that she had to perform another trivial chore for her mother and complaining that she was already late, Mariana opened the letter with a resigned look on her face that indicated that it was another parental demand, utterly onerous and inconsiderate, that she was having to meet. But her little act of displaying her resentment vanished before she had finished reading the first sentence, for, pausing after the opening line—"Considering that you have without leave and without explanation been absent for two weeks . . ."—she saw the look of consternation that had come over her mother's face and was herself filled with a vague fear. The father had been dismissed from his post. Uttering a short, sharp cry, Sonia left the room while Mariana had yet to read the paragraph that stated that Felipe Gamboa's communist activity had been noted and consequently his accumulated pension deductions would be forfeited and he would be ineligible for any other government post. Without reading that paragraph, Mariana followed her mother to the living room where she had collapsed in a chair and begun to lament her fate.

"Mother, what are we going to *do?*" she cried, dropping the letter and the envelope into her lap.

But her mother appeared to her to be jabbering nonsense and seemed not to hear any of her practical questions. Deciding that, although she had a good excuse not to go to school that day, staying at home would be a greater agony, and having also on her mind the thought that perhaps Federico might have returned, Mariana fetched her books and left the apartment.

Sonia did not see her go, for just then she was imagining herself huddled against the closed doorway of a shop at night with her poncho gone threadbare. Dogs nosed about her cold body, rats sprang up from the gutter and snapped away bits of her clothing and were about to attack her flesh. Then the shopkeeper was kicking her when he came to open the shop and found her there.

When many such horrors had played themselves out in her mind, a calm descended upon her. She stared at the familiar objects around her. She stood up and walked about the two bedrooms, looked into the tiny kitchen and the cramped bathroom. There was dust everywhere. The lid of the trashcan in the kitchen stood at an angle above the heaped-up rubbish with decaying food sending out its rotten smell; onion skin, zucchini peel and the leaves of a cauliflower were strewn on the floor around the trashcan. A pile of dirty clothes lay abandoned in the corner of the bathroom; the sink was turning gray with dirt and had bits of toothpaste stuck in it; there were long strands of hair in the bath.

The small, cluttered apartment, which was stiflingly hot in the summer and made her suffer from a sense of claustrophobia, often making her wish they had more money and could move to a larger space, giving her the fantasy of airy rooms and long corridors, sometimes creating in her the thrilling thought that she lived in a mansion, suddenly, now that she walked within the confined space in her despair at her vanished husband and his dismissal from his job, her little apartment became a precious place. One more month, and she would not have the money to pay the rent. Seeing that she could lose it, the apartment's dimensions became enlarged in her mind and its rooms, offering security and privacy, took on a new charm and became a dear possession.

Chiding herself for neglecting her housework and letting the dust accumulate, she busied herself energetically. She dusted and wiped, swept and sponged; she took the trash out and washed the kitchen floor; she scrubbed the bath and the sink and polished the mirrors; and as she went about restoring a glow to surfaces, it seemed to her that she dwelt in a luxury apartment. She must go to her brother. Beg him to help her out for a month or two. Find herself a job. Do something. Anything. To keep her dear little apartment.

She sorted out the pile of dirty clothes. Underwear, slips; a cotton frock of Mariana's, one of her own; a couple of Mariana's T-shirts and a pair of her jeans; two sets of bed-sheets and pillow cases; one of Felipe's shirts and a pair of his trousers.

When she went to empty the pockets of the trousers, she found in one a soiled handkerchief and in the other, the left pocket, a quantity of torn-up pieces of paper. She remembered that he had been wearing these trousers on that last Friday when he returned from work and went into a rage, beating her and getting her to beat Mariana. The fragments in her hand all had numbers inscribed on them. Funny, what could they be? She walked to the kitchen, laid the bits of paper on the table and shuffled them around to see if she could not fit the pieces of this jigsaw puzzle together. She managed to match a few of them but it was impossible to arrange them all to form the page before it had been torn up. All she could see was numbers. Lots of them. Several of them indicated an incredibly large sum. It had to be money. So much money! But what was Felipe doing making up these big sums? He'd never said anything about that much money. What had he been calculating? With so much money. How could he dream of so much money?

He must have won the lottery, that must be it!

The explanation seemed to her to solve the mystery of his disappearance. Seeing some of the larger figures with several noughts at their end, Sonia's mind burned with the thought of enormous wealth. All that which should have been hers to share! She cast her mind to previous weeks and began to believe that Felipe had been unusually quiet and that when he talked it had invariably been to complain of their poor situation: it was, she felt convinced, the behavior of a man with a secret, one who was plotting a big change in his life; she remembered, too, that he went out for several hours on Sunday afternoons, telling her that he was going for a walk, often adding bitterly as he went, "That's all I can do, go for a damn walk while everyone else takes his family out in a car." That must have been another trick of his, Sonia now considered. What walk? He must have got himself a mistress. The money must have come to him some weeks earlier, and he had taken his time plotting his move, putting on a great act of being poor. Especially on that last Monday morning when he put on a really miserable face and asked her for the bus fare. She imagined how his face must have changed when he was out of the door of the apartment, a broad smile spreading across it, and how he must have laughed to himself that he had fooled her when he reached the bottom of the street and hailed a taxi. The longer she stared at the bits of paper the more vividly she saw him in his new life of luxury in a house surrounded by a large garden, with a young mistress. Some pretty thing she must be. Some cheap whore.

Sonia did not share her conclusions with anyone, not wanting to be pitied for her husband's ungrateful and treacherous deed. Henceforth, any question about him met with only one answer from her: "God took him away." As if the husband's great error obliged her to serve a period of penance, enforcing her to suffer pain to the same degree that she imagined he experienced pleasure, she resigned herself to hardship. When she went from door to door in the nearby commercial street, asking if there was not some job she could do—washing dishes in a restaurant, shelving cans in a supermarket—she felt the humiliation of each rejection as a sort of public contrition that had necessarily to be performed before the husband's sin could be atoned. Finally she found a job as a cleaning woman in a bank, and scrubbing the floor on her hands and knees gave her an inner satisfaction, as if she were a pilgrim to Our Lady of Guadalupe who must climb the 365 stone steps to the hilltop church on her bare knees in order to be worthy of grace.

At her school Mariana heard Federico's absence explained by rumors that were malicious in proportion to the envy that had been harbored by the person with whom they originated. Two boys especially, Gerardo and Emilio, who had scorned Federico's success with girls by forming a gang given to expressions of empty male bravado and who had shown their contempt for Federico's popularity with the teachers when he did well in the tests by making ignorance appear a particularly virile virtue, were the authors of several of the worst rumors. Getting some of the younger boys, who were anxious not to be bullied by Gerardo, to say that Federico had once tried to sell them pot, they spread the notion that he had been caught dealing in the street. Three unattractive girls who lived in a world of frustrated fantasies did not mind admitting that Federico had constantly pestered them and one swore that she had seen him trap Mercedes in a corner once and pulled up her skirt to thrust his hand between her thighs, and so a new rumor began to go the rounds, that Federico lived among whores and had become a pimp. At first Mariana laughed away all the stories. They were too ridiculous, and too obviously false. During the last year, when they were not in class, he was alone with her for much of the time and could have had no opportunity to give his attentions to another girl. As for drugs, she had never heard him talk about them, he did not even smoke cigarettes. But as the days, and then the

weeks, passed, she became confused and did not know what
to believe. She was bewildered by the circumstantial details
attending some of the rumors—but always of a kind that was
impossible to verify—which made it hard to reject them out
of hand. Not wanting to hear what was being said and yet
eager for the next piece of gossip, she felt terribly oppressed.

She sought release from the oppression by imagining Federico as the great love of her life, remembering the times with
him as periods of ecstasy. She would think of herself as a
figure in some legendary romance obliged to pine away during
the absence of her lover who had been cast by fate into an
involuntary exile. Or, moved by self-pity and finding the
sensation gave her a sharp pleasure, she would imagine him
as a brute, a vain man who had thought only of his own
pleasure and discarded her no sooner than she had gratified
him. Her recent memories, undergoing a constant revision as
she reacted to the untruths being broadcast about Federico,
became distorted, so that the truth perceived by her mind was
as much a lie as any of the rumors.

One fact she would never remember again was that it had
been she herself who had felt a strong desire for sexual
possession. Inexperienced and timid, Federico had not had
the nerve to kiss her on the lips, never having done so with
anyone before, and it had been Mariana, once at dusk in the
park, who, pretending she saw something curious in his ear,
had brought her face close to his in order to examine the ear,
and then, moving slightly, had allowed her mouth to brush
his cheek and stop against the corner of his lips. Even then,
at their subsequent meetings, Federico was not emboldened
to take the lead and she invariably resorted to some subterfuge
in order to get him to kiss her. With a mixture of horror at
having bad thoughts and a thrilling anticipation of fulfilling
her desires, she would pass hours when alone in bed with
fantasies of making love. And on that fateful Friday night
when he had been waiting for her outside her apartment
building and the two walked down the street, it was she,
holding his hand, who had pulled him toward the dark
entranceway and, leaning against the wall, had drawn him
into an embrace; it was the first time that kissing him she had
pressed her tongue into his mouth, finally liberating him from

his timidity, and in that moment's frantic urgency of instinct
she had lifted up his hand and placed it against her breast.
What pained her that night was not merely that her father
had pulled Federico away from her but that her own aroused
desire should be so quickly frustrated and be succeeded first
by punishment and then by Federico's disappearance.

"You want information about him?" Gerardo said to her
one day during the morning recess. People had begun to
lose interest in what had happened to Federico. Sensational
scandal had become boring. Gerardo wanted to strike while
he still had the opportunity, before all interest in Federico
was dead.

Mariana stared at Gerardo's light-complexioned face and
the thought crossed her mind that while he was well built, his
wet, rubbery lips, straight black hair and small black eyes
made him look repulsive. His friend Emilio, shorter and
suffering from acne, shuffled nervously next to him. "What
information?" she asked.

"Can't talk here," Emilio said in a hoarse whisper.

"Meet us after school," Gerardo said, looking around,
making out that he did not want anyone to overhear them.
"By the gate."

She could see through their act, but asked, "You know
where he is?"

"By the gate," Gerardo repeated, beginning to walk away.

Emilio leaned his face close to her. "After school," he
whispered, and turned to follow his friend.

When she left the building in the afternoon, she could see
Gerardo from a distance, his tall, broad-shouldered frame
making him stand out in the milling crowd of kids many of
whom hung around in groups or leaned against the parked
cars, and in that moment she recalled the various incidents in
which he had been involved, each one increasing his notoriety
as a bullying braggart. He had been suspended from the soccer
team for repeatedly injuring the shins of other players; he
used foul language in class to impress the girls with his
independence and daring, but only succeeded in embarrassing
them and being shunned by them. It was a pity, Mariana
thought walking up to him, he had such an ugly face with a
chin that was perpetually wet from saliva dribbling down

from the corners of his mouth; but Emilio, standing behind him, had even less to make him attractive with his shock of curly, untidy black hair, a stooped back and a face like the skin of a jackfruit.

"You said you had information," she said to Gerardo, coming up to him.

"You hear that, Emilio?" Gerardo turned to his friend. "The lady wants information."

"Such as what, the price of bananas?"

The two boys laughed. They had apparently worked out a routine.

"Quit fooling around," Mariana said.

"Do I ever fool around?" Gerardo asked Emilio.

Before Emilio could attempt another wisecrack, Mariana said, "To hell with you, then." And she made to walk away.

"Hey, don't you want to know about Federico?" Gerardo shouted after her.

She stopped, turned round and said sternly, "I'll listen if you'll stop acting like clowns."

"I told you I had information," Gerardo said. "But I can't give it here."

"Why not?"

"Because you won't believe me without proof, and I've got the proof locked in a box at home."

She remembered he lived a block away from Federico's street, on the way to her own apartment.

"You want to come and see it?" Gerardo asked.

"The proof," Emilio added.

"What sort of proof?"

"You want to come or not?"

Now it was Gerardo who pretended to walk away. Looking over his shoulder, he saw that Emilio had come up behind him and that Mariana had begun to follow them. He said to Mariana across the short distance, "You'll see for yourself that Federico was planning to lay his hands on big money and run away."

Mariana quickened her pace and caught up with him as he continued to walk on. "How do you know?" she asked. He grinned at her, and she looked away from his ugly mouth while hearing him say, "I told you I got proof."

"You better believe him," Emilio said, remembering to play his part.

When they arrived at the apartment, Mariana asked, "Where's your mother?"

"Gone to the country," Gerardo answered, "to be with a sick sister."

Mariana felt a moment's apprehension to be alone with the two boys in the apartment. It was precisely the opportunity she had often longed for in recent months, for her mother to be away so that she could take Federico to her own bedroom. She must watch out, she determined to herself, these two could be up to some trick. But forcing herself not to show her concern, she demanded rather loudly, "Okay, where's this great proof of yours?"

"Hey, hold on," Emilio said, "what's the hurry, relax, will you?"

"Yeah, let me get some Coca-Cola," Gerardo said, going off to the kitchen.

Mariana was about to protest that she could do without his hospitality but the hurried walk had made her thirsty.

"Gerardo," Emilio shouted through the door, "can I put on a record?"

"Sure, be my guest," Gerardo shouted back.

Before Mariana could say that she had not come to hear a concert, Emilio picked up a record and said to her, "Heard the Spinsters' latest?"

"No," she answered. "But what I came here for . . ."

"Ah, quit being nervous," Emilio said, "you're with friends, the school's superstars." He put the record on with the comment, "This is the greatest."

The four members of the British rock group were all males and their lead singer, Johnny Verve, affected an American accent as he yelled out the lyrics. Gerardo returned, clutching three full tall glasses in his hands, holding them out in front of his chest. The electric guitar had just begun a vibrant solo. Gerardo found one of the glasses slipping and he hurriedly brought his hands down on a table and placed the glasses there. This unexpected action confused him: pleased with himself that he had not let the glass fall and that he had succeeded in putting all three of them down without spilling a drop of their content, he had looked up at his guests as if to see admiration in their faces for his deft maneuver, but going to pick up the glass to offer to Mariana he could not remember which was the one in which he had mixed rum with the Coke. Realizing that it would be fatal to hesitate, he passed the glasses with a bravado that Emilio interpreted as confidence in knowing what he was doing. Accepting his drink, and in order to set an example for Mariana to follow, Emilio shouted over Johnny Verve's renewed bellowing, "Just what I need!" and took a long swallow. His drink tasted unmistakably of rum, and he threw a smile at Gerardo as a silent expression of his thanks, for he assumed that his friend must have decided to add a little rum to their own two drinks as well.

"You like the album?" Gerardo asked Mariana.

Without realizing it, she had been moving her body jerkily to the music, and the thought had occurred to her that this was what some kids talked of doing, going to one another's apartments to hear records, something that she had never experienced, and here she was with two guys listening to the Spinsters' latest. Seen that way, she really was having a great time. It would be a terrific story to tell her girlfriends; only no one was going to be envious when she revealed the guys were Gerardo and Emilio. But even if they had been handsome, she hadn't come to have fun. Knowing that she must sacrifice her pleasure, she drank the rest of the Coca-Cola, put the glass down, and said to Gerardo, "The album's great, but I don't have time for the rest. What about the information?"

Emilio, seeing her finish her drink, drained his glass too and said, "Come on, Gerardo, give the lady what she wants. She needs it badly." He grinned stupidly at his friend.

"Okay," Gerardo said, "come to my room and see for yourself."

Mariana and Emilio followed him down a corridor and into a small room with a bed in a corner and opposite it a little table with a stool. Gerardo brought out a wooden box from under his bed. He took out a key from beneath the mattress just below the pillow and with a great show of ceremony unlocked the small padlock on the box. He held up a school exercise book. Mariana's first response was disappointment; instead of some magical revelation, she was being shown a commonplace object.

"This is the proof," Gerardo said, showing the cover of the exercise book and pointing to Federico's name on it. She recognized his handwriting. Gerardo turned the pages, skipping over the ones on which Mariana could see Federico had copied down the history notes the teacher had written on the blackboard and stopping to let her observe Federico's doodles. She saw her own name written many times in different scripts and often the symbol F+M within a heart.

"Now, look at this," Gerardo said, arriving at a page full of little sums under the heading, "Money equals Independence." A list of foreign currencies was inscribed as a column: dollars, pounds, francs, marks, rubles, sucres, contos, pesos, cruzeiros . . . The symbols denoting some of these currencies were scattered about the page in between the impressive sums. Above one sum was the heading "What I'd do with One Million Dollars". At the bottom of the page were the words WHAT I REALLY NEED and below this was the number 9 followed by a series of noughts that went right across the page and apparently would have continued had the page been wider.

"Well, what does this prove," Mariana asked, taking the exercise book and holding it against her bosom, "except that he was daydreaming in class?"

"Haven't you heard?" Gerardo said in a voice indicating surprise that she was ignorant of a common scandal and noticing in that moment that Emilio had sat down on the edge of the bed. Mariana stared at Gerardo who went on, "Your great friend Federico—excuse me, your one-time lover . . ."

"Don't be obscene!" she interrupted loudly.

"Hey, who's being touchy? Okay, boyfriend then. Well, he stole money from his parents. He robbed his own father."

"That can't be true," she cried. "Stop playing games with me."

"Games, she calls it," Gerardo said turning to Emilio, but the latter was leaning back on the bed and had closed his eyes. "Listen," he went on, looking at Mariana, "it was his own mother who told me. Go and ask her yourself if you don't believe me. I went to see her when Federico had been absent over a week. I like to know what's going on, see? She broke down and cried like a baby. He stole from his father's wallet and ran away."

"I don't believe it!"

Gerardo snatched the exercise book from where she still held it near her bosom and, waving it in front of her, said, "The next day I looked inside his desk and found this. You can see how he had been working out a plan. He was looking for a break, see? He was looking for a little capital. To start him off on the road to independence. And he found it right in his father's wallet."

Emilio, his eyes rolling as he tried to resist the dizziness that had come over him, raised himself from the bed, remembering the part he had been rehearsed to play. Since Mariana, and not he, was supposed to be under the influence of rum by now, his job was to push her accidentally so that she fell on the bed; instead, Emilio found that he had an imperfect control over his movements and could not precisely remember what he was meant to do, and so, putting on a forced joviality, he made a roaring sound and fell against Gerardo, clasping him from behind. Mariana was shocked to see Emilio's eyes leering at her while he clutched Gerardo round his chest with his head over the taller boy's shoulder.

"Hey, stop that!" Gerardo shouted, trying to wrench himself free. Emilio, however, held on to him, and the two staggered about the room, Gerardo pushing back to be rid of him and he pressing forward to prevent him from so doing, until the two hit the edge of the bed and together collapsed upon it with Emilio being slightly crushed by his friend falling on him and the taller Gerardo hitting his head against the wall, so that the two of them yelled out simultaneously. Seeing Emilio extricate himself from under Gerardo and jump upon him, straddling him across the thighs and beginning to bounce there, Mariana picked up the exercise book, which had fallen to the floor, and quickly left the room and fled from the apartment.

Some days later, while she was walking back from school, she happened to look back and saw that Emilio was following her. She pretended not to have noticed him and quickened her step. On subsequent days she frequently ran into him at the school. He always seemed to be coming out of some place that she happened to be walking past, but he never stopped to speak to her, giving her the impression instead that he had some urgent business to attend to. One day she stopped him and said, "I never see you with Gerardo any more."

He looked at her silently, hoping she would remark the infinite sadness on his face, and then said, "It would be best if you didn't know the truth."

"What about?"

"Rumors get spread."

He did not want to tell her that after she had left the two of them on the bed, they had ended by fighting. Gerardo had accused him of ruining his plan to seduce Mariana and he had countered by accusing Gerardo of making him drunk, and in the fight that followed Emilio had received more blows than he could inflict. Going away, Emilio had realized that, given his small body, his only weapon for advancing himself in life was cunning.

"What rumors?" she asked.

Emilio was determined not to compromise himself with a blatant lie and relied upon innuendo to do the work. "I don't think I should be telling you," he said.

"Emilio, what are you talking about?"

"I'm talking about nothing," he said, "but everyone else is."

"Saying what?"

"I don't believe any of it myself. But rumors are rumors."

"Oh, for God's sake, what rumors?"

"That you go to guys' apartments," he said, watching her closely to see how her face reacted. "That you get taken to the bedroom."

"Is that what Gerardo has been saying?" she asked, unable to restrain the anger from showing on her face.

"Listen, I told you nothing. Nothing, okay?"

He observed to his own satisfaction that she looked visibly disturbed and, in order to appear to be consoling her, said, "To tell you the truth, Mariana, I myself don't believe any of that nonsense. Okay, so I was there with you the first time you went into Gerardo's bedroom, but I don't believe what people are saying. I didn't even want to tell you about it, it's all lies. You don't have to take it to heart. As I say, it's all lies."

After this occasion, Emilio began to play the role of her devoted friend, meeting her in circumstances which he led her to believe were fraught with danger to himself. Gerardo would murder him if he found out. "I can be with you for only a couple of minutes," he would say, looking around anxiously, "but I have to tell you what I heard Benito say to the boys of what Gerardo had told him . . ." Thus, day after day, he piled untruth upon untruth and, attempting to cover his tracks, spread the same falsehoods among his friends, so that each person, passing on the gossip as if it were his own remarkable discovery and for that reason not attributing it to a source, but instead keeping it mysterious to heighten the sense of his own importance, unwittingly contributed to fostering a general belief in whatever perverse lie had originated with Emilio. Mariana began to depend upon him as an old faithful ally. His acne-ravaged face and stooping back made him hideously unattractive, and she invariably found herself looking over his shoulder when talking to him; but what was ugliness if his heart was pure and he was a valuable friend? Even the girlfriends who had been close to her now affected a coldness toward her, and she detected sarcasm in their voices. Emilio at least was always honest.

Emilio was convinced that he had made himself indispensable to her. Very soon he maneuvered himself into a position where he was the only friend she had. He realized that instead of manipulating her with the ultimate aim of inflicting revenge upon Gerardo, her dependence on him changed the picture dramatically. Why bother with Gerardo when he had Mariana where she could be used in a far more exciting way—for his own gratification? He withdrew from the school's political intrigues, for now the direction of his secret plan had taken a new turn. Instead of being a character actor, he was going to be the hero.

A young uncle of Emilio's, visiting from the country where he had a small dairy farm, had recently told him that if he wanted to get rid of acne he ought to find himself a woman, adding, "It's not enough to jerk off every time you go to the bathroom." Had Emilio's face not already been covered by pink-headed pimples, the uncle would have seen him blush. Emilio suffered from a ferocious need to empty himself and each day he sought to add a novelty to his experience. The basket of dirty clothes in the corner of the bathroom had offered variety for a time. He had stuffed his mother's bra with balled up T-shirts and placing it on the floor had pressed his chest against it, or crushed her malodorous panties against his nose, while his hand energetically went about its business. A large jar of recently opened cold cream had suggested first a means of exotic lubrication and then the idea of thrusting his member into the jar a moment before ejaculation. Recovering from that extraordinary sensation, he found a great thrill in smoothing out the surface of the cream to remove the evidence of its having been violated. Later, when he saw his mother come out of the bathroom, as she did each night, with cold cream freshly spread upon her face, he was overcome by a powerful desire to repeat his earlier performance. But the uncle's words stung him and, seeing his wretched face in the mirror, he concluded that the uncle must be right.

Once he had determined that the object of his plan of attack was the conquest of Mariana and no longer the punishment of Gerardo, it took Emilio some weeks to work at his strategy before he could begin to hope for success. What he could not have known was that Mariana, while she still harbored a fantasy of a passionate romance with Federico, with whom she imagined she had had a prolonged union rather than merely the two or three minutes in the entranceway on that Friday night which really had been the extent of any sexual intimacy she had enjoyed with a male, was herself not so rigidly upright that she could be toppled only after a long campaign but that she was already in a precariously leaning position, for her fantasy was but a disguise of urgently felt desires, and she needed only fresh male breath to touch her lips for her eyes to close and for her arms to open. The experiences that were advancing her to womanhood were subtly transforming her character, or perhaps, with maturity, her true character was beginning to assert itself, and she was not what she had seemed to be, a clever, strong-willed girl, but a dull, ordinary person whose perception did not comprehend the reality, accessible to a truly stronger will, outside the very narrow world in which she lived, meekly accepting its sordid circumstances as her fate. Her memory of the past was distorted and short-lived, her imagination changed the less pleasing images of the present to make them acceptable, and in her small world in which routine trivialities constituted an absorbing drama there was not the room for a larger ambition.

Stealing a few inconspicuous coins a day from his mother's purse, Emilio accumulated enough money to be able to tell Mariana one day that he had some important information to convey to her that could only be given where they could not be seen. He suggested going to a movie in the afternoon, adding casually that the money was no problem. She was astounded. What could be so important, so hard to whisper in broad daylight with no one around to overhear? He remained inscrutable. She enjoyed the melodrama, believing herself to be at the center of other people's imaginations. She felt a little thrill in going to her teacher and telling her that she suffered from menstrual cramps, instantly winning the middle-aged woman's sympathy and permission to take the afternoon off.

Soon after *The Albatross of Desire* began, Mariana thought herself the most privileged of the girls at her school: was she not doing what most dreamed of, sitting in a cinema with a boyfriend and watching a romantic movie in Technicolor? She had never thought of Emilio as a boyfriend, but looking at the close-up of the dark-haired hero on the screen, she turned her head very slightly to see Emilio's profile and told herself that he was not *that* ugly. Gradually her idea of Emilio began to take on a new shape; she saw less of his actual physical presence and more of an abstract notion of a man, and the fact that by bringing her to the movie he had already done more than Federico had ever been able to do was decidedly a mark in his favor, speaking eloquently for his real concern for a girl's happiness.

Seeing the hero kiss the heroine for the second time made Emilio nervous; he had resolved that after the second kiss and certainly by the moment when the two lovers reached out with their lips to each other the third time, he was going to hold Mariana's hand; and then, when some intense drama took place on the screen, he was going to raise her hand to his lips. He was in a considerable panic not being able to make the first of the moves he had promised to himself; in his failure to play out the prepared scenario he felt the sweat trickling down from his armpits and was afraid that his breathing was audible.

The heroine, walking up the steps to her apartment in a happy mood after a wonderfully charming dialogue with her lover in his convertible under a starlit sky and a crescent moon, suddenly stopped, and the camera held her horror-stricken close-up for a second before a man in a black suit leaped at her and stopped her incipient scream by throwing his black-gloved hand across her mouth. Mariana gave a little scream and flung a hand across Emilio's chest to hold his arm, putting her head against his shoulder.

"Is he going to kill her?" she whispered to him.

"No, it's okay," he said, turning his face to speak softly into her ear and feeling the pleasant sensation of her hair against his mouth.

"Can I look now without being scared?" she whimpered.

"Yeah, it's okay," he said to her hair.

She turned her head without raising it from his shoulder and continued to see the movie, and after a while he felt emboldened to adjust the position so that he could have his arm behind her shoulder and stroke her smooth flesh just below the short sleeve of her right arm, making a new resolve, to kiss her on the cheek when the hero returned to clasp his girl. He just hoped that the black-gloved villain, who looked like a dangerous criminal, wasn't going to frustrate his plan.

But the heroine having been abducted, the plot became complicated with the story now imposing upon the hero the burden of a quest in which he must suffer a thousand afflictions before the happy ending. When the moment finally came, however, Emilio lost his nerve and found himself staring stupidly at the screen; but just then, with the lovers' faces separating briefly and the camera showing the smiling, moist-eyed heroine, Mariana suddenly turned herself, threw her arms over his shoulders and held her head against his, saying, "Oh, I'm so happy for them!"

The lights went up and before he could take advantage of

her spontaneous gesture everyone was standing up and making for the exits. Mariana's eyes seemed brimmed with tears, and he was thrilled by the fact that when they left the cinema she was holding his hand. "It was such a lovely story," she said, smiling at him, no longer seeing him as the Emilio she had known at school but as a young man who had paid her the wonderful compliment of taking her to see a movie that she now kept repeating was great.

She wanted to talk about it. There were a thousand questions she wanted to know the answers to: how soon would the hero and heroine get married, how many children would they have, would the villain go to jail . . .? Emilio wished he had the money to take her to a café so that they could sit over a Coca-Cola. It was only four o'clock in the afternoon. He often spent a couple of hours after school playing soccer with the boys and therefore his parents would never ask him where he had been. But he had no more money and, annoyed with his poverty, found it difficult to concentrate on Mariana's questions.

"Will you walk me home?" she asked, still holding his hand. "We can talk on the way."

He cheered up at the thought of her not expecting him to take her to a café and began to talk with fresh animation. She became excited by his explanations to her questions and was sorry that they had reached her apartment building. They remained standing outside for some ten minutes during which time each new idea begun to bring the discussion to a conclusion, only led to another thought that needed to be examined. Suddenly Mariana said, "Why are we standing here? Let's go up and have a cup of coffee."

What would her mother say? he wondered aloud. Oh, she would not be back till eight. She worked at a bank after it closed at four, Mariana informed him, again taking his hand and quickly leading him up the stairs. He noticed that the small living room that they entered was much tidier than the one in his own home. The straw mat on the floor had worn thin and was ragged at the edges but it possessed the dignity of an antique and did not at all appear to be an item of furnishing the family was too poor to replace. A slender glass vase shaped like a lily caught his eye from where it stood on a doily in the center of a low circular table, a slight diagonal crack on the greenish glass of the empty vase. Mariana had run into her room and switched on her radio, regretting she did not possess a stereo system, and coming back, hurrying toward the kitchen, was asking him why had the movie not continued until the hero and heroine got married. Could anything still go wrong and upset their plans? He followed her ringing voice, muttering, Naw, a happy ending is a happy ending. But suppose the villain escaped from the police? That wasn't impossible, was it? While she spoke, she noticed that the jar of instant coffee was almost empty; she could not take a teaspoon from it without her mother noticing, for, having so little money, her mother carried a precise inventory of their shortages in her mind. She turned round just as Emilio was entering the kitchen and, striding toward him, grasped his hand and led him back into the sitting room and toward her own room, saying, "I just remembered! There's something very funny I want to show you."

The bed in the corner was neatly made up; a small stack of freshly laundered clothes was piled on a chair.

"Everything's so tidy here," he remarked.

"Oh, that's my mother," she explained, "she's got a mania for keeping things clean. She never was like this before. Oh, here it is," she added, bringing out a little book.

She had written in capital letters on the cover: ETERNAL FRIENDS. Copied out in a neat hand on the first page was a quotation:

> If you are my friend fast and true
> Share with me your private mind.
> Tell me your most secret wish, and you
> An eternal friend in me will find.

In the following pages, she had persuaded her schoolfriends to inscribe their secret wishes, each one signing herself as "eternally yours".

She flipped through the pages, amusing Emilio with some of the extravagant statements contained on them. A few were long, written in a pious tone, beginning irrelevantly with a solemn declaration that the person they loved the best was their mother; some, like Clara Tijerina's, were starkly to the point: "A millionaire husband, a mansion, a Mercedes Benz, and a private plane to fly to Disney World. Eternally yours."

But turning a page, Mariana threw her hand across it and said, "Oh, no! You can't see this one." Had she quietly moved to the following page Emilio would have said nothing but, hearing her remonstrance spoken in a voice that was touched by a fake alarm and ribald laughter, he insisted on reading the page.

"Oh, but you *can't!*" she repeated, keeping her hand firmly across the page.

"Come on, Mariana, let me see it!"

She refused, laughing. He persisted, his hand on hers, their heads close together.

"All right," she finally said, "but on condition you don't see the name of the person who wrote it." He accepted the compromise, and read while she held her hand over the name: "Every night my cunt aches and I dream of a cock two meters long O God I wish to be fucked and fucked don't you eternally yours!!!***!!!"

Emilio was both amazed and embarrassed, and he covered up the moment's awkward feeling by bellowing out in laughter. Mariana put the book away, inwardly pleased with herself for having been so daring with a boy but saying aloud rather smugly, "Don't get the wrong idea. Most girls are not like that. We want to remain virgins."

While his conversation with his male companions was often graphically bawdy, Emilio was stunned into a bewildered silence on seeing Mariana show him the coarse words, almost as if she had spoken them herself. After spending weeks plotting by slow encroachments to win her attention, he was confused to find that she appeared to be leading him on, and his misery was that he did not know how to take advantage of the situation. He wanted to say something, make some gesture, in order to make an impression on her, like the hero in the movie had done when he pressed a button and the top of the car folded itself away automatically and he, pointing to the moon, said how it shone brightly on people in love. But Emilio could think of nothing and could only say, "I got to be going."

She had forgotten to ask him what was the important information that he had said could be conveyed only in the darkness of a cinema; and he forgot that what he had gone up to the apartment for was a cup of coffee.

On the following day he began to steal coins from his mother's purse again. He even offered to run errands that involved going to a shop so that he could pocket the odd coin from the change. Nightly he counted the accumulated money and calculated how many days it would take before he could invite Mariana again to the cinema. But three days after he had been with her she came to him and said, "I have to make you an apology. The other day I said come up for a cup of coffee and I never got round to making it. I completely forgot! I feel terrible about it. You want to come today for it?" That morning she had noticed that her mother had finally purchased a new jar of coffee.

The school's politics turned to other concerns. New alliances formed among the boys and girls, who found new subjects for scandals. Federico was forgotten and consequently Mariana's position became inconspicuous.

Emilio was able to take her to the movies again a week after she had him over for coffee, but in the meanwhile she had inveigled him to accompany her home regularly. She had hit on the idea that they could do their homework together, putting on a scene when he came the first time for coffee that she had no head at all for geometry and wished someone could help her solve the problems. He obliged and heard her call him Mr Big Brain or Mr Born Genius.

Emilio, who talked among his male companions as if he had sampled every whore in each of the city's brothels, was earnestly literal in Mariana's company. If she, leaning against him as they pored over Euclid, read aloud the problem that baffled her, he gave all his attention to arriving at a solution and made a deliberate attempt to stifle from his senses the potent feminine odor the memory of which, when he was alone in the bathroom of his own home, made him dextrously practise again his old vice. But when they went to her apartment after the second movie—the event coincided with the jar of coffee being again low—she resorted to the device she had used with Federico, without remembering the former occasion and indeed without consciously thinking that she was engaged in anything but the welfare of the young man, of seeing something curious in his ear that needed to be examined closely. "What is that?" she suddenly said, fixing her eyes on his ear and bringing her face near his shoulder; he feared that she had discovered some new deformity on his face, but her nose was nearly touching his jaw and just then she put up one hand to his opposite shoulder and flicked the index finger of her other hand across his ear, saying, "Only a mosquito," and adding, while simultaneously tugging toward herself the hand that firmly held his shoulder, "I hope it didn't bite," so that his lips fell against her forehead and his hands instinctively clasped her back, and she, bringing her free hand to hold his other shoulder, said softly, "What are you doing, this isn't the movie, you know," raising, as she spoke, her head with a quick jerk in such a way that the final word was spoken against his lips.

The young man, thus initiated into the preliminaries of carnality, finally lost his inhibitions and began to accompany her regularly to her apartment after school. Her eyes closed in Emilio's embrace, the lover in her imagination was the hero of the first movie they had seen together; and even when she saw Emilio's ugly face and felt his sweat-soaked slippery body as he lay on her in the moment of exhaustion, she could not abandon the fantasy of a beautiful and mysterious romance; seeing him rise out of the bed, his narrow skinny chest and thin legs making him appear ridiculously like a pygmy as he hopped into his pants, she witnessed instead the lover her girlfriends at school talked about incessantly as the man of their dreams. They could only talk; *she* had the unique happiness of daily possessing him.

Six weeks after they had begun to tackle Euclid together and still some three months from her seventeenth birthday, Mariana found herself pregnant. Emilio's discovery of her condition coincided with the beginning of the long holiday when he normally went to his uncle's farm in the country. He decided this time to persuade his uncle to take him on as a permanent worker, a plan his parents did not object to since they knew that if he received a certificate of matriculation after one more year at school it would only be a worthless piece of paper. There were no jobs to be had, except menial ones. His going to the farm would save them the expense of feeding and clothing him for another year.

Mariana, too, did not return to school after the holidays. She found a part-time job as a sweeper in a supermarket, a move that greatly impressed her mother as proving that she was at last learning to be responsible and acquiring a real understanding of money. When Mariana realized that she could no longer conceal her condition from her mother, she announced it to her, anticipating the alarm that an independent discovery might cause her, and was shocked by the mother's response. Mariana had expected a scene charged with violence and repeated demands to know the identity of the father, with her repeated refusals to divulge the secret leading to blows and being locked up in her room until hunger and her mother's persistent verbal abuse forced her to confess; and she had imagined being dragged through the streets, her hair a mess, her face stained with tears, dressed in soiled clothes, pulled along by the wrist until her mother brought her to Emilio's parents' apartment where she demanded they surrender their son to marry the girl he had got pregnant. Emilio was the last man Mariana wished to marry: the shock of her pregnancy had made her perceive something of the reality in which she lived. Emilio was far from being the hero of her imagination. He was ugly, ugly. She would be humiliated if anyone found out that he had been her lover, that he had been the first man to whom she had willingly, and with great ardor, given her virginity.

But her mother's behavior surprised her. Instead of demanding the identity of the father, she said, "Mister Millionaire has gone to live in a palace, it's all that money he came into." At first, Mariana thought that her mother had not heard her correctly and was about to repeat her confession when her mother said, "All that money, what's a baby to him? What's a wife to him, a daughter to him, in his palace with his young mistress?" Confused, Mariana believed her mother to be talking of Emilio and looked aghast at her as she continued, "He was a crafty one, moping around with his clumsy body, secretive as the devil, waiting for his chance. One lottery ticket, and poopsy-poo! Goodbye to the office, goodbye to the family. God, all that money!"

Mariana turned away from her, realizing with the reference to the office that her mother had been talking of the missing father and beginning to understand that she was losing, or perhaps had already lost, her mind. In the following months the mother never once alluded to Mariana's pregnancy, and even when the daughter was born her response did not convey any emotion, whether of happiness or outrage, connected with the event.

To Mariana the potential for a rich and beautiful life still seemed accessible, for its images were ever present in the world around her and it seemed that a slight manipulation of a trick was all that was necessary and she could be afloat in luxury. She returned to work longer hours at the supermarket only a month after the baby was born, moving languidly from aisle to aisle, sweeping the floor but imagining to herself that she had just left her car outside and had come in to buy three kilos of prime beef and some bottles of foreign wine for a dinner party which would see her seated at the head of the table in her pale blue silk gown, with a diamond necklace across her bosom. But she dared not go too close to the rows of bottles in case the end of her broom accidentally knocked one off the shelf; even a bottle of domestic wine would cost her a fortnight's wages, but a foreign one . . . she shuddered at the thought of working for six or seven months in order to pay for the damage. Once, Iván, the store manager who spent most of his day in a glass cubicle at the end of the checkout counters, had caught her daydreaming in front of a shelf containing cans and jars of exotic foods, wondering what exquisite tastes lay sealed there that some of them, like a little glass jar hardly larger than a thimble, cost more than a bottle of imported whiskey, and had said sharply to her, "Get on with your work!" His large round head with close-cropped black hair and black-rimmed spectacles, which kept slipping down his nose so that his eyes, appearing to be blank, became larger and penetrating each time he pushed the glasses up, terrified her. She quickly resumed sweeping and saw him walk away, his khaki trousers wrinkled about the seat and his large belly, falling over the belt, shaking like a mass of jelly. But he had let her work longer hours when she had come back after having her baby and could not afford to be seen slacking.

She took her breaks in the room at the back of the produce section where, among crates and jute sacks and piles of returned bottles, the workers had a small area in a corner where they could make coffee, with a lavatory nearby in which the toilet seat was missing and the washbasin was pocked with rust. Half a dozen of her fellow workers were always to be found by the stove, waiting for the water to boil, exchanging gossip. At first she considered them as coming from an inferior world, for it seemed unthinkable that women twice her age should have no expectation than to spend their days pushing a cart piled high with canned goods and placing the cans on the shelves, but she soon became accustomed to the small talk mainly about the heroine of the latest soap opera on television or about one another's children, and she found herself perfectly at home in their company.

Someone always made an outrageous remark about Iván. He must take five kilos of beef home every night to fill that stomach of his. Why doesn't he ever smile? I'll tell you why. Once he smiled and all the eggs cracked and trickled down the counter and flooded the floor. It was good to laugh over the silly jokes. Esmeralda was so funny when she said his wife has a sign over the bed with "Special Reductions" written on it. What a crazy group. Mariana wished the coffee break could be longer.

Esmeralda was shocked to discover that Mariana did not have a TV set and pitied her for missing the soap opera. "How can you know what we're talking about?" she asked.

"Oh, I get to know the story from what you say," Mariana answered.

"But you don't even know what Joanna *looks* like!" Mariana had seen pictures of the soap opera's heroine in a magazine. "That's not the *same thing*!" Esmeralda exclaimed. She had to come to her house on Sunday, Esmeralda insisted, it was a crime not to see *Joanna's Sacrifice*.

The part of the city where Esmeralda lived was twenty minutes away by bus. Mariana took her baby with her. The bus dropped her off halfway up a hill which was covered with wooden shacks, some of them painted bright pink or dark green. On the roof of almost every shack was a television aerial. Scores of children ran wildly in the street and filled the air with their screams. Men sat in groups outside some of the shacks, playing cards. From one or two doorways a woman or an older girl came out and emptied a container of dirty water. A vacant lot between two shacks was piled high with trash. Like all the others in the street, Esmeralda's door was open and, like them, the loudly turned-up sound of the TV set came from it. A commercial for a sports car was reaching its roaring climax when Mariana entered.

A young man sat on a wooden crate against the wall. Esmeralda lay on the floor with two pillows under her head. The room glowed red and green from the image on the TV screen which Mariana was astonished to see was in color. Esmeralda raised her stout little body and stood up to welcome Mariana to her house. She immediately wanted to hold the baby. "What a cute little darling!" she said to the baby, swinging it in a rocking motion in her arms. "Sit down, sit down," she said to Mariana, stooping to pick up one of the pillows and throwing it at Mariana's feet. "This is Alfonso," she remarked, slightly jerking her head in the direction of the young man. Mariana looked down at him. He briefly raised his head, mumbled the word, "Pleasure," half swallowing it, and continued to stare at the screen. The yellowish-green image just then cast a deathly light on his face, and he looked to be twenty or twenty-five, it was hard to tell. Mariana sat down enchanted by the wonder of color television which she had never before seen except in shop windows. An airline commercial was showing a quick succession of images of the capitals of Europe and of people in the first-class section of a jumbo jet being served a gourmet dinner. The baby began to cry and Esmeralda returned it to Mariana. "I'll go quickly make some coffee," she said. Mariana rocked the baby but it would not stop crying. Alfonso sighed loudly. Mariana undid two of the buttons of her blouse and gave a breast to her baby. She glanced at Alfonso and saw him turn his head away quickly to stare again at the screen. Another commercial was on the air: a beautiful blonde, her pink body glowing in a white gown, a handsome young man, holding before each other's face crystal glasses filled with ice cubes and an amber liquid, between them a table with an ice bucket and an open bottle of imported whiskey.

"What time is it?" Mariana asked, buttoning her blouse, the baby asleep in her lap.

"Another fifteen minutes," Alfonso said without looking at a watch and without taking his eyes off the screen. Later, while she herself had her eyes fixed to the screen, she was aware of his head turning to look at her but was too absorbed in the drama to pay him any attention.

Esmeralda came in with three mugs of coffee on a tray and, glancing at the TV where a sports program had resumed, repeated Alfonso's words, "Another fifteen minutes." She began to describe the plot of *Joanna's Sacrifice*, giving a summary of the episodes that Mariana had missed. Alfonso made a loud sucking sound, drinking his coffee while he watched young men in immaculate slacks playing golf in a tournament in California. Mariana felt her head spin with the details of Joanna's story. There were so many characters, she was completely lost. She was afraid she would never be able to follow the story. On the screen she saw a ball roll across the grass and fall into a hole. A great cry went up from the crowd. A man threw up his arms, a golf club in one hand, while the commentator shouted that the twenty-two-year-old player had now taken his winnings for the year past one quarter million dollars. "But her brother is not her real brother, see?" Esmeralda was saying. "And as for who Joanna will marry . . .!" The question was of the highest importance and the greatest mystery. Mariana could feel her heart thumping as the imagery of a fantastic world of wealth and power, love and treachery filled her mind. "Five minutes now," Esmeralda said, seeing the sports program show highlights of an equestrian event in England. "It is just incredible, just incredible," she went on. "Do you know the script is kept in a bank vault? And all the technicians have to swear an oath of secrecy and take a lie-detector test every week. Just incredible. *No one* knows what is going to happen next!"

Before Mariana knew it, the sports program and the commercial break were over and she was watching the much talked-about drama. She was amazed to find that she was able to follow it without any difficulty straight from the start, but soon she forgot her amazement and her own self altogether. The moment Joanna appeared she knew that *she* was Joanna. She lived in a beautiful mansion with a marble staircase, gilt-framed mirrors, fresh-cut flowers on all the tables, and servants who brought even a glass of water on a gleaming silver tray with a pink rose on it. One unbearable, tense event followed another. Now Joanna was in the arms of a man she did not love, handsome though he was, but must suffer his kisses because of his hold over her father's business, now she was almost falling into the trap set for her by the man she took to be her brother, and now she was running into the ocean, her hair flying behind her, running away from her problems. Mariana identified with her so absolutely that she was suddenly surprised to hear a baby crying and shocked to find that the baby lay in her own lap.

The episode ended leaving the audience with a terrible dilemma. Would Joanna have the baby that she realized toward the end of the episode she had conceived by the man she did not love, handsome though he was? The final scene showed her lift the telephone receiver to her ear, punch a number rapidly with her forefinger, and say a moment later, "Dr Almagro, please. This is urgent."

What was she going to ask the doctor? They would have to wait till the following Sunday to discover the answer. And all that week, during the coffee breaks at the supermarket, they returned to the same question. Was Joanna going to ask Dr Almagro to commit the crime of performing an abortion? Would he counsel her to have the baby which was a gift from God? What was Joanna going to *do*? On Thursday Manuela said she had gone to the church and asked the priest about it. They could forget about Joanna having an abortion. The priest had told her it was definitely out of the question. The actress would be excommunicated, the director and the cameraman as well. Mariana thought Manuela was clever going to ask the priest about it; why hadn't she thought of it?

Mariana went to Esmeralda's house for the eight Sundays that followed and brought the tortured story of *Joanna's Sacrifice* to an end. She had never been so entirely absorbed. The days and the weeks vanished quickly. Life seemed to her to be full of excitement. And Esmeralda had become her fast friend. She made up so many jokes about the other girls at the supermarket, it was incredible.

All the time she was at Esmeralda's, Alfonso sat there as though he were only a shadow cast in the room through the open door. Mariana assumed he was Esmeralda's boyfriend even though he looked ten years younger than Esmeralda's thirty-two and she already had five children, the first of them when she was fifteen. But on the day of the final episode, when both Mariana and Esmeralda ended up with tears in their eyes on seeing Joanna enter the cathedral on her father's arm to marry the man whom she had thought she did not love, handsome though he was, and then realized that she really and truly loved him and no one else, after the booming organ had died away and a commercial for a shampoo had come on, Alfonso suddenly said to Mariana, "I'll see you to the bus stop."

Just then two of Esmeralda's children, two boys of five and seven, came running into the room, asking for money to buy ice cones. "Ice cones?" Esmeralda said sternly to them. "*Ice* cones? So that you can spend the night coughing? You go right out and play and come back in an hour for hot milk."

When the children had gone, Mariana answered Alfonso, "You don't have to bother, really."

He was looking at the TV screen and, turning his eyes to the floor, mumbled, "I got to go to Miraflores."

Esmeralda was surprised and said, "You didn't tell me you had plans."

"It's nothing," he explained to her. "I just promised some guys I'd be with them. Just knocking around, see?"

Esmeralda seemed satisfied with the answer.

When Mariana's bus arrived, he came with her though she knew that he needed to catch another bus if he wanted to go to Rua Miraflores. "I'll change at Braganza," he said, taking the seat next to her. That struck her as logical. She looked out the window as the bus accelerated and braked and honked its way through the crowds of children in the street. She wanted to talk to Alfonso but could think of nothing to say. Her mind was a complete blank. She thought of Joanna. What would happen to her now? There were some things in the drama that puzzled her. But she did not want to ask Alfonso the questions that came to her mind. He'd think her stupid. But nothing else suggested itself to her mind. She was annoyed with herself for remaining silent.

After ten minutes, he surprised her by saying, "Your baby's really pretty." She beamed a smile at him and he added, "But then she gets her looks from her mother, right?"

Mariana did not know how to take that compliment and he surprised her still more by asking, "Do you like to dance? A figure like yours, you must be a born dancer."

"Oh, I don't know about that!" She did not know how to respond to his flattery and did not want to commit herself. She felt a secret thrill but thought she must be careful. Esmeralda had never explained her relationship with him and she had assumed that he was her lover; but then, he was too young for Esmeralda, and if by chance she was mistaken in her assumption then she ought not to scare him off, for he was quite good-looking and just the right age for her. She glanced shyly at him and said, "I mean, I haven't done a whole lot of dancing."

"We could fix that," he said. She wondered whether he was going to invite her to a dance, but he went on to ask, "You got someone to look after the baby?"

"Well, my mother. She's home most of the time."

"That's good," he said, and appeared to be working out something in his mind. Mariana felt certain he was trying to determine when he could invite her, and in that moment thought that she would not really be doing anything wrong to Esmeralda, not stabbing her in the back or anything horrible like that, just going dancing; it wasn't robbing anyone's lover or anything underhand like that, was it? "That's good," he repeated. "You could be dancing like a pro in no time, your figure is a natural for it."

The additional flattery pleased her. Then he surprised her by saying, "There's something I got to take care of first. I'll fix it easily, just give me a couple of days. I'll be seeing you." The bus arrived at Plaza Braganza and he stood up, saying before he walked away, "You got rhythm in your figure. You'll be sensational, you'll see."

He was really very smart. Funny she hadn't noticed how good-looking he was while they'd sat watching the drama the last two months. A real fast operator, she thought him, the kind of quiet guy who won your heart the moment he opened his mouth. Fancy talking to *her* like that, praising her figure and everything! He had sneaked glances at her all those weeks while they watched TV and then suddenly he is as good as telling her he's fallen for her. She imagined that what he needed to take care of first was his situation with Esmeralda. Was it her fault that he preferred her to Esmeralda? It was just like the problem Joanna had had in an earlier episode, having to choose between a girlfriend and a man who promised romance. She remembered what Joanna had said to her friend. "I was born to cause sorrow." The words were really deep, incredible how deep they were, just *her* situation! Long after she had returned home and gone to bed, she kept thinking of the new excitement that had entered her life. Alfonso's words kept returning to her, producing a thrill each time: she was going to be sensational.

Esmeralda looked terribly depressed the next day and said nothing at all during the first coffee break when everyone was excitedly talking about the conclusion of *Joanna's Sacrifice*. Mariana wondered whether Alfonso had already told Esmeralda he was leaving her. She felt bad. It made her miserable to see her friend look so depressed. But what could she do about it, she hadn't led Alfonso on or anything, had she? During the afternoon's coffee break Esmeralda came up to her and said, "I've got to talk to you." They went and sat next to a pile of jute sacks, away from the others. Mariana felt nervous and her heart quickened its pace. Should she be noble and tell her friend that she was not going to accept Alfonso's proposal, that she valued her friendship more than a flirtation with her lover? Or should she say like Joanna, "I was born to cause sorrow," and leave the older woman to her suffering? She saw that Esmeralda was about to speak and turned her eyes away from her to the letters stencilled on a crate of oranges. But immediately she was staring wildly at Esmeralda, drawn to her face by the shock of what she heard.

Alfonso had been stabbed to death in a street at the back of Rua Miraflores late last night.

"Oh no!" Mariana cried. "How could it have happened? Oh my God, *why*?"

Esmeralda explained in short phrases, pausing to wipe the tears that she could not stop shedding. An evil world out there. Men desperate for money. Alfonso was one of a gang. What could he do? No one gave him a job. He was an honest boy at the start. But you can't spend your life shining shoes in Plaza Independencia. You need money. You need things. He had to take them where he could find them. It wasn't his fault. He was a good boy. He was just sucked into the underworld. What else could he do? He was on to a racket with a gang of men. A big machine that ran the vice in Nuevo Soho. They got protection money from gaming houses. Fixed the games. Trapped the tourists who came to gamble. Supplied strip bars with girls. Got the girls to go with men loaded with money. Alfonso was working on a plan. He was going to make a quick packet and start a tobacco shop. Settle down to a clean life. Some girls he had found for the strip bars. They were in his control. He'd worked on them. Collected money from them. The machine found out. The machine is quick with its justice. Just two men in a dark street. One knife. They left him next to a trashcan.

Mariana cried with Esmeralda. During one part of the story her weeping was uncontrolled, and when Esmeralda had concluded, she clasped her shoulders and said, "Oh Esmeralda, I'm so sorry, so very sorry for you!"

Her mother's distraction growing, she lost her job as a cleaning woman at the bank, where she had begun to leave puddles of soapy water in the corners, and Mariana timidly approached Iván to ask him if she could work longer hours, full time instead of just threequarters. He pushed up his black-rimmed spectacles, stared at her, then gazed down the aisle of wine and liquor behind her shoulder and said, "I'll talk to you later." He resumed his scrutiny of numbers on the long rolls from the cash registers, deftly working an adding machine. It gave him enormous pleasure to compute the daily take; although his own monthly wages were a minute fraction of what the supermarket's cash registers rang up in a quarter of an hour, it excited him to see the very large sums, as if they represented his personal wealth in some secret foreign bank account; he enjoyed imagining that he was really the president of the corporation that owned the supermarket and had taken on the humble guise of a store manager just as kings in fairy tales appeared among their people disguised as beggars.

"When?" Mariana asked.

He was irritated to find her still standing there, and said, "I'll decide that."

Two days later, just when it was almost time to close the supermarket, a child knocked down a row of beer bottles. After he had talked to the boy's mother about the damage, Iván sent for Mariana. "You got yourself an hour's overtime," he told her.

All the other workers left ten or fifteen minutes after the store closed and she stayed on to clean up the aisle. He watched her from his glass cubicle while finishing his own work, adding up the very last receipts of the day, over which he always spent an hour after the store had closed and he had seen all the workers off. He kept a sharp eye on the workers making sure everyone went and that no one sneaked out with some stolen item hidden in his clothes. Now he looked up again and again from his numbers to make sure Mariana was doing her job and not getting any ideas. She was finished in twenty minutes. He saw that she was a frightened little girl who only wanted to earn a bit more money; he did not have to worry about her shoplifting. "Go make me a cup of coffee," he told her, "if you want to earn a full hour's overtime." He stared at her for a moment as she walked away and then turned again to the numbers before him.

A thought had nagged him for some months and would not go away. It came back now, somehow triggered by seeing the girl walk away. He needed money to send his daughter to college. She was such a bright kid and it was tragic not to be able to afford a proper education for her. His two boys were growing up fast too. He needed more and more money every day. He had been the manager of the supermarket for eleven years. The company respected him. He followed orders precisely. Once, when the company's policy was not working too well and there was a cash-flow problem, he had suggested a system of rotating special reductions on items of particular local interest. It was a simple man's idea of marketing, but it had worked, generating a surprising increase in the cash flow. He had been emboldened to make similar suggestions from time to time, usually with successful results. Recently, either through forgetfulness or through unconscious daring, he had put all the canned fish on special without consulting the company; the product, which had not moved for months, was sold out in a week. Since then the company allowed him a little discretion and, as long as the cash kept flowing, it did not discourage his occasionally putting a dead product on special reduction. He was too cautious and conservative a manager to cause the company a problem. However, worrying about his own pressing need for money, the thought had suddenly come to him that he could take a product that sold well at the regular price—say, bananas—and tell the company that he had had to put it on special before it rotted, and pocket the difference. The idea was so simple, no one would detect the fraud; on the other hand, he feared the simplicity might make the detection all the easier. His mind was thrilled by the temptation and, reminding him how hard he worked, argued convincingly that he was really owed the extra money; at the same time his mind was terrified that the real name for its preoccupation was embezzlement.

He heard a sound and looked up from the numbers on his desk. It was Mariana, returning with a mug of coffee. He was reminded of air hostesses on TV commercials, walking brightly down the aisle to offer drinks to the passengers. He had never been in a plane. He asked himself why should he not have what everyone else in the world took for granted. Mariana came up to the cubicle and placed the mug in front of him, putting her hand through the circular hole in the glass that surrounded him. Everyone bought dollars on the black market and went on foreign vacations, Miami and Paris, even all the way to China. He saw Mariana's hand place the mug and withdraw, and for a second it froze there in his mind, the fingers and thumb inside the hole in the glass as if they still held the mug, the palm still seeming to possess a softness that her daily labor had not yet spoiled. The hand withdrew and he felt it had plucked something from him. A dormant emotion, a buried longing. People had so much money they thought nothing of setting up a mistress in an apartment. His wife was getting old. After three children she had no patience with his fantasies. If he wanted another child, she would make it, but he could not forget his ideas of fancy positions and a kiss here and a suck there. Make it. The words put him off. They had nothing to do with desire. "Okay," he said to Mariana who still stood outside the cubicle, "you'll get an hour's overtime pay."

"Thank you very much, Señor Iván," she said, smiling brightly.

She had a pretty mouth, well-shaped teeth, and he said, "Okay, you've got the extra work you wanted. An hour's overtime every day."

She thanked him and went off, very pleased with herself and thinking that he was really a kind man. He was generous behind the grumpy, stern façade. One extra hour on double pay. That was better than two more hours in the morning. She thought herself extremely lucky.

He saw her go away cheerfully and her smiling face remained with him. But what had he done? he suddenly asked himself. Committed the company to additional cost. How could he justify that? He was always being reminded to cut labor costs. He would have to tell her she couldn't have the extra hour. The work just wasn't there. He hadn't noticed before how pretty she was. The kind of girl you could never tire of kissing. Lovely her fingertips, lovely her mouth, lovely her flesh. He tried to concentrate on the numbers before him. If only one of the figures, so minuscule in the company's reckoning of its daily national intake, could be his each day, what a wonderful difference it would make to his own life. He forced himself to stop dreaming. He knew he was incapable of carrying out a fraud. As a schoolboy he had never cheated even when he saw that most of the boys at the top of the class got there by cheating while his honesty kept him near the bottom. During adolescence he envied the other boys when they talked of their sex life but when he went out with a girl he repressed himself with thoughts of respecting her honor. When he married, he, and not his wife, was a virgin, though he assumed that she was too. He had been born straight. Fantasies and temptations besieged him and criminal thoughts nagged his mind, but he remained straight.

The next day he could not bring himself to tell Mariana that she could not have the overtime, putting off having to see her disappointment until near closing time. A drunk walked in, staggered toward the liquor aisle, and, before anyone had seen him, had crashed against a shelf of whiskey bottles, sending a dozen of them smashing to the floor and himself falling among them and passing out. His hands and face were cut and some blood floated in the pool of stinking whiskey. The police and an ambulance had to be called. It took till closing time for things to return to normal. Though Mariana and two other women had taken away the broken bottles and mopped up the floor, it still smelled strongly of whiskey. It needed to be washed with a strong detergent, otherwise he would have no end of complaints from the next day's customers. And so, when closing the store, he told Mariana to wash the floor.

On the following day he again procrastinated telling her that there was no regular overtime work for her to do. When it came to closing time, he sent for her with the intention of giving her the bad news. She came at once and he found himself saying to her, "The returned bottles need counting. There's some mistake in the receipts. I need the bottles counted correctly." She went off to the room at the back of the produce section where the crates of returned bottles were kept. It was boring work alone in that ill-lit space but the thought of the extra money kept her cheerful.

Iván was astonished at what he had done. All he had meant to say to the girl was that he had no overtime work for her; instead he had invented a bogus job for her to do. When she had gone away and he had begun to work on the cash receipts, he was amazed to see what his fingers were doing on the adding machine. *Altering* some of the figures! He tore the paper out and began again. Before he could resume feeding the numbers into the machine, he paused and held his head in his hands. What had come over him to fall so unknowingly into deception? He must get a hold on himself. He was not a criminal. Never would be. He would die a poor old man who had never done anything wrong in his life. The bitter thought also came to him that his life would be over without one singularly happy memory to cheer him in his old age. He would never escape from this dreadful treadmill of endless servitude. He would receive no honors for having remained a lawabiding slave. He shook his head. What was he thinking of? There was work to do. But the bitterness that had entered his heart was pumped out to the rest of his body, affecting his mind. He needed a cup of coffee to calm himself and see things clearly again. Stop these foolish thoughts.

He heard the bottles clinking as he approached the room at the back. He must tell her to stop the useless work. Give her a conto and tell her to go home. He wasn't going to make any more mistakes. Her hands were among the bottles, slapping the top of each as she counted. She wrote down a number on a piece of paper and proceeded to count some more. Hearing his footsteps, she looked round. "Is there anything you want?" she asked. Her clear voice, resonant with young feminity, sent a searing current through his chest. He stopped some six paces from her and stared at her. "Do you need me for anything?" Her voice seemed to crash into him, breaking the wall behind which he had cast all his foolish and idle fantasies and dreams. Now they came flooding out, demanding gratification. But he merely stood and stared at her pathetically.

The look reminded her of Emilio after she had provoked him to kiss her and he, overwhelmed by the experience, stared at her with his eyes shot with lust but unable to make a move, and she had put her hand to his fly, saying, "I know what boys do when they're alone and think of girls." He had let his head fall on her shoulder and moaned when he felt the clasp and pull of her hand and heard her say, "Is this how you do it?" Iván had the same desperate look. But she dismissed the thought. Iván was an older man, married with children. He could not want what Emilio had wanted, it was stupid of her to have such a thought.

Iván forced himself out of the clutch of the demonic power that possessed him. He jerked his head violently, looked away from Mariana, and said, "I want a cup of coffee, a cup of coffee, that's all." She walked to the stove, saying, "I'll bring it to you in a minute."

He returned to his cubicle, hearing his own breath come loudly. Quit being ridiculous, he told himself. He knew that when he had stood there after hearing her voice that seemed to inflame his skin with its breath he had wanted nothing more than to rush at her and to crush her in his embrace. "Just quit it!" he said aloud, angry with himself that there was a part of him over which he had no control. But what was his life going to be? Dull conformity. Nothing but doing the right thing. With no memory of one exhilarating moment. The regret of never having dared. An old age with nothing, not even money.

She brought him the mug of coffee and again saw that look in his face. She assumed it signified some complicated thought to do with running the store, some business anxiety that she could never know. But back home that evening she kept seeing his face and wondered whether a man who was nearly fifty was any different from a boy of sixteen when it came to wanting a woman. She was surprised that the idea of such an old man, who was also fat and wore glasses, and whose appearance was far from attractive, did not repel her in any way; for all these disadvantages were cancelled out by the other idea, that he was her boss. Although she told herself to stop having stupid thoughts, the possibility intrigued her.

At closing time the next day she went to him and asked, "Do you want me to count the bottles again today?" He had begun the day with the firm resolution to remain on the straight and narrow path that had been his life. There was his daughter to think of; the future of his boys depended on him: he owed them all the sacrifice of the rest of his years. But hearing Mariana's voice and seeing her lovely face, his resolution collapsed and before he could think what he should say to her, he had already said, "Yes." She smiled and asked, "Will you be wanting a cup of coffee, too?" He nodded his head, not being able to speak just then, for a commotion of desires had his ordinary, responsible self bound and gagged, her clear, young voice again breaking the wall of his self-control that he had labored to repair.

She had not yet begun to count the bottles when she heard him enter. He had hurried after her. His breath was loud. She saw him staring at her. Helpless and lost. "You want your coffee already?" she asked, and could not help the little laugh that accompanied her voice. He was struggling with himself, fighting for self-control, shouting within himself to go back, but he could not take a step, could not even control his loud breathing. "Why, you look like you need something stronger than coffee," she said, walking to him, looking concerned. The expression of her anxiety intensified his inner turmoil. He went to raise his arms and to take a step toward her, but the combination of the raging feelings and the voice within him that still begged him to be prudent had the effect of making him want to move simultaneously in her direction and away from her. Instead, he collapsed to the ground. Fearing he had had a heart attack, she ran to him and, bending down, unbuttoned his shirt and began to massage his chest. "Are you all right, is it your heart?" she asked gently. A soft moaning came from his mouth, his face shone with sweat. He raised his head a little, lifting his left arm to her hair, searching for her neck. She eased herself forward a little and sat down at a slight angle to his body, her right shoulder leaning toward his face. She felt his hand caressing her head, slowly drawing it closer toward himself. "What are you doing?" she said in a whisper. He lowered his hand to her back and pulled her, so that her bosom fell against his face, his mouth against the coarse cotton of her blouse and the thick bra behind it. "Señor Iván, you're hurting me," she whispered, but he seemed not to hear in his agitation. For a minute she remained caught with her bosom against his face, and then strained herself to get a little away from him to ease the discomfort she had begun to feel. He was moving in a convulsive sort of way. She turned her head and looked down his body. He had unzipped his fly. She gave a little laugh seeing that he was doing it himself, working his hand rapidly. She was about to move her hand to replace his, but stopped. It was amusing to see a man humiliate himself. And she grasped something else. He would now go in terror of her scorn.

For a week she said to him at closing time, "I guess you want me to count the bottles again." Nearly the same scene occurred each day, though without the dramatic collapse of the first occasion, concluding always with her amusedly watching his action of self-abuse. He gave her more money than the overtime was worth and one day presented her with a gold chain. In his mind he was building up an elaborate fantasy that he kept a young mistress whom, on the next Sunday, he would take to a hotel which rented rooms by the hour, and he enjoyed rehearsing the most tender scenes in his imagination. When the weekend came, he postponed the idea of the hotel, saying to himself that he needed more money. He had to have an expensive present for her in anticipation of receiving the gift of her body. She mustn't think he was using her as his whore. He wanted her to feel special. Admire his generosity. Be proud to be his mistress. And love him for his nobility.

But that Sunday never came, and what was supposed to follow—a double life, one of the ordinary hard-working head of a decent family, the other a dream of luxury come true, its hours spent in exquisite debauchery, its wonderful enclosed world full of splendor and charm, and endlessly rich—never transpired. His attempt at embezzlement was so crude that he was detected within a few days. The ordinariness of his life had given him no experience of cunning; his character was too simple to engage successfully in the devious; and his mind was incapable of anything clever. He was sentenced to five years in prison.

From these early experiences of her adult life in which she associated herself with people without education and without hope of economic advancement, Mariana grew accustomed to her own low condition. She merely lived from one day to the next, preoccupied with her daughter, enjoying the gossip at work. Her brain was too dull to think that hers was the life of a very ordinary person or to arouse in her feelings of bitterness and resentment that the romantic expectations of her youth had so quickly been dashed, and consequently she did not see the reality of her daily struggle as an unusual hardship. It was enough for her for someone to remark how beautiful her daughter was, accompanying the comment with "just like her mother," and she was happy, or for some middle-aged man to become her lover, and her fantasy of a romance was amply gratified. All her lovers were ugly, brutish men who offered her little tenderness and made of the sexual act another occasion to commit violence, demanding from her a shocking perversity or a ferociously bestial coupling. With time Mariana assumed that this was normal behavior, and when a girlfriend said in some general context concerning the relations between the sexes, "Ah, men, they are such beasts!" Mariana took her to be referring to their actions in bed, thus having her own idea of men reinforced by the independent observation. She gave birth to her second daughter when she was twenty-three, and was once again abandoned by the father of the child. She was scarcely outraged or even disappointed. To her, that was life.

There was a short period soon after she had turned twenty-five when the vaguely conceived thought that something was not right with her life worried her. She could not put the idea together in a precise language, for it came to her mind in confused glimpses and imperfect images. There was the shadowy image of *a husband* who, not existing in reality, took on a ghostly presence; he was closer to her own age and was the father of her daughters; he worked in an office, brought home a good paycheck, and was the gentlest of souls. Surrounding him were other ill-formed images of a happy family life, and she felt that the way she lived with her two daughters and her mother in the small apartment was not the way things should have turned out. There was something wrong there. But when she observed the way Esmeralda and the other women whom she knew lived, she saw that the storybook ideal of the family, with a caring and a loving male at the head of it, did not exist. When she compared their condition with her own, it seemed to her that she enjoyed a superior standard, a conclusion that convinced her that she was only imagining that there was something wrong with her life. Nothing was wrong really. Imagine being Serafina who had been forced into vice for eleven years by a man who took all the money she made and then abandoned her when her body lost its attraction, leaving her, at thirty-two, a prematurely aged woman fit for no job but cleaning floors. And Esmeralda had gone through worse when she had been young and so beautiful people used to tell her only a duke from Spain would be worthy of marrying her; a man had tricked her, swept her off her feet (according to Esmeralda), drove her round town, gave her presents, all in one crazy week at the end of which he had her trapped in a house off Rua Miraflores. Mariana had been horrified to hear Esmeralda say, "You think all men want to do with a whore is to screw her? You're wrong there! Some men get a bigger thrill from seeing cruelty and will pay more to see it. You can't know what it's like to lie naked in bed with a piece of raw, bloody meat on your stomach, pretending to be asleep and knowing a huge dog is going to jump on you for the meat. That's when the men who've paid to watch begin to howl like a pack of dogs themselves. God, the secret desires of men!" She would have been forced to remain for more than the seven years she spent there had the police not raided the house for drugs. After six months in jail, she was at last free; and though some of the men she had taken as lovers made their money from criminal connections, she never again let go of her own independence. Mariana admired her but, seeing her in her little shack and knowing her story, invariably felt pleased with the circumstances of her own life which had been so fortunate.

She saw a young couple in the supermarket one day and thought that the woman looked familiar. They had loaded the cart with groceries, bottles of wine and a large prime rib of beef, and were pushing it toward a checkout counter. The young man, wearing a beige lightweight suit and a pink tie, had a hand on the woman's shoulder while he talked amiably to her, his other hand on the cart, with a gold watch conspicuous at the wrist; the woman, who had both her hands on the cart next to his, displayed diamond and emerald rings on her fingers, and looked extremely elegant in her pale blue dress while she listened to the man with a bemused smile upon her lips. Of course, it was Clara Tijerina! Mariana suddenly recognized her friend from school. The eight years that had passed had scarcely changed her; she was perhaps a little fuller at the bosom, slightly wider at the hips, but the only thing really different about her was that from being a simple girl from a modest family she had been transformed into a lady.

Mariana instinctively began to walk toward Clara in order to say hello to her. But walking past the glass cubicle in which the store manager sat, she caught a reflection of herself and stopped. She was wearing a gray plastic coverall, an old piece of dark green cloth was tied over her hair as a scarf, she carried a broom in her hand. For a very brief moment the image of herself as a teenager passed through her mind, and although she could not see for herself how much she had

altered and begun to be a dumpy little woman who had
already lost her youthful beauty, she was not so blind as to
see no change at all. Her conscious thought that she did not
want to be seen by Clara the way she was dressed suppressed
the unconscious realization that had tried to assert itself in
that brief moment, that she would not be recognized, or, if
Clara did remember her, she might not wish to acknowledge
her friendship with a poor shopgirl in front of her smart
husband. It would be better to approach her if she came alone
to the supermarket.

But somehow her day was spoiled. When it was too late,
she wished she had not drawn back but had gone and greeted
Clara. When had she got married? Did she have children?
Where did she live? She would have loved to have found out
all about her. And then gradually—but again in not too
precise and coherent a way—envy began to provoke images
in her mind. Had she been able to follow her thoughts clearly,
she would have known that what she was really thinking
about was the contrast between her own life and Clara's and
experiencing the resentment of not having had the same luck;
that seeing Clara had stirred deep within her mind a despair
that she had been cheated of a real happiness. Instead she
made herself miserable with fantasies, seeing herself sitting at
a dresser and removing from her fingers the rings she had seen
on Clara's, imagining the handsome young man to be her
own husband. But when the fantasies had exhausted themselves, they buried with them the resentment and the despair;
and in this manner her mind acquired an enormous reservoir
of bitterness without her brain ever being aware of it. From
time to time she fell ill and remained comatose in bed, but
she never understood that the illness was not a physical
ailment but a profound depression—as if her body refused to
participate in the petty routines that constituted her life. She
became moody, spoke less and less, slowly growing fat and
ugly without noticing the years as they passed, taking away
her hopes for a happiness like Clara's, until, at the age
of thirty-four, she was unrecognizable from the lively and
beautiful Mariana last seen by Federico.

*

Nuevo Soho had changed. New high-rise buildings on Rua Miraflores had replaced the studios, making the street a commercial center. Where artists had once dawdled, bankers and executives busied themselves with currency deals, international loans and the export trade, sitting all day in the great towers of concrete and glass doing business worth hundreds of millions of U.S. dollars. In the side street where Popayan's shop had been, an entire block had been razed to the ground to make way for an enormous hotel that offered the facilities of a convention center to international business; holding on to his property the longest, Popayan had extracted a high price for it and thus acquired for himself an undreamed of wealth at the age of seventy-nine, and had removed himself to a one-room apartment where he spent his days poring over certificates of deposit and accounts of his investment in stocks and bonds, working out with a pencil on a piece of paper how much more he was worth and suppressing for ever the troubling images of the past that he had known to contain the catastrophe of the future. Only once had he been startled by forms that suddenly possessed his imagination, a representation that he recognized of the self's combat with its shadow, but he had quickly snatched up a newspaper and turned to the page full of numbers giving the closing stock prices. After that he was never without a sum before his eyes.

When the hotel was built, Mariana found a job there as a cleaning woman, being attracted to it by the higher pay. One of her friends in the staff canteen had been Patricia who was a few years younger than herself and who, even when wearing a maid's uniform, managed to highlight her attractive figure and always made up her pretty face to cause a quiet sensation in the minds of men who passed her in the corridors. About two months after Mariana had begun working at the hotel, Patricia stunned her with the news that a businessman from São Paulo had proposed to her. Patricia had often talked about her dream of a millionaire falling for her and had developed the trick of pretending a room was empty when she knew that a man was alone in it and opening it with a master key, and then acting surprised and confused and offering her apologies for disturbing the guest, and adding

almost coquettishly that if there was anything she could do
. . ., thus giving the man an opening he might wish to exploit.
Mariana had been scandalized, and Patricia had said, "A man
won't notice you unless you appear as a temptation." She had
been noticed twice, receiving on the second occasion a gold
necklace that the man had purchased to take home to his wife
but offered to her instead in a reckless moment. Mariana was
shocked, but not so much as when Patricia came bursting
with the news of the marriage offer. "It's a miracle!" she
cried. "I'm going to have a husband! He's worth millions,
millions!" Mariana was thrilled for her, but on later reflection
wished she herself had been the lucky one.

Her luck instead, some months after Patricia had gone
away to her happiness and had been forgotten, was to meet
Pascual who had just lost his job as a porter at the hotel.
Unshaven, supporting a huge belly, and too often drunk, he
disgusted her, but his helplessness drew her to him, and in
the unthinking manner in which she existed, before she knew
it, he had come to live with her and had made her pregnant.
Her third daughter was now two years old. She despised
Pascual. He would return to his wife for months at a time,
reform himself, and then take to drink again, lose his job, and
come back to Mariana. She wanted to have nothing to do
with him, and still, from time to time, when her already dull
brain was not too deadened by the drudgery of her work,
harbored the fantasy that her real life was yet to come, when
she would be the wife of a rich young man. She did not
perceive the wrinkles that had begun to mark her face and
was unaware of her obese condition. It was impossible for
her to realize that the reason why she felt pleased when
Pascual broke again with his wife and returned to her was
that deep within her mind she knew that he was the only man
who would, after his brutish fashion, make love to her.

She came out of a room she had finished cleaning and
slowly pushed the cart with the sheets and towels, and the
vacuum cleaner, down the corridor toward the next lot of
rooms to be cleaned. A young man in a dark blue suit and
shining black shoes with chrome buckles went past. He carried
a black leather briefcase with polished brass fasteners. He
was dark-haired with a handsome, clean-shaven face, and had

the manner about him of a man of the world. Mariana continued on her way. The man hardly noticed her though his eyes had caught hers for a second. What he saw was the familiar figure he had seen in hotels all over the world, an uneducated woman from the country's slums doing a job she was lucky to get.

He unlocked the door of a room and went in. Throwing the briefcase on the bed, he picked up the telephone directory and quickly turned its pages. He phoned the airport. Had they found his luggage yet? This was impossible! Yes, the Eastern flight from Miami. They would call him back. He repeated his name: Federico Chagra.

Federico's life was so routinely consumed by banal ironies which made surprising coincidences commonplace events that to him any reflection on destiny would have been boringly redundant; it would scarcely have amused him to be reminded that the hotel he was in stood on the very ground where eighteen years earlier he had walked out of an old man's shop not knowing whether he had been made a fool of or given an extraordinary gift. And yet, such remained his superstitious dread of the future, he still wore the little brass book on a chain round his neck, the amulet Popayan had given him that Federico had often considered worthless but never had had the courage to remove.

On the day when Ernesto Vivado had driven him away from Daniela's house and had sung aloud the words, "Excitement, women, wealth!" in answer to his question where they were going, Federico had been thrilled and at the same time frightened. Ever since he had come out of Popayan's shop, the amulet clasped round his neck and the cheap parody of a magician's cloak on his back, he had run into a succession of accidents, each one apparently a mistake on someone's part and seeming at first to condemn him to a frustration of his desires, but then unexpectedly giving him what he longed for. When Vivado echoed his wish, he began to be convinced that none of the recent occurrences had been accidents; for it was impossible, he thought, that each of his wishes should be followed by an unbelievable complex of coincidences that fulfilled the wish. Had Popayan given him a magical power? Did the magic reside in the amulet or in the cloak or had it been transmitted by the old man's touch, his eyes, his breath, conveying some terrible secret to his soul? Federico could be certain of nothing. Sitting in the car, filled by the exhilaration induced by the changing scenery as Vivado drove fast up the curving mountain road, entering the unknown that existed only as the expression of his wish and as yet was mysterious, he fingered the amulet as if he expected to experience an electric charge or some sharp sensation that was a sign that the tiny brass rectangle gave him the power to create his own future. But the metal was cold and provoked no unusual feeling in his fingertips. However, he was not disappointed to receive no sign, knowing that if a thing possessed a mystery it did so only so long as the mystery remained its secret; and all he could do was to believe in its existence: that would be *his* secret. He resolved to remain prudent and not to make wishes extravagantly or indiscriminately for fear that thought-less excess might lead to his losing the power; and he feared, too, that there might be some horrible price to pay at the end, a pain to suffer for each granted wish. There were stories he had read, fairy tales, in which the possessor of a magical power was also given a knowledge of the curse that must overtake him when the magic had been exhausted. Vivado's boisterous accompanying of the opera on the cassette player while he drove at a dizzying speed up the mountain road distracted Federico from thoughts that were both exciting and gloomy, and the idea that was beginning to form itself in his mind, that perhaps he had not been given a power to have his wishes come true so much as been cursed by an evil that must finally damn him, was drummed out of his mind by the full orchestra and chorus loudly filling the car with the climactic tragic episode of the opera.

The road rose higher as if it formed diagonal lines up an enormous triangle. The mountainside was covered with flowering vegetation and thin streams that fell like white vertical lines. The air was moist and cool. They ran into a silvery fog and Federico asked, "Shouldn't we slow down? I can't see a thing." Vivado pressed on, saying, "I have built-in radar." In a few minutes, like a plane cutting through cloud, the car had risen above the fog and they seemed to be floating over a vast sunlit plateau with a sky above them of a clearer, darker blue than earlier. Pampas grass with its long feathery white stems and arcing fronds grew along the roadside; lush meadows undulated to the distance; here and there a small lake sparkled in the brightness. On the horizon straight ahead of them four mountain peaks thrust their white jagged tops into the blue.

"See where we're going?" Vivado said, glancing at Federico. "Those mountains seem very close, don't they? You could drive the whole day and not reach them. Perhaps it's only because the road keeps turning away, but the mountains have a way of receding. The world here surprises you with illusions, it's very curious."

"But what *is* there?" Federico wanted to know.

"Everything you could wish for," Vivado answered. "There are valleys that you can't see from here, with little settlements, some of them probably still not touched by Spanish influence. There was a madman named Sandoval in Pizarro's army who coming to this region had the vision of himself being crowned king. A fairly normal form of hallucination among men who had abandoned their own world and been driven into the unmapped regions of the dark underside of the earth by a lust for gold."

Vivado shifted down to second gear and for a few moments concentrated on negotiating a sharp bend. "Nothing remains of that madman now," he continued when the road had straightened, "except his name after which the place where he settled is known. His delusion seems to have been nothing more than a wish to put an end to his wanderings. Who knows why people go crazy?"

The road swept down into a pine forest and the view of the mountains was lost.

"Sandoval is now my kingdom," Vivado said, and laughed. "What I learned early in the movie business is that people crave for an alternative world to the one in which they live. They'll go any distance to see if it isn't to be found somewhere."

A series of bends had his full attention and while coming out of one and entering another he said, almost as an afterthought to what he had spoken earlier, "Even beyond death, I suppose."

They entered a long straight drive of smooth red dirt bordered by cypresses, with a lake some fifty meters to its left. The reflection of the dense pine forest which covered the slopes across the lake made the water appear black. To the right there were paths in the woods, and Federico caught a glimpse of half a dozen people on horseback.

"Americans or English," Vivado said, seeing them too. "They always go for horses. Whereas Scandinavians go for the sun—you'll come across them lying naked in little clearings in the woods, grinning stupidly in the brightness."

They arrived in front of a large stone house, and at last Federico asked, "Why have you brought me here?"

Vivado looked surprised and said, "Don't you want a job?"

"A job? I didn't ask for one."

"Daniela said you wanted a job."

Federico understood that that had been Daniela's tactful, or perhaps only convenient, way of getting rid of him. He found his surroundings enchanting and decided that he might as well go along with Daniela's fiction. Keeping to himself the observation that there had been a mistake, he thanked Vivado for the opportunity. It occurred to him that if the unexpected happened, it did so only to advance the process by which his wish was to be granted. The words *excitement, women, wealth* were still ringing in his mind.

Vivado, who himself rarely spent more than a few days at Sandoval, being at that time engaged in enlarging his empire, and sometimes did not reappear for half a year, put Federico in the hands of the general manager of the resort, a man named Pedro Candia who first employed him in his office in the disappointing, and somewhat demeaning, position of an errand boy, his most strenuous task being to fetch his boss a cup of coffee several times a day.

There was interest in learning to drive a car—an old Fiat in which Candia could send him to take instructions to the workers on distant parts of the resort; and there was some diversion in learning foreign phrases, especially English, from the visitors; but Federico could hardly count these as representing the excitement he had wished for. He was not disappointed, however, that the new circumstances of his life were monotonous and boring, for he knew by now that the time of ordinary reality was not the time of the world of magic, that, indeed, there was a distinct idea of time for every different activity—as he could see in the image of the sportsmen on the lake, sitting still in their boats with a fishing rod in their hands, who hardly ever looked at their watches, while Candia stopped his endless typing every so often and held up his wristwatch before his eyes. Federico had learned from his experience with Daniela that the few days he had waited for her to come to him were a much longer time than the months he had spent alone in her house when she went away to the States. Its very concept perhaps only a persuasion of the mind, time was created anew in each consciousness, the conception changing with the experience, being a response to varying degrees of pleasure or pain, and when this felt presence of the nonexistent became too unbearable an oppression, one turned to magic—a dream, a drug—for deliverance.

In order to assist the magic that Federico presumed was secretly and mysteriously in his possession, he would dress up in his leisure hours, wearing a brightly colored T-shirt and a pair of slacks or sometimes one of the suits Daniela had bought him, and walk on the paths to the cottages at the hour when the resort guests would be coming to the main house to sit with drinks on the patio. Perhaps he would thus encounter a beautiful woman—and his fantasy saw her in a variety of guises: a perfect Scandinavian blonde, a black-haired Italian type from Argentina, an American heiress from Florida; sometimes, when no one appeared, the trees seemed to his excited brain to be changing to beautiful women, the cries of birds their warm, sensuous voices, and the breeze carried to his nostrils the perfume of their bosoms and the maddening odor of their sex, so that he breathed in deeply through his open, eager mouth the air that his mind had transformed into visions. More often middle-aged couples walked past him, scarcely noticing the dreamy, self-absorbed youth. Once, wearing a double-breasted suit, he wandered into a clearing where he came upon a group of men and women lying naked on straw mats; they had seen him, and in order not to give them the impression that he had been spying on them he pretended to a botanist's interest in the shrubs and slowly circled the clearing, bending down before a number of bushes to examine their foliage and flowers. The sun worshipers paid him no attention. Two of them were reading magazines, the others lay flat on their stomachs or their backs. Federico caught a glimpse of a woman of about fifty-five, her skin marked with brown splotches, her breasts shrunk to deflated sacks, her thighs blue with veins.

Candia saw him in his double-breasted suit one day, was struck by his handsome appearance, and put him in charge of receiving the guests when they came to the main house in the evening to relax with a drink before dinner. Federico greeted them with a serious air, never smiling or giving his voice any other tone than one that indicated resigned indifference, and showed them to their seats. He quickly withdrew from them and, making a sign to a waiter to attend to their wishes, placed himself at a discreet distance as though he wished to remain invisible. His intention had only been to secure for each guest his privacy, but the impression he gave was of a person stricken by some profound melancholy. The women looked frequently where he stood behind a horsetail palm, his face turned to the lake, and when they saw his eyes and the overwhelming sadness that they read in the unblinking stare, they longed to hold his head against their breast. What could his grief be that his lips trembled as he stood in his proud silence? The women made up a thousand fictions about the sad youth. Chronicles of passion fluttered their pages in their minds, whole chapters sighed and whispered in their breasts, and in others blood flowed.

If Federico paid them no attention it was because the youngest of the women was in her mid-forties and, to his perception, ancient. He found more pleasure in observing the fantasies that engaged his mind and kept him in a state of patiently enduring a present that seemed to his inner vision to be unreal. One day when the guests had all gone to the dining room and he was standing by a column at the end of the patio, watching a waiter clear the tables and straighten the furniture, one of the women returned and walked briskly up to him. "I left my purse behind, I wonder if you have found it?"

She was tall and square-shouldered, with sunken cheeks, very thin lips and blue eyes that seemed to have receded in their sockets.

"Where were you sitting?" Federico asked.

The woman looked around and pointed to a chair. Federico began to walk toward it but she said behind him, "No, it wasn't there. I must have sat there yesterday. Yes. It was *there*." Federico, who had stopped and turned to look at her, saw her point to another chair. The purse was stuck between the cushion and the backrest. When he had brought it to her, she took it and patted his arm with a bony hand, saying, "Thank you so much, I'm much obliged to you."

"It's nothing," Federico said.

She was about to go away when, appearing as if she had suddenly had an unexpected idea, she stopped and said, "Can I ask you a question?"

Federico stared at her and nodded his head.

"It's a personal question, I hope you don't mind my asking it."

Federico's face indicated that he did not.

"What do you think of Gabriela Mistral?"

Federico lowered his eyelids in an effort to remember. The name was vaguely familiar but had sunk too deep in a fold of his memory for him to recall quickly.

The woman thought he had lowered his eyelids because the name had evoked some line of Gabriela Mistral's poetry and brought back some sad memory.

"I mean, of course, what do you think of her as a poet?" she said to encourage him to consider Gabriela Mistral objectively, without suffering from any personal associations her poetry might evoke.

Federico remembered his literature teacher—the histrionic Señor Lobo who used to declaim verses at the top of his voice and then order the class to stand up and recite the lines in chorus, walking up and down the aisles tapping the bottoms of the boys with a ruler—and raised his eyes and repeated Señor Lobo's words: "A great treasure, a . . . jewel, yes, a jewel on the highest peak of the Andes sparkling over South America."

"I'm so glad you think so," the woman said, beaming at him, patting his arm, and impressed by the young man's poetical turn of phrase. "I wonder if I can make a terrible imposition on you," she added after a pause. "You see, I'm trying to translate her poems into Swedish. As you can hear, my Spanish is far from perfect."

Federico was surprised by this declaration, for she talked correctly though with an accent. "There are some poems," she continued, "where I find myself quite lost. If you could spare me a few moments, perhaps tomorrow morning, at ten, say, I shall consider it a great favor if you came and helped me with some of the lines."

"I can try," he said, and finding his answer both brief and trite, found himself adding, "But you must know a poet's passions are a mystery of the heart."

"Indeed, that is so," she said, finding his words charmingly poetical. "And it's so kind of you to offer to help a weak prosaic mind like mine. The name is Erika Hannum. And yours, you don't have to tell me, everyone knows it's Federico. Such a beautiful name in Spanish! Northern European versions of it are dreadful, I'm afraid, but *Federico*—one finds oneself caressing the consonants, sighing over the vowels and expressing an amazement at the end."

Federico watched her go away to the dining room, noticing her bluish hair was cut short like a man's, and thought she must be some eccentric scholar. He kept worrying about Gabriela Mistral all that evening, but he could only think of Señor Lobo's words and, trying harder to have a more specific recollection, ended by seeing an oversize emerald set in a gold bracelet on an old lady's wrist.

He pondered the two alternatives before him when he went to Erika Hannum's the next morning: he could either confess straightaway that he knew nothing about Gabriela Mistral or pretend that he knew her poetry so well that it was too difficult to explain it in simple terms. He still had not decided which course to adopt when he arrived at the cottage.

Erika Hannum greeted him with the words, "Ah, the beautiful poet of Sandoval!"

Federico was astonished to see that she wore a loose blouse over shorts and went about the cottage in bare feet, her long white legs striding energetically about the floor. The curtains were drawn across the windows and it was dark in the sitting room when he entered; even so, it was impossible not to notice the thick strings of varicose veins that ran down her legs and the slack mottled skin of her arms.

"Anders has gone fishing," she said of her husband. "That's his only passion."

Federico had expected to see a table covered with books and papers and for Erika Hannum to be wearing a dark gray smock and gold-rimmed spectacles. But he saw no evidence of scholarly industry. Instead there was a bottle of vodka on the table in front of the sofa and he noticed that she had a small glass in her hand. She raised it to her lips, tilted her head back, quickly jerked her hand to empty the glass, while striding to the table where she put the glass down, turned round to face him, put her hands on her hips in a decisive movement, smiled, and said, "What can I get you? A cup of coffee perhaps? Or some maté? Or would you like to share my vice?"

He was still nervous about having to answer questions about Gabriela Mistral and said, "No, nothing, thank you."

"Ah, I see you prefer to drink dreams and not the insipid liquids we mortals must swallow!"

He had no idea what she meant and stood looking apprehensively at her. She threw herself onto the sofa, turned to sit upright in it, leaned forward to pour herself a drink and, patting the seat next to her, said, "Well, come and sit down."

He stepped forward hesitantly, wondering whether the moment had not come when he should confess that he knew nothing about Gabriela Mistral. "Ah, how softly you walk!" she observed. "The world is only clouds at your feet."

Federico sat down gingerly, finding himself tense, so that his weight seemed to remain suspended over the sofa rather than sunk in it. "How depressing it must be for you," she said, seeing the odd manner in which he sat, "to have to suffer the surfaces of reality, how very sad when your soul longs for the flight into eternity."

He gazed at her with a silent questioning expression, too

nervous to demand of her what she meant by these extraordinary words, and she confused him still more by asking, "What poetry is there in my face that you look at me with such divine intensity?"

He turned his face away and wondered how he should make his confession to her. Somehow it seemed inappropriate to declare bluntly that he was ignorant of Gabriela Mistral's work. "I have to tell you," he began and looked at her; but he aborted his confession, for he saw an ugly leer on her face, reminding him of the lustful way in which old men stared at beautiful young girls, and he realized at last that he had been lured for a purpose other than scholarship.

"What, what do you have to tell me that it trembles like a butterfly on your lips?" she asked eagerly, expecting to hear some priceless poetical sentiment.

Federico burst out crying.

"What is it?" she asked tenderly, holding his shoulders. "Is the world so hard, so unbearable? Oh, my poor darling poet!"

His crying became a convulsive sobbing and she drew his head to her bosom where, finding his cheek pressed against a ribcage where a younger woman would have had breasts, he cried all the more loudly. But he cried not because he was revolted by the idea of being seduced by a much older woman; the thought that had brought on his despair was that what was happening was *nothing less* than the precise granting of his wish: he had simply wished for women, not for beautiful, young women. He ought now to have concluded that his amulet possessed no power, that some of the recent events of his life had been so absurdly farcical and perverse, and so unlike the destiny he wished for himself, that they were nothing but a series of accidents; instead, Federico's belief that Popayan had given him a secret magic was reinforced: he interpreted the present event only as the working of that magic.

From stroking his head against her bosom, the old lady had moved her bony hand to his thighs. It took Federico a few moments to feel the sensation emanating from that region. Why, in the wretched circumstance in which he found himself, he should get an erection he was at a loss to understand. What followed, considering that she was forty years older than he was, and Federico still legally a minor, could have been an example of child abuse, did he not think at the crucial moment that far though the act was from his idea of making love to a woman it was certainly superior to the self-abuse to which he had had to resort in recent months.

When leaving Sandoval a few days later Erika Hannum told an acquaintance of the pleasure she had enjoyed with the young man, and it was not long before Federico began to receive hints from her and, after her, from others. The ruse employed by each one was transparent and he could easily have prevented putting himself into the situation that he had suffered with Erika Hannum; but he obliged each of the ladies, believing that it was his particular fate to do so since he must accept the granting of his wish even if it realized itself as a cruel joke.

Without knowing it he had become an accomplice of the invisible agent created by his own imagination: having founded his belief on a delusion become a faith by the circumstantial evidence whose ambiguities he could interpret only in a manner that reinforced the faith, and never observing that the philosophy embraced was a self-deceiving fraud, he had trapped himself into doing that which his own prophecy demanded and saw the ludicrous turn of events in which he found himself as a solemn and rigorous working out of a wished-for fate.

On his next visit to Sandoval Ernesto Vivado was amused to discover the amorous regard in which Federico was held by some of the older women, but he decided to put an end to the young man's forced labor of love, not wanting an immoral reputation for his resort. In his enterprise of serving the dreams of mankind and making available to the debauched vanity of human wishes the gratification of its secret lust, his business included the selling of vice and cruelty; starting as a movie distributor and then a consultant to Hollywood, he had acquired a worldwide range of concerns, making the forbidden his special territory. His office in Brussels monitored the demand for arms by countries banned from buying them on the open market, and found ways of supplying them; in Panama he ran a corporation that seemed to deal legitimately in foreign currencies while it carried on its real business of laundering the money acquired corruptly by politicians and criminals in the Americas; he had set up a tourist agency in Hong Kong that had a good share of organized prostitution all across the Far East from Singapore to Tokyo. A deity of the underworld, Ernesto Vivado was constantly on the move, encircling the globe with a prescribed regularity, circumventing everywhere the restraining laws of civil order and subverting them to create new grounds for the flourishing of evil. Everywhere except in Sandoval. For Sandoval was his own private vice that took the form of a need to keep the resort scrupulously virtuous and honest, so that coming there whenever he could to indulge his fantasy that he did no wrong he could persuade himself afresh that he had created an unblemished world in which no one suffered.

"Time for a change, what do you think?" he said to Federico. "I have a small operation in West Palm Beach in Florida. You'll enjoy living there among the rich."

"What will I do there?" Federico asked.

"Oh, nothing that you haven't been doing here," Vivado answered with a charming smile.

A few days later Federico accompanied his mentor to the city where he spent two nights in Vivado's penthouse with a view of the Andes. In a country with a tortuous bureaucracy that obliged one to an indefinite wait while the forms of any application for a government service were processed, it took one phonecall from Vivado to have Federico's passport ready in twenty-four hours and another for him to get his visa to the U.S.A. two days later. Federico enjoyed his brief residence in the city of his birth, lounging on the penthouse terrace in the evening, watching the snow cover on a distant peak of the Andes turn golden as it reflected the setting sun. Thoughts of his own past did not trouble him. He had no curiosity about his parents. Mariana came to his mind, but only as a valued object that he had left hidden somewhere and could repossess when he wished to do so.

Then the thrill of flying to Miami. The exhilaration as the plane lifted off from his native land as if in a furious urgency to abandon that world. The marvel of its steep rise which within minutes seemed to humiliate the highest peaks of the Andes, inducing in Federico the feeling that it was he himself who possessed that incredible power. And then the arrival in Miami. The smooth silent world of American efficiency. The tall, beautiful girls as they walked from a recently landed flight from the Virgin Islands, two striking blondes stepping over the blue carpet with such naturally purposeful confidence. Federico was filled with enchantment. He could have hugged the immigration officer when he returned his passport for he struck Federico as the guardian of some magical castle to which he was unquestioningly granting him admission.

He took a cab to the city where he had to meet Vivado's agent, Bill Radner, who from behind the cover of a real estate business, with a private helicopter ostensibly to take his clients on an aerial view of ranches, assaulted the state with cocaine and prostitution. Federico kept reminding himself that he was in America. The thought was incredible. He was amazed at his good luck. The cab was overtaken by a gleaming red Mustang convertible with its top down and driven by a young girl, her blonde hair swirling about her head, and as she passed the cab she glanced at its occupant and, seeing the young man staring at her in wonder, waved a hand and threw him a gorgeous smile. She accelerated away, leaving Federico with a vivid impression of freedom. A freedom that was his too now by the simple miracle of finding himself in America. And he would have money. Vivado had hinted at the riches he could acquire. Excitement, women and wealth were nearly now within his grasp, and he passed a forefinger over the brass rectangle at his neck.

"Hey, you look great, just fabulous," Bill Radner said to him, squeezing his hand. In the background his secretary was answering an inquiry on the phone, describing a condominium, and she smiled prettily at Federico when she caught his eye. Almost every face he had looked at since landing in America seemed to be welcoming him. Happiness was choking him, making him nearly speechless.

Radner gave him a packet of instructions, with directions to proceed to West Palm Beach and whom to contact there. "You look to me like you were born for the job," he said, and laughed. Then he leaned his head forward a little, looked seriously at Federico, and added, "There's no turning back now, you know."

What could he mean? "In this world, you don't ask any questions, okay?" was the answer.

But Federico saw no reason to turn back from enchantment.

When he arrived in West Palm Beach the next day, Radner's instructions took him to a part of town which, with its concentration of cheaply built apartment complexes, was little more than a glorified shanty town but which appeared to Federico as a privileged tentacle of civilization. There, on the ground floor of a five-story apartment building, he found his contact, the person identified in his packet of instructions as "The Shuttle Columbia".

A grossly overweight woman in lime green polyester slacks, who walked with the help of a stout stick, brandishing it when she did not lean on it, answered to that description and said in the gentlest of voices, "Call me Miss Molly." Her small hand was soft and limp when Federico attempted to shake it. She wore a black wig on a large head, creating a startlingly incongruous effect, making her round white face appear ghostly and featureless, her eyes being two tiny dots and her mouth a thin line. A wrinkled mass of white fat fell from her chin to her neck, quivering like jelly, and in spite of the air conditioning that had the room quite refrigerated, sweat had collected in the wrinkles. She stood holding her stick in the fist of her left hand, hitting the ground with it in a pounding action. "Let me look at you now," she said, raising her right hand to Federico's chin and turning his face from side to side. "Not bad, not bad a-tall." She pinched his arm and then slapped the palm of her hand against his chest. "Good and firm, not too tough, not like them string beans from Puerto Rico." She lowered her head and seemed to stare at his waist. "Guess you're okay in that department there." She walked round him and thwacked his buttocks with her stick, so that he reacted by taking a step forward. "Fine, that's fine."

Intimidated by her enormous presence, he was unable to question her words and actions. But the blow to his behind opened his mouth and he said, "What's the idea?"

She ignored his question and slowly walked to a small desk. She pulled out a drawer and took a key from it. "Your apartment's upstairs," she said.

Federico was installed in one of the six efficiency apartments on the fifth floor. The other five were occupied by silent, sad-looking young men whom he never got to know though he soon understood that he was one of them, all their lives controlled by Miss Molly who assigned them to her network of clients of rich old women.

Federico was not shocked when the realization came to him that he had been sent to America to sell his body, with 90 per cent of the profits going to Vivado's empire. As at Sandoval, where he had performed the same service free, he accepted his situation as a necessary debt to be paid for his wishes. He had wished for women and he was given a new one every night. Some of the women asked for him again and, imagining him to be a real lover, gave him expensive presents—gold watches usually, but also cases of whiskey, jewels, clothes, and once a Lincoln Continental. Somehow Miss Molly always knew when he had received a present and obliged him to surrender it to her, though she appeared to be scrupulously honest in letting him have his 10 per cent of the proceeds when the object was sold. He got the impression that, from her cold room, Miss Molly controlled more than the lives of the six men on the fifth floor.

For fifteen months Federico's existence was a dream in the lives of old women for whom the expensive hours spent with him constituted a more poignant reality than the emptiness of their widowhood or country club rituals with their husbands who had long ceased to take an interest in their bodies. To Federico it seemed that only other people led a real life while he himself, caught in a remote corner of a design which he continued to be convinced was of a magical weave so fine that it for ever remained mysterious, must believe his own real life to have become suspended for a necessary period during which he must submit himself to the fantastic demands of his destiny. Hurricanes in the Gulf, civil war in Central America, and other disasters that afflicted humanity meant nothing to him; he remained untouched by contemporary events whether they were the invasion of one country by another or a man being implanted with a mechanical heart: he had closed himself completely within the circle of his own self and grimly looked only inward. If he watched the external world with deliberate care, it was not to see what was happening in it but to keep himself alert to the minutest twist that might reveal to him some modification of the fate that governed him.

Occasionally, when he wearied of the excessive gratification of their desires that the old women required of him, he wondered whether he should not, once and for all, put his power to a conclusive test by asking of it an unambiguous happiness, one that was not an ironical and mocking interpretation of his desires but truly answered his wishes. But each time he stopped himself from doing so, terrified that he might commit some error without realizing it, and consequently perpetuate the original error of subscribing to a faith whose unpredictable and treacherous inflictions upon him he continued to perceive as a perfectly logical unfolding of a destiny, for he interpreted each event only in the narrow language of the accepted faith which reduced explanation to ideas already known to him.

He did not ask for a relief from the perversity of lovemaking to which he seemed to have become condemned. In fact, the more his situation caused him anguish the greater he believed his ultimate prize would be. His early delusion, that he was to discover a beautiful freedom in America, had quickly foundered when he saw that the figure of the Statue of Liberty had been replaced for the occasion of his immigration by Miss Molly. He resigned himself to a present so repetitive and dull with its faking each day of novelty and thrills that his life would have seemed meaningless could he not remind himself of the secret he possessed and continue to believe in a glorious future.

On his way to Europe Vivado stopped in Miami for a meeting with Bill Radner, and in the course of the conversation Radner happened to refer to the small operation in West Palm Beach. Vivado decided that that was like a branch line on a railway which did not generate enough traffic and, looking at the accounts, ordered it to be closed at once, with Miss Molly to be sent to Bangkok. It was then that he remembered Federico to whom he had not given any thought for over a year. On a whim of the moment, only because he needed to make a call to his office there that afternoon, he arranged for Federico to be sent to Brussels.

Vivado's caprice governed Federico's fate, and in this manner Federico spent the following thirteen years being suddenly moved from place to place, now to Hong Kong, now to Taipei, or back to South America for a spell, convincing him each time that he was about to achieve in the world he was newly entering the full realization of his dream but discovering each time that it was only another period of anguish and boredom that had to be endured. Once, in his despair, he had held the little brass rectangle between his forefinger and thumb and cried, "Give me a sign, some proof!" But he had stopped, not wanting the gift that he still believed in to be compromised. He was in Brussels then and had recently returned from Seoul with two senior men from the corporation who had gone to South Korea to effect a shipment of American arms to Iran; he knew little of the business and had no notion of the enormity of the crime that was being committed. The senior men had taken him along to perform two crucial tasks when incriminating papers had to be carried from one office to another, and should there have been a government agent among the Korean contacts the discovery of the papers on his person would have sent him to jail for many years. Not knowing what he did, Federico carried out the orders with cool efficiency. And so, back in Brussels, a few days after he had spoken to his amulet, when the corporation gave him a bonus of twenty-five thousand dollars in one-hundred-dollar bills, the only thought that filled his mind was that this token of wealth was a sure proof that the magic he possessed had a real power.

He needed no further hint to encourage him and bore the ennui of the present with the greatest indifference, smiling inwardly at the secret glow within him that was his constant companion and comforter when his daily life offered no escape from tedium. The corporation surprised him with large gifts of money, for he never understood what he had done to merit such unusual rewards, being always kept on the obscure fringes of Vivado's empire where the commands that he obeyed involved him in actions so isolated from the cause that initiated them and the effect they were calculated to produce that he never knew what exactly he had undertaken; but he never questioned the gifts, believing that any literal reason would be incidental and finally irrelevant for the real reason was that his magic was working. After the fifth such gift of money he ceased even to be surprised, having become accustomed then to the idea that his bank account should continue to swell until his wish to possess real wealth had been fulfilled.

On the occasion of his thirty-fourth birthday he was shocked to realize that although he had, for eighteen years since he had run out of his parents' apartment, led what by common standards was an exciting life, made himself a considerable fortune, and had sex with hundreds of women, he was alone and unloved. He had many acquaintances on three continents but not a single friend. All the women he had gone to bed with had been old; even Daniela, the youngest of them, was over forty when, at sixteen, he first slept with her. He had never enjoyed the simple, devoted love of a girl his own age, not known the simple dreams of ordinary young people in love. In an important sense, the knowledge of which pained him, he had remained a virgin. The reflection depressed him. He had missed a vital experience of youth and it wounded him to think that he had never known what it was like to be in love. A doubt dimly entered his mind and began to torment him with the question whether he was not already being punished for the excess of his wishes by being excluded from the more poignant pleasures of an ordinary, but true, love. His relationship with Mariana would surely have developed into that, for it had begun so naturally; they had reached the stage when they were happiest when alone with each other, and it would not have been long before they had begun to say they loved each other, and then there would have been talk of marriage, of children, followed by the joy of their two bodies coming together in a natural coupling of the human species. How perfect that would have been, how *right*! He had thrown away the chance of that simple happiness, believing at first that he could return to find it waiting for him to grasp whenever he wished. But the years had vanished, bringing him a hideous debauchery instead of love, substituting his common human self with the monster of desires. He was assailed by regret.

But what was he moaning about? He thought of the wealth he had already acquired, and asked himself what would he be now if he had stayed and found the simple happiness that he was being so sentimental about—at the most a clerk in some wretched office with not enough money to buy meat more than twice a week for his family. Although he told himself to be thankful for having escaped that misery, the regret did not leave him, but unexpectedly surged in his mind when he seemed most assuredly in command of the world he had created for himself.

He was unable to sleep on planes, and the night flight from Miami, made longer by the stopover in Panama, where severe weather kept the plane grounded for two additional hours, had tired him. After calling the airline about his missing luggage, he had removed his clothes, locked the hotel room and fallen asleep. The phone awoke him in the afternoon. His luggage had been found and would be delivered to the hotel. Federico rang room service and ordered sandwiches and beer. "No, cancel the sandwiches," he quickly added. "Make it steak, rice and beans." He suddenly felt like home cooking.

While eating in his room he went over in his mind the details of the business he had come to accomplish, but the meal, evoking associations of his youth, made him soporific and he went back to bed. He lay drowsily for a while, seeing images of himself as a schoolboy and of his life with his parents. For some reason the cleaning woman he had passed in the corridor when arriving at the hotel earlier in the day came to his mind, but then also did some of the people he had seen on the plane, and he let the image slip out of his mind and be replaced by more from his youth. He remembered within how short a walking distance he was from his parents' old apartment. Would they still be there? For a moment he had the fantasy of entering the apartment, staggering them with his cultivated presence and placing before them more money than they had ever seen. Perhaps later, he thought, beginning to fall asleep, and just when unconsciousness overcame him he had the image of Mariana as he had held her in the dark entranceway.

When he awoke, darkness had set outside. His watch showed that it had gone ten o'clock. He wondered if he had failed to adjust it after leaving Miami but, calling the receptionist, he found he had the correct time. He remembered to ask the receptionist if his luggage had arrived. It had. Presently a porter brought it up.

Federico showered and changed. He was amazed at how long he had slept. A profound, dreamless sleep. Years seemed to have been encapsulated in the hours. He turned off the hot water and let the cold stream shock his head into full awakening.

Having dressed, he left the hotel and walked toward Miraflores. The street was deserted, its great towers of banks and offices empty, though lit up. Coming to the end of the street, he entered his old district where he found a bar where a few men sat drinking. He got himself a beer and some fried chicken and bread. The poorly dressed, unshaven men seemed oddly familiar, and he wondered whether they might not be his former schoolfellows. But they were eyeing him suspiciously, almost aggressively, with a contempt for his rich man's looks that could never be their own. Federico remained silent and left as quickly as he could. There was nothing to be gained by proclaiming his identity.

Realizing that he was only ten minutes away from his parents' apartment, he walked in that direction, deciding to have a look. Some of the buildings he recognized from the past, but others had been replaced by taller ones. Coming to the street where he had lived, he became confused, not being able to find the building. He had made some mistake, he thought, and went back to the beginning of the street to look again at its name. No. It was the correct street. Then he saw that where his building had been there was now a gap. The foundations of a new building had been laid down and in the darkness he had to look closely to see its steel skeleton. He walked back to Miraflores and just when he had reached the street where his hotel was located it occurred to him that he should have gone to see if the building in which Mariana had lived still stood. But then, coming to the hotel and seeing in its international image a symbol of commercial power, he told himself to stop being sentimental, it was useless to loiter on the outskirts of his dead past when his present life was here. He was about to enter the hotel but stopped and had the sensation of entering another room in the same space. He stepped back and looked down the street. Not a single building stood from eighteen years ago, there was no landmark to confirm an identification, but he was convinced that this was where Popayan's shop had been. Deliberately entering the hotel with an urgent step to shake off the memory of the past, he remembered all too sharply his appearance before Popayan and, taking the elevator, he touched the amulet at his neck and felt a pain surge in his breast. He hastened to his room, quickly removed his clothes, and fell into bed. A rush of perspiration had broken from his body, especially at the neck and chest. Convinced that it was a slight indigestion brought on by the greasy fried chicken, he got up, took an aspirin, and returned to bed. He regretted eating in the cheap café, the sort of establishment he had not entered in over a dozen years. Some obscure nostalgia dimly evoked by entering the area of his childhood must have driven him to order such a meal. He burped, and his nostrils picked up a sour smell that immediately brought to his mind the recollection of going to the same café with his father when he was a small boy, perhaps six or seven, and being kept busy with fried chicken while his father drank beer with the men. The memory of that time now disturbed him; he was filled with a loathing for the images of his own early past and yet could not be pleased with himself for having escaped it and made for himself so rich and exotic a life that even a sketchy description of it to his former friends would be beyond their imaginative comprehension. But a subtle distress had entered his mind. The more he deliberately congratulated himself at his unique fortune the more he secretly feared that the cost of it had been the committing of a profound wrong for which he must one day begin to pay the price of infinite sorrow. Perhaps that time had already begun. Whenever he had thought of his parents and the terrible pain that he must have caused them, he had quickly dismissed them from his mind with the thought that one day he would visit them with a trunk full of money and provide their old age with unimagined luxury. They would forgive him. No, no, his father would insist and his mother agree with him, there was nothing to forgive, he had done no wrong, they were proud of him, it was an honor to call him their son! But now, having walked up their street in a moment of idle curiosity which, however, unknown to him, was the outer frivolous disguise of a deep and painful guilt, and having seen that the building where they lived had been demolished, his fantasy of visiting them in some vague future could no longer be nourished. He heard his father curse him, he saw his mother as a heap of silent misery.

To cast them out of his mind, refusing still to recognize the distress that caused his body's agitation, he forced himself to think of the business that had brought him back to his native country. As always he had been given no precise instructions as to what he must do, only told to contact someone, this time one Roberto Quintano. There was some island in the Pacific they had to visit together. Having no specific idea of what he had to do, Federico could not distract himself for long with the work he had come to perform for Vivado; nor would images of his recent experiences in Europe fix themselves in his mind, which kept being invaded by his past, imbuing him incomprehensibly with a painful remorse.

The figure of the cleaning woman he had passed in the corridor earlier in the day flickered through his mind again and was replaced by other images of the day, each one apparently trivial and meaningless. But suddenly he saw himself leaving his old apartment and walking to meet Mariana and then going to the park with her. He saw her vividly as she was then, and in the turmoil that now filled his mind she became transformed into some divine gift that had been given him and that he had so callously abandoned, and he began to believe that all the countless older women he had been obliged to make love to, each one a negation of female beauty, had been his punishment for his early presumption that he could return to Mariana simply by wishing for her when the realization of his fantastic dreams had become exhausted. He lamented the disappearance of all that time. Eighteen years vanished, with only an accumulated wealth to prove that he had lived through them. Years without feeling, without love. And now he was stricken by grief that he could not have any of that time back, that no amount of his wealth could purchase a second of it. The ordinary life that he should have lived, finding a commonplace happiness with the woman he loved, suggested itself to his mind as a wonderful existence that could never now be his.

He found himself sobbing, and while that part of him which had long sold itself to the pursuit of fantastic pleasure scorned this maudlin outburst, the other part that had become overwhelmed by a sense of loss hung its head low and saw no shame in the spirit's despair. Federico snatched at the amulet as if wanting to wrench it from his neck and cried for the simple life he had thrown away, and as the violence within him broke in unrestrained and louder sobbing he wished he could be back with Mariana as she was eighteen years ago. He felt a sudden sharp pain at his neck. In his agitation, he had pulled hard at the amulet. The chain had momentarily dug into his flesh, causing the pain, and broken. Federico stared at the little brass rectangle in his hand. He got out of bed, walked to the window, opened it, and threw the amulet out into the night. He returned to bed and fell into an undisturbed sleep.

In the Violet Glow of Sunset

And even in that moment, when he held the joyous Herminia in his arms and saw over her shoulder the boat enter the small bay, he observed, as his mind performed the instantaneous calculation of Herminia's age, how his own years were suddenly frozen with the present moment forcing a recognition of its potency, compressing all his past into a trembling anxiety, as if all that long time had only engaged him in a suspended reality and he had remained motionless like the marine iguanas lying dead still on the rocks with their backs to the sun. Instantly arriving at Herminia's age, even to the precise number of days after her sixteenth birthday, he lost a sense of his own age—what was he, fifty, sixty?—and felt ageless, with no expectation of mortality, but a remote sense of an unending future in which the days declined, sending the sun on one more voyage through the underworld, but there was no final termination of time, and human memory, escaping from the fires of cremation or leaping out of the interred skull, became a current in the atmosphere, a charged breath that must again be the fuel of human blood and human passion. I am never I, the voice of Domingo Maturana again possessed Gamboa's brain, only a coincidence within this flesh. He let the voice die, watching the two men in the boat; but the dead man's whisper persisted, only these desires that own our bodies construct a desperate formula of the self, held by an outrageous belief—and Gamboa, with Herminia in his arms and his vision blurred, was sitting again with Maturana, the old man's stick across his lap, his head bowed, spitting his words at the ashen dust, making exuberant pronouncements about the self's immersion into non-being—a coincidence within the flesh, he repeated, or an extraordinary romance invented by the soul bemused by the potential of surprise in the predictable, just as the sun's rising is an astonishing event, we awake before dawn to witness its novelty.

"You go into the house," Gamboa said to Herminia when she withdrew from him and turned her head to look at the boat now proceeding slowly in a wide loop across the bay.

But why should he then find himself reconnoitering the recesses of memory, an espionage maneuver confounded by the self come under the suspicion of being a double agent who must deny a documented existence but whose other identity, supported by fictitious papers, flaunted a convincing circumstantial evidence of an alternative life? For, in this sense, was he not himself the surprise of his own predictable expectations, discovering in the exquisite forgery of thought, which converted simple apprehensions into a surreal havoc, that forlorn resident who claimed a portion of the self, making shadowy appearances in melancholy dreams or in moments, as now, of distraction, when one sensed an unspeakable menace in ordinary perception?

"Go," he said again to Herminia, seeing in her the Mariana before she had become defiled in his eyes, but Herminia stood a little longer beside him, enchanted by the trim boat and by the excitement that deliverance was at hand.

The boat stopped some ten meters from the beach. The man in the cabin turned off the motor, the other threw out the anchor.

"Hey, Roberto," the man on the deck called to the other, "I thought no one lived here."

"That's right, everyone was evacuated."

"Well, look there."

Far up on the road, which they had not distinguished during the first general impression of the island when they entered the bay, next to one of the huts, which had remained invisible because they first made for the cove where the sea lions were and could see only when they had turned back from the cove in a slow wide loop, Roberto now saw the distant group from which, just then, a young female figure detached herself and entered the hut.

"See *her*, Federico?" he said, coming out of the cabin.

"Why were they left behind?" Federico asked.

"God knows. Just happened, I guess. Some mistake."

"What are we supposed to do now, waste our time shipping them out first?"

"Well, we'll see," Roberto said. "They could save us time. Instead of commuting back to San Bernardino, we could stay in one of the huts and have them cook for us."

"Roots in a gravy of ash is what we'll get, I should think."

"No, they'll have goats," Roberto said optimistically. "And there's that girl, Federico," he added with a grin. "I tell you what, I'll do a deal with you. Equal share of the loot. What do you say?"

"What is *that*?" Federico exclaimed, seeing a figure that seemed only grotesquely that of a man and more of a hairy beast begin to walk away in a loping gait up the hill.

Federico was reminded of the little gray-haired old man in San Bernardino's only bar—an ashen floor with a tarpaulin roof, a few crudely constructed chairs—who, having a new audience for his old stories, had him and Roberto listening to his tales on the previous evening for far longer than either cared to spend with him. But each time he seemed to conclude a story and they thought they could escape, he launched on a commentary that had them beguiled and listening to him with a sense of fearful anticipation, as if they were on the verge of hearing some extraordinary revelation. What did they think, he asked, his round, owlish eyes staring, his finger pointing to the empty space between the two men, that these islands were fragments of the world they had come from? Bits of the same old earth torn away from the continent and floating out on the ocean? Do not be deceived by the facility with which you can transport yourself, with the nice illusion of such navigation that the surface you travel over is constant and continuous, that time is only a material zone requiring you to put your watches back an hour. These are enchanted islands. The bones of shipwrecked sailors from centuries past have still not shed their flesh. Roberto laughed. The man glared at him with enormous pity. Oh, you will find a good many skulls if you dig deep enough! But watch out for the human beast in his innocent depravity, and know that the excuse that brings you here, giving you a semblance of control over your actions, is only the disguise of other impulses buried in your soul, twitching there, silent and shadowless, releasing a laughable memory and driving you toward the final atrocity of time. The man spoke as though he were scolding them for presumptions they had not professed. You cannot know what identities you have not already outlived, so do not laugh when I tell you that these enchanted islands are also the station of terror so incandescent the hardiest human spirit dissolves in it as if it had only been an illusion.

Roberto was not laughing now, watching the curious figure disappear over the hill. "Why didn't we think of bringing a gun?"

Federico did not answer. He was observing the man who had begun to walk toward the beach, and felt unaccountably irritated by his situation. Each time in the past when Vivado had sent him to a new destination—America, Europe, the Far East—Federico had excitedly anticipated a turn of events that would place him in that magical realm where the idealized longings of his vanity would be realized, and even when the reality had proved to be an ironical mockery of his wishes he had continued to expect a subtle change in the terms of his existence that would transform ugliness to beauty, the predatory old ladies of West Palm Beach, for example, becoming compliant maidens. No perfect happiness had ever come to him and the ideal young woman of his fantasy continued to exist only as an unobtainable form in his imagination. And since the day of his recent return to his native city, when remorse had entered his mind and he had in his emotional agitation cried at the loss of what he began to believe had been his real life, he had experienced a collapse of will, and proceeded, when the next day dawned and he had to contact Roberto Quintano, to go on with the necessary business without finding any interest in it or caring to know what it was that he was doing but merely, like an overtired laborer, going through the required motions while his heart and mind were elsewhere.

Perhaps it was owing to his altered mental state that he disliked Roberto from the start. At twenty-six Roberto was the first younger man he had met who had made him realize that, though only eight years older, his own youth was well behind him, that a new generation already existed of smart, successful men. Roberto had a degree in business, read books on geology as if they were novels, had the oddest hobby Federico had ever known, land surveying, carried a portable computer in a briefcase, and, what seemed to vex Federico the most, was married to a general's daughter who was only twenty-three and had already given him two children. He seemed to possess a complete happiness, but it was not an envy of it that made Federico dislike him. Roberto talked endlessly, and in a boastful tone that Federico found sickening, of his conquests of society women, and repeated his favorite line, always with a self-satisfied smile on his face: "She was another one who said no one had ever given her such a terrific orgasm." Or he would say, "You know, Federico, there are so many women who never had an orgasm until I screwed them, I think the government should give me a decoration!" Federico was revolted but obliged himself to smile. "You should hear the cry from their throat, then, when I take them to the climax, a delicious little scream of pure pleasure." Disgusted, Federico soon developed the technique of detaching himself from the painful presence of Roberto's voice, giving him only the appearance of a bemused friend.

Roberto had rolled up his trousers and, carrying his shoes in his hands, had waded through the water to go to the beach. Federico followed, looking around at the small bay and the rising land of the island, images flickering through his mind of his arrival in many foreign lands to which he had carried the precious luggage of his expectations, while here, so much closer to home, he was stepping, reluctantly and without any declared motive, on a land that already proclaimed its desolation.

But within a minute a new tension possessed him. The man who had been walking down the road stood just above the beach, and Federico, climbing up behind Roberto, heard him say, "I was afraid we had been abandoned." Federico stopped and stared at the man, and though he was much changed he immediately recognized him as Mariana's father. Noticing, as they exchanged the first few words, that Gamboa had not identified him, Federico decided not to reveal himself. There was no point in recalling a former animosity.

As they walked toward the cottages Gamboa described how he and his daughter had been left behind when the ship came to transport the islanders to the mainland. Federico's heart quickened at the mention of the daughter. "My poor girl was going mad with the thought of having lost all hope of happiness," Gamboa said. "So was I, to tell you the truth, with the knowledge that it had all been my fault."

"There was a third figure we saw just now," Roberto said, looking at Gamboa, who anticipated his question and answered, "Oh, that's Baltazar, he's a harmless little soul." But he did not add that he had ordered Baltazar to make himself scarce and the harmless little soul had run off in a state of anxiety and fear.

They had come to the huts and Gamboa excused himself by saying, "Let me go in for a moment and see what we need to take with us."

When they were alone together, Roberto asked Federico, "What do you think, we should take them back to San Bernardino straightaway or wait till we've got some work done?" Federico was still bewildered at having come upon Mariana's father on this remote island and, expecting soon to see the greatest mockery of all his wishes, a Mariana more than twice the age when he last saw her and transformed to someone other with none of her original beauty, remained pensively silent. "So as not to waste a trip?" Roberto added.

Federico was staring up the hill and at the blue sky above it. What he had observed of the island so far had been barren and possessed a forbiddingly inhospitable appearance. He and Roberto had been sent to it to make a preliminary inspection, to report on its basic geography before a team of surveyors was commissioned. Federico had no interest in the job, finding that he hardly had any will with which to pursue enthusiastically the schemes proposed to him by Vivado or one of his lieutenants. Merely allowing himself to go along with what was required of him and hoping that the time would pass when he would no longer suffer, as he had acutely begun to do, from a sense of having become estranged from his own world, he was vaguely consoled by the thought that his energetic and resourceful companion would provide the skill and the momentum for the present job to be completed. Roberto was full of ideas, and on the trip from San Bernardino had elaborated the fantasy of discovering some new species of animal life on the deserted island that would change previously held ideas of natural history, saying excitedly, "You don't have to be a scientist to hit on a new truth." When Federico had pointed out that they did not even know what it was they were going to inspect, and for what purpose, Vivado's project being secret, Roberto had quickly rattled off a series of possibilities that included, Federico was shocked to hear, serving an unfriendly foreign nation, and then added, "One thing I've heard a lot about is that the big powers are looking for dead parts of the world to dump nuclear and chemical waste, and my guess is that this is what Vivado has for sale, a chunk of the dead world." Federico dismissed the thought as coming from an inventive imagination, but Roberto had also said, "Don't you know, Vivado is in with all the tyrants of South America? And those sons of bitches who have killed thousands of their own people just to stay in power will sell their mother's grave if that is all that's left of the land for a U.S. or Soviet chemical dump in exchange for a bank account in Switzerland. You're dealing with men with evil dreams."

Federico turned his gaze away from the hill to Roberto and was about to answer that perhaps they ought to take the stranded islanders back to San Bernardino straightaway, but he was checked by seeing a look of astonishment and pleasure light up Roberto's face and heard him say softly, "Hey, we're going to stay right here."

And now Federico, too, saw the girl who stood in the doorway, and he could not suppress the cry that escaped his lips. Eighteen years of his life seemed to dissolve like a meaningless dream, for there she stood, the very Mariana he had embraced before her father separated them. All those years during which he had sought a fantastic reality had been nothing but a delusion of an anxious vanity, a life lived with apparitions. Could it be that no time had passed and those eighteen years were merely a compressed presentiment attending a moment's idle wish that distracted him from the happiness he already possessed with a larger promise? His hand reached involuntarily for his neck and he remembered the amulet he had thrown away: he recalled with a terrible shock that in the passionate despair that had overcome him that night he had cried at the loss of his real life and, snatching the amulet from his neck, had wished to be again with the Mariana of eighteen years ago, not with the Mariana who would have grown old but that Mariana still only sixteen, as if he had left her but for a minute, so that her presence would restore to him his lost years. And here she was! All at once his mind was dazzled, confused, and tormented as one question succeeded another—was she real, was he at last to grasp his final prize, was the magic, after all these years of trying him with false conceits, at last going to let him resume his simple life, or was he face to face with a new disguise that was about to draw him into a worse evil than he had known before?

"I'm Roberto." The young man walked across the few steps and held out his hand to Herminia, a gesture that annoyed Federico who, entranced by the vision of his Mariana, was unable to move or speak though in his mind he had rushed to her and embraced her with the passion of his youth. Herminia came out of the doorway to take Roberto's hand. "And my friend is Federico," he said when she had withdrawn her hand. She did not move toward Federico but smiled at him from a distance and said, "What happiness to have you come for us!" Before Federico could respond, her father called her from inside the cottage and she went to him.

"Herminia," Roberto repeated softly the name her father had shouted aloud. "What do you say, Federico, isn't she a most desirable piece of property? You know, I always had the fantasy of being alone on an island with a beautiful girl. Now, if you could only take the old man away . . ."

Herminia! Had Gamboa changed her name? Federico had no time to think for he had to prevent Roberto from committing any foolishness, and he said, "I think we'd better do the work we've come for and not fool around."

"What's the matter with you, don't you like girls?"

"Do me a favor, Roberto. Don't try anything with this girl."

"*You* don't have to, you're old enough to be her father."

Federico's annoyance with Roberto's display of male bravado turned momentarily to anger, but he restrained the impulse to fling himself at the younger man. "I'll explain to you later," he said in a calm voice, "but, believe me, it's important you leave the girl alone."

"No one tells me what to do."

Federico maintained his restraint and said, "I'm not telling you anything, just asking for a very important favor."

Before Roberto could answer, Gamboa came out of the hut. "I thought we'd have a little meal before we go," he said cheerfully. "If there were time, I could slaughter a goat and make a feast. But just a few eggs to keep us nourished, what do you say?"

"It's only an hour across to San Bernardino," Federico said. "I think we should set out at once. We could take the food with us if you like."

"But Herminia has it all set out," Gamboa said, and gestured with his hand toward the open door.

"Only an hour to get across," Roberto remarked as he entered the hut, "so what's the hurry? We have all day."

A cloth was spread upon the ground and they sat around it eating boiled eggs and corn bread. Light from the door fell diagonally across Herminia's head, and Federico, sitting opposite her, saw the right side of her face defined sharply by the brightness while the other half remained in shadow. She seemed delighted by the company, for she believed they had come for the sole purpose of delivering her from a life of infinite solitude and in her mind no two handsomer men could have come to her rescue. She listened with pleasure to Roberto talking about how charming it must be to live a simple life, and was it not true—he appealed to Federico—there were millions of people in cities dreaming of an island paradise, for—he observed to Gamboa—you have space here and a precious silence, complete freedom in fact without any of the corrupting temptations of society. While Herminia longed for the very city life that he affected to despise, it pleased her to listen to his praise of the solitary life for it was as if he indirectly praised some exceptional virtue in herself. Gamboa thought it a sign of good manners that he should speak so well of a life from which he had come to release them, for his words sounded like an extended compliment to the patience with which they had endured almost an eternity of non-being. But Federico loathed him, hearing his chatter only as an attempt to make himself appear charming to Herminia, and he could see that she was being taken in by him. He himself could hardly speak a word, being still in a state that was partly shock and partly terror that his dreams, taking him on an extravagant odyssey which with almost a perversely deliberate malevolence had given him not the life he sought but a parody of it that was now vile and now farcical, had brought him to the very point in his life from which he had fled. Only Mariana's name had been changed to Herminia. Knowing neither how Gamboa had come to the island nor the circumstances of Herminia's birth, and remembering how once he himself believed that he possessed a magical power, he wondered now whether Gamboa was not indeed in possession of some magic that had enabled him to keep Mariana unaffected by the passing of time. But to what purpose should nature and the cunning of man connive at such a scheme? The succession of appearances that had been granted him in his desire for life now invited him to confront the supreme irony, making him observe that an image of reality and an appearance of it coincided in the same object. It was his mind only, with its consciousness of time which engaged vanity in the catastrophe of desire, that drew distinctions. Fearing he had become trapped among subtle illusions, he was anxious to leave the island and to take Herminia where he had last seen Mariana and thus be able to grasp a past moment and to will the future that had already happened to cancel itself out as being nothing more than a chain of events projected as a hypothesis of happiness but then rejected for containing too strong an element of improbability.

But Roberto was saying, "If, as you say, you were born here and have seen nothing of the world, may I make a small request? All I ask for is a little tour. I should hate to lose the opportunity of having the only surviving native of this island show me its main points."

He threw Herminia an ingratiating smile, but Federico complained, "How can you be so stupid, Roberto? These people have been waiting for years to leave and now that the hour has come you want to prolong their wait! That's cruel, to say the least."

"Oh, another hour or two won't matter," Herminia said, taking Roberto's side, instinctively expressing an allegiance on noticing a latent antagonism between the two men.

"And I say no!" Federico insisted. "We have work to do. The sooner we can deal with your problem the better."

"You forget, Federico," Roberto remarked coolly, "*I* am the geologist, and I can't think of a better preparation for my work than to be given a tour of the island by someone who knows it."

"Oh, come off it, you're only seeking to delay working." Federico did not know how else to state his objection.

"That's an insult, Federico, but as these good people are my witness, I shall not lose my temper as easily as you have lost yours. And for no good reason at all!"

Having thus established that he was a reasonable man, Roberto looked at Gamboa and said, "Why don't *you* resolve this question? Is it too much to ask for a little tour before we take you back?"

But Herminia intervened, saying, "It's nothing, an hour more here. Why quarrel about it?" She felt as if she had to defend Roberto against the older man's attack.

"Well?" Roberto said to Gamboa.

Gamboa quietly stared at the two men, stood up ponderously, and slowly walked out of the hut, deep in thought. The repetition of Federico's name had provoked a buried memory within him that yet remained elusive, and he felt troubled. Coming out in the bright sunlight, he suddenly saw in his mind an ill-lit street and then the headlights of a car illuminating youthful lovers at the entrance of a building and he remembered the Federico he had violently torn away from his daughter.

"Well, have you decided?" Herminia's voice reached him, and he saw that the three had come out of the hut. He stared at Federico and then at his daughter. At last he spoke in an answer to Roberto and Herminia.

"There's a third person on the island, more animal than man. When we saw your boat coming into the bay, I found a pretext to send him away. That was cruel, an unpardonable mistake. We have a chance to right the wrong. Why don't the two of you go and find him?"

Before Federico could think of an objection, Roberto and Herminia had begun to walk up the hill, and Gamboa, gesturing to the stone bench where he used to sit with Domingo Maturana, was saying to him, "Let's sit down here while we wait."

From a distance the two figures seemed to Federico to be scampering up the hill like two children released from school. He grieved that while he had rediscovered Mariana, she had yet to see him as Federico, obliging him to wait until she had exhausted the adopted role of Herminia and reverted to the self she had as Mariana. He went to the bench where Gamboa had already sat down and said, "You should not have trusted your daughter with that man."

"I had a daughter once whom I trusted," Gamboa said, and even before he could pronounce her name his words caused Federico's blood to surge to his brain.

"I never saw her again after that night you parted us in the street," Federico spoke in a low voice, holding his head in his hands. "Never, never." He wanted to add, "Until now." But he waited to hear from Gamboa what must be an incredible revelation.

"Nor I after that weekend."

Now the two looked at each other, seeing in the other's face the features of the outcast, the sadness of infinite exile marked there by his birth, and before each could tell his story, both understood the havoc of destiny that came disguised as accident, error, and coincidence.

Roberto paused at the top of the hill and turned to look down on the bay which presented a picturesque sight from that height, and his eyes, following the curving line of the beach up to the road and from there to the cottages, saw the two men sitting on the bench, and he said to Herminia, "Where do you think we're likely to find this Baltazar?"

"I know his favorite spot," she answered. "It's not far from here, some muddy pools, he lies on their edge for hours at a time."

"This place is so beautiful," Roberto remarked, continuing to walk. "I tell you what. Let's make your Baltazar's favorite spot our *last* stop. I want to see *your* favorite spots first."

They had come over the top of the hill, out of view of the bay and the cottages. She took a childish sort of pleasure showing her things to a new friend. "That'll take hours," she said, "days actually, if we saw everything."

"What's an hour, or two or three hours?" he said, stopping to look at her face as he spoke. "When I gaze into your eyes, it's as if time didn't exist. Don't you think when people are happy with each other as we are, nothing else matters?"

She understood that he had paid her a compliment and had an instinctive recognition of his real meaning, and walked on, a little confused as to what she should think. He saw the slightly disturbed expression in her eyes as she turned away, and quickly walked up to be next to her, reflecting with inward pleasure that she was so inexperienced and naive he would only need to make a couple more trite advances, like the cheap shot about her eyes that appeared already to make an impression on her, and he would have her. It was going to be his fastest conquest yet. He looked at his watch and made a bet with himself, thirty minutes and she was going to be crying with pleasure in his arms—okay, Roberto, here we go!

He looked around for a likely place that offered seclusion, shade, and a little grassy area to lie down upon. They had reached a field covered with pink flowers but the ground from which they sprouted was hard and rocky.

"You know," he said, putting his hand to her arm, squeezing it softly, and releasing it, "if you had lived in the city all these years and came here, you'd think you'd come to paradise. Especially," and he held her arm just below the elbow and kept his hand there, "when you found there someone so perfectly beautiful you realized everyone else had been a fake copy."

She felt his hand slide down the length of her forearm and move slowly up toward the elbow again, a slight pressure from his fingertips creating a pleasant sensation. "I've been told of all the lovely things in the city," she remarked.

"Have you also been told about love?" he asked, dropping his hand to hold hers.

She stopped and looked boldly into his eyes. He raised his

other hand and placed it on her shoulder, coming closer to her, seeing behind her some bushes in the near distance toward which he thought he should soon begin to guide her. "I've been *told* so much," she said. "One day I will know, and then I will be able to *choose*."

"But that day has come!" he cried eagerly, moving slightly closer to her, deciding that any more roundabout talk was a waste of time. "Fate has chosen for you." Lowering his voice to a whisper and moving closer still, he added, "My beautiful Herminia, all our past was a dream from which we have awoken for this moment, this enchanting moment of truth." He let go of her hand in order to put his arm around her shoulder, but in that moment she stepped back and turned away from him.

"How can you be so certain of what fate has chosen for me?" she asked. "That friend of yours, that other man, Federico, who's so quiet, what about him?"

"You can't be serious," Roberto said, coming up to her. "He's so much older than you."

She remained quiet, and he changed the subject, asking, "What are those bushes? They seem to have pretty flowers on them. Can we go and have a look?"

She turned her face toward the bushes and stared at them for a long moment. She had long learned to read the shadows among which Baltazar lurked, and although to any other eye the prospect was only one of spiky leaves and small yellow flowers in terraces of light and shade on the undulating land, she could see Baltazar there as clearly as one can a fish in transparent water. So, he was not on the edge of the muddy pools but following her. Just as well, she thought, for in that moment her intuition made plain to her Roberto's intentions, bringing her the knowledge of human corruption and of the arrogance of male conceit which displayed an outward dashing form, expressing itself in a sweet flattery. When she had first seen him with Federico, she could have hugged the two men for coming to rescue her from her solitude and had immediately found them the handsomest men she had ever seen; but in the short time she had been acquainted with them, she was already beginning to perceive subtle differences of character and to have a sense of their rivalry that made one quiet and morose and the other an aggressive seeker of opportunity, and the expectancy of happiness that she had experienced on first seeing them was already becoming dissipated. An obscure awareness was seeping into her mind, which was perhaps only a fear of the unknown, that the world she hoped to gain might cause her to regret the loss of the world she possessed.

"We can't go there," she said, seeing the still shadow that was Baltazar, and moved away in a direction opposite to the bushes. "There's an albatross nest there."

"That's too far inland," he said, coming up to her and again holding her arm.

"No, only some thirty meters from the cliff. They make their nests where they're protected from the wind." She shook her arm to free it of his hand and began to walk faster.

Breathless from trying to keep up with her, he found it difficult to think of an arresting proposal until, coming to the area of the old ash pits where clumps of vegetation grew on the rims of the large circular hollows that had been dug in past years to extract the nitrate and were now full of muddy water, he said, "Can we rest for a few minutes? This city boy is not used to such vigorous hiking."

"Be careful where you step," she said. "Some of that mud is soft, and the mud in those hollows is liquid."

The path on which they walked was spongy, and he saw that on either side of it the ashen earth was a dark gray with black areas on it still damp from recent rains, and a little beyond that the pools looked like great chunks of obsidian. She was striding ahead of him, having decided after discovering that she did not want his ardent companionship that she should cut across to the cliff and take a shortcut back to the cottage, and he looked up to where she proceeded energetically up an incline and doggedly followed her. At the top was the tree where she used to bring her father his lunch, and, reaching it, she waited for Roberto who appeared to her comical as he labored up the slight slope. Behind him, among the hollows of the ash pits where the high sun caused them to appear alternately a bright whitish gray and solid black, she saw a shadow slip behind a rock and knew that Baltazar was keeping on their trail.

Roberto reached her, panting and sweating, and, finding the ground beside the tree grassy and smooth, sat down, saying, "I hope you know a shortcut back. I'm dying of thirst."

She looked down upon him, amused by his discomfort, and said mockingly, "I thought you wanted to see the sights."

"Well, sit down and point them out to me."

She remained standing and, raising her chin, spoke in a clear voice that she knew would carry across the hollows. "We must find Baltazar and tell him we want to take him on the boat. He is to come with us."

"Aren't there any springs here?" he asked. "A drop of water somewhere?"

She laughed and said, "How simple you are! You wanted so much to see the island, and now all you can think of is water."

He suspected that she did not mean simple, but weak, and realized that he was losing what he believed to be his advantage over her. Looking at his watch, he saw that he was close to losing his bet with himself. He stood up quickly and walked to her, saying, "Oh, it's all right, I can wait till we get back." He held her hands, standing in front of her, and, adopting an ardent manner, added, "A little thirst, hunger even, I can bear anything when I have you."

She pulled away her hands and stepped back, for she had discovered within herself an admonitory voice that cautioned she keep her distance from him. Only so short a time ago, when she had excitedly walked away from the hut with Roberto, she had possessed a natural spontaneity that allowed her to act uninhibited by thoughts of right or wrong; the absence of temptations in her simple world had not required her to develop a moral faculty and in the naivety of ignorance she had enjoyed a crude freedom; but in this short time, while a part of her behaved as her former self, there was a good portion of her mind being rapidly instructed by instinct and being permeated by civilized behavior as if it were a virus she had contracted from the coming of the outsiders. She was beginning to dislike Roberto's little declarations, and thought of Federico, whose outburst, when he had tried to prevent Roberto from going with her, had seemed to her the flaring of an older man's envy but now struck her as a kind of warning. He had been so quiet when they were eating, and she had twice caught him glancing shyly at her. As she stepped back from Roberto, the thought of the restrained Federico made him appear the more cultured of the two, his quieter manner contrasting pleasantly with Roberto's brashness and assertiveness. The odd thing now, however, was that she could not remember what Federico looked like, and in that moment's attempt to recall his face her imagination created the figure of a dark, melancholy, but terribly attractive, man. She decided they must return to the hut at once.

"What's this?" Roberto demanded. "You said the view from the cliff was spectacular, we haven't even got there and you already want to return." He assumed an expression of disappointment and of being let down.

"Father will be getting worried, and besides you're not used to this land. You're dying of thirst, you just said."

"But the view from the cliff, at least that!"

"Oh, that's on the way, let's go!" She made to walk off briskly.

"Oh, come on," he said, grabbing her arm and forcefully pulling her toward him, having resolved that in the deserted island there was no difference between an open space and a secluded spot—each offered the same privacy.

"No!" she cried aloud in a screaming voice. "Let me go!"

He held her tightly with both his hands and attempted to kiss her. She shook her head, turning it away from his face, crying, "Stop it, let me go! No, I said, *stop* it!"

Holding her strongly at the back by his right arm, he caught her head with his left hand and stopped its rapid motion. He pressed his mouth to her cheek and tried to turn her head so that he could possess her lips. She brought her hands to his chest and pushed him with all her strength. Freeing herself from his embrace, she made to run, but he, recovering quickly from a moment's imbalance, rushed at her and, grabbing her by the waist, knocked her to the ground. She screamed when her head hit the ground but he flung himself at her and, pinning down her flailing arms, again tried to kiss her. She began to kick her legs in order to extricate herself from under his weight. He was now in a rage of lust and succeeded in clasping his mouth to hers, and, believing she would become passive and submissive as soon as he could deploy his unfailing technique, he freed one of her arms to press his hand on her breast. She threw up her hand to his head and pulled his hair. Obliged to let go of her breast, he slipped to his side as he tried to grasp her waist. She rolled a little away from him, but he, both his hands now at her forearm above his head, rolled back with her and the momentum took him right over her until he was flat on his back and she on the top of him. She pounded his chest with her fists and then, realizing that she was no longer pinned down and noticing also the shadow that had fallen across the ground, quickly stood up. He raised himself on his elbows and was about to fling himself up when he froze, the emotion of lust at once replaced by one of terror.

Baltazar stood a few paces from him, his arms held up above his head, a large rock between his hands. Herminia drew back and looked away. Roberto stared at the unfamiliar beast slowly advancing upon him; his mouth hung open, but the cry of terror choked in his throat, his body anchored to the ground disregarded the command of his will to rise and confront his enemy, Roberto helplessly watched the monster grow as he approached nearer.

Herminia kept her eyes away and scarcely flinched when she heard the crash of the rock against the skull and the loud cry released by Roberto's throat a second before and seeming to continue, pouring out of his body with his blood. She began to walk away, breaking into a short run, then walking hastily, then running again. When she looked back, she saw that Baltazar was dragging Roberto's body by his feet down the slope toward one of the hollows of the ash pits. She stopped and watched him pull the body to the edge of the hollow where he pushed it into the soft mud. Stepping into the mud himself, he pushed the body to where the mud was a thick, black oozy liquid, where it slowly sank.

Federico and Gamboa had told each other their stories and sat in silence, each disturbed in his mind by the remembrance of his and the other's improbable past; neither could believe that the events that constituted for each his life possessed a discernible logic, and yet, unwilling to see himself as the victim merely of chance, each was obliged to posit the further belief that some profound mystery had designed the events with some as yet unknown end as the final resolution of meaning that would come as a revelation. The fact that they had been brought together in an extraordinary and unexpected way seemed to the two men an indication of some remarkable coincidence of destiny that was perhaps readying itself to spring an unimagined surprise. But, for the present, there was no release from ignorance: the mind remained perturbed by foreboding, fearful that the imminent revelation might only be a joke in bad taste.

They were startled to see Herminia coming running down the hill, and before they had risen from the bench she was standing in front of them, her hair dishevelled, her cheeks begrimed and her frock covered with dirt. Her face trembled as though her teeth chattered with cold; her eyes looked wildly at the two men. "What happened?" Gamboa cried, and Federico, in the same moment, asked, "Where's Roberto?"

She looked down and began to flick at the dirt on her frock. Then she raised her head and fixed a long stare at Federico. "Herminia," her father said in a pleading voice, "what happened?"

She went and sat down on the bench, her knees well apart, her hands clasped between them, the fingers intertwined, and head bowed. "We were looking for Baltazar near the old ash pits when Roberto . . ." She paused, looked up at Federico and then at her father, and lowering her head again continued: ". . . suddenly grabbed me by the shoulders and tried to kiss me. I struggled and managed to get out of his embrace. But he threw me down on the ground, fell on me."

Gamboa flinched; a sudden pain seemed to stab Federico's chest.

"He was crushing me with his weight. I fought to get out from under him. He got madder and madder. I was crying to him to stop, to let me go. But he was pressing down on me, his hands holding my arms, his knees dug into my thighs to prevent me from kicking my legs. He freed one hand to put it all over my body, to squeeze what he could grab of my flesh. He was too mad to think of anything but what he wanted from me."

"Where is he now?" Gamboa spoke aloud, filled with anger by his daughter's account.

"He was off balance for a moment," Herminia went on. "I succeeded in pushing him off, but he swung himself back with such force that he rolled over me. A large rock lay to the side. Just when he was over me, I gave him a hard push, and he fell to my other side. His head struck the rock and he went still. I stood up. Shaking, boiling with anger. He began to stir, to moan, holding his head. Then he saw me and that mad look came to his eyes again. He made to move, looking madder than before. He was going to attack me again. He began to rise and I could see that he was determined not to let me go until he'd got what he wanted. And then quickly, before he was on his feet again, I found myself running to the rock. I don't know how it happened. What came over me, what gave me the strength. I don't know. But I picked up the rock and smashed his head with it. Broke his skull. Killed him."

Now Gamboa came and sat next to her and put his arm around her shoulder. "Feel no remorse," he said tenderly. "You did right, you did absolutely the right thing, O my poor, brave daughter!"

Federico came and stood near them and said, "We'll bury him, and when we get to the city I'll report an accident."

But Herminia had not finished her story. "Just nearby, one of the old ash pits is full of thick liquid mud. I dragged his body and pushed him into that black grave. I don't know why I did that. I was mad. I was very mad."

Federico was shocked by what he heard. He felt no sympathy at all for Roberto, but was astonished by the young girl's swift and complete revenge and imagined it must be the work of pure instinct in one who had never been exposed to civilized ideas.

"There is no reason to detain ourselves on this island," Gamboa said after a short silence.

"First we'll have to go and pull out Roberto's body from that muddy pit," Federico said. "How deep is it?"

Herminia looked at him in alarm and heard her father say, "What, just to bury him again!"

"I wish never to see him again," Federico responded, "but

we have no choice." He pointed to the boat far down to their right and added, "That boat won't start without an ignition key. And that key happens to be in Roberto's pocket."

Gamboa noticed that Federico's disclosure made no impression on Herminia; she who had been so exultant on seeing the boat arrive seemed unconcerned that her deliverance was to be delayed. The poor girl must be suffering from an unbearable shock, he reflected, her innocent mind forced to perceive the vileness of man and then persuaded to commit murder in self-defence, all in so short a time that she could not be expected to have a sense of her present reality. His own reaction to the news of the missing key, that another outrage had been inflicted upon him by chance, replacing what had appeared to be a certain liberation with a prolonging of an uncertain future, painful though the thought was, had quickly been succeeded by his anxiety for Herminia, for her liberation, more than his own, was what really mattered, and now his poor girl was in a daze of horror. He was stricken by grief that she should have been subjected to such suffering from one moment to the next. When he had given her and Roberto the excuse to go away together, he had not been blind to the importunate young man's flirtatious gestures, but he had decided not to be the father he had been to his other daughter, not to be in the way of her natural inclinations, and had been persuaded also by the thought that when they returned to the mainland it would be to a life of poverty unless some miracle were to occur, and therefore a promising relationship with a suitable young man was not to be discouraged. He realized now that his selfish calculation, especially as it was based on no knowledge of the young man's character, was the direct cause of her suffering; his guilt intensified when he remembered that the excuse he had given them, to go and find Baltazar, had been a lie, his humane concern for Baltazar a sham, for he despised that creature who too precisely represented in his mind the idea of life given to a deformed body for no other purpose than the infliction of humiliation and pain, a grotesquely caricatured image of himself. Had he only taken Federico's side and insisted on immediate departure, they would all have been on San Bernardino by now!

"You need to rest," he said to Herminia, not knowing what words could console her and draw her away from the horror in her mind.

But she surprised him with the firmness of her voice. "No, we must do what we have to. There's no point in prolonging the delay."

Federico, too, was struck by her cool determination. She had the same spirited manner as Mariana, forthright and decisive. It seemed incredible to him that she should have experienced what she just had and not be shattered by it, but instead be showing more resolution than either of the two men. Silently they began to walk up the hill, their feet scarcely making any sound on the ashen dust of the road.

She showed them the rock where it still lay, the blood on it not quite dry. Federico was amazed to see how large it was. Too heavy certainly for a girl of Herminia's age. But perhaps fear gave one the strength one did not normally possess. He saw the great quantity of blood that had flowed on the ground. The image must have registered on his mind at that moment, but the force of it would only strike him later, that while there was so much blood on the gound and on the rock itself there was not a stain upon Herminia's person or her dress.

They came to the edge of the hollow and she pointed to where Roberto's body had been sunk. Gamboa stared at the black mud. "That's two to three meters deep," he said. "I don't know what we're going to do."

Herminia had seen Baltazar's shadow and knew he crouched behind a distant rock. She realized what he must understand in his simple way as he saw her point to where Roberto had been killed and where sunk, that she was explaining to them what she had seen him, Baltazar, do. And so she threw her hands to her face and cried aloud, "Oh, I wish I had not killed him, I wish I had not killed him!"

Gamboa quickly stepped up to her and held her in his arms, saying, "My poor darling, you are not to blame."

She hoped Baltazar understood what she meant. All her life he had been a figure of ridicule or an object of exaggeratedly condescending sympathy, and yet, now that she had observed the benevolence of his animal nature, she feared there might be emotions within his primitive breast which had bred in his mind an inexplicable terror, and therefore she believed she owed him a restorative understanding. But her feigned hysteria on his behalf released an emotion within her that had earlier remained blocked, that of a fear of what life held for her, and she began to sob.

"No, my sweet, dear child," her father whispered in her ear, "you have done no wrong, no angel in heaven is more innocent than you."

Federico was greatly moved and, touched almost to tears himself, turned away. He noticed then that the hollow in which Roberto's body lay was divided by a ridge from another next to it, but that the latter was lower and seemed to be shallow, judging by the mud, which was gray and slightly cracked in places and not liquid black as in the former. When Herminia appeared to have recovered somewhat and he could impose upon Gamboa's attention, he pointed to his observation and said, "Suppose we dug a channel across the ridge, wouldn't the liquid mud flow down into the lower hollow?"

The only tools on the island were two pickaxes and a quantity of hoes. One of the wheelbarrows, abandoned when there was no longer the need to transport nitrate to the beach, was still serviceable, not having rusted through. And with these implements Gamboa and Federico began the following day to dig a channel between the liquid-mud-filled hollow in which Roberto's body lay and the lower one with its bed of nearly dried mud. It was very slow work. The softer, but not liquid, mud formed a solid wall around the hollow and had to be dug out and carried away. It was dangerous working in that area for the soft mud appeared to be solid and in the eagerness to get the job done it was tempting to step upon it. The only sensible way in which to do the work was for one man to make cautious advances upon the soft mud while the other, a length of rope in hand for an emergency, carefully observed the operation. It took them two days of digging to form a long enough channel for the stagnant mass of the thick liquid mud to begin to trickle toward the channel. At this point they realized that they would need to make the channel at least two meters deep if the bulk of the mud was to move, and that at the same time they needed to keep the farther end of the channel dammed up to prevent the flow of liquid mud from interfering with their digging. The compacted mud a quarter of a meter below the surface was surprisingly hard and it took them two more days to reach the depth they thought necessary before bursting the dam.

They worked long hours, from soon after sunrise to sunset. Herminia brought them boiled eggs and goat's milk for their lunch and stayed with them in the afternoon, insisting on at least being the one who stood watching with the rope if they would not let her perform any labor. During these times and in the evenings when they sat outside the hut after the meal, Federico found himself reflecting on the years he had lost and wondering whether the reincarnation of Mariana in Herminia was not indeed a second chance at life. Seeing that she was still obviously in a state of shock from her recent awful experience, he dared not make any advance but hoped that she would naturally form an affection for him. He had, he believed, won Gamboa's trust by showing himself to be selfless in the arduous labor he performed, and perhaps, he imagined, she too was touched by his working for her freedom.

On the fifth day they burst the dam. At first nothing happened. Then the liquid mud appeared to heave slowly. Federico ran to a tree and tore the longest branch that he could reach and, returning to the hollow, attempted to agitate the mud. Sluggishly it moved. They stood staring at it for fifteen minutes. A thin line of mud made for the channel and, like glue on the rim of a jar, began to trickle down toward the lower hollow, sticking to the side before reaching the bottom. But a little later a larger mass entered the channel, sucking behind it a still larger quantity, and suddenly the mud began to flow as smoothly as oil. Federico almost gave a cry of triumph but, noticing that Herminia stared apprehensively at the center of the hollow, restrained himself. For nearly an hour they watched the mud flow evenly and its level fall by a good two meters. Then the flow became a trickle and soon ceased altogether, for the surface of the mud had reached the floor of the channel.

"We should nearly be to the bottom," Gamboa said. "Maybe there's another meter in the center, but not half that depth for most of the hollow."

"There's only one way to find out," Federico said, taking the rope from Herminia and tying it round his waist.

"You're not going to walk into it!" Herminia exclaimed in an alarmed voice.

"Only one small step at a time," Federico said, flinging the end of the rope to Gamboa.

He gingerly eased his way down the side of the hollow where he thought the mud was hard and dry. But it was deceptively damp and his heels sank through the surface and he found himself knee deep in the slimy substance.

"I don't think that's a good idea at all," Herminia commented.

Federico pulled his right foot out and took a tentative step, his foot breaking the surface with a squelch. The sensation he felt as his leg cut through the slime was one of utter revulsion, but he clenched his teeth and completed the action. Still no more than knee deep. He took a step with his left foot. Three or four more similarly cautious steps and the mud was above his knees.

"I think that's enough, you should come back," Herminia called to him. He rather enjoyed hearing her concerned voice and threw her a brave smile.

"If the center is not much deeper, we should be able to find the body," he said, staring at the black mass in front of him.

His next two steps, a fraction longer than the earlier ones, brought the mud a little way up his thighs but caused no problem. He pushed his right foot forward again and slowly lowered it, seeking the solid bed, but it was not where he had anticipated it would be and, in the expectation that in the next millimeter his foot would land upon it, he continued to lower his foot until his trunk was bent forward, and, before he could check himself, his left foot had involuntarily risen from the ground as he tried to keep his balance. He went crashing head first into the mud. Herminia screamed. Gamboa pulled at the rope. Federico was dragged back a little, and the action of his trunk being snapped back by the rope brought his head out of the mud and let his now vertical body sink until his feet hit the ground. The mud came up to just below his chin. He looked around, his eyes wild with fear.

"Hold that rope," Gamboa cried to him.

"Oh, for God's sake, come out!" Herminia shouted.

Federico turned himself and, finding the rope where it held him under the mud, caught it in both his hands. After three or four steps, which seemed to take a terribly long time, he had risen to the higher gound where the mud was below his waist. When he finally climbed out of the hollow, they decided to return to the hut for the day. The channel needed to be deeper. They would resume the next day.

During all those days Baltazar had watched them at their labor. He kept to himself and understood things in his own crude fashion. Only Herminia knew where he was but she never revealed the fact. She knew too that he would sneak away to the hut in the afternoon to find food for himself and so she deliberately left something for him. It was almost as if she was conniving with him to keep their secret, and she worried that he might not understand that he himself had nothing to fear.

Baltazar watched with wonder Federico's attempt to wade into the liquid mud and saw the three go away a little later. He came down from behind his distant rock and squatted on the edge of the hollow, staring at the spot where he had pushed the body into the mud. Had Federico entered the hollow from two paces farther to the left he would have stepped right on it. Baltazar could not comprehend why they were trying to dredge up the body. His rudimentary knowledge of the world around him was little more than the functioning of raw emotions within him, principal among them fear. Some mysterious dread attended the drowned body. He had heard Herminia's words but remained puzzled, not having the capacity to interpret the motives of others. No explanation penetrated his brain but it enlarged the area of his ignorance and intensified his fear.

He darted up from where he sat on his haunches and then, standing bent with his hands on his knees, stared at the sucking, hissing sound coming from the channel which had made him jump. The earth there was loose, and while the mass of liquid mud had appeared to remain stagnant after its level had been lowered, some of it was forced by pressure to trickle into the channel, gradually loosening the earth there; and now the force had dislodged a good quantity of earth which, even as Baltazar stared at it, moved forward as a lump and created a wider passage for the mud to flow through. The continuous black flow carried the earth with it and after half an hour the channel had deepened and the liquid mud began to pour through it. An hour later, as, amazed and terrified, Baltazar stood watching, the outline of Roberto's body appeared on the dark surface.

The mud ran out of the channel. Baltazar had sat all afternoon hypnotized by its flow. The body, thick with black slime as though wrapped in a sheet of black plastic, lay a few paces from the edge of the hollow. Baltazar looked over his shoulder where the slightly rising undulating land led to the cliff. The sun was low, near to setting. He slipped down from the edge and entered the hollow. He held the body by its ankles and pulled it out with some difficulty, for it was heavy and slippery. Looking around, he saw the rope lying where Federico had dropped it. Securing the body with the rope, Baltazar found that he could easily drag it along the ground.

He arrived at that part of the cliff from where he knew there was a sheer drop into the ocean. From here the large birds took off into the wind. He untied the rope. The sun was touching the horizon, its great eye throwing across the water a red beam which, spreading out over the ocean, transformed the blue to a vibrantly glowing violet. Baltazar stared at the sinking sun; then he pushed the body over the cliff. It dropped straight down the enormous depth. The water burst into a large flower where the body hit it and then, almost immediately, calm returned to the surface where the violet now turned an inky purple, the sun having set.

Herminia came to the hollow the next morning with the two men. When they had somewhat recovered from the shock of what they saw, Federico asked her, "Are you certain it was in this hollow that you threw the body?"

"It had to be," she answered, looking up at where the rock lay which had killed Roberto, and Federico, following her gaze, understood that it was the shortest distance between the two points.

The soft slimy mud that covered the floor of the hollow

had kept no evidence of someone stepping across it, but she had observed, which the others had not, the muddy smears on the rim, confirming what she had already guessed.

"But the body can't vanish just like that," Gamboa said.

"Either it was not put into this hollow," Federico speculated, "or, if it was, it was taken out of it. On the other hand," he paused, pursuing a new thought, "when the mud broke through after we left, we don't know with what force it flowed. Could it not have carried the body with it?"

"It's possible," Gamboa conceded.

"It *has* to be!" Herminia agreed emphatically. "There's no other explanation."

"In that case, we have a problem," Federico said, looking at the lower hollow which was now filled with the mud. "There's no way we can empty all that. We could be at it for weeks and not get anywhere."

They returned to the hut. Herminia thought she would go to Baltazar and try to find if there were not some way to make him communicate to her what he had done with the body. The poor creature must live in terror. Was that why she was trying to protect him? She could not have answered to her motives. Her excitement at the prospect of being liberated had died and been replaced by a despair, or perhaps a diffuse sorrow that she could not understand, but she was filled with a resentment for the world beyond the ocean that had sent to her simple life only elements of viciousness. Hurt by the thwarting of her expectations, she reacted with a suppressed anger that took the form of hating what she could not possess. But she kept her anger to herself, and her father, seeing her embittered face and interpreting that to be sadness born of frustration, suffered deeply for her. Coming down the road and seeing the boat anchored in the bay, he said in a low voice, "Why do I continue to be punished at every turn?"

"We were due back in the city by today," Federico said. "They are bound to send out a search party in another week. We'll be all right."

"I must wait, always wait," Gamboa mumbled to himself, but kept the excess of his self-pity and raging despair to himself so that his body boiled with indignation and by that afternoon he had taken to his bed with a fever, his brain affected by an exquisite delirium.

Federico could think of nothing to say when he found himself alone with Herminia. "A search party is bound to come soon," he had repeated, but she had not appeared cheered by the consolatory words, and he was unable to utter the many thoughts that had come to his mind. He wanted so much to tell her that she represented the salvation of his life, that without her he saw no living reality for himself, for only she could restore the past he had squandered and give to him the only future that could have any meaning. But he dared not speak a word of this, knowing that while he saw in her the Mariana he loved she must surely see him not as the Federico whom Mariana had eagerly drawn to her embrace but as an older man from whose lips any declaration of love was very likely nothing more than the seizing of an opportunity to seduce an innocent young girl. And even if she listened to him seriously, without her mind being prejudiced by what she had already experienced with Roberto, he feared that she would state objections that had not occurred to him and thus prevent a relationship that might otherwise naturally grow between them. For this reason he was not unhappy to be stuck on the island. He was given time, but he must not precipitate the issue.

She went in the afternoon to look for Baltazar and after walking for two hours found him in the little cave above the ocean where she had often gone with her father. He had seen her coming and sat crouched in a corner. She held out a basket to him, saying, "Some bread. Some eggs. *Eggs*," she repeated, holding one out. She placed the basket near his feet.

Some bedclothes that she had herself given him some time earlier, taking them from the things abandoned by the islanders who had left, lay heaped on the ground. She realized that he had brought his few belongings to the cave after her father had exiled him from the settlement on the arrival of the two men; she must tell him that he could return to the hut he had occupied. Her father's state of mind, which she had observed becoming distracted long before the startling symptoms of a breakdown appeared, was such that he would not know, or knowing, care.

She took a pillow with a threadbare covering and placed it next to Baltazar to make a cushion for herself to sit on. He had begun to chew a piece of bread and was digging his thumbnail into the shell of an egg.

She did not believe he possessed a sense of right or wrong but nevertheless said in a gentle voice, "You did no wrong, you know that, don't you? You were only protecting me. You have been my friend ever since I was born, isn't that so? No one was looking to punish you. What was it then, fear, fear that the dead man would talk when we found him? That's why you took the body and dragged it to the cliff. Isn't that what you did?" She could tell from his look that she had hit upon the truth, and paused to reflect that they had lost the chance to escape and there was no telling when rescue from the mainland would come, if it ever did. "I know the signs you leave behind," she went on. "But that's all right. I'm no longer impatient to go. They'll come for us, the other tells us. They'll come sooner or later."

She talked on in her quiet, soothing voice. Baltazar had stopped eating and looked at her with eyes that appeared to her to be sad. She could not tell what he understood. Perhaps it was only the gentle tone of her voice that gave him a comforting sense of security and he listened enraptured as though he were a child being told a fairy tale full of mystery and wonder. And then he did a surprising thing. He moved up to her and placed his head on her thigh. She remained still, suppressing a moment's shock, and continued to talk. He turned, so that his cheek was against her thigh and his curled body on the floor beside her. He fell asleep as she talked. She put her hand to his head and stroked his fine hair. His breath came in an even rhythm.

In the evening, after the sun had set, Gamboa went out and sat on the bench. At first he attributed to the weakening light the fact that he could not distinguish things too clearly, but then he realized that his withdrawal to his room earlier in the day, lying sweating and being tormented by vivid dreams and a chaotic succession of voices, had not been a submission to the depression that overcame him after the failure to recover Roberto's body, not a benumbed resignation to his fate, but a symptom of illness, and he laughed bitterly to himself with the reflection that a search party would come in a few days, that he would be transported to the mainland, that rehabilitation would be at hand, only for him to die when that moment came.

Federico walked up from the beach where he had taken a swim and had gone into the boat to see one more time if he could not work the radio. All he could understand was how to switch on the power and turn the dial and hear a number of short-wave stations which went *squeak, peep-peep-pip* and burst into popular music or a news program, but though he played with all the knobs and checked the various wires coming from behind the radio, he could not discover how to use it to send a distress message. Seeing Gamboa on the bench, he went and sat next to him and described his frustrating attempts with the radio. "It's probably something very simple staring me in the face that I just can't see," he said. "It's very frustrating. I know a search party is bound to come. But if only I could work the radio, it would come sooner. This agony would be over."

Gamboa did not respond and Federico did not proceed with his attempt at conversation. But a few minutes later he was surprised to hear Gamboa say, "Yes, I forgive everyone." Federico looked at him and saw his head swaying as he said, "All the crimes committed against me, all the undeserved punishments, to everyone who stabbed my flesh and tortured my spirit, I say I forgive you."

Before Federico could ask him what he meant, Herminia came out from preparing the evening meal and announced, "We can eat soon." Federico stood up and she said to him, "Are you any good at gardening? We need to do some hard work soon. Otherwise we'll only have weeds to eat in another month."

"I hope we'll be rescued long before then," he said with a laugh calculated to discourage her pessimism.

"Maybe," she remarked. "But we mustn't count on it."

The next morning he worked with her in the vegetable and corn patches. Her fingers moved with remarkable agility and precision among the plants. He observed that her strong body was imbued with a strong spirit, a will that was not too easily going to bend to a purpose foreign to it.

Gamboa heard Herminia's distant voice telling Federico what to do and later in the day, when the two men sat on the stone bench outside the hut, Gamboa said, "Are you prepared to wait a few years?"

Federico stared at him, not understanding what he meant, and Gamboa added, "I will go and talk to your father. If you are serious, that is. The dear girl is so intelligent, she should go to college, don't you think? I have no objections, mind you, young people should do what they wish. An engagement at this stage would be proper, but not marriage. Let me discuss this with your father. What do you say?"

"That would be the correct thing to do," Federico answered in a calm voice, suppressing the shock he experienced.

Gamboa nudged him with his elbow and laughed. "Tell you what," he said, "let's not involve the mothers in this. They'll only mess things up. We'll keep it strictly a business among men, what do you say?"

"You have a good point there," Federico assured him.

"Do you know what comes after life?" Gamboa looked at Federico with great seriousness and then, his face about to burst with laughter, he answered his own question: "*An after life!*" His whole body shook with laughter and tears ran down his cheeks.

The next morning when he was again with Herminia in the vegetable patch, Federico said to her cautiously, "Have you noticed, your father's keeping to his room and comes out only at sunset. He doesn't seem to be able to tolerate bright light for some reason."

"It's worse than that," she said quietly. "He's very ill, and not only that, he's lost his mind."

Federico leaned on the hoe with which he was digging a furrow and said, "I'm sorry." She continued training a tomato plant on a stick she had embedded next to it, and he added, "I didn't realize you knew the worst of it."

"It's obvious a man's ill when he loses his appetite. Besides, he calls me Mariana and asks if I have passed my exams."

"And what do you answer?"

"That everything is coming out all right. It makes him happy when I say that, and he eagerly sips his chicken broth."

For the third consecutive afternoon he saw her go up the hill, along the ashen road, a basket in her hand, and, not having anything to preoccupy him, he decided to follow her when she had gone over the crest of the hill. He kept well behind her, frequently losing sight of her and having to guess in which direction she had gone. At one point he saw her walking in the far distance across a field covered with small pink flowers, and a succession of associations flickered through his mind—a landscape glimpsed from a train in Europe, a pointillist painting, an image of himself with Mariana in a field of pink flowers—which last was a memory of an imagined event and not of a real past experience, and he was startled by the sudden recollection that the image represented a fantasy held by his mind a long time ago and now, springing its precise occurrence in his present reality, obliterated the intervening time and seemed to suggest that he had immediate access to the gratification of his wish. It was not Gamboa but he who deserved to lose his mind, having squandered his years in a fantastic perversion, mortgaging his reality to purchase an illusion, for now that he believed he had come to his senses, he perceived how fragile and elusive was the present with the hope it offered, that it were best, should the image of this charming moment be shattered and its promise vanish, that the mind finally left holding nothing not suffer the ignominy of truth but bear it as the folly of a deranged vision. But seeing Herminia disappear as the land at the end of the field dipped down and then appear again on an incline, his soul was in ecstasy, a state he had entered when he first saw in her the form of Mariana, and he could not tell whether the ecstasy was a knowledge of the joy of paradise or the disguise of a mortal affliction.

He came to the high rocky western edge of the island. The land fell away in a sloping mass of large broken rocks cut cleanly by the wind and the ocean. Iguanas lay sunning themselves on the rocks. Farther down, the land ended abruptly in a massive cliff with a sheer drop to the ocean of some two hundred meters, and high above there an albatross floated in wide descending loops. He had seen Herminia disappear among the broken rocks. Something of a path was visible and he could detect the direction she had taken. Fearful of causing her displeasure, he decided to withdraw and return to the beach.

Herminia sat in the little cave, talking to Baltazar while he ate the food she had brought him. "Father's very ill, you know. I have to take care of him, too. The poor man has had so many shocks. I only hope they reach us in time. Then we can all go to our new life, wouldn't that be wonderful?" She glanced at his face and read his look to mean that he feared the change. "Oh, you will be all right, I will always be with you! There'll be so many people there who'll be our friends. We'll be a big family. You'll like that, won't you?" Her enthusiasm and encouragement did not alter his expression, and she added, "I know this is your home. Mine too, I suppose. All this ocean and sky. Sometimes I'm afraid of the life to come."

He came and curled up on the ground in front of her, placing his head in her lap, and she continued to talk to him, stroking his head, knowing that she talked more to herself, expressing the confusion in her mind which now longed for the life promised her and now feared the loss of the world she possessed.

Another four days passed with no sign of a search party coming for them. Although Federico's anxiety grew with the passing of each day, for he feared that some error back at the office, such as a simple failure of one department to communicate vital information to another, might lead to his indefinite incarceration on the island, the absence of a rescue boat nevertheless also relieved him, giving him more time in which to hope that Herminia would develop an attachment to him. He remained attentive to her and labored in the garden to make a good impression on her, but scrupulously refrained from giving her a hint of his enormous passion for her. He longed to clasp her in his arms and to tell her that he could have no life without her, that if she did not promise to be his then he would rather perish in the loneliness of the island than resume a miserable life on the mainland.

He saw her go away in the afternoon, up the hill with the basket in her hand. He wished he could call to her, have some wonderful news to give her which would fill her with joy and make her come rushing to embrace him. But as she

disappeared over the hill he was left with his empty mind
and idle body. He wandered down to the beach and waded
through the water to climb aboard the boat and to find there
something to do to pass the time.

Gamboa had not awoken that morning. Herminia had
patted his cheek and raised his head to compel him to take
some of the broth she held before him in a bowl. He had
swallowed a little and then fallen back, turning his head away
as though reluctant to nourish his body.

Federico turned on the radio in the boat. The cabin filled
with the crackle and hiss of static. He turned the dial and the
static was replaced by a muffled dialogue in Japanese. He
wondered if there were a Japanese fishing fleet in the area.
Not likely, he thought; illegal in these waters; but what if a
ship were just passing by on the other side of the island right
then? He stared at the radio and cursed it for not showing
him how to use it to send a message. Suddenly the Japanese
voices disappeared and a loud buzz took their place. Before
Federico could reach the dial, the buzz stopped and was
replaced by a popular Peruvian female vocalist singing a
recent hit. There was a lovely gaiety to her voice and a
lingering sensuousness to the cadences. Federico had the sensation of being caressed by her voice and leaned back with
his eyes closed. The song ended. Three notes sounded from a
trumpet, a clock struck twice, and a male voice began loudly
and rapidly to read the news. A political crisis in Bolivia. A
Soviet submarine incident in Swedish waters. A man had won
forty million dollars (the news reader emphasized the words
in an incredulous tone) in the Illinois state lottery. In soccer
news. . . But though the voice continued and was followed
two minutes later by a popular song, Federico heard no more.
His heart was louder in his ears and he could not believe what
he was staring at. It was six or seven days, he could not tell
exactly how many in that excited moment, since they had
abandoned the search for Roberto's body and he had been
coming every day to the boat and sitting right here trying to
work out how to send a message on the radio, and all that
time, right in front of his nose, had been the ignition key.
Roberto had never taken it out. Federico could not understand
how he had not seen it before. Now, having noticed it, it

seemed the most conspicuous thing in the cabin. He could not imagine that he had been so stupid as to believe that Roberto had taken it; perhaps he had seen him do so at some previous time and his mind had retained that recollection and mistaken the place where it had occurred. But for that error of memory they could all have been on the mainland by now! Instead, they had labored vainly for five days to recover Roberto's body, and the additional frustration and despair that had accrued had been enough to push Gamboa into a depression from which he did not appear likely to emerge sane, and God only knew what havoc had been wrought in Herminia's mind. "How stupid, how incredibly stupid!" Federico berated himself as he left the boat and hastened to gather the lost souls of the island.

He touched Gamboa's arm, shook it gently. "Can you hear me? I said the key, I found it, it's still there! We can go, do you hear?"

Gamboa opened his eyes and looked at him as from a great distance. "I ..." he said in a hardly audible voice, "your father ... he does not think ..." But he fell silent and his eyes took on a helpless look.

Federico left him and went in search of Herminia, thinking how impossible it would be to transport Gamboa to the boat if he could not walk. They would probably have to leave him and get men from San Bernardino to come and fetch him. But he did not want to think of this problem just now, anxious as he was to find Herminia and to give her the good news.

He was out of breath by the time he reached the top of the hill and decided to slow down his pace. After all the time that had been wasted, it was absurd to succumb to such desperate urgency. Expecting to find Herminia where he had followed her up beside the cliff, he proceeded at a steady pace. It was a two-hour walk from the hill. The time seemed long when he thought only of the happiness that would come over Herminia's face when he told her the news but it seemed to disappear when he was engrossed in other thoughts. From certain points on his walk he could see the ocean to one side and on the other the expanse of the undulating land of the island with its patches of pink flowers and the gray areas of volcanic ash. One rock near the path had cracks on it that shaped themselves in his mind into the form of an eye and he was reminded of the image on Popayan's shop window, instantly filling his imagination with a series of images of a complex association. All those years he had spent not daring to believe that Popayan had mysteriously transmitted to him a magical power and yet secretly hoping that his wishes would be granted; and the anxiety of not knowing whether the unfolding destiny, with its perplexing ambiguities that confounded rational speculation, was not what his life would have been without the intervention of magic; the events of all those years mocked him now and filled him with a new fear. He had made an evil bargain, he was convinced, thinking of Daniela, and how could he be certain that he had been released from the obligation to pay for other subsequent gratifications of his wishes, vile though the form of each success had been? He could not argue in his defence that never had he been gratified in the manner in which he desired. It was seeing the field full of pink flowers that most filled him with dread, for he remembered again once wishing to be in just such a place, and on an island too, with Mariana. The fact that Herminia was not Mariana did not console him, for in his mind she was more Mariana than Herminia. What if, now that he had the key to their escape, the evil that he had sold himself to still extracted a price and fate granted him one of his earliest wishes—killed off Gamboa, got rid of Baltazar, sank the boat, and said, "Is this what you wanted, Federico, a field of pink flowers and Mariana?" The idea which was once the perfect picture of paradise in his mind now struck him as the unendurable image of a hell he was about to fall into, and he began to repeat with his labored breath, "Herminia, Herminia," as if by obliterating Mariana's name he could invalidate that wish, a desperately superstitious chanting to exorcise the evil in case it still possessed him.

All was serene on the island. The iguanas lay motionless on the rocks. A solitary albatross floated high in the sky. Water spurted in bubbles among the rocks as if some subtle fermentation were in progress. He looked for a likely spot where Herminia might have ensconced herself and found it without difficulty, for a faint path was visible among the rocks. He saw the cave-like formation from some ten meters away and made for a high rock near it. Climbing up it gingerly, he crouched and looked into the cave. What he witnessed provoked an unexpected horror within him.

Herminia sat with her legs crossed, holding Baltazar's head in her lap. She seemed to be speaking to him but the words did not reach Federico. She rocked as she spoke. Federico turned his eyes to the ocean. He saw her on the day she had taken him and Gamboa to show them where Roberto had attacked her and she had killed him, and he perceived clearly now what his mind had then registered but what he had not seen at the time, that there were no bloodstains on her clothing, and he understood suddenly that Baltazar had been the killer. She was protecting him and had been coming every afternoon to offer him a strange kind of love in order to drive away the terrors from the unfortunate creature's mind. Federico looked into the cave again. Just at that moment she pulled up Baltazar's head to her bosom in a feverish gesture and rested her cheek against his forehead. Federico wanted to cry out to her that they were saved, that they could leave the island at once. But he crouched there, open-mouthed, unable to utter a word, staring at the spectacle that filled him with both fear and loathing. She lowered Baltazar's head to her lap again and resumed talking to him. Federico wondered whether the coincidence of her looking exactly like Mariana when she was sixteen was not a cunning forgery contrived by nature, for in that moment she appeared in his imagination to have become transformed to the likeness of Baltazar, an animal of the island, so that he had the passing conviction that her outer form was a deception. He had been a victim of the conceits of his mind before. He looked more intently. Loose strands of her hair hung on one side of her face as her head was bowed and the angle of the light cast a fine mesh of throbbing shadows on her cheek, giving to that part of her face a sudden loss of dimension and thus both thinning out and making more prominent the features that remained solid, with the nose unexpectedly elongated, so that Federico was reminded of an ibis. But then a slight shifting of her head threw the light fully on her face, and in the moment that the shadows vanished he saw first a round radiance and then the flashing of her eyes, as if a large cat had been alerted to the presence of her prey. Could it only be that she held Baltazar in her lap to console him? Or was there some passion peculiar to the natives of the island that was common to their blood and alien to his?

Federico withdrew from his observation, coming down from the rock, and began to walk back. Evening had fallen by the time he reached the hut where he found Gamboa's condition unchanged. Herminia arrived some twenty minutes later and he looked hard at her but could only see in her the features of Mariana. When he told her that they were free to go, her joy at the news was so spontaneous that he was prepared to believe that he had been deluded by what he saw in the cave. They decided to go to San Bernardino in the morning to fetch help so that her father could be transported to his country.

Federico knew how to operate the boat but he was an inexperienced sailor and had no knowledge of navigation other than to make straight for the visible distant destination, and when he set out with Herminia the next morning, they had not got out of the bay when, approaching the four whale-backed rocks, he ran into a submerged rock which tore out the underside of the boat and forced it to be thrown on its side. They crawled out of the cabin where water was already gushing in. Before he could reach for the lifejackets, she had already dived into the water, and Federico, grabbing hold of a lifejacket for himself and hastily putting it on, followed after her. The outer point of the curving bay was in fact less than thirty meters away and they gained it in a few minutes. The sea lions were barking in a loud chorus in the nearby cove and from their ledge on the rock at the opposite side of the bay a flock of birds had flown up as if on an urgent mission. Herminia had begun to walk over the rocks toward the beach. Federico stood for a few minutes, watching the boat sink, and then followed Herminia, and by the time he had caught up with her on the beach there was not a sign on the water, when he looked in the direction of the whale-backed rocks, of the boat sunk there.

Baltazar had seen their departure and now, hidden in one of the abandoned cottages, he observed their return.

Federico blamed himself for not looking where he was

going, but Herminia, though she despised him for his pitiable incompetence, did not accuse him of his failure, preferring in her anger to remain silent.

Gamboa was sitting up in bed when they reached the cottage and he said quietly to his daughter, "I could eat a little bread and a boiled egg." Herminia went to see if she could find any eggs and Federico, going to the vegetable garden, saw that the plants needed to be watered. Later in the day Baltazar, wearing only a strip of dirty cloth around his waist, brought a bundle of firewood and added it to the much diminished pile at the back of the cottage. Federico discovered that two goats had strayed into a corn patch; seeing him attempting to catch them, Baltazar slipped between two rows of corn and emerged a moment later, his arm tightly round a goat's neck. Federico saw an opportunity to catch the other goat and he leaped toward it, but though he succeeded in copying Baltazar's method and had his arm round the goat's neck, he found he did not have the strength to hold the creature. Baltazar tied his goat to a tree and returned to stalk the other one and quickly submitted it to the vice of his arm. He gestured to Federico to follow him and presently showed him a gap in the fence of the pen at the back of one of the abandoned cottages that Federico had made his own. In a short time Baltazar had found enough material in the discarded debris behind the cottages to improvise a provisional repair. A rooster flew up and perched on the fence, his head turned rapidly as if in a quick inspection of the captive goats; he retracted his neck and then flung it out, crowing loudly, and then jumped off the fence while redundantly flapping his wings, and scuttled off to where some hens and chickens were pecking at the ground. Baltazar looked at the hens. Federico watched him make some inscrutable deliberation and then seize a hen and kill it in an instant. His action was so quick that Federico did not precisely see what he had done. One moment Baltazar was lunging to the ground to seize the hen, the next he was sitting down and plucking its feathers. When he had finished and was turning the denuded bird about in his hands to examine his work, Herminia came out of her cottage and took it from him without showing any surprise but almost as if she had charged him to have a hen ready for her pot and had come out assuming that he would have completed the job. In the evening Gamboa expressed interest in the smells reaching him from the kitchen.

Herminia and Federico did not mention the loss of the boat in the weeks that followed. Gamboa recovered sufficiently to take an occasional stroll to the beach. He stared at the water, trying to make cohesive a disintegrated memory but, seeing nothing on the calm blue surface, concluded that he had only imagined that a boat had come to take him away. He seemed to Herminia to have regained his lucidity, but that was perhaps because he said so little. Baltazar, too, she believed to have recovered from the terror that had afflicted him. The shock of seeing her go, seemingly abandoning him, and then observing her return after the wreck of the boat appeared to have restored his sense of immediate reality, and the way he was constantly doing things for her gave Herminia the impression that he was expressing gratitude after his own fashion, though it could have been only a desire to remain close to her. But for that deep torment that none of them would speak of, that pain of unending exile, they appeared to be a happy little family. Federico and Baltazar each lived in a cottage of his own, and Herminia with her father, and the four went about the simple routine that had become established.

Having lost his possessions on the boat, Federico wore only a pair of shorts that had already frayed at the edges. His chest and shoulders were a very dark brown after weeks working under the sun, and black hair covered his face and hung from his head to his shoulders. Herminia, seeing him once at a distance in the faint light of the evening as he stooped to pick up something, momentarily mistook him for Baltazar but realized her error as soon as he stood erect. They had begun to share a companionship born of the need to keep the garden flourishing. No longer believing that he had access to his former life, he forced himself not to think of her as Mariana, even though, after the failure to leave the island, he dreaded suffering some unexpected irony that made him the victim of the very thing he might inadvertently have desired. Herminia still secretly hoped for present deliverance and, though she thought of him as a likable enough partner should her future offer her no escape from the island, she was too young to despair of an alternative, happier future, and therefore deliberately inhibited the development of any emotion. Federico misunderstood her reluctance to respond to any idea not connected with the garden or the goats and the chickens as an inability to express her feelings and was easily persuaded that the feelings must be too profound for her to be able to put into words, leading him to conclude that she must be in love with him without as yet her mind having a clear conception of her emotions. Why else should she sigh with such emphasis when he simply remarked that it was a fine day? He attributed her inability to respond with emotional warmth to her inexperience bred of long solitude. It did not occur to him, however, that he with all his experience of the world had no experience at all of love, and consequently it was impossible for him to realize that his interpretation of the young girl's feelings was not a true psychological perception but only a projection of what he himself would like her to feel. But believing that she must be in love with him, he had no doubt that he himself was in love, and in this he was like an adolescent who converts every sign in his own favor and yet is not bold enough to take the initiative and remains harrowed by fear that the girl might be outraged by even an innocent advance. It was the first time in his life that he had fallen in love, really in love, as he repeatedly told himself, deleting from his mind the idea that he had wished to rediscover the image of the girl he retrospectively believed he ought to have loved and, finding her likeness, was merely permitting a delusion to fulfill his fantasy. He thought that he had abandoned Popayan's magic, but his belief that he was in love was still a tacit belief in that magic and if he had examined his own mind closely he would have had to admit that his hope for success was really only a hope that the magic would serve him and that this time it would not, as with Daniela and the old women of West Palm Beach, answer his wish with a fraudulent twist.

Gamboa intuitively apprehended Federico's passion for his daughter but said nothing. He knew that Herminia was not Mariana but had difficulty dissociating the two, and sometimes even confused Herminia with Paulina. He had found Domingo Maturana's cane and supported himself on it when he walked, and sometimes, sitting with the cane in his lap, repeated half-remembered fragments of Maturana's speeches as if he talked to another Gamboa. You were a simple man. One of the hundreds of millions in this world. Hey, Felipe, you still there? He laughed softly to himself. Imagine being chosen for such a life, a real honor, eh? Another thousand contos a month. But do not make the mistake of thinking that this is uniquely your destiny. What nonsense you talk, Domingo! You have a complicated way of making a joke. I do not see your heart, nor with what trouble your blood flows through it. And do not memories that are not your own disturb your sleep? O Domingo, I am myself! The invisible wounds on your flesh. Who wove the shirt you wear that sets your skin aflame when you are cold? O Domingo! You loved my daughter and she's dead. My exile is eternal. How terrible to know that, what horror to live with the abomination of truth! We shall arrive at the doors of heaven as surreptitious aliens and be marked even there as undesirable residents, indulged perhaps for what we have suffered, but despised for our presumption to belong to the commonwealth of fulfilled souls. Domingo, I only wanted another thousand contos a month, I never hurt anyone, envied no man his wife, never questioned my rulers. Religion made the mistake of giving us revelations when its proper function was to keep us ignorant. Do you hear me, Domingo, my wishes were not excessive, I was without the sin of pride, did not lust after fame. Take this stick and beat me. After such knowledge. After such. So many selves that must be driven out of the body. But see if you cannot devise an anarchy to replace memory. Here, take this stick.

Herminia saw her father sitting by himself and heard the murmur from his lips and remarked his new habit of quietly laughing to himself. She was resigned to his incapacity to enter any sort of comprehensible dialogue, but their island life did not entail the exercise of more than a primitive mental power and therefore she was not too concerned by the apparent loss of his mind. She was touched to see Federico sit with him in the evenings and talk to him of their life in the city, a time so remote, and some details of which that she caught so puzzling, that it seemed like farfetched episodes from the history of a tribe long extinct, and in her own way of perceiving phenomena unknown to her of a place she had never visited she understood how ordinary events drew a person into improbable situations until his reality became unbearable. She looked at the horizon and imagined there was an invisible line there where fantastic forms skirmished in a ceaseless endeavor to invade and overwhelm commonly held beliefs. These thoughts were unformed, of course, coming to her only as vaguely sensed apprehensions, but she had inherited from her grandfather Maturana a sharply attentive mind and already comprehended that large abstractions, some of them intolerably obscure, lurked behind the simple succession of material facts. When the ship had taken away the inhabitants of the island, she was then mentally still a child and her cry of indignation and despair at the loss of a chance of freedom had been the reaction of one who confronts suffering for the first time; in the short time since then she had matured in excess of her years, having of necessity become an adult; two hours with Roberto and a fortnight nursing Baltazar and her father while she attempted to keep simple her relationship with Federico, knowing that it could not remain so, had given her insights normally purchased only after prolonged experience.

Baltazar looked in amazement at the hands that had held him and the bosom that had pressed against his head. She had exorcised the demon that had possessed his mind, but once released from the anguish he no longer had a memory of it. Bringing the firewood, he watched her in the green light of the vegetable garden; or taking the goats to their pen, he heard her voice as she talked to Federico. He wanted to place his head in her lap again and feel her warm cheek rest on his forehead. But the other man was ever present with her.

Federico was awakened each morning by Herminia's voice when she talked to the goats when she came to the pen behind his cottage to milk them. He watched her stealthily from one of the three narrow slits that served as windows, letting the sea breeze through but keeping the sun out. Seeing her milking the goats aroused his sexual passion, and though he could have wished for no greater happiness than to go and embrace her, he kept firmly to his resolve to refrain from expressing even a word of tenderness for fear that she would interpret his sincere feelings as the exuberant declaration of an opportunist. But there one morning came Baltazar.

She had just entered the pen and had not yet begun to milk the goats and was calling to one of them, *Come, Tatti, tippy-tippy milky-do,* clicking her tongue and snapping her fingers while the goat stared at her with apparent indifference, when she saw Baltazar. "I haven't milked them yet," she said, assuming that he had come to herd them to a pasture. But he came and stood in front of her and stared at her face with that quiet look of his which on a normal human being would be a calculated one of infinite sadness. "Why, what is it?" Herminia asked. Baltazar slowly raised a hand and softly touched her hair. "What do you want?" Her voice was gentle, solicitous, as if trying to elicit from a child a want it is unable to describe. His fingertips touched her cheek for a moment, his mouth hung open, his eyes stared. She took his hand in hers and said, "The bad dream has come back, is that it?" He moved closer and clasped her, placing his head on her shoulder. Federico, watching unseen from the window, was stricken by a sudden violence in his breast for he saw not a tormented creature that needed to be comforted but an animal no longer able to keep away from the object of his lust, recognizing in Baltazar's moves the very gestures he had himself rehearsed so often in his mind. But he heard Herminia say, "Come, enough of this, you're a confused little boy, aren't you?" Still believing that he was in need of consolation, she did not disengage herself from his embrace. Federico wanted to rush out and tear Baltazar away from her, but he remained frozen, unable to move, astonished that she should not push the revolting animal away from her body but instead continue to talk to him in a tender voice as if to a lover. Baltazar, his arms around her back, slipped down until his knees were on the ground and, clutching her tightly from behind, pressed his face to below her stomach. His animal lust nuzzled at her sex, Federico clearly saw, but still he could not move and realized that he could not do so because Herminia made no attempt to repel the beast. The pressure of his hands and the mouth panting below her evoked in her a sensation that touched off an alarming knowledge, as if another beast were within her, and shocked by what she felt, afraid of that internal tension, she bent down and put her hands forcibly on his shoulders to push him away. Doing so, she fell to the ground where he, a pure unrestrained beast now driven by animal hunger speedily to seize his opportunity, possessed and suddenly crazed by her smell, had her on her back in a moment, tore off the dirty cloth from around his waist and jumped on her. This was when she cried aloud, and her cry unfroze Federico. He ran out to save her, shouting out her name as he ran. He saw her legs thrashing wildly and between them Baltazar's agitated hairy buttocks, and even as he was rushing to pull away the animal the image came to his mind of himself making love to Herminia at some future time, and while he was yelling at Baltazar and had pulled him away from her he saw himself as he made love to her and saw his own buttocks become as hairy as Baltazar's and knew the association would always be present of Baltazar's ugly behind and that he would never be able to dissociate himself from him.

Baltazar slipped out of his grasp as he wrestled with him and stood panting, his eyes wild, his penis still erect, a creature of enormous ugliness. Federico stood up, his mind in a rage, the blood loud at his temples, hating the ugly animal as he stood there with no knowledge of shame. Herminia had withdrawn to the corner where the goats were and stood as if in a daze. Federico went to her. "Thank God I came in time," he said, but if he expected her to fall into his arms to express her relief and eternal gratitude he was disappointed. She simply stood there, staring at him. "Oh my poor darling!" he cried, holding her shoulders. "My most perfect love!" But she remained frigid. He did not see that her eyes were filled with suspicion and refusal, that she understood his declaration as the claiming of a reward which should have been hers to bestow and not his to demand, that she could not love a man who would always remind her of the gratitude she owed him, whom she would always see as coming on the heels of Baltazar, a shadowy twin; not knowing the thoughts that rushed through her mind, he interpreted her silent stare as a natural reaction to what she had just had to endure and, cursing Baltazar for being the cause of her suffering, he turned to see the naked beast still standing there, panting. He looked at Herminia again. Was it fear that still lingered in her eyes? "I will always protect you," he said, moving to embrace her. She stiffened, her hands pressed against his chest. He sensed her rejection but believed it indicated little more than her present agitated state of mind. He turned again to Baltazar who still stood there with his mouth hanging open. All the wrongs of his life seemed to Federico in that moment to be concentrated in Baltazar and a rage now possessed him that was so monstrous that he walked grimly toward him, saying coldly, "I am going to kill you for what you have done." Baltazar read the expression on his face, grasped the meaning of the tensed muscles of Federico's arms, and perhaps also understood the words. He turned on his heels and ran. Federico rushed out of the pen in pursuit.

Gamboa saw them, thirty meters apart, running up the hill. He had been asleep until a few minutes earlier. Herminia's scream and Federico's shouting had reached him and become mingled with a dream. Presently he heard water splashing and knew Herminia must be bathing. Soon they would have breakfast together and he must tell her of the life he had enjoyed in the city. Why had he never talked of that? He must tell her of their apartment in Quinteros, on the *top* floor, with a view of the mountains, and that car, metallic blue it was, in which they went for weekends to their lovely little cottage in the mountains and sometimes to their beach house. What were those two fools running for? Gamboa laughed. He thought them very funny.

In spite of his awkward gait Baltazar was the faster runner, for Federico, who might have overtaken him in a short sprint, was unaccustomed to physical exertion and was soon out of breath, not able to keep up a strenuous pursuit in his bare feet. But the strength of his will gave him the energy to follow, and although Baltazar increased the distance between them, Federico kept after him, and the farther they went into the island the more determined he grew that he would not turn back until he had killed the beast. Two or three times Baltazar slipped out of sight. On the first occasion Federico thought he had lost him and feared that he himself might be the victim of a surprise attack, and had stood motionless, his eyes and ears alert until a slight noise gave away Baltazar's location behind a rock where he crouched, so that Federico learned to read the geography about him to discover where Baltazar might be resting. Once, believing he must have slipped into a crevice between two large rocks, Federico approached the area slowly, hoping at last to catch up with his adversary, but as he got there he heard a bird fly up from a bush farther away and hover in the air, flapping its wings and making a loud squawking noise, and Federico realized that Baltazar must be there.

From the cliff, past the cave, Baltazar made again for the interior where the sloping land was covered with cacti and thorny bushes, a part of the island that Federico had not seen before. Baltazar slipped through the forbidding terrain with greater facility; Federico, short of breath under the hot sun, was momentarily overcome by the futility of his pursuit. The position of the sun indicated it was late in the morning, perhaps only an hour from noon, and he had been pursuing the creature for at least three hours. But his doubt was soon succeeded by a renewal of rage, and the longer he was engaged on his hunt the stronger his obsession grew. He did not know in that unfamiliar landscape that Baltazar had drawn him into the desert where the sun was fixed and timeless, and time itself was inflicting a mortal violence on living matter.

When Herminia saw a small boat enter the bay in the afternoon, the first thought that occurred to her was that just as she and her father had paid for the freedom of the islanders by being left behind during the evacuation, so Federico and Baltazar must now pay the price for her own and her father's liberation. The man in the boat was surprised to see the two of them on the beach with a small bundle between them as if they had been waiting to catch a bus, and he said that he had expected to find two young men instead. "What two men?" she asked innocently. The man named Roberto and Federico and said they had been sent by the company to do a preliminary survey of the island. "It is the island of Santa Barbara, isn't it?" he asked. "Yes, it is," she answered, "but no one has come here. Not for months and months, not since everyone was taken away and my father and I were left behind by mistake. I thought you had come for us, at last. What should

I know of your two men? No one ever came to save us."

The man thought it very strange as he ferried the unexpected passengers to the larger vessel beyond the whale-backed rocks. He knew nothing of the earlier evacuation of the island, and Herminia, watching anxiously when they sailed past the area where Federico had wrecked his boat, told him about it and how they came to be left behind, adding in her relief as they went beyond the whale-backed rocks, "Now at last we will be free!" The man pointed to Gamboa and asked what was the matter with him that he did not talk. "What would *you* have to say in this situation?" she asked, and the man, struck by a combative sharpness in her voice, thought it best to say no more. But climbing aboard the vessel, Gamboa suddenly said to the man, "Supposing the agreed figure is three thousand contos per month for the first three years and an additional thousand per month for each succeeding three years, what would be the total sum *with interest* at the end of eighteen years *plus correction* for inflation and added to that the bonuses that would normally accrue and a nominal allowance for lost promotion opportunities?" The man stared at him in bewilderment. Gamboa laughed and said, "I'll tell you the answer. It's two million one hundred and seventy-six thousand contos. Mind you, I'm saying nothing about the damages, you know, the *punitive* damages. I think we are talking about five million at least." He was beside himself with laughter. But soon they were sailing away and Herminia, glancing back at the island, smiled bitterly to herself as she thought of the two left behind.

And now Federico was no longer so much the pursuer as the one being drawn into an unimaginable wilderness where the giant cactus trees cast grotesque shadows. And among those shadows the fluid form of Baltazar appeared like a phantom he felt obliged to follow. The late-afternoon sun seemed to be splitting his skull. He had not eaten anything all day, nor drunk any water. He could not say whether he was possessed by some extraordinary hallucination or that some unchecked turbulence of emotions had brought on the inchoate symptoms of lunacy whose first attack was viciously ferocious. Lizards darted across the desert floor, twice he had seen snakes coiled in the narrow shade of rocks. The blistered soles of his bare feet burned, his tongue was swollen. It was no longer a matter of being driven by a will that urged the body to pursue its enemy but of the body become incapable of stopping its stumbling after the flickering shadow in front of it.

They came out of the harsh landscape to scattered rocks where iguanas lay and then to a line of sand dunes and finally to a small beach. Federico stumbled to his knees in the sand but continued to crawl. The sun was low on the horizon and the red beam from its eye was already beginning to cast a violet glow upon the ocean. Baltazar stood on the water's edge, panting loudly, exhausted, wanting to fall in the encroaching tide. He could see stingrays in the shallow water and stepped back as a little crest of foam swept over his feet and then flowed back into the ocean, agitating the coarse sand with a sucking sound. Federico looked up at him and raised himself with a great effort. He staggered toward Baltazar. There was no strength left in him, no will, but still the body was moved to press forward. Baltazar had begun to approach him and his gait was almost precisely the same as Federico's, an unwilled, powerless staggering. They halted within a pace of each other. Federico raised his hands above his head, his arms stretched up. Baltazar too raised his hands above his head in an identical manner. Simultaneously, the two leaned forward. Trying to check his balance, Federico put his right foot forward and Baltazar found himself doing the same. Each let his arms swing out so that their hands collided, a weak slapping of palms, and then the fingers loosely intertwined. Their faces came opposite each other, the noses almost touching. Each tried to push the other. But there was no sense of pressure, or weight, as if their flesh were all water. Their hands clasped, their arms fell slowly to the left and then slowly to the right and repeated the motion twice more. They were panting almost into each other's mouth. Their legs gave way simultaneously and they fell on their side, Federico on his left arm, Baltazar on his right. Attempting to wrestle, they only succeeded in holding each other's arms and their foreheads knocked against each other, while their legs, trying to kick, could not so much as twitch and lay helplessly, their thighs pressed against each other. In the distance on the ocean a sea swell surged toward the shore, lifted itself high from the surface, broke and crashed thunderously, and swept swiftly up the beach, dispersed on the sand, a tongue of it creeping under the two bodies locked in a senseless embrace. Another swell had already formed out on the ocean and behind it yet another, each succeeding one gathering more volume and energy than the one before it. Marine iguanas, having charged their bodies with sunlight all day, came down to the beach to enter the high tide and to be drawn into the waters that nourished them. The rushing water knocked some of the stingrays onto the sand where they flapped helplessly until the next wave submerged them again. There would inevitably be some who would be flung too far out to make it to the water again and that accident of nature had no other consequence than to add to the decomposing matter on the beach.